hundred romance novels. Her books regularly appear on best-seller lists and have won several awards, including a Prism Award, a National Readers' Choice Award, a Colorado Romance Writers Award of Excellence and a Golden Quill Award. She is a native Californian but has recently moved to the mountains of Utah.

DUTY OR DESIRE

BRENDA JACKSON

TEMPTING THE TEXAN

MAUREEN CHILD

MILLS & BOON

First Published in Great Britain 2019
by Mills & Boon, an imprint of HarperCollinsPublishers,
1 London Bridge Street, London, SE1 9GF

Duty or Desire © 2019 Brenda Streater Jackson
Tempting the Texan © 2019 Harlequin Books S.A.

Special thanks and acknowledgement are given to Maureen Child for her contribution to the Texas Cattleman's Club: Inheritance series.

ISBN: 978-0-263-27200-0

1219

MIX
Paper from
responsible sources
FSC™ C007454

This book is produced from independently certified FSC™ paper to ensure responsible forest management.

For more information visit: www.harpercollins.co.uk/green

Printed and bound in Spain
by CPI, Barcelona

DUTY OR DESIRE

BRENDA JACKSON

Acknowledgments

To the man who will forever be the love
of my life and the wind beneath
my wings, Gerald Jackson, Sr.

To all my readers who love the
Westmorelands and their friends.

To my sons, Gerald Jr. and Brandon. Please
continue to make me and your dad proud.
I love you guys.

To my family and friends who continue
to support me in all that I do.

Ask, and it will be given you;
seek, and ye shall find;
knock, and it shall be opened unto you.
—Matthew 7:7

Prologue

The doorbell sounded and Bane Westmoreland wondered who the latecomer could be. All his family and friends who'd been invited to celebrate his and his wife Crystal's housewarming party were accounted for.

Upon opening the door he found an older couple, in their late sixties, standing there with a baby in their arms.

Bane was certain he did not know the couple. "Yes, may I help you?"

The man spoke. "We hate to impose but we were told Peterson Higgins was here tonight. We are the Glosters, his deceased brother's in-laws."

Bane nodded. "Yes, Pete is here. Please come in."

The man shook his head. "We prefer not to, but we would appreciate it if you could tell Peterson we're here. We would like to speak with him. We will wait out here."

Bane nodded again. "Okay, just a minute." He circled

around the room before finally finding Pete in a group in the family room.

"Excuse me, guys, but I need to borrow Pete for a minute," Bane said to the others. Once he got Pete aside, he told him about the older couple waiting outside. Pete placed his cup of punch aside and quickly moved toward the front door.

When Pete returned about half an hour later, he was carrying a baby in one hand and a diaper bag in the other. Everyone's attention was drawn to him when the baby released a huge wail.

It seemed all the mothers in the room hurried toward him.

"Whose baby?" Bane's cousin Gemma was the first to ask, taking the baby from a flustered-looking Pete.

"This is my nine-month-old niece, Ciara," he said, noticing how quickly the baby girl quieted once Gemma held her. "As most of you know, my brother, Matthew, and his wife, Sherry, were killed in that car crash six months ago. This is their daughter. Sherry's parents were given custody of Ciara when Matt and Sherry died. But they just gave me full custody of her, citing health issues that prevent them from taking proper care of her. That means I'm now Ciara's legal guardian."

Pete looked around the room at the group he considered family and asked the one question none of them could answer.

"I'm a bachelor, for heaven's sake! What on earth am I going to do with a baby?"

One

Five months later

"I hate that I'm leaving you like this, Pete, but my sister needs me."

Sheriff Peterson Higgins stared at the older woman standing across the kitchen. He'd known something was wrong the minute he walked through the door.

Well, he had news for Bonnie. He needed her, too.

Pete suddenly felt like a class A bastard for thinking such a thing after she'd just tearfully explained that her sister had been diagnosed with breast cancer. Of course he understood her wanting to go be with her only sister during this time. Even if her leaving would put him in a bind, the last thing he wanted was for Bonnie to feel guilty about going to her family. Somehow, he would find the right person to live-in and keep his fourteen-month-old niece while he worked.

Of course, that person couldn't really replace Bonnie.

Bonnie McCray had been his mother's best friend. When Renee Higgins had died, Pete had been sixteen and his younger brother Matthew twelve. Renee had asked Bonnie to always be there for her sons and Bonnie had kept that promise. And when Pete's father passed away three years later, Bonnie wouldn't hear of Pete not fulfilling his mother's dream of him completing college. Bonnie and her husband, Fred, agreed to look after Matt while Pete studied.

It had been hard going to college full-time and making sure the cattle ranch his father had loved remained productive. Luckily, his two best friends, Derringer and Riley Westmoreland, had a huge family of cousins and brothers who'd pitched in and helped out. They also made sure Pete hired the best people to help run things while he attended university.

After he completed college with a degree in criminology, he discovered ranching wasn't in his blood but a career in law enforcement was. He found out ranching wasn't in Matt's blood either when his brother went into the military immediately after high school.

Even so, Pete refused to sell the ranch that had been in the Higgins family for generations. Instead he leased part of the two hundred acres to sharecroppers, and for the other parts he hired a foreman and ranch hands. That freed Pete up to work for the sheriff's office, a job he'd secured after college thanks to Riley's oldest brother, Dillon Westmoreland.

Pete loved his career, and the ranch was making plenty of money, which he'd split with Matt before Matt's death.

A pain settled around Pete's heart when he remembered the phone call almost a year ago telling him Matt and Sherry had been killed in a car crash. Luckily, three-

month-old Ciara hadn't been with them. It had been Matt
and Sherry's "date night" and the baby had been at home
with a sitter.

Sherry's parents, who lived in New Hampshire, had
wanted full custody of Ciara and Pete had seen no reason not to give it to them. Matt had adored his in-laws,
thought they were good people who treated him like a
son instead of a son-in-law. Besides, Pete knew with his
bachelor lifestyle, the last thing he could manage was
taking care of a baby. When Sheriff Harper retired a few
months before, Pete had been selected to replace him.
That meant his plate was fuller than ever.

Things had been working out and he'd made a point to
call and check on his niece every weekend. He enjoyed
hearing about the development of her motor skills and
how much she liked to eat.

But five months ago, out of the blue, Sherry's parents
had shown up in Denver to say that health issues meant
they needed him to serve as guardian for his niece. They
assumed his bachelor days wouldn't last forever and they
thought a much younger couple would have more energy
to raise their granddaughter.

At thirty-six, marriage was the last thing on Pete's
mind. However, he gladly gave his niece the love, attention and care he knew Matt would have wanted him to.

Now at fourteen months, Ciara Renee Higgins was
ruling the Higgins household, and Pete was glad Bonnie
had been there to help out as a full-time nanny. Her husband had passed away a couple of years ago and with her
only son living on the East Coast, Bonnie had welcomed
the opportunity to take care of others again. As far as
Pete was concerned, she'd been a godsend. He honestly
didn't know what he'd have done without her and wondered what he would do now that she would be leaving.

"May I make a suggestion, Pete?"

For a minute he'd been so deep in thought he'd forgotten Bonnie was standing there, waiting for him to say something. "Yes."

Bonnie smiled as she placed a serving tray on the table with soup and a sandwich. His lunch. He made a habit of swinging by the ranch at noon each day to spend time with Ciara. Although Bonnie's job was to take care of Ciara, she always prepared lunch and dinner for him, as well. Where did she find the time to do such things? On the days when Bonnie returned to her own home, Pete took care of his niece by himself. Ciara required his full attention and would let him know when she felt she wasn't getting enough of it. It was only during her nap time was he able to grab a nap of his own.

"Hopefully, I won't be gone any more than two months, and I know of someone who could replace me."

He doubted anyone would be able to replace Bonnie. "Who?"

"A woman I met a couple of months ago at church. She recently moved to the area and she and I have become good friends."

He nodded as he walked over to the table to sit down and eat. "Where is she from?"

"Charleston."

He chuckled. "Good grief. Don't tell me we have another Southerner invading these parts. Bella is enough."

Bella was married to his friend Jason Westmoreland. Everyone thought of her as a real Southern belle. From the time she'd arrived in Denver it had been obvious that she was a woman of refinement. It didn't take long for word to spread that she was the daughter of a wealthy business tycoon in Savannah, Georgia. Although Bella had adjusted well, at times she still looked out of place amidst the bunch of roughnecks in these parts.

Bonnie placed a small salad near his sandwich. "Yes, another Southerner." She then poured iced tea into his glass.

He looked up. "Thanks. And what makes you think she will be good with Ciara?"

"Because she taught prekindergarten for a few years and before that, she worked with younger babies in a nursery at a hospital in Charleston. She's had us over for tea several times. I always take Ciara with me and the two of them hit it off. You of all people know how Ciara can be."

Yes, he knew. If his niece liked you, then she liked you. If she didn't, she didn't. And she normally didn't take well to strangers. "What makes you think she would be interested in keeping Ciara until you return?"

"Because I asked her," Bonnie said with excitement in her voice. "I didn't want to leave you with no one at all, and then not with just anyone."

He appreciated that. "When can I meet her, to see if she'll be a good fit?"

"I invited her to lunch."

Pete paused from biting into his sandwich. "Today?"

Bonnie smiled. "Yes, today. The sooner you can meet her, the better. I would worry sick the entire time I'm in Dallas if you and Ciara weren't taken care of properly."

At that moment the doorbell sounded. "That's probably her," Bonnie said, smiling, as she swiftly left the kitchen.

Pete began eating his sandwich, curious about the woman Bonnie was recommending. He figured she would be around Bonnie's age, which meant she could probably cook. Having home-cooked Southern dishes once in a while was a nice thought.

"Pete, I'd like you to meet Myra Hollister. Myra, this is Sheriff Peterson Higgins."

Placing his glass down on the table, Pete stood and turned to offer his hand to the woman, then froze. Standing in the middle of his kitchen beside Bonnie was the most gorgeous woman he'd seen in a while. A long while. And she was young, probably no more than twenty-two or twenty-three. She had a petite figure and was no more than five-three. She appeared even shorter than that when standing across from his six-three height.

She had skin the color of rich mocha and features so striking he felt like he'd been struck in all parts of his body. Perfect hazel eyes stared back at him and a smile curved a pair of delectable lips. Fluffy dark brown bangs swept across her forehead and a mass of curly hair fell past her shoulders. When he finally moved his gaze from her face it was to check out the legs beneath her dress. They were as gorgeous as the rest of her.

He couldn't ignore the spike of heat that caught him low in the gut. The power of her femininity surrounded him, actually made his heart skip a couple of beats. He wanted to groan in protest.

"It's nice meeting you, Sheriff Higgins. I've heard a lot of wonderful things about you," the woman said, offering him her hand. Her Southern accent was just as perceptible as Bella's.

"Thanks," Pete replied, fighting back a curse. The moment their hands had touched, a hard hum of lust had rushed through his veins.

Bonnie wanted him to hire this woman as a live-in nanny? She had to be kidding. There was no way he could do that, even on a temporary basis. This was the first woman he'd been attracted to since Ellen.

That placed him in one hell of a dilemma.

Myra Hollister tried hiding her excitement at possibly being hired as Ciara's nanny. She adored the precious little girl she'd gotten to know. And when Bonnie mentioned her need for a replacement, Myra had been glad to help. It would certainly solve some of her own problems for a while.

First off, she would get a salary, which meant she wouldn't have to touch her savings. And since her lease ended next month, moving in here was great, too. Hopefully without her own address, her brother wouldn't be able to find her. The latter was the most important thing and would definitely buy her the time she needed before returning to Charleston for a face-off with Baron.

"How old are you?"

Sheriff Higgins's question reeled her concentration back in. "I'm twenty-four but will be turning twenty-five on Christmas Day."

Myra studied his very handsome features, which she'd noticed the moment she'd walked in. She figured he was either thirty-five or thirty-six, which would put him at Baron's age. She'd encountered good-looking older men before. Her brother's friends were all eye candy and, like him, they were all womanizers who thought women were good for only one thing. Long ago she figured it must be an age thing. Even Baron thought that way and he'd been married to Cleo almost four years. She loved her sister-in-law and regretted how Baron and his mother, Charlene, were treating her. Myra was convinced Cleo would have left Baron long ago, but he swore he would fight her for custody of the kids if she left him.

Pushing thoughts of Baron from her mind, Myra placed her concentration back on the man standing in front of her. He had chestnut-colored skin, broad shoulders and long legs that looked good in his pants.

He also had a gorgeous pair of dark brown eyes that seemed to be staring at her in disapproval. Why? Although this was what she considered an informal interview, she had dressed appropriately. She was wearing one of her church dresses with heels.

And why had he asked about her age? Hadn't Miss Bonnie given him a rundown of her credentials and experience? What was the issue? She could tell by the frown on his face that there was one.

Automatically, she slid her hands to the back of her hair and fluffed it away from her neck, something she did whenever she was nervous. And she shouldn't be feeling nervous, not when she was qualified for the job. If truth be told, probably overqualified.

"You're a lot younger than I thought you would be," he finally said, after staring her down. "Sorry, but I don't think you'll work out."

Myra blinked. He didn't think she would work out?

She was being dismissed because of her age? Maybe now was the time to remind him that there were such things as discrimination laws, but then she figured that would only make the situation worse. She glanced over at Miss Bonnie, who was giving the sheriff a shocked stare.

Deciding to reassure him, because she truly needed the job, she said, "I don't consider myself too young to care for your niece, Sheriff Higgins. I've worked at a day care and also in the nursery at the hospital. And once I finish my thesis, I'll have my PhD in child psychology."

If Myra thought that information would impress him,

then she was wrong. He remained expressionless when he said, "All that's nice, but I regret you wasted your time coming here today."

Although she didn't understand what was going on, all she could do was take the man at his word. Besides, he might think of her as young, but she was strong. Only a strong woman could have put up with her brother's foolishness for the past six months and not have broken. Fighting back the anger she felt, she said, as politely as she could, "I regret wasting my time coming here today, as well. Good day, Sheriff."

Giving Miss Bonnie an appreciative smile, she added, "I can see my way to the door." Then Myra turned and walked out of the kitchen.

"Would you like to tell me what that was about, Peterson?"

It wasn't the tone of Bonnie's voice alone that let Pete know she was upset with him. She never called him Peterson. "I stated it already and there's nothing more to tell. I thought the woman you were recommending was an older woman, closer to your age. She's way too young," he said, before sitting back down to the table to resume eating his lunch.

"Too young? For heaven's sake, she's nearly twenty-five. Women her age are having babies every day. How can you think she's too young when you've gotten Charity Maples to babysit for you a few times and she's only seventeen?"

He shrugged. "The key word is *babysit*. I don't need a young nanny working for me. Have you forgotten I need a *live-in* nanny?"

"At the moment what I think you need is your head examined. Myra Hollister is more than qualified to be a nanny, and what's the problem with her living here while taking care of Ciara?"

He didn't say anything and then he wished he had come up with something. If he had, Bonnie might not have slung out her next accusation. "You're afraid, aren't you? You're afraid that a young beautiful woman will remind you to live again."

He glanced over at her, which wasn't hard to do since she'd come to stand by the table. "I don't know what you're talking about. I am living."

"No, you're not—you're breathing. I, more than anyone, know that a part of you stopped living the day Ellen died. It's been twelve years, Pete."

Every muscle in Pete's body tensed. He, of all people, knew just how many years it had been. A man would not forget the day his fiancée died when she was thrown from the horse she'd been riding. Pete doubted he would ever forget that day for as long as he lived.

A man had come into the dress shop where she worked a month earlier and tried flirting with her. She'd told him she wasn't interested and was engaged to be married. He had begun stalking her and Ellen hadn't told Pete anything. Then the man had intentionally thrown a firecracker to spook her horse. At least he'd been arrested and was still serving time for Ellen's death.

"I know how long it's been, Bonnie. What's your point? You act as if I don't date."

"Yes, you date, though rarely."

She was right. However, his excuse was a good one. He was too busy. Besides, some women saw a man in a uniform as a trophy to win and he didn't intend to be a prize in any contest. He sighed as he shifted his gaze from Bonnie to the window.

Bonnie moved around the table to stand by him, intentionally blocking his view. She stood there, a force to be reckoned with, her hands on her hips, giving him that infamous Bonnie McCray glare.

"You've just dismissed your best prospect for a nanny. I didn't even know about that thesis for her PhD. That makes her more than qualified."

He drew in a deep breath. "What do you even know about her?"

"She's living in Denver temporarily, trying to deal with grief. Her parents died a few months ago while vacationing in Morocco. The tour helicopter crashed."

"That's tragic," he said, shaking his head, feeling bad for the woman. Losing both parents at the same time had to be hard on a person. He recalled years ago when the same thing had happened to his best friends, Derringer and Riley Westmoreland. The cousins had lost both sets of parents the same day in an airplane accident. He recalled how devastating that had been.

"Yes, it was tragic," Bonnie was saying. "Her family owns a huge corporation in Charleston, but she's not in the family business or anything."

"How did she decide on Denver?" he asked,

"Someone she knows from college owns a house here and she's leasing it for six months."

He nodded. "Well, I wish her the best, but like I said, she's too young to stay here. I'm sure there are other women out there. An *older* woman I can hire to live here as a nanny."

"Myra could live here as Ciara's nanny, Pete. Don't think I don't know why you're behaving the way you are. I've got eyes. I knew the moment she walked into the room that you were attracted to her."

He wouldn't bother denying anything because he'd

learned long ago that Bonnie didn't miss a thing. "And what if I am? I've been attracted to women before."

"Yes, and the few you've dated were women you deemed safe. For some reason you're afraid if a pretty young woman like Myra got underfoot that she might thaw your frozen heart."

First she accuses him of breathing instead of living and now she's saying he has a frozen heart.

His heart wasn't frozen. He just wore a thick protective shield around it. Pete refused to ever go through the pain he'd felt when he lost Ellen. Pain that could still creep up on him even now, twelve years later. Had Ellen not died, they would be married by now with a bunch of kids and living in this very house where he'd been born. They would be happy, just as they'd been that day when they'd been sixteen and had decided to be boyfriend and girlfriend forever.

Forever...

For him, forever was still going on. It hadn't died the day Ellen had.

"Have you forgotten about that dream you shared with me, Pete?"

He didn't have to wonder what dream she was talking about. "What does that dream have to do with anything?"

She sat down in the chair beside his. "Because in that dream you said your hands had been tied and Ellen was untying them for you. Not only did she untie them but then she tried to push you out some door."

A part of him now wished he hadn't shared any details about that dream with Bonnie. But he had done so mainly because it had bothered him to the point where he'd awakened in the middle of the night in a cold sweat. He'd gotten up to go into the kitchen, needing something to drink and found Bonnie in the living room, sitting in the chair, rocking Ciara back to sleep. While downing a glass of lemonade, he had told Bonnie about his dream and she'd listened and said nothing.

It had been the next morning when she'd told him what she thought the dream meant. Ellen was trying to release him, free him from all the plans they'd made together. She wanted him to enjoy life. To live and love again. To do more than just breathe.

Pete sighed deeply. He hadn't accepted Bonnie's interpretation of the dream then and he wouldn't accept it now. "I don't want to talk about that dream, Bonnie."

"Fine, Pete. But you need to accept that I'm leaving and your niece needs a nanny. I honestly don't think you're going to find another person more qualified than Myra Hollister, especially not in two weeks."

He slid back his chair to stand. "I intend to do just that, Bonnie. I'm determined to find someone more qualified."

He had to.

Two

Myra looked up from reading the morning paper and sipping her herbal tea. She tipped her head to stare at her cell phone. It was ringing and she didn't recognize the ringtone. Granted, she hadn't assigned a specific sound to everyone who called her. Only those that mattered. She was about to ignore the call and then remembered it might be Sheriff Higgins.

She had run into Miss Bonnie and Ciara at the grocery store two days ago and had been so glad to see them. Ciara's chubby arms had automatically reached for her and she'd been happy to hold her. That had been the first time she'd seen Miss Bonnie since that day a week ago when the sheriff had turned down her employment as a nanny.

According to Miss Bonnie, the position hadn't been filled and she felt the sheriff would come to his senses soon enough and realize Myra was the best candidate.

Deciding to appease her curiosity, she clicked on the phone. "Hello."

"Gosh, Myra, you had me worried there for a minute."

"Wallace? Why are you calling me from another number? One that I don't recognize?"

Wallace Blue had been her father's protégé. The man Elias Hollister had groomed for years to replace him at the company whenever that time came. At least her father had the good sense not to make Baron his successor, recognizing at an early age that her brother lacked the skills, knowledge and compassion to ever head a company the size, depth and magnitude of Hollister Enterprises.

Her father thought his only son's lack of character stemmed from Baron having been raised by his mother, who'd been Elias's first wife. He thought Charlene had raised her son to be just as callous, calculating and cruel as she was. Myra hadn't known just how true those allegations were until her involvement with Rick Stovers.

She should not have been surprised that Baron's behavior would get worse after her parents died unexpectedly. The first thing Baron had done was go after Wallace, who'd been in place to head the company. Rumor had it that Baron, along with his devious mother, had gotten to the stockholders after obtaining damaging information on their pasts. Baron and Charlene had threatened to expose the information if the stockholders didn't vote Wallace out and put Baron in as Myra's father's replacement.

"It's a burner phone and I wanted to check to make sure you're okay," Wallace was saying. "Your brother is more devious than ever and I think he might have put a tracker on my regular phone. He's desperate to find you."

Myra could believe that because in two months, when she turned twenty-five, the entire company became hers and there was nothing Baron or the stockholders could do about it. It was Baron's intention that she not show up at that meeting where she would take control of the company, appoint Wallace as the CEO and show Baron the door. How he planned to stop her was anyone's guess, but she didn't want to take any chances.

"I can't understand why you're still working there," she said.

"Because while I'm here I can make sure Hollister Enterprises stays profitable until it's time for you to take over. Otherwise, Baron will bankrupt it. All Baron's friends are working here and they don't know what the hell they're doing."

Myra believed Wallace. Her father had said often enough that Baron had no business sense and as far as Myra was concerned the men he hung out with, mostly frat brothers, were just as bad. "Well, let Baron continue to look for me. I think this is the last place he'll think to look. According to Cleo, he thinks I'm somewhere in Spain, which is why Charlene tried to have my passport revoked so I couldn't return to the States."

"Don't put anything past her, Myra. Over the years she's been known to have bed partners in some pretty high places."

Myra could believe that. Baron even bragged about his mother's past lovers and how she could get some of them to do just about anything for her. Baron and Charlene disliked Wallace because they saw him as taking Baron's place in Elias's life. Baron and Wallace were nearly the same age, and yet as different as day and night. Wallace, whose father had been Elias's best friend since childhood, always carried himself with professionalism and honesty.

"So, what's going on with you?" Wallace asked her, breaking into her thoughts.

She shrugged, not surprised he'd asked. She considered him the big brother Baron had never been. "Not much. Paula needs to turn this house back into an Airbnb for the holidays, so I'll be moving out in a week."

"And going where?"

"Not sure. There's a woman I've met who relocated from Savannah," she said, thinking about Bella Westmoreland. "She owns a private B and B. I plan to talk to her about moving into one of the rooms there for two months. Just till Christmas. I told you why I'm avoiding hotels."

"Yes, because Baron could trace your whereabouts if you don't," Wallace said. "I just hate you're on the run like this. If your father was alive, he—"

"But Dad isn't alive, Wallace, and we need to carry out his wishes like he would want us to do. I'm fine, just a little inconvenienced."

She and Wallace knew the truth. She was being inconvenienced a whole lot. It was never her desire to get tied to the family's business. Her father had always respected her decision. But she'd known, because he'd told her, that if anything happened to him and her mother simultaneously, the company would become hers. He'd instructed her to make sure Wallace was CEO so he could run things. And that was what she intended to do. Her twenty-fifth birthday couldn't get here soon enough. Now, if she could only stay hidden from Baron until then.

"You still working on your thesis?" Wallace asked her.

She moved back to the table to sit down. "Yes, but not as much as I should." Then, because she wanted to share her disappointment with someone, she said, "I interviewed for a nanny position last week."

"That's great. How's that working out for you?"

Knowing Wallace figured she'd gotten the job, she said, "I wasn't hired. The guy thought I was too young."

"Too young?"

"Yes. I think he was looking for an older, matronly woman."

"Too bad, it's his loss. You're good with kids and would have been a great nanny."

She believed that, too. At that moment her doorbell rang. "Thanks. I have to go. Someone is at the door."

"Okay. Make sure you check to see who it is before opening it, Myra."

"Okay. I'll talk to you later." She clicked off the phone and headed for the door.

Pete couldn't believe he was here, but it had taken his best friend Derringer Westmoreland to help make him realize that just like Bonnie had said, Myra Hollister was the best person to be nanny to Ciara. Besides, he was running out of time.

Bonnie would be leaving town next week and so far, the women he'd interviewed had been so lacking in certain skills he'd quickly shown them the door. Then there had been Ciara's reaction to each of them. She had taken one look and started screaming her dislike.

According to Derringer, Jason's wife, Bella, and Myra Hollister had become friends. Bella had invited Ms. Hollister to one of those Westmoreland family chow-downs, something the Westmorelands got together for every Friday, and the one thing they'd all been amazed about was how the Westmoreland kids had taken to Myra and she to them. It was as if she was a modern-day Mary Poppins.

Something else Derringer had said had helped Pete see reason. If he truly wanted what was best for Ciara, then he would get the best. It would be up to him to keep things professional between him and his nanny. He had to agree with that. All he had to do was remember his relationship with Ms. Hollister was strictly business.

He intended to make sure it stayed that way.

So here he was on Myra Hollister's doorstep with Ciara in tow. It was his day off and he hoped Ms. Hollister was still interested in the job. He glanced down at his niece who was smiling happily at him.

Suddenly the door opened and Myra stood there with a surprised look on her face. "Good morning, Sheriff Higgins."

He was about to ask if he could come in when Ciara released a happy scream and all but jumped out of his arms into Ms. Hollister's. He tightened his hold on his niece as she tried twisting out of his arms.

"You can let her go. I have her," Myra Hollister said. Ciara not only went to the woman but wrapped her arms around her neck as if Myra Hollister was her lifeline.

He'd seen the interaction between Bonnie and Ciara numerous times and had seen the bond developing between them over the months. But he hadn't been prepared for this, although he'd been forewarned.

"Hey there, Ciara, how are you, sweetie?" Myra asked her, and that's when Ciara pushed back to look up at the woman while smiling brightly.

Myra Hollister lifted her eyes over Ciara's head to look at Pete, who could only stare back at her. Today she looked even younger. The legal drinking age in Colorado was twenty-one, and he could see her getting carded easily. Few would believe she was twenty-four without proof. She was wearing her hair down and around her shoulders as she had the other day, and he wondered if the curls were as fluffy as they looked.

"Would you like to come in, Sheriff Higgins?"

"Yes, if you don't mind."

"Not at all," she said, stepping aside for him to enter, propping Ciara on her hip.

"She's heavy," he said, reaching for his niece once they were inside. Again Ciara rebuffed his outstretched hands and clung to Myra.

"She's fine. Come in by the fireplace. Glad to see you have her dressed properly."

"Of course," he said, taking off his Stetson and hanging it on the hat rack by the door.

It was October and the temperature was below freezing. Did she think he didn't know to dress his niece for the cold weather? Granted, he would admit Bonnie had made it easy for him by laying Ciara's clothes out the night before.

"Would you like something to drink, Sheriff Higgins? I have tea, hot chocolate and coffee."

When she sat down on the sofa with Ciara, he sat in the chair across from her. "No, I'm fine."

He knew from Bonnie that Myra was leasing this home. He liked the community and recalled it had once been his area to patrol when he was a deputy. The people were friendly and because of a neighborhood watch program, crime had been practically nonexistent.

"I want to apologize for my behavior the other day. I didn't mean to offend you." He decided to get it out there. He wished he wasn't noticing how good she looked sitting there in her leggings and pullover sweater. Or how at eleven o'clock on a cold Monday morning she reminded him of a bright ray of sunshine.

After removing Ciara's coat, hat and mittens, she adjusted his niece in her lap, looked him dead in the face and said, "Yet you did offend me, Sheriff."

He blew out a slow breath. He needed to explain his actions as best he could while leaving out a couple of vital details. Like his intense attraction to her. He'd hoped it had been a fluke, but when she'd opened the door just now, he'd seen that it hadn't been. At least he was doing a better job of controlling his reaction today than he had last week.

"I apologize for offending you. When Bonnie told me about you, I assumed you were an older woman. I hope you can understand my surprise when you walked into the kitchen."

"Even if I wasn't what you expected, I'm sure Miss Bonnie told you about my qualifications. I still don't understand why there would be a problem even if I'm considered *young* to you. I used to work in a day care. I worked in a nursery at a hospital taking care of newborns and I'm getting my PhD in child psychology. What else did you need, Sheriff?"

He had to tighten his lips to keep from saying he didn't need anything else, but it would help tremendously if she didn't look like a goddess. And then, as if things needed to get more interesting, his niece took hold of the front of Myra's sweater. That caused a dip in the fabric, exposing a generous portion of Myra's cleavage. He nearly swallowed his tongue when he said, "I don't need anything else. I think that would do it…if you're still interested."

She didn't say anything for a moment, like she was mulling it over, trying to decide. Then she said, "Yes, I'm still interested."

He felt relief at that. "Good. However, there are a few questions I need to ask to finish the interview process."

"Ask away."

"First, I want to offer my sympathy in regards to your parents. Bonnie told me what happened." He saw the sadness that appeared in her eyes. She and her parents must have been close. A cop was trained to read people even when they didn't want to be read.

"Thanks, Sheriff."

He wished he didn't have to ask the next question but there was no way around it. She needed to know what her working environment would be like. "You will need to move in with me for two months." He paused, deciding he didn't like the way that sounded. "Let me rephrase that."

"No need," she said, smiling. "I know what you meant. And yes, I'm aware that because of your unorthodox work hours, I'll have to move into your place as a full-time nanny to Ciara. In fact, moving into your place works better for me."

He lifted his brow. "Why is that?"

"Because my lease on this place expires in a week, and I would have had to find someplace else to stay. I won't have to do that if I move into your place to take care of Ciara. Then around the time Miss Bonnie will be returning, I'll be heading back to South Carolina."

He nodded. She was right. It would work out well for her. That meant she would leave Denver around the holidays. She'd mentioned her birthday was on Christmas… just like his.

She shifted positions on the sofa and Ciara shifted with her, without taking her eyes off the flames in the fireplace. Funny, she'd never been so attentive to his fireplace. Then he saw the colorful flames emitting from the logs. He smiled his understanding about why such a thing was holding his niece's attention since it was now holding his.

"Did you know, Sheriff, that babies have the ability to recognize colors at eighteen months?" Evidently she noticed he was staring at the flames as much as Ciara.

He glanced back at her. "Is that a fact?"

"Yes. However, I suspect Ciara has a jump start since it's quite obvious she can detect colors now. I also suspect it won't be long before she notices similarities and differences in shapes, sizes and texture of objects."

He nodded again. "She's already begun talking and thinks I'm her daddy. She's even called Bonnie Momma a few times."

"Does that bother you? That she calls you Daddy?"

He had to be honest that yes, it did. "I don't ever want her to forget Matt and Sherry."

She shifted in her seat again, in a way where Ciara could still keep her gaze on the flames. "Can I be blunt with you, Sheriff?"

He nodded his head. "Yes."

"Chances are she's already forgotten them."

His jaw clenched and unclenched. He preferred she not say such a thing because he definitely refused to think it. "You don't know that."

A hint of sadness appeared in her eyes. "Yes, I do. She was only three months old at the time of their accident, right?"

"Yes."

"Then what she remembers most is their scent."

Although he didn't want to agree with her, he knew what she said made sense. "Like I said, I don't want her to forget them."

"What you mean is that you want her to remember them."

As far as he was concerned, it meant the same thing. Evidently she didn't think so, but he refused to spar with her. Besides, there was one other thing they needed to cover before he felt totally comfortable hiring her.

"When Ciara gets older," she continued, "around three years old, that would be a good time to begin establishing her parents' likenesses into her memory with pictures. There's nothing wrong with her calling you Daddy. When she's old enough you can tell her the truth."

He didn't say anything for a moment. Instead of appreciating her insight, he resented it. He was hiring her as a nanny, not a social worker. He and Ciara would do just fine without her dotting every *i* and crossing every *t* for them.

"There's another matter I want to discuss with you."

"Oh?" she said, moving her gaze from his to smile down at Ciara. His niece had finally gotten bored of the fire and was glancing around the room. Myra Hollister held Ciara firmly in her arms and he was amazed that Ciara hadn't given her any pushback. Usually, she was ready to get on the floor and move around to see what she could get into. The Higgins household had gone through a lot of changes since his niece began walking three months ago.

"And what matter is that, Sheriff?"

"Our relationship." When he realized how that sounded, he quickly said, "Our *working* relationship. I think I need to define it."

He saw the way her brows scrunched up. "Why?"

Her words pretty much confirmed she honestly didn't have a clue. Maybe that was a good thing. But still, he needed to make sure they had an understanding about a few things.

"Why do you think you need to define our working relationship, Sheriff?" she asked again.

Pete drew in a deep breath. "We will be living under the same roof. I'm a single man and you're a single woman."

"And?"

"People might talk, Ms. Hollister."

She looked even more confused. "Why would they? I'm sure people around here know your profession. You're the sheriff. You're also the guardian to your niece. Why would anyone have anything to say about you hiring a temporary nanny until Miss Bonnie returns?"

He shifted in his seat. "Like I said. I'm single and so are you."

"So is Miss Bonnie."

Pete frowned. Was she deliberately being obtuse? "I've never had a *young*, single and beautiful woman living under my roof before."

She stared at him for a moment and then cocked a brow. "Although I don't consider myself one of those real proper Southern belles, I was raised to adhere to conservative protocols. Is there something about your reputation that I need to be concerned with, Sheriff?"

Her question threw him. "Why would you think that?"

"Because you're evidently worried about my reputation and what people will think with me living in your house."

Is that what she honestly thought? "I assure you there's nothing questionable about my character."

"And I assure you there's nothing questionable about mine. And as far as anyone suspecting something going on between us while we're living together, that is the craziest thing I've ever heard."

"And why is that?"

She rolled her eyes. "First of all, you're not my type. Second, you're older than anyone I normally would date."

Well, damn. She'd pretty much put him in his place by telling him she was not in the least attracted to him. There was only one thing he could say. "I'm glad because you're not my type either, and you're younger than the women I'd typically date."

"Great! Then we don't have anything to worry about. I honestly don't care what people might say or think about me living with you. However, if you're concerned about what they might say, then I suggest you find yourself another nanny."

Myra meant what she'd said, although she could understand why someone would think she could fall for the sheriff. After all, he was a very handsome man. Instead of being dressed like a lawman, today he was wearing jeans and a Western shirt. When she'd looked out the peephole and seen him earlier, standing on her doorstep, tall, broad shouldered, ruggedly built with a Stetson on his head, she'd drawn in a deep breath to slow her pulse. He was her idea of a Denver cowboy ready to go off and tame a bunch of wild broncos.

But the bottom line, handsome or not, she could not and would not be attracted to him. She could appreciate a man's good looks without losing her mind over him; especially an older, good-looking man, thanks to her bad experience with Rick.

But she couldn't deny the sensations that had gone off in her stomach when Pete had described her as young, single and beautiful. Did he really think she was beautiful? And why did the idea of him thinking such a thing give her a warm feeling? She couldn't let his words, or her reaction to them, go to her head.

Her time in Denver was limited and like she'd told him, she would be returning to Charleston in a couple of months. But she'd stay there just long enough to boot Baron out of the company and return Wallace to his rightful place as head of Hollister Enterprises. Then she intended to take a monthlong vacation in Paris. She would definitely deserve it.

"I see I've offended you again."

She glanced over at him and her stomach contracted. Why did he have to look regretful and sexy at the same time? "Yes, you have. I'm beginning to think you enjoy doing that."

"I assure you I don't. I just didn't want you caught off guard. You're new here and I know this town."

She nodded. "And I guess that means you have a reputation to uphold, and I understand that. Well, guess what? So do I. But obviously you think your reputation means a lot more than mine."

"I never said that."

No, he hadn't insinuated such a thing, but she also hadn't given much thought to them sleeping under the same roof until he'd made such a big deal out of it. "Like I said. If you're worried about what people think, then I'm not—"

"I'm not worried." He stood and she watched how he easily slid out of the chair to stand up to his six-three height. "You will work out fine if you still want the job."

He then offered her an amount that was a lot more than what she had figured on earning. That would certainly help keep her tucked away from Baron until she was ready to return home. "I accept your offer, Sheriff. Will I be expected to do laundry and cook, as well?"

He lifted a brow. "Can you cook?"

She lifted her chin. "I can hold my own. I can't cook as well as Miss Bonnie, but considering how *young* I am, Sheriff, I might surprise you."

"You're not going to let me forget about the big deal I made with your age, are you?"

"No time soon," she said, unable to hide her smile.

She looked down at the little girl she held in her arms, deliberating over placing her concentration on Ciara before she looked back at him. "But that's your hang-up, Sheriff. I'm sure you will get over it. I'm looking forward to taking care of Ciara until Miss Bonnie returns."

"I'm glad."

He smiled for the first time since she'd met him. All she should have seen was a friendly smile, but when his lips had curved, she was struck with a spike of feminine awareness. Why had his smile caused that reaction in her?

She didn't know. The best thing to do was to get rid of him to ponder the reason in private. She stood after putting on Ciara's coat, hat and mittens. "So, I guess that's it. I will be reporting to your place on Friday. That will give Miss Bonnie a chance to help me get acclimated to Ciara's schedule and my duties while she's gone."

"Do you need help moving out of here?" he asked, glancing around. She watched him while every hormone in her body seemed to sizzle. And all because he'd *smiled*?

"No, I don't need any help. Most things here belong to the owner, who is a college friend of mine. I just need to pack my clothes."

"Okay." The sheriff reached for Ciara and seemed disappointed when his niece's head dropped back against Myra's chest, as if she wasn't ready for Myra to relinquish her.

He tried again. "Come on, Ciara. We need to leave before the weather gets any worse."

When his words wouldn't budge his niece, he then said, "We'll have cookies to eat when we get there."

Evidently mentioning *cookies* had been the magic word since Ciara extended her arms out for him. The sheriff threw his head back and laughed while cradling Ciara close.

Myra's heart skipped, and she knew why. Baron had twin girls and he'd never shown them that much compassion. Yet he hadn't thought twice about threatening to take custody of them just to hurt Cleo.

"Looks like you know how to handle her, Sheriff Higgins."

He chuckled. "I do my best. And from here on out I prefer for you to call me Pete."

She nodded, swallowing the lump in her throat caused by the deep, husky sound of his voice. "And please call me Myra. I'll see you to the door."

At the moment, she didn't care if it seemed as if she was rushing him out. Mainly because she was. All the man had done was smile. She didn't quite understand her reaction, and she was never good at dealing with unknowns.

But when they reached the door and Ciara looked at her beneath her fluffy little cap, Myra was a goner. In truth, the little girl had captured Myra's heart the minute Myra had held her. She refused to think about what could happen to Ciara if she was left with the wrong nanny. Unfortunately, not all nannies were dependable and competent.

"We will see you on Friday."

Myra met Pete's gaze over Ciara's cap. "Yes, you will see me Friday. I should arrive by noon."

"Good. We'll be waiting."

Once again his deep, husky voice played havoc with her ears, sped up her heartbeat and tempted her to close her eyes. Moments later when the pair had left and Myra had closed the door behind them, she leaned back against it and drew in a long, deep breath.

"I will *not* be attracted to Sheriff Peterson Higgins," she said aloud, issuing the command to her brain and

expecting her body to cooperate. Opening her eyes, she
drew in a deep breath, confident that her brain and body
now understood each other.

Pete had barely made it inside his house before Bonnie began grilling him. "How did it go? Did she still want
the job? Do you feel comfortable about her being here?
Did you hire her?"

He placed his Stetson on the rack before turning with
Ciara in his arms. Bonnie didn't waste any time taking
his niece from him.

"Things went well, and yes, yes and yes to your other
questions."

Bonnie smiled. "I knew things would be all right once
you talked to her yourself."

Pete wasn't sure things would be all right, but he'd gotten tired of unintentionally offending Myra and figured he
needed to stop while he was ahead. Bottom line, she was
qualified to take care of Ciara and anything else would be
up to him to keep in check. He knew now more than ever
that doing such a thing wouldn't be easy. Sharing space
with her even with Ciara with them had been hard. He'd
been aware of every breath and every move. How would
he handle her being here with him in this house alone?

If anything, what she'd told him should help. He wasn't
her type and was too old for her liking. He shouldn't be
offended by her comment since he was the one who'd
made such a big deal of the age thing. But he had news
for her; the twelve-year difference in their ages didn't
mean a damn thing. Bonnie had reminded him that his
own father had been ten years older than his mom, and
old man Arnold was fifteen years older than Ms. Viola
and they'd been married for close to seventy years.

Pete wondered why he was wasting so much thought

on this issue. The important thing was that he and Myra
had an understanding. Well, sort of. Deep down he believed she felt the entire subject had been ridiculous since
she wasn't the least bit interested in him, and he shouldn't
be the least bit interested in her.

But he was, though. The best thing to do when she
moved in was to stay out of her way and make sure she
stayed out of his. His home didn't have split levels. His
master suite was at the end of a long hall and Myra should
have no reason to venture that far down the hall since the
bedroom she would be using had its own private bath and
Ciara's room was next door to hers. There was another
guest room and his office next to Ciara's room.

On the other hand, he would have to walk down the
hall and pass by both bedrooms to get to the living room
and other parts of the house.

"When will Myra be moving in?"

"We agreed on Friday. That will give you time to pack
and take care of things you need to handle at your place
since you'll be gone for a while. If you need me to do
anything while you're gone, let me know."

"I will and I appreciate it." Bonnie glanced down at
Ciara who'd fallen asleep in her arms. "Let me lay her
down. It's not even her nap time yet. What did you do to
her to tire her out?"

"I didn't do anything. In fact, once she saw Myra Hollister, Ciara forgot I was alive."

Bonnie chuckled. "You sound jealous."

Did he? Was he? Possibly. He wasn't used to Ciara being
so taken with anyone she wasn't accustomed to seeing on
a regular basis. "I have no reason to be jealous, Bonnie."

"Oh, by the way," Bonnie said as she headed down
the hall, "Zane's here checking on the horses. Told me
to tell you he would stop by before leaving."

"Fine." Zane was one of Derringer's older brothers. Although he was a married man now, Zane once had a reputation as one of Denver's most notorious womanizers. But then so had Derringer and Riley. Only difference was that Zane's reputation had been a lot worse. He'd also been dubbed an expert when it came to women and was known to give out advice on the topic.

Pete removed his jacket before walking over to the window. Snowfall was predicted tonight. He couldn't wait until Ciara got older and he could build a snowman with her like he'd done with Matt while growing up. Those had been fun times when both of their parents had been alive and their only worry was making sure their homework was done before going to bed.

He saw a movement out the window and recognized Zane walking toward the house. Zane, Derringer and their cousin Jason were partners in a lucrative horse breeding and training business, along with several of their Westmoreland cousins living in Montana and Texas. The partnership was doing extremely well financially, with horse buyers extending all the way to the Middle East. One of their horses, Prince Charming, had placed in the Kentucky Derby a few years ago. Since then, potential clients had been coming out of the woodwork in droves. As a result, they'd needed more land to hold the horses. Since Pete had more property than he knew what to do with, he'd leased a portion of it to the Westmorelands.

Pete had never sought out Zane for advice on the topic of women before, but maybe he should run this situation regarding Myra by Zane. Hell, doing so couldn't hurt.

Myra glanced around her bedroom. Although she had four days to pack, there was no use waiting until later.

Like she'd told Pete, she didn't have much stuff and the majority of her items could fit into her luggage.

Pete.

She couldn't stop remembering the exact moment he'd suggested she call him Pete instead of Sheriff. She knew his real name was Peterson but that he had been called Pete since he was a baby. That information had come from Miss Bonnie, who'd told her a lot about him.

Myra also knew he'd been engaged once and his girl-friend from high school had died just weeks before their wedding. She'd been participating in a local parade when she was thrown off her horse.

Myra had been saddened by the story and a part of her heart had gone out to the man who'd lost the love of his life so close to their wedding day. That had been twelve years ago and she wondered if he was now seriously in-volved with anyone.

She picked up her phone when it began ringing, rec-ognized the ringtone. "Hello, Bella."

"Myra, how are you?"

"I'm fine. What about you?"

"Doing okay but I hear there will be a snowstorm beginning tonight. I hope you're prepared," Bella said.

"I am. Besides, staying inside will give me a chance to work on my thesis."

"How is that coming?"

"Great. I'm hoping to turn it in around this time next year."

"That's outstanding. Another reason I'm calling is to invite you to the Westmorelands' chow-down on Fri-day night."

"Oh, thanks for thinking of me again, but I'm mov-ing on Friday."

"Moving?"

"Yes. I've been hired to be Sheriff Higgins's temporary nanny while Miss Bonnie is away."

"That's wonderful. You'll be perfect, and Pete will go to work each day knowing Ciara is in good hands. The girls will be disappointed not to see you on Friday."

Myra laughed when she thought of Bella and Jason's twins. She had won them over, along with a few other Westmoreland kids, with her magic tricks when she'd attended their Friday night chow-down a few weeks ago.

"Well, I'm going to have to pay them a visit once I get settled at the Higgins place. Then I can bring Ciara along."

"Oh, they will enjoy that, and we'll look forward to your visit."

"So, what's on your mind, Pete?"

Pete glanced over at Zane Westmoreland, whose long legs were stretched out in front of him as he took a sip of his beer. His wife, Channing, was expecting their first child and yet Zane had just finished telling Pete that *Zane* was the one craving stuff.

"I need your expert advice on something."

Zane lifted a brow. "What?"

"Not sure if you heard that Bonnie's sister has cancer and she needs to be in Texas for about two months."

"Yes, Bonnie mentioned it when I first got here. I told her that I was sorry to hear that."

"Her leaving means I have to hire a nanny until she returns. I found one, a woman name Myra Hollister, but I detected possible problems."

Zane raised a brow. "What kind of problems?"

"She's a very beautiful woman."

Zane nodded. "I met Myra a couple of weeks ago when Bella invited her to one of the Westmoreland chow-downs, and you're right, she's a beautiful woman. She's also single and so are you, so what's the problem?"

"She's younger than me by twelve years."

"And?"

Pete took a sip of his own beer. "I want things to remain professional between us while she's living here."

Zane lifted a brow. "Why wouldn't they? Or, why *should* they if you're attracted to her?"

Pete frowned. "Who said I was attracted to her?"

Zane chuckled and then shook his head. "Oh, you want to be one of those, do you?"

"One of what?"

"A man in denial."

"I'll admit to being attracted to her. A little."

"A little?" Zane shook his head, ginning.

"What if I told you that she's not interested in me?"

"And how do you know that?"

Pete took another sip of his beer. "I warned her that people might talk, with her being young and single and living under my roof. She told me not to worry about it since I wasn't her type and that I'm older than the men she would normally date."

Zane snorted. "At twenty-four she's probably not sure what type of man is her type, and maybe it's time for her to date men your age to see what she's been missing. If I were you, I'd see that as a challenge and prove her wrong on both accounts."

"Why would I want to do something like that?"

The room was quiet for a moment and then Zane said, "You know what I think your real problem is, Pete?"

In a way, Pete was afraid to ask because the great know-it-all-about-women Zane Westmoreland was known to tell it like it was and not sugarcoat anything. "What?"

"Your problem is denial, plain and simple. You desire the woman, so admit it and stop trying to fight it."

Pete didn't say anything, then he said, "I have to fight it, Zane."

"Why?"

"Because I don't want it. I'm not ready for it."

Zane frowned. "I'm sure you've dated and desired women before, Pete."

He nodded. "This is different." He met Zane's intense gaze for a long moment and only someone who knew him as well as Zane did would feel the depth of his turmoil.

"Ellen would want you to move on with your life, Pete."

If another person told him that, Pete would be tempted to ram his fist into the nearest wall. "You don't know that."

"I do know it and I'm wondering why in the hell you don't. Have you forgotten that Ellen used to be one of Megan's best friends? She hung around our place just as often as you did. She was a wonderful girl who didn't have a selfish bone in her body. There's no way she wouldn't want you to move on with your life. I think the problem is one you're bringing on yourself."

Zane took another sip of his beer and then added, "Apparently Myra Hollister is capable of making you want to move on and—"

"Hey, wait a minute. Things aren't that serious. We're talking about an attraction and nothing more."

Zane shook his head. "But there *is* more, Pete. Attraction and desire aren't the same. A man doesn't desire every woman he's attracted to."

When Pete didn't say anything, Zane said, "If you're trying to stop desiring her, don't bother."

"Why?"

"Because you can't get rid of something you won't acknowledge having. You have a thing for the woman, so admit it. You desire her, too, so admit that, as well. And if you don't want either, then don't hire her as your nanny because the more you're around her, the more you're going to desire her."

Pete met Zane's gaze. "Too late. I have hired her." He paused a moment and then said, "I don't want chaos in my life, Zane."

Zane drew in a deep breath. "Any chaos will be of your own making. Desiring a woman is a healthy part of being a man, Pete. If you want to waste those emotions, go ahead. Doing so won't eliminate this problem you have but will only increase it. If she stays here and you try to fight your desire, then eventually you're going to snap."

Pete frowned. "I'm a lawman—I don't snap."

"You're a man first and you will snap." Zane stood. "I'm going to give you the same advice I gave myself a few years ago."

"What?"

"Stop trying to fight emotions you're supposed to be feeling. Sooner or later you're going to have to accept there's a reason Myra Hollister has the ability to make you feel things that other women can't."

Three

Myra slowed her car and took a deep breath when she came to the marker for the Golden Glade Ranch. She thought the same thing now that she'd thought when she came this way for her initial interview. Sheriff Pete Higgins's ranch was simply magnificent.

It sat on what she figured to be over two hundred acres of land. On one side of the ranch house were rows and rows of pear trees, which fared surprisingly well in Denver's cold weather. On the other side she saw herds of beautiful horses running in a gated area.

Inwardly, she asked herself—for the umpteenth time since putting the last piece of her luggage inside the car—if she was making the right move. Now it went beyond just her personal finances. She was dealing with her peace of mind. A part of her had hoped Wallace would call so she could tell him the change of plans. That she'd been hired as a nanny after all. Then she would tell him about her misgivings.

Knowing Wallace like she did, he would probably find it amusing that she had finally met someone who interested her...even though she felt the man *shouldn't* interest her. Not only was it bad timing, it was a bad situation all around.

It was days like this that she missed her parents more than ever because she would have talked to them, as well. They had never tried forcing her to date anyone. What made her happy had made them happy and she'd appreciated that.

This would be her first holiday season without them and instead of celebrating like she knew they'd want her to do even without them, she would be returning to Charleston to fight her brother for the company he was trying to take away from her.

As she continued down the long drive, her thoughts returned to her present predicament, which was being nanny to Ciara. It would only last two months, and chances were Pete would be gone most of the time. After all, he was the sheriff of Denver. And when he was at home, they probably wouldn't see each other much.

If she really believed that, then why was she feeling like she was about to have an anxiety attack?

Finally, she brought her car to a stop in front of Pete's home and drew in a deep breath. She would take care of Ciara and then she would be gone. Why was she suddenly feeling like these would be the longest two months of her life?

Pete was convinced that when it came to women, they had a language all their own. And it was one they'd deliberately created so a man couldn't understand. He'd always thought that while hanging around the Westmoreland ladies. Now he was even more convinced, seeing how Bonnie and Myra interacted. He had a feeling that if Ciara was older, she would be right there, too.

Just like she'd said she would do, Myra had arrived at lunchtime. He'd been standing at the window staring out when he'd seen her car pull up. He wouldn't deny it; he'd been waiting for her. Mainly to help with any items she might need to get out of the car. At least that was the lame excuse he'd told himself. She hadn't needed help and the one piece of huge luggage had been easy for her to roll inside. He had looked forward to helping her get settled and showing her around, but Bonnie had appeared. She'd let him know she would be showing Myra around and that he wasn't needed.

He had escaped to the basement where his man cave was located, although now it mostly resembled a baby cave. Ciara's toys, along with her playpen and swing, took up a lot of the room. Derringer had recommended the swing. It was great on those days when a football game was on. All Pete had to do was wind it up every twenty minutes. And thanks to Flipper, one of Bane Westmoreland's Navy SEAL friends, who was a master diver and a tech wiz, Pete had a remote for Ciara's swing. He could rewind the swing without moving off the sofa. How sweet was that?

However, today Pete wanted to move around. Specifically, he wanted to go upstairs to the main floor to see what was going on. Footsteps were constantly grating across the ceiling and he figured Bonnie was showing Myra around. It was his house so shouldn't he be doing that?

He glanced over at Ciara in the swing. She looked like she didn't have a care in the world. She didn't. She wouldn't. Not even when she reached the age of twenty-one, thanks to the trust fund he and her grandparents had established from the proceeds of her parents' insurance policies.

She did look sleepy, though. Maybe he should take her upstairs and put her down for her nap. Pete rubbed a hand across his face. It was pathetic that he was looking for any excuse to leave the comfort of his man cave and go upstairs to see Myra Hollister.

If he didn't know any better, he'd think it was a deliberate ploy of Bonnie's, to keep him separated from Myra. Had Bonnie picked up on his attraction to Myra again today? Had she felt the heat while he watched Myra get out of her car wearing a pair of skinny jeans, knee boots and a dark gray pullover sweater? She'd looked good. Too good. If he hadn't been desperately in need of a nanny, he would have backed out of the arrangement. Too late. The plans were finalized. Myra would be in his home, under his roof, sleeping in the bedroom down the hall from his, starting tonight.

Over the next two months he would try like hell not to notice her. Other than being courteous when he saw her, he would pretend she didn't exist. Her goal was to take care of his niece. His was to bury his head in the sand and refuse to acknowledge he was attracted to her.

That he desired her.

There, he had admitted it. According to Zane, the first step in fighting your desire for a woman was admitting it. Until just now, Pete had refused to do so. But it had become clear to him when she'd gotten out of the car today.

How could he desire a woman this much? He wished he could blame it on something he ate or drank, or on his lack of sleep. He knew it was none of those things.

When he heard footsteps coming down the stairs to the basement, he quickly straightened up on the sofa, rested his arms on his thighs and leaned toward the huge flat-screen television on his wall. He needed to present the impression that the football game had been holding his attention for the past hour and a half.

Glancing over at Ciara, he saw she was wide-awake and looking at him. If he didn't know better, he would have said she'd known what he'd been thinking a few moments ago. He was tempted to say, *Yeah, kid, your uncle wants your nanny, but she's off-limits and needs to stay that way, so don't worry—I got this.*

"Peterson?"

He cringed. Why was Bonnie calling him by his full name again? Heck, he hadn't done anything. She had no idea about the naughty thoughts that had crossed his mind. If she had, she would have reminded him Myra was there for Ciara and not for him.

He turned to the two women, giving them a look as if he was annoyed being interrupted. "Yes?" he said, standing to his feet.

Bonnie gave him the same kind of look his niece had given him just seconds ago. It was one of those I'm-onto-you looks. "I've shown Myra around and will leave you to cover the rest."

The rest? What else is there? Instead of asking, he said, "All right. I can do that."

"Great! I'll put Ciara down for her nap while you do." Bonnie took Ciara out of the swing.

"I would hate to interrupt you watching the game," Myra said.

He looked at her and wished he hadn't. Standing in the middle of his man cave she looked like that was where she belonged. That didn't make sense. They called it a man cave for a reason. Women didn't belong.

"No problem. My team is so far ahead I doubt the Gators can make a comeback."

She crossed her arms over her chest and frowned at him. "I guess that means you're for the Buckeyes."

"Yes, that's what it means."

"Too bad. I'm Florida all the way."

He lifted a brow. A woman who liked football? "That's too bad."

"We'll see."

Bonnie chuckled. "I think the two of you need to take it outside, and while you're out there, Pete, please show her around."

"Yes, ma'am." He watched Bonnie climb the stairs with a sleeping Ciara in her arms. He then turned back to Myra. "After you."

He couldn't help feasting his gaze on her curvy thighs and delectable-looking backside in her jeans as she climbed the stairs. Drawing in a deep breath, he gave himself a second to compose himself before he followed.

"All this land is yours?" Myra asked, glancing over at Pete.

He nodded. "Yes, every single acre we covered is mine. All two hundred of them. My great-grandfather bought it back in the early nineteen hundreds. He, Raphel Westmoreland and another man by the name of Titus Newsome all settled here together."

Pete had given her a walking tour of the area around his house, which included a huge barn and several smaller houses. They had saddled up and were now on horseback, covering the outer areas. He told her he leased the majority of his property to others, preferring to spend his time on law enforcement.

"How close are you to the Westmoreland property?" she asked him when they brought the horses to a stop near a creek.

She looked at him and there was that smile again, the one that curved his lips while making her acutely aware of him as a man. He sat beside her on his horse, a huge chocolate-brown bronco he called Satin, and she knew why. His coat was so smooth and shiny it looked like satin. Although she'd assured Pete that she was a pretty good rider, he'd still given her a docile mare named Tally. She'd tried keeping her eyes off Pete during the ride, but he looked more cowboy than sheriff today, wearing a Stetson, sitting on the back of a horse.

"Do you see the roof of that house through the trees?"

She leaned forward and squinted. "Yes, I see it."

"That was the Newsome property. In a way it still is since Dillon Westmoreland's youngest brother, Bane, married Crystal Newsome. The Westmoreland spread begins where the Newsome property ends. However, because of the shape of my property, there is Westmoreland land that backs up to my line in the north pasture. That's owned by Riley Westmoreland and he's built a monstrosity of a house there. The Westmorelands own so much land in this area that we call it Westmoreland Country. I'm just a neighbor."

She heard what Pete said but knew he was more than just a neighbor. "I heard you're best friend to both Derringer and Riley Westmoreland."

He chuckled. "Boy, how did I get so lucky?"

She smiled. "I've met most of the Westmorelands."

"I understand you've been to one of their chow-downs."

"Yes. I enjoyed myself. They were kind and there are so many of them."

"Yes, they're a huge family. I'm close to all of them since we grew up together. I can recall clearly the day the cousins' parents died. I was hanging out with Derringer when he got the news."

Myra could just imagine. She knew how hard it was to lose both parents, but to lose your parents and your aunt and uncle at the same time had to have been devastating for all of them.

They continued riding and he showed her a lake on his property. "This was originally called Magnolia Lake, but Derringer's great-grandfather Raphel renamed it after the woman he loved, Gemma. Now it's Gemma Lake and it runs through the properties owned by five neighbors."

"Why did the landowners keep the name?"

"I'm told Raphel Westmoreland wasn't the only one who loved Ms. Gemma. Everybody in these parts did. She had a big heart."

"Thanks for giving me such a personalized tour." Myra checked her watch. They'd been gone for almost two hours.

"You're welcome. You'll be here two months so it's good that you know your way around. Even when I'm at work I'll only be a phone call away. Ciara is my family. I want to do right by her and take care of her the way I know my brother would want."

Myra nodded as they trotted their horses back toward the ranch. "You and your brother were close."

"Yes. Extremely close. When our parents died, all we had left was each other. I was four years older than Matt, and he thought I was his hero. I tried not to let him down."

"I'm sure you didn't."

He didn't say anything for a moment, then, "I understand you have an older brother."

She wondered where he'd gotten that information. It wasn't something she had mentioned to anyone in Denver. But then, she figured she didn't have to mention it.

Pete was the top cop in Denver. Regardless of Miss Bonnie's recommendations, he would still check her out. She couldn't blame him. She was thankful a routine background check wouldn't tell him everything. It would definitely not reveal her deep, dark family secrets. She knew publicly Baron was trying hard to make it seem like their relationship was a close one. It was just the opposite. Definitely nothing like the one Pete had had with his brother.

"We're okay," she finally said. "He's my father's son from another marriage and because his mother was always bitter about my father divorcing her, she tried turning Baron against Dad."

Why had she told him all that? She could have easily lied. Not wanting to think about Baron, but feeling the need to keep the conversation flowing between her and Pete, she said, "I understand Ciara's grandparents found it difficult to keep her."

"Yes, and after having her here with me for almost six months I can see why. They're an older couple and Ciara can be a handful. Their intentions were good but I'm glad they decided to bring her to me."

He didn't say anything for a minute and then added, "Granted I wasn't in the best position to take on a baby either, but thanks to friends and Bonnie, I made it work. I had a lot to learn. I am still learning. Ciara keeps me on my toes and you will see there is never a dull moment around her. It seems she learns something new every day."

Myra could feel the love he had for his niece in his words. "I don't want you to worry when you're away. I will take good care of her."

"And that's all I ask."

And she had no problem doing what he asked. She enjoyed Denver, and she was far from Baron's ruthlessness.

He had teamed up with Charlene's present lover, who had somehow convinced him that if he kept Myra away that he could run the company without interference from her. Thanks to her sister-in-law, Cleo, who'd overheard the two men talking, Myra knew of those plans. And she knew about how he'd planned to get Rick to help him keep Myra away.

Did Baron really think she would let Rick back into her life? Still, she didn't need drama in her life. That was when Myra decided to leave without Baron knowing where she'd gone. Her plan was to return after her birthday when she could take over the company. With the help of friends, she'd faked a trip to Europe and that was where Baron was presently looking for her. She was safe as long as he continued to be misled. She'd been careful about using a new phone and not using her credit cards.

"Ciara and I are dining with the Westmorelands later. It's chow-down Friday," he said. "I would ask if you want to go but I'm sure you have a lot of unpacking to do."

There was no need to tell him about Bella's invitation, which she had turned down for that very reason. Besides, Myra was certain the only reason he'd mentioned it was to be nice. "You're right, I need to unpack."

Moments later, when they walked back inside the ranch house, they could smell Bonnie cooking dinner in the kitchen. "Did you forget to tell her that you and Ciara are going to the Westmorelands for dinner?"

He removed his Stetson to put it on the rack by the door. He looked at her with his eyes a charismatic shade of brown.

"I told her, but it wouldn't matter with Bonnie. Besides, you have to eat. Any leftovers go to the freezer for another day."

A loud cheer made them look toward the kitchen to

see Bonnie appear with Ciara in her arms. "Down Bon-Bon," Ciara said, trying to wiggle out of Bonnie's arms.

Bonnie placed her on the floor and the baby happily raced across the room to them. As if she couldn't decide which of the two she wanted, she grabbed hold of one of each of their legs. But it was Pete who she smiled up at. "Up, Da-da." Laughing, he leaned down and picked up her, placing her atop his shoulders.

Myra had thought Pete's smile from earlier was mesmerizing but the one covering his face now was so captivating it nearly took her breath away. To breathe she had to look away. Glancing across the room, she looked at Bonnie, who seemed to be watching her and Pete with considerable interest.

Myra cleared her throat. "Do you need my help with anything, Miss Bonnie?"

Bonnie smiled. "No, I'm almost finished. Besides, now that your tour of the place is over you probably want to unpack."

"Yes, I need to do that."

"Before putting the food away, Bonnie, make sure you leave some out for Myra."

Bonnie lifted a brow and shifted her gaze from Pete to Myra. "Aren't you going with them to the Westmorelands?"

Myra shook her head. "No, I need to unpack and get settled. You're still going back to your place tomorrow, right?"

Bonnie shook her head. "No, I plan on returning to my place tonight."

"Tonight? I thought you were staying until tomorrow evening," Pete said, and Myra could tell he was just as surprised as she was. When Miss Bonnie had given her the tour, she'd said she wouldn't be returning to her place until late tomorrow.

"Yes, that had been my plan, but I got a call that one of my church members is sick. I want to check on her before I leave. Besides, I have no doubt in my mind that Myra is capable of handling things until I return."

Myra appreciated the vote of confidence. "Thanks, Miss Bonnie."

Myra glanced over at Pete at the same moment he looked at her. Their gazes collided and she felt a whoosh of air leave her lungs at the same time she heard him draw in a sharp breath.

Had she imagined it?

He quickly broke eye contact with her and asked Bonnie, "Do you know who won the game?"

Bonnie smiled. "Derringer did call to see if you were licking your wounds so I guess that means your team lost."

"Yes!" Myra said, clapping her hands. "Go Gators!" She couldn't help but laugh when Pete gave her a not-so-nice glare. "Sore loser, Sheriff Higgins?"

"You win some and you lose some. In the end, my team will win more than lose. I can't say the same for your team."

Myra fought back a grin. "We'll see about that, won't we?"

"Yes, we will." And with Ciara still sitting on his shoulders, he moved toward the hall leading to his bedroom.

Pete placed Ciara in the playpen he had set up in his room. They spent a lot of time in here or in his man cave whenever Bonnie returned home and it was just the two of them. Because his bedroom was so spacious, the play-

pen didn't take up much of the room, although it was
plenty big enough for his niece to enjoy herself.

He shook his head, grinning as he recalled Myra's reaction to hearing her team had won…and his had lost.
Most women weren't into football so having someone to
watch the games with would be…

He paused in the process of unbuttoning his shirt.
What in the world was he thinking? They would not be
watching football games together. He could just imagine sitting beside her on the sofa, sharing a beer or iced
tea. He shook his head. That wouldn't be happening. He
had to make sure their relationship remained as it should
be. He was the employer and she was the employee. This
house was her workplace and taking care of his niece
was her job.

With that thought firmly planted in his head, he
glanced over at his niece. She was playing with her blocks
so he went into the bathroom to strip and shower. It had
taken a lot of getting used to having Ciara here with him.
He'd had to learn how to dress her, undress her, feed her,
entertain her. Hell, he even sang to her before she went
to sleep at night. He still thought the hardest thing he'd
had to do was change her soiled diapers. It still was and
he couldn't wait until she was completely potty trained.
He knew Bonnie had been working on that, and Ciara
was catching on but wasn't totally there yet. He hoped
Bonnie had told Myra to continue the training during the
time she would be away.

Myra.

As he stepped into the shower and moved beneath the
spray of the water, he admitted she looked good sitting
astride a horse. He figured she'd gone to riding school.
That was pretty obvious by the graceful way she'd held
the reins. Tally, the mare he'd selected for her to ride,

had liked her. He could tell. Even Satin had liked her and usually his bad-tempered horse didn't like anyone. But Satin had let Myra touch him without trying to bite her fingers off. Amazing.

He would admit that at one point, when she'd picked up speed as if to get Tally to go faster, he'd panicked, hoping she wouldn't try to race the horse anywhere. All he could think about was Ellen. Granted, a human element had caused her accident. Nevertheless, the memories still managed to invade his mind, causing him concern.

Getting out of the shower, Pete dried off and slid into the clothes he'd taken out to wear to dinner at the Westmorelands. For years he'd had an open invitation to their chow-downs. However, he'd never made a habit of going because of work hours. And then, when the brothers and cousins began meeting women, falling in love and marrying, he preferred not to constantly be around a bunch of happily married people. Although he was happy for his friends, being around married couples only reminded him of what he would never have. What had been taken from him.

Because Ciara should be around kids sometimes, he'd tried to attend the dinners at least once a month. That way she could play with the Westmoreland babies. There was quite a number of them and nobody seemed to be slowing down. Derringer had told Pete the other day that he and Lucia were having another baby and Riley and his wife, Alpha, had announced baby news, as well. It would be their first. But the biggest news had come from the youngest member of the Westmorelands, Derringer's sister Bailey. She presently lived in Alaska with her husband. Bailey had called the family yesterday to let everyone know that she and her husband, Walker, would be having their first child in late spring.

Pete shook his head, finding it hard to believe that Bailey Westmoreland, former holy terror, was having a baby. Hell, he was still reeling at the thought that she'd settled down and married.

He glanced over at Ciara. She was still playing with her blocks. Then, as if she felt his presence, she glanced over at him and smiled. He smiled back and winked at her. She tried imitating what he'd done and instead she blinked both eyes, then laughed at herself. He couldn't help but throw his head back and laugh, too.

It had taken some getting used to, but he would readily admit that his niece had become the brightest part of his life.

Four

Myra closed the dresser drawer and glanced around. She had finally finished unpacking and had put all her things away. This bedroom was larger than the master suite of the house she'd been leasing the past few months. The huge window provided a stunning view of the mountains.

Another thing she liked about the room, in addition to its close proximity to Ciara's room, was the huge four-poster bed that reminded her of the one that had been in her parents' home. She sighed wearily. That was another thing she had to do when she returned to Charleston. Reclaim her parents' home. It was hers, but of course Baron felt he had every right to be there.

She had contacted her attorney, who had sent him a certified letter advising him that he needed to vacate the premises by the end of the year and that everything on the inventory sheet better be accounted for. She could just imagine what his reaction would be when he got the letter. Honestly, it wasn't her problem.

She glanced at the clock. A couple of hours had passed since Pete had left for the Westmorelands, taking Ciara with him. He had dressed his niece and bundled her up for the cold weather. He had knocked on Myra's bedroom door to let her know they were leaving. She had placed a kiss on the little girl's cheek and told her she would be there when they returned.

"And you're sure you don't want to go?" he'd asked her.

"Positive," had been her quick response. "I've still got a lot to do here." Truly, she didn't, but the last thing she wanted to do was ride in the same car with Pete Higgins anywhere. Being on a horse beside him had been bad enough.

"Then we'll see you when we get back," he'd said, before heading down the hall and out the door.

He hadn't said when that would be but she knew from attending one of those Westmoreland dinners that they could last for a long time, well into the night if the men decided on a poker game. She recalled Pete saying he would be working tomorrow so chances were, he wouldn't be participating in any card game. And she'd discovered that when it came to his niece, he was very considerate of her needs. He would probably want her sleeping in her own bed at a reasonable hour.

Leaving her bedroom, Myra walked down the hall stopping in front of a bulletin board. Bonnie had explained this board held the numbers of those to call in case of an emergency. There were also photos tacked to the board. One was a group photo. Bonnie had told her the photo had been taken the night Pete had taken custody of Ciara. She recognized members of the Westmorelands that she had met, and Bonnie had pointed out Bane's friends and their wives, as well as Westmorelands from Atlanta, Montana and Texas, and their newfound cousins, the Outlaws from Alaska.

Moving away from the wall, she continued down the long hall until she came to the living area. It made her feel good knowing there were some families, like Pete's and the Westmorelands, where family meant something. It was sad that her brother's greed was the driving force behind everything he did.

Myra had just sat down on the sofa and grabbed the remote when the front door opened. Pete entered the house with a sleeping Ciara in his arms. Myra stood. "You guys are back."

He nodded. "Ciara can't keep her eyes open past eight, which is fine since I need to get in bed, as well. I have to be to work at six."

She moved to take Ciara from him and was surprised when he drew back. "I've got her. On those days when I'm off, I like doing everything for her. I guess you can say it's our uncle and niece time."

"Oh, okay. Just call me if you need me."

"Sure thing." He headed down the hall with a sleeping Ciara in his arms.

He didn't call her and when some time passed, she figured he'd gone to bed himself. Then he reappeared, walking into the living room with his shirt out of his jeans and in his bare feet. She tried not to study his masculine build.

Before she could say anything, he said, "She woke up when I got her jammies on and got fussy. I ended up rocking her and singing her back to sleep."

An image of Pete, in that rocking chair in Ciara's room, touched Myra even more.

"What did you sing?" she asked, wanting to know.

He chuckled. "Well, it wasn't your typical lullaby, that's for certain. It was a Michael Jackson tune."

"Which one?" When he told her, she asked, "Oh. What made you decide on that one?"

Was she imaging things or was his gaze focused on her mouth? Specifically, her lips. Or did she only think that because her gaze was focused on *his* lips?

He slid into the recliner chair across from the sofa. "Matt was a big Michael Jackson fan. I remember visiting him when Ciara was not even a month old. A part of me was proud of how well he'd perfected the role of daddy."

He paused as if remembering that time. "Every night before putting her to bed, he'd rock her to sleep singing that MJ song. When I asked him why he'd selected that particular song, he said that because of his job in the army, there would be times when he would be gone away from her. Depending on the assignment, it could be for long stretches of time. That song was his way of letting her know that no matter where he went, or how long he'd be gone, she would never be alone because a part of him would always be with her."

Myra fought back tears while imagining Pete's brother conveying his love to his daughter that way. She could tell the memories touched Pete and she appreciated him sharing them with her.

The room was quiet before he said, "Whenever I sing that MJ song to Ciara, it's as if she's remembering Matt singing it to her. She settles down and quickly drifts off to sleep."

Myra didn't say anything. She couldn't with the hard lump she felt in her throat. "I think that's special, Pete," she was finally able to say.

He raised a brow. "Do you?"

Why did he sound unconvinced? "Yes."

"Why? Aren't you the one who told me just the other day that Ciara won't remember her parents?"

She heard the bitterness in his voice. "Yes, but that's just visually. Auditory memory is another story. That's why pregnant women often read to babies who're in their wombs, talk to them, play music to them. Babies can relate to sound. I'm sorry if I gave you the impression Ciara wouldn't remember anything about her parents."

He stood. "No harm done." Then, as if he wanted to not only change the subject, but also to end conversation between them completely, he said, "If I don't have an unusually busy day tomorrow, I should be home by five."

He was so tall that she had to tilt her head back to look at him. "Okay, Pete. Ciara and I will be here waiting."

Too late she realized how that had sounded. "What I meant is that we—"

"I know what you meant, Myra. I'll see you tomorrow. Good night."

"Good night, Pete."

Myra watched him walk out of the room. She practically held her breath until she heard the door close behind him.

"Well, do you believe me now, Sheriff?"

Pete studied the image on the mini video recorder. It wasn't the best quality, but it served the older woman's purpose. For months she'd claimed a ghost was trying to scare her out of her home. Of course, since there wasn't any such thing as ghosts, he'd figured the eighty-four-year-old woman was just seeing things. However, when she'd called today, he'd told his deputies he would go visit Ms. Katherine. The last thing he had expected was proof.

"How did you get this?" he asked.

"That boy who cuts my grass, Olson Thomas's teenage grandson. He set up the recorder for me." She gave him an I-told-you-so smile. "What do you say to that?"

Honestly, Pete didn't know what to say. But he was still certain that no matter what the video showed, there was no such thing as ghosts. "I'm going to need to keep this and have the lab analyze it. In the meantime, I need to take a look around."

"Certainly, Sheriff. And how is that pretty little niece of yours?"

He smiled at the older woman who he'd known all his life. "Ciara is doing fine. Thanks for asking."

"I understand Bonnie had to leave unexpectedly and you have a temporary nanny."

"Yes, that's right."

"Have you noticed just how pretty she is?"

Pete smiled. "I notice just how pretty my niece is every time I see her."

The older woman frowned. "I am not talking about your niece, Sheriff."

He held back a chuckle. "Then I can't imagine who's prettier than my niece."

"What about that woman staying with you?"

He met her gaze. "Oh. You mean my temporary nanny who's living with me to take care of Ciara?" he asked, feeling the need to establish the facts.

"Yes, that's the one."

He nodded. "You think she's pretty?"

"Yes."

He shrugged. "I hadn't noticed."

Thirty minutes later he left Ms. Katherine's house even more baffled. When he'd seen the video, he'd figured it had been a couple of neighborhood teens. Everyone knew of her claim of seeing ghosts. Now, after walking around her backyard, he wasn't 100 percent sold on that theory. He hadn't seen a single footprint.

When he came to a stop sign, he recalled how Ms.

Katherine had tried goading him about Myra. When he'd told Myra people would talk about them living under the same roof, Ms. Katherine had headed that list.

As he turned the corner to head back toward his office, he thought about his live-in nanny. It had been a little over three weeks since Myra had moved into his place and so far, so good. They had established a routine where he pretty much avoided her when he got home from work. He'd also put an end to his drop-in visits at home for lunch.

Myra would have dinner prepared, and he'd been surprised what a good cook she was. Granted she was into cooking healthy foods. Instead of frying chicken, she would bake it, and he was eating more salads and fewer starches. She also served herbal tea in place of sweet iced tea. He'd decided not to complain and now he'd gotten used to it. He left the table with his stomach full. After dinner he would get his niece and take her with him to the man cave. Evidently, Myra thought the basement was off-limits since she never ventured down there. Then around seven, he would return upstairs and give Ciara to Myra to get her ready for bed.

Later he would meet them in Ciara's room where he would rock and sing his niece to sleep. Afterward, he would retire to his own room, shower and go to bed. He made it a point to get up and leave for work before Myra got up the next morning to avoid seeing her.

It did bother him, however, that Myra never sat down and ate dinner with them. When was she eating? Before he got home every day? When he and Ciara retired to the man cave after dinner? After he went to bed? Pete felt he had every right to be annoyed about the distance since Bonnie would share dinner with him and Ciara.

His only problem with their living arrangements so far

were those nights when he went to bed but couldn't get
to sleep. He would lie awake, staring up at the ceiling,
hearing her movements beyond his closed bedroom door.
He knew when she would wake up to check on Ciara, or
when she needed a drink of water or milk at about three
in the morning.

He would lie in bed and remember how she'd looked
when he'd gotten home that night, recalling her outfit,
regardless of whether it was a dress, skirt and blouse, or
a pair of leggings with a pullover sweater. She had the
figure for anything she put on her body. She could wear a
potato sack and he would still give her a second look. And
then there was her hair. Some days she had it pulled up
and some days she wore it down. It didn't matter how she
wore it, it looked good enough to run his hands through.

She didn't wear makeup when she was home. Honestly, she didn't need it since her skin appeared so smooth
and soft without it. And she always wore a smile that
seemed to come naturally. His attitude or disposition
never seemed to faze her. It was as if she'd made up her
mind that he was inconsequential. The reason she was
there was to take care of Ciara and she could ignore the
rest. Including him.

Especially him.

He was well aware that she went out of her way to
avoid him as much as he was trying to avoid her. So far
they were doing a pretty good job at it and he should be
happy. But instead he had to fight down his desire whenever he saw her. That took a lot of work. More than he
wanted to put up with.

Since he was off work most weekends, they had agreed
those days would be Myra's days off. Because she had
moved into his place, she didn't have a house to check
on. Instead she had spent the first two weekends with

Leola Miller, an older woman who'd lived next door to her rental and whom she'd befriended.

Telling himself he was being considerate, he refused to go to bed on Sundays until he knew she was back, safely under his roof. Deep down he figured it was more than that. He would be sitting in the living room on the sofa and the moment she walked through the door an emotion he wasn't used to feeling would stir inside him. That first time, she'd been surprised to see him waiting up for her and had told him he didn't need to do that. He'd told her he did and without any further explanation, he'd gone to his bedroom. That second time, she'd known what to expect and had merely thanked him for caring for her safety. Her words of appreciation had broken the ice and before going off to bed he'd inquired about Ms. Miller's health. Although it had lasted less than five minutes, it had been the longest conversation they'd shared since she had moved in.

The Westmorelands had invited them for Thanksgiving dinner. She'd declined, saying she'd made plans that would include the entire weekend. She would be leaving early Thanksgiving morning and wouldn't return until Sunday afternoon.

A part of him had wondered what those plans were and with whom she had them, but because he had no right to ask, he hadn't. But that hadn't kept him from imagining things, like that guy named Wallace coming to town. The thought hadn't sat right with him, but what she did was her business.

Myra smiled when she opened the door to Bella Westmoreland. After a couple of days of snow over Thanksgiving, the sun was now peeking through the clouds. Although it was still cold outside, the temperature was a lot better than what it had been. Myra had enjoyed her girls' trip this past weekend to Breckenridge with Rekka. They hadn't spent time together in ages.

She had reached out to her college friend weeks ago after hearing about her recent breakup. She had been careful to pay only in cash, and Rekka had covered the hotel. Rekka was getting on with her life and seemed to be doing a good job of it. Myra was proud of her friend.

"Come in. I'm glad to see you," Myra said to Bella, widening the door to let her in. "I just put Ciara down for her nap. Come sit by the fireplace."

The one thing she and Bella had in common, being Southern girls, was getting used to the Colorado weather. At least Myra didn't have to get used to it too much since she would be leaving to return to South Carolina next month.

"Thanks," Bella said, peeling off her coat and handing it to Myra.

Myra had heard the story of how Bella had moved here to claim the inheritance her grandfather had left, ended up staying and meeting Jason. Myra thought Jason, and any of the male Westmorelands for that matter, was a good catch. Not only were they handsome, but they were also thoughtful and kind.

She had a feeling Pete would be a good catch, too. He was handsome, but the verdict was still out for thoughtful and kind. At least he exhibited those behaviors to his niece. Bottom line, he ignored Myra most of the time. But then, wasn't she trying to ignore him, as well?

"Would you like a cup of tea?" Myra asked.

"I'd love a cup. Thanks."

"I'll be right back."

Moments later Myra returned with two cups of tea on a serving tray she'd found in one of the cabinets.

"Thanks," Bella said. She took a sip, smiled and said, "This is delicious."

"Thanks. So what brings you out in the cold today?" Myra sked, taking a sip of her own tea.

Bella settled comfortably on the sofa. "Two reasons, actually. First, I wanted to see how you're doing since it's been over three weeks since you started here as nanny."

Myra braced her back against the sofa's cushions. She liked Bella and had from the first. There was a genuine kindness in Bella that was lacking in other people. Myra could see how Jason had fallen in love with her. "So far, so good. I've established a routine for Ciara, which is pretty much the same one Miss Bonnie had. She's such a happy baby and a joy to keep."

"That's good news. I knew you would work out well. The girls just loved it whenever Pete would bring Ciara over for a visit. She is such a happy baby and I'm glad Pete's putting her first."

Myra nodded. "He definitely loves her, that's for sure."

Bella took another sip of her tea and then said, "The other reason I'm here is to tell you about the Westmoreland Foundation Charity Ball next month."

"A charity ball?"

"Yes. The Westmoreland Foundation was established years ago to aid various community causes. The charity ball is one of the ways they do so. I was selected as this year's chairperson. The ball holds special meaning for me since it was the first event I attended in Denver and the one where I met Jason."

Myra was always moved by the sparkle she would see in Bella's eyes whenever she mentioned her husband. It was love, through and through. Myra wondered if there was a man who'd put that same sparkle in her eyes one day. She doubted it. Besides, she had so much to do before the year ended and romance was not on the list.

"I'd love to attend but I'm not sure I'll still be here. When is it?"

"This year it would be New Year's Eve night."

Disappointment settled in Myra. She would be gone by then. "Sorry, I won't be here then."

"Oh." She could see Bella's disappointment, as well. "I wish you could extend your visit. I would love for you to meet some of the other Westmorelands. They all fly in for the event."

Myra wished she could but she couldn't. When she arrived back in Charleston, she would officially be twenty-five and removing Baron and putting Wallace in charge was her priority. "I have business I need to take care of in Charleston during the days following Christmas, but if I finish it in time, I will try and come back."

Bella beamed. "That would be great and I hope you truly will come back. There's nothing like starting the New Year off right."

Myra agreed. "Now I have a request to make of you."

"Sure, what is it?" Bella asked, a smile curving her lips from corner to corner.

"I need to stay here in Denver through Christmas, and not leave until the day after. Miss Bonnie will be returning the week before Christmas and I'll need to find somewhere to live for about week. Will you have any accommodations at your bed-and-breakfast inn?"

"I will definitely hold a place for you, but you're welcome to move in with me and Jason."

Myra shook her head. "I can't possibly do that. A room at your inn would work for me. Just let me know how much it will be."

"Nothing. I don't charge for when the family, friends or business associates of the Westmorelands come visiting."

"I have to pay you something."

Bella shook her head. "No, you don't and we won't discuss it any further. Besides, I doubt you'll be needing a room. There's no way Pete will let you leave here without a place to stay. That's just not Pete."

Myra decided not to disillusion her, but it could very well be Pete. To him she was just a paid employee whose time ended when Bonnie returned. He had no reason to care where she would be living after that. Deciding to change the subject, she asked about the twins.

"The girls are fine and of course they are excited with our news."

Myra lifted a brow. "What news?"

An enthusiastic look shone on Bella's face. "Jason and I are expecting another baby, or babies. Everyone thinks I'm nuts for even wanting twins again."

"Congratulations!" Myra said, leaning in to give Bella a hug. "I am so happy for you."

"Thanks. I'm surprised Pete didn't mention it. We announced at the chow-down Friday night."

It was on the tip of her tongue to say that she and Pete didn't have that kind of relationship. They barely talked. Other than asking her about Ciara's day, he never said anything except casual comments about the weather.

"Well, I am happy for you."

Bella smiled happily. "Thanks. Oh, I almost forgot. There's another reason I stopped by. Pam's acting school is hosting a Wild West festival. They are having a lot of games for the kids and even baby activities. It's for all ages, including adults. Pam is even getting her sister, the one who's a Hollywood actress, to fly in and participate. I think it would be great if you brought Ciara."

Myra knew that Dillon's wife, Pam, used to be a movie star and now she owned an acting school in town. From what she'd heard, Pam also held several social events at her school that benefited the community. The Wild West festival was one of them. "Sounds like fun. When is it?"

"Friday night. We're canceling our regular chow-down, which means all the Westmorelands will be on hand to help. I'm sure Pete will be lending a hand, as well."

If he had planned to do so, he definitely hadn't mentioned it to her. But he truly didn't have to since she was not privy to his personal schedule.

Bella glanced at her watch. "I hate to rush off but I have a couple more stops to make. Thanks for the tea."

"You're welcome," Myra said as she walked Bella to the door. "And thanks for your visit."

Five

The moment Pete entered his home, Myra came into the room with Ciara walking beside her as she held her hand. When his niece saw him, she said, "Da-da," before racing across the room as fast as her chubby little legs could carry her. He automatically bent to capture her in his arms. His little bundle of joy.

Had it only been six months ago that Ciara had come into his life, changing it forever? Honestly, he could barely remember what he'd done before her. When he came in from work, he would go down to his man cave, but he still did that. Now he had company. He also had home-cooked meals and didn't have to eat dinner alone at McKays, the popular restaurant in town.

After hugging his niece and smelling the sweet apple scent of her hair, he looked over her head at Myra, who was watching them with a tender expression on her face. Why? He always greeted his niece each day with a hug.

Usually Myra would appear from the kitchen carrying Ciara in her arms. On those days he would automatically take her from Myra, giving him the opportunity to smell the woman's honeysuckle scent, as well.

"Hello, Myra," he said, standing to his feet with Ciara in his arms.

"Pete. Are you ready for dinner?"

"Yes. What did you prepare today?" Not that it mattered. After skipping lunch, he was hungry enough to eat a horse.

"I made a meat loaf with green beans, squash, rice and yeast rolls."

Pete nodded. It all sounded good. Why was she still standing across the room? He figured since he was holding Ciara, she had no reason to come closer. He intended to remedy that right now. Crossing the room to her, he handed Ciara back, intentionally leaning in to get a whiff of that honeysuckle scent. "If you don't mind holding her while I wash up?"

"Of course, I don't mind."

He moved away, then turned to her. "I prefer that you eat dinner with me and Ciara every day."

She lifted a brow. "Why?"

"Because I want you to." With that said, Pete moved toward his bedroom.

Because he wanted her to...

Myra watched him leave, not sure what to say. What if she didn't want to? She hadn't thought dining with him every evening was a requirement.

It didn't matter that Bonnie had mentioned she would join him and Ciara for dinner and that it was time she used to bring him up-to-date about anything she felt he needed to know. Myra had been fine telling him everything when she handed Ciara over to him when he got home. They had established a routine. So why was he changing it?

Looking down at Ciara, she said softly, "There are days when I don't understand your uncle, sweetie. If he wanted me to join you guys for dinner, then why didn't he say so that first night?"

Not expecting Ciara to respond, she hugged her and headed for the kitchen. She had already set the table for one, so after placing Ciara in her high chair, she moved around the kitchen to put another place setting on the table. She could hear Ciara practicing some words she'd been teaching her. The little girl was a quick learner and the things she could comprehend always amazed Myra.

Myra knew the moment Pete entered the kitchen. Glancing over at him she saw he'd taken a shower. The top of his head still glistened with water. Ciara, who'd been busy with blocks, began clapping and said, "Da-da back."

He went over to her, lightly pinched one of her cheeks and said, "Yes, Da-da is back."

Myra looked away; otherwise she knew she'd get emotional. Whether Pete knew it or not, what he'd just said was monumental. He was acknowledging that his brother was gone and wouldn't be returning. However, Matt had left him with this special gift and allowing her to call him Da-da was something he could deal with. He would tell Ciara the truth as she got older.

He sat down at the table and so did she, after putting a small plate of food in front of Ciara. Before Bonnie left, she'd told Myra that Ciara was ready to feed herself. Myra had continued to show her the proper way to use a spoon. Although the end result was somewhat messy, Ciara managed to put more in her mouth than on the floor.

They were in the kitchen's eating nook instead of the huge dining room. Bonnie had told her Pete preferred the smaller area since it was normally just him and Ciara and Bonnie. After placing their food on the table it occurred to Myra just how small the area was. Just how cozy.

"Is anything wrong?" he asked, sitting down at the table.

She looked at him. "No. There's nothing wrong." She quickly finished what she was doing and sat down.

Before Pete could reach for anything, she said, "Just a minute, Pete." Then, glancing at Ciara, she said, "Grace, Ciara."

Ciara didn't disappoint. She bowed her little head and said the recitation Myra had been teaching her to say all week. When she finished by saying the "Amen," Ciara lifted her head, smiled and began clapping her hands.

Myra heard Pete chuckle. "Well, I'll be," he said in amazement, glancing over at her. "When did you teach her that?"

Myra was glad he was pleased. "This week. Today I decided to put it to the test. She did good, don't you think?"

He nodded. "Yes, my girl did excellent. Thank you for teaching her that."

"You're welcome."

They began eating in silence and then after a short while he asked her, "How did your day go today, Myra?"

She tried looking down at the food on her plate and not at his face. The last thing she needed was to get mesmerized by his eyes or turned on by his lips. Both had the ability to render her senseless when she dwelled on them for long.

"My day went fine. The usual." After she said that it occurred to her that he probably didn't know what "the usual" was. So, she said, "We got up around eight, ate breakfast, did our classes and—"

"What classes?"

She glanced up and the moment their gazes connected, she felt her muscles tighten as desire warmed her to the core. It was desire, she recognized it, although she wasn't used to the reaction. But she knew what it was. It was there whenever she looked at him. There whenever she lay in her bed at night and thought about him.

At first the desire bothered her and she appreciated that when she woke up in the mornings, he was gone. Then she had all day to pull herself together by staying busy. Then when he walked through that door in the evenings and she looked at him, her torment would start all over. Heaven help her. What was there about Sheriff Peterson Higgins that got to her?

"Myra?"

She blinked upon realizing she'd been sitting there staring at him. He probably thought she was a nitwit. "Yes?"

"What classes are you teaching Ciara?"

She swallowed and broke eye contact with him to glance over at Ciara and smile. The little girl was doing better with the spoon today. "Her colors and shapes. And in addition to her saying grace, we learned another song this week, but we're not ready to share that with you yet."

He seemed amused and the husky-sounding chuckle caused a frisson of fire to rush up her spine. Eating dinner with him wasn't a good idea. Not when he was this close, sitting right there in front of her.

"Okay," he said, smiling broadly. "I'll take your word for it."

His smile did it to her again and she nodded. She

couldn't help a smile touching her own lips. "Bella stopped by today."

"She did?"

"Yes. She wanted to tell me about the Westmoreland Charity Ball. She's chairperson this year."

"That's what I heard, and I told Jason we better have something stronger to drink than tea," he said, chuckling again.

Myra grinned, not sure how to take this side of him. This was the longest conversation they'd ever held and he seemed to be in such a good mood. "Tea isn't the only drink Southerners drink, you know."

"You could have fooled me," he said, grinning as well, tilting his head to acknowledge her teacup and the tea in it.

She laughed as she took a sip. Moments later she said, "Bella also told me that she and Jason are having another baby."

Another huge smile spread across Pete's lips, making Myra's heart skip a few beats. She still didn't know how a man's smile could affect her that way.

"Yes, and I'm happy for them. I remember the first time I met Bella. I was a deputy and got called out to her grandfather's ranch on official duty. Someone had thrown a huge rock through her living room window with a note telling her to leave town."

"Did you get the person who threw the rock into her house?"

"Yes, we got them."

"Them?"

"Yes, it was two."

She waited to see if he would fill her in on the rest and when he didn't, she decided to change the subject. It

was then that she told him about the Wild West festival.
He seemed interested.

"Not sure if I'll be able to attend since I might be
working that night, but you should take Ciara. It sounds
like a lot of fun."

"I think I will." Bonnie had mentioned that periodi-
cally Pete worked nights. Myra couldn't imagine having
him home during the day and being underfoot.

She glanced up at him and caught him staring. "What?
Is something wrong?"

He shook his head. "No, nothing is wrong." He broke
eye contact with her and began eating again.

Drawing in a deep breath, she then asked him the
same question he'd asked her. "So, how was your day?"

Pete wasn't sure Myra eating dinner with him and
Ciara had been a good idea after all. He could barely eat
with her sitting right there. But then, that was why he'd
suggested she eat with him. He had wanted her close. He
was tired of her conveniently being absent during meal-
time when he would sit and wonder where she was and
what she was doing.

Although it was pure torture, he liked glancing up
from his meal every so often to see her sitting there. She
looked pretty today like always, and he hadn't realized
until now just how much he liked the sound of her voice.
He also liked sitting here sharing a meal with her. Holding conversation. That was when he remembered she'd
asked how his day had gone.

"It was pretty busy. First off, I answered a call at Katherine Lattimore's house. She's in her eighties and a retired
teacher here in town. She claims she gave up teaching
after the likes of Bailey and Bane Westmoreland." He

heard the sound of Myra's soft chuckle and it seemed to caress his skin.

"I understand those two cousins used to be a handful while growing up."

"Yes, and whatever you were told, believe it. Derringer, Riley and I were constantly covering up for them to keep them out of trouble. Bailey and Bane, along with the twins—Aiden and Adrian—were the terrible foursome."

"So what was wrong with Ms. Lattimore?"

Pete found himself sharing Ms. Katherine's ghost story and liked how Myra would tilt her head, listening attentively. "So, there you have it. She actually captured a ghost on video. Now it's my job to find out what in the heck is going on."

"How do you intend to do that?"

"Not sure yet," he said. "And by the way, this food is delicious." He truly meant it.

"Thanks."

"Who taught you how to cook?"

She shrugged what he thought was a beautiful pair of shoulders. "In college I assisted at a homeless shelter's soup kitchen for an entire year. Various chefs would volunteer their time and they often held cooking classes. It was fun." Not only had she learned her way around the kitchen, she was also educated on how to eat healthy foods without sacrificing the delicious flavor.

He decided to ask the one question he'd pondered. "How did you become a Gators fan? Did you attend the University of Florida?"

She smiled and he swore he felt the brilliance of it spread to him. "No, I didn't, but Wallace did."

His hand tightened on his glass. He recalled the name on her Facebook page. He also recalled the man it belonged to. "Wallace?"

"Yes, Wallace Blue. He works for my father's company and attended the University of Florida. I went to a small all-girls university in Boston for college. My school didn't have a football team so when I wanted to learn about football, Wallace was eager to teach me."

I just bet he was, Pete thought and wondered where the anger toward a man he didn't know came from. "Do the two of you still date?" A part of him regretted asking the question, but it was too late to take it back.

"Date?" She laughed. "Wallace and I have never dated. We're good friends. He's like another big brother to me."

A part of Pete was glad to hear that.

"What about you, Pete?" she asked. "Why are you a Buckeyes fan? Did you go to Ohio State?"

Her question gave him pause and he stopped eating for a minute. Drawing in a deep breath he glanced over at her and said, "Yes, but just for a year. My dad died and I came home to attend college here. But I traveled back to Ohio whenever I could to see Ellen."

"Ellen?"

He met Myra's gaze across the table. "Yes, Ellen, my fiancée. When we graduated from high school, she and I left Denver to attend Ohio State together."

He waited for the next question. The one that usually followed whenever people heard he'd once been engaged. People who didn't know him well enough to know the full story of what had happened.

When she didn't ask, he glanced up and saw her eating. "Aren't you going to ask what happened?" He wasn't sure why he'd prompted her. For all he knew she'd already heard the story. Bonnie might have told her.

She looked up at him. "Not unless you want to tell me."

He thought about her response. In the past, people had

asked him about it even when he hadn't wanted to tell them. "Ellen was killed two weeks before our wedding day. She was an excellent rider and participated in the Martin Luther King parade every year. That year someone tossed a firecracker near her horse's feet. The animal panicked and threw her."

"I am so sorry, Pete."

"Thanks. So am I."

Silence covered the table and he glanced over at Ciara. He'd just shared a part of his past, but Ciara was his future. Making sure she grew up happy was what he intended to do for the rest of his life.

He also knew something else. This was the first time he had mentioned Ellen's name to anyone without a feeling of deep pain in his heart, without bitter agony settling into his every pore. And without the need to look back and cling to those memories of her.

What could that mean? He needed time to himself to think through some things, possibly resolve issues within himself. Pushing his plate back, he said, "Dinner was great, Myra. Look, I need to go check on a few things and meet with my foreman so I might be a while."

"Okay."

He then left the kitchen, grabbing his Stetson off the rack on his way out the door.

Myra watched Pete leave and released a breath when she heard the sound of the door closing. She felt bad for him and regretted that she had reopened wounds for him. Bonnie had already told her how he'd lost his fiancée, so why had she wanted to hear it from him?

It had been heartbreaking. After twelve years he still hadn't gotten over her death.

She glanced over at Ciara and the mess she'd made.

At least she hadn't gotten any food in her hair and hadn't thrown any off her plate. She had eaten every single bite. Myra got up from the table. It was time to clean up the kitchen and then clean up Ciara.

She didn't have time to consider the feelings Pete's story raised.

A couple hours later she was done with both and yet Pete still hadn't returned. His truck was still parked outside, which meant he hadn't left the property, but he could very well have gone off on horseback after meeting with his foreman. Holding Ciara closer to her chest, she moved away from the window. The only thing they could do now was to wait for him to return.

It was getting dark and Pete knew it was time to head Satin back toward home. The ride had done him good since he'd needed to clear his head about a few things.

He had loved Ellen since he'd discovered what love was. They'd been so close and had known what they wanted out of their lives. He'd looked forward to their wedding day as much as she had because he'd seen it as the start of what would be the best days of their lives.

And then all his hopes and dreams, his future, had ended because of someone's cold-bloodedness. It had taken years to stop blaming himself, but there were times when his mind would play the "if only" game.

He closed his eyes and tried to remember their last days together. As time passed it was getting harder and harder to recapture the memories and that bothered him. Then he'd had that dream, the one where she'd come to him as if to free him. He hadn't liked it and he'd fought the meaning behind it.

Until Myra walked into his kitchen.

He hadn't expected the emotions he'd felt that day or

since. He hadn't known he was capable of finding another woman as desirable as Ellen. Nor had he known he could dream of Myra while fighting to keep Ellen in his heart. He'd found the attempt exhausting. Did that mean it was time to move on?

What had Bonnie said? That he'd been breathing and not living? He could now say that she'd been right about that. He'd made love to women to release primitive urges and nothing more. However, being around the Westmorelands on Thanksgiving and seeing how happy they were with their spouses had made him wish for things that he had turned his back on. Things that deep down he knew Ellen would want him to have, even without her.

During dinner he and Myra had shared a real conversation over a meal. He had enjoyed talking to her, listening to what she had to say. Looking at her. Noticing how she was looking at him. He figured she had no idea what that look had done to him. How his blood had stirred each and every time he'd caught her staring.

He had desired her from the start, but according to her he wasn't her type. He was older than the men she normally dated.

Maybe Zane was right and he should take her words as a challenge, especially knowing how she'd been sneaking those looks at him. He smiled as he headed Satin back toward home.

Myra Hollister had no idea that things were about to get interesting in the Higgins household.

Myra glanced at the clock when she heard the sound of Pete returning. He'd been gone for nearly four hours. She had gotten Ciara ready for bed and rocked her to sleep, singing the song Pete usually sang.

Instead of going to bed herself she decided to wait

up for him to apologize. It was her fault he'd had to talk about his fiancée. Needing to see him before he went to his bedroom, she walked out of the kitchen.

"Pete?"

He turned and she could tell he was surprised to see her. Even though it was still pretty early, usually after making sure Ciara was tucked in for the night, she would escape to her bedroom and watch television until falling asleep.

"Yes?"

"I want to apologize."

He lifted a brow. "Why? What did you do?"

She nervously licked her lip. "I made you talk about something that brought back painful memories for you."

"You don't have anything to apologize for, Myra."

"I feel like I do."

"Well, you shouldn't. Is Ciara asleep now?"

"Yes."

She could tell from his expression that he regretted not being there to put his niece to bed. "You missed dessert," she told him.

"Did I?"

"Yes."

"What was it?"

"Peach cobbler."

He nodded. "I love peach cobbler."

"I used those peaches Bonnie told me about in the freezer."

He nodded. "It's not too late. I think I'll have some cobbler now," he said, walking toward her. When he got close, she moved out of his way so as not to block the entrance.

Instead of passing by, he stopped. He stood right in front of her, and the way the lamp shone on them, she could look deep into his eyes.

"I don't bite, you know," he said.

She wasn't so sure about that. She could feel the essence of him in every pore, nerve and pulse. "Yes, I know you don't."

He was still looking at her, not having moved an inch. She was about to tell him good-night when he said, "Come eat some cobbler with me."

Not sure she'd heard him correctly, she said, "You want me to eat some cobbler with you?"

The corners of his mouth edged up, displaying that smile that did crazy things to her. "Yes. If you don't, I might end up eating the entire pan myself. I need you to stop me if I try doing such a thing."

She couldn't hold back a grin. "You love peach cobbler that much?"

"Afraid so. Bonnie didn't warn you?"

"She did mention it was your favorite."

"It's more than my favorite. It's one of those things you can become addicted to if you aren't careful."

She doubted he knew that he was effectively pushing her buttons and making her wonder just what other things he could become addicted to if he wasn't careful. She was standing there imagining a lot of things and when his gaze dropped to her mouth, the hormones in her body seemed to burst to life. "That sounds like a big problem for you, Pete."

"It is, so will you join me in the kitchen to make sure I don't overdo it?"

Myra nervously licked her lips. Things were getting pretty hot here in the living room and she didn't want to think what the temperature might be in the kitchen. Honestly, she should have the good sense to tell him that his eating habits weren't her concern, but that would be a lie. Hadn't she made sure all his meals were healthy ones?

Not that he looked out of shape or anything. If he looked any more in shape, she would go bonkers.

"Since you presented it that way, then I guess I will," she said. Turning, she went to the kitchen, knowing he was following her.

Six

"That's it, Peterson Higgins—no more. You've had three servings already," Myra said, laughing, as she guarded the pan of peach cobbler on the counter. "I thought you were joking about eating the entire pan."

He stood in front of her, grinning from ear to ear. "You should not have baked it so well. It's delicious."

"Thanks, but flattery won't get you any more peach cobbler tonight. You've had your limit."

He crossed his arms over his chest. "I could have you arrested, you know."

Crossing her arms over her own chest, she tilted her chin and couldn't stop grinning. "On what charge?"

The charge that immediately came to Pete's mind was that she was so darn beautiful. Irresistible. But he figured that was something he could not say. He enjoyed this playful side of her and would admit to enjoying this spirited side of himself, as well.

It had started out with them sitting down and eating

the cobbler and him commenting on how good it tasted. That got her to talking and she told him about those weekends she'd spent with Ms. Miller and that one of the things they did was watch old movies and how much she enjoyed it. He tried to remember the last time he'd watched a movie. A new one or an old one.

She snapped her fingers in front of his face to reclaim his attention. "If you have to think that hard about a charge, then that means there isn't one."

"Oh, there's one, all right. How about harboring someone else's property?"

She rolled her eyes at him. "How about it? Do you honestly think you can make that charge stick?"

"Oh, you'll be surprised what all I can do, Myra."

She tilted her head to the side as if to look at him better. "Do tell, Pete."

Her words—those three little words—made a full-blown attack on his senses. He drew in a shaky breath, then touched her chin. She blinked, as if startled by his touch. "How about 'do show,' Myra?"

Pete watched the way the lump formed in her throat and detected her shift in breathing. He could even hear the pounding of her heart. Damn, she smelled good, and she looked good, too. Always did. He'd noticed the leggings and pullover sweater when he'd arrived home earlier. She looked comfortable and sexy as hell.

"I'm not sure what 'do show' means," she said in a voice that was as shaky as his had been.

He tilted her chin up to gaze into her eyes, as well as to study the shape of her exquisite pair of lips. "Then let me demonstrate, Ms. Hollister," he said, lowering his mouth to hers.

The moment he swept his tongue inside her mouth and tasted her, he was a goner. It took every ounce of strength he had to keep the kiss gentle when he wanted to devour her mouth with a hunger he felt all the way in his bones. A part of him wanted to take the kiss deeper, but then another part wanted to savor her taste. Honestly, either worked for him as long as she felt the passion between them.

He had wanted her from the moment he'd set eyes on her, but he'd fought the desire. He could no longer do that. He was a man known to forgo his own needs and desires, but tonight he couldn't. Not when they were out of control. She might deny it, but he could tell from the way she was responding to him that need was driving her just as much as it was driving him.

He heard her moan and the sound sent even more heat spiraling through him. Wrapping his arms around her waist, he pulled her closer, loving the feel of her body pressed against him. It was as if she was melting into him. It had been a long time since he'd tasted this much passion in a woman. He doubted she knew just how potent she was, just how she was driving him to the brink. It was as if he couldn't taste her enough, hold her close enough. He wanted to absorb her into his skin, his entire body, as their tongues tangled.

Knowing if he didn't stop kissing her now he would have her spread out on the counter, he ever so slowly broke off the kiss. But not before swiping another lick across her lips with his tongue. Whispering close to her ear, he said, "Peach cobbler isn't the only thing I could become addicted to, Myra."

Then, taking a step back, he dropped his hands to his sides and stared at her. She wore passion well. "Don't cook dinner tomorrow. I'm taking you and Ciara out."

"Oh."

He dragged in a deep breath, pulling the luscious scent

of her through his nostrils. "I'll check on Ciara before going to bed."

"Okay. Good night."

"Good night, Myra." Pete turned to leave the kitchen and as hard as it was for him to do so, he didn't look back.

Myra somehow made it to a chair and sat down at the table before her legs gave out. She'd been kissed before, but never like this. Never with slow, seductive strokes. He'd taken her mouth in a way that seemed effortless yet unquestionably thorough. And she had accepted the stroking of his tongue with ease, as if she'd known it would spread through her bloodstream. And when he'd finally lifted his mouth from hers, she'd wanted to cry in protest.

Drawing in a ragged breath now, she heard the sound of Ciara's door closing and knew he had left his niece's room. Would he go on to his room like he'd said he would, or would he come back into the kitchen to give her another mind-drugging kiss? Did she want him to? She held her breath, wondering what move he would make, and released it when she heard the sound of his bedroom door opening and then closing. He hadn't just kissed her; Pete had devoured her mouth in a way that still had her head spinning.

Standing, she got busy and covered the rest of the peach cobbler and put it in the refrigerator. She wanted to be in her bedroom with the door closed just in case Pete did decide to come back. He said he didn't bite, but he did a good job of licking and sucking.

And the kiss had gone on and on. It'd seemed neither of them had wanted it to end. She'd become enamored with his taste. He obviously knew what he was doing, and she'd merely followed his lead while his mouth and tongue coaxed hers into moaning.

Just thinking about it now was increasing the beat of her heart and had erotic awareness curling her stomach. Tonight, she had undergone a sexual revelation, instigated by a man she'd initially decided wasn't her type and was older than those she would normally date.

Date? Now, that was a laugh. When was the last time she'd gone out with anyone other than Wallace? And just like she'd told Pete, Wallace was more like a brother to her than Baron ever had been.

Moments later, after tidying up the kitchen, she headed down the hall to her bedroom. Once inside, she leaned against the closed door and touched her lips, still feeling a tingling sensation there.

She had to put Pete and that powerhouse of a kiss out of her mind and move forward on the resolve that it couldn't happen again. No matter how enjoyable it had been. She would get a good night's sleep and hopefully in the morning she would be able to think straight.

"So, how's that new nanny working out for you, Sheriff?"

Pete rubbed his eyes as he glanced up from the computer screen. He'd been rewatching the video Ms. Katherine had given him. Although it was a long way from being 4K ultra HD, he could still detect a willowy feature that seemed to be floating around her backyard. He and his men had agreed there was definitely something there; they just didn't know what.

His gaze lit on the man standing in the doorway of his office. Pete and Detective Lewis Tomlin had grown up together in Denver. They had started the police academy at the same time, and then Lewis left to work as an FBI agent for a couple of years. "She's working out just fine, Lewis," he said, leaning back in his chair with the palms of his hands bracing against his neck. "She's doing a great job taking care of Ciara and she's a darn good cook. Thanks for asking."

He knew the questions should end there but wouldn't. Lewis's grandmother was one of Ms. Katherine's cronies, so Pete was sure he'd heard something. It didn't take long to find out what. "I heard she's pretty."

Yes, she was definitely that, Pete thought. She was pretty and tasted like heaven on earth. He'd had to force himself to get that kiss they'd shared out of his mind. He had gone to bed thinking of it, had dreamed sweet dreams reliving it, and had awakened that morning yearning for another.

"You heard right," he said, seeing no reason to lie about it.

"Heidi and I would like to meet her."

Pete frowned. "Why?"

"She's only with you temporarily, right?"

"Yes."

"Well, we hear she has a ton of experience taking care of kids. She might come in handy."

Pete lifted a brow. "You're looking for a nanny?"

Lewis chuckled. "No, but Heidi and I are planning to get away for a few days by ourselves and are looking for someone to keep the kids for us."

"When are you planning this trip for?" Pete asked him.

"The second week in January. We want to head up to Aspen for some skiing."

"Sorry, but she won't be around. She plans to leave sometime around the holidays to return south."

"Well, if she changes her mind let me know."

"I will."

Lewis moved on and Pete thought about their conversation. Specifically, the part about Myra leaving. Why was the thought a downer? He shook his head, deciding not to dwell on that. What he wanted to do was think about that kiss some more, how easily their mouths had fit together.

He had left her a note on the kitchen table this morning with directions to McKays, deciding to give her a little break from being in the kitchen tonight. She deserved it. He'd taken Bonnie out to dinner with him and Ciara plenty of times. No big deal. But deep down he knew it was a big deal. At the end of her stay in Denver he wanted her to reach the conclusion that he was her type and not too old for her to date.

Then what?

He rubbed his hand down his face. He hadn't thought that part through yet. At that moment his cell phone went off and he quickly clicked it on. "Sheriff Higgins."

"Pete, this is Bane. Crystal said you called."

"I did and thanks for getting back to me. I remember you mentioning a while back that Flipper had developed some sort of special high-tech video camera."

"Yes, that's right. You know Flipper—whenever you can keep him out of the water, he's inventing some high-tech gadget or other."

"If possible, I'd like to use it in a case I'm working on. I think it might be helpful."

"Then you're in luck. Flipper and Swan will be here this week. They're coming to town with the baby. I'll tell him to bring it when he comes."

"Thanks, I appreciate it." Pete knew Flipper and his wife recently had a little girl. "And by the way, how're Mac and Teri doing? And all your other SEAL teammates?"

Because Bane was so close to his teammates, namely Viper, Coop, Mac and Flipper, all the Westmoreland family and their friends had gotten to know the guys pretty well.

"The McRoy household is doing fine. I talked to Mac the other day and he said the twins are climbing all over the place and getting into anything that's not nailed down. I told him to stop whining. He wanted sons and now he has two."

Yes, now Mac had two sons and four daughters. "Well, I'm glad he got what he wanted and I heard the ranch they bought in Texas is pretty damn nice."

He talked to Bane for a few minutes more and before ending the call, he asked about Bane's family. Bane and Crystal were the parents of three-year-old triplets: two sons, Adam and Ace, and a daughter, Clarisse. Adam and Clarisse had been named after Bane's parents.

Turning his attention back to the computer screen, Pete jotted down some notes but again his mind began wandering. He'd never allowed a woman to interfere with his work before. He would push thoughts of Myra to the back of his mind. It wouldn't be easy, but he was determined.

"Welcome to McKays."

Holding Ciara in her arms, Myra smiled up at the waitress. "Thanks. I'm meeting someone here. Sheriff Pete Higgins," she said, glancing around the restaurant. This was her first time here, but she'd heard it was one of the most popular eating establishments in town.

"He's already here and asked for a high chair for the baby. Please follow me."

"Thanks."

Myra was led to the back and around several couples dining. It seemed a number of them recognized Ciara and smiled to greet her by name. Myra figured Pete must have brought his niece here often for her to be so popular. When they rounded a corner, she saw Pete the moment he saw them. The minute their eyes connected she felt like she was burning from the inside out.

He stood and smiled and she could no longer ignore the deep attraction she had for him. She had awakened that morning giving herself a pep talk. Although she had enjoyed their kiss immensely last night, she knew it couldn't happen again. First of all, she was his employee and living under his roof. The last thing she wanted to indulge in was an affair with her boss. Okay, she would be honest with herself and say she would love to indulge in one, but it wouldn't be right. Besides, the man was older and not her type. But he could kiss the panties off a girl without much effort. And there he stood, looking as handsome as sin and with a body to die for.

"Da-da!"

Ciara stretched her hands out and he took her out of Myra's arms. Myra watched the little girl wrap her arms around his neck tight and kiss him on the cheek. It was obvious she'd missed him. This was the first time Ciara had seen her uncle since dinner yesterday. Myra could tell Pete had missed his niece, as well.

"Hello, Pete."

"Myra. I hope you found this place without any problems."

"I did," she said, sliding into the seat at the booth. "I'm glad you wrote down those directions for the short cut. GPS would have probably had me in the middle of rush hour traffic."

"Yes, it would have. How was your day?"

Myra could tell him she had spent a lot of the day thinking about the kiss and trying to convince herself it was one and done. She'd pretty much succeeded, too. But it was hard sitting across from him and staring at his lips and recalling what they'd done to hers last night.

"It was great. That song I taught Ciara at the beginning of the week, she has it down pat now. But please don't ask her to sing it. She gets loud and stuck on what is obviously her favorite part. I don't think you want to get her started in here."

He laughed, placing Ciara in the high chair. "I'll make sure I wait until we get home."

Her breath wobbled at what he'd said. It was as if they were a couple and he was referring to his house as their home. She tried forcing the thought to the back of her mind, but his smile was mesmerizing her.

At that moment the waitress brought them their menus. Myra broke eye contact to look down at it. "What do you suggest?"

"I would say their meat loaf but yours even tops the one here."

"Thanks, that's a kind thing to say."

"I wouldn't lie to you." He then said, "Since we've taken meat loaf off the list, I suggest their pork chops. For Ciara, I usually order the kids' meal ravioli. She seems to like it."

The waitress took their order and Myra glanced around, noticing how crowded the place was and the number of people staring at them. She glanced back at him and knew he noticed, as well. Before she could say anything, he said, "If you recall, I gave you fair warning."

Yes, he had. Not that it mattered for her, but he was the town's sheriff and happened to be single. People were probably curious as to what was going on in his life. Although Denver was a large city, certain parts were pretty close-knit and it seemed this area was one of those.

That was fine because at that moment the waitress returned with their food.

* * *

Pete smiled as Ciara entertained them during the meal. She hadn't burst into any songs, but she was trying to tell him about her shoes. He didn't quite understand what she was saying and Myra had to translate. That meant he got to look into her face without it being so obvious he was doing so.

He had been anxiously watching the entrance to the restaurant and remembered the exact moment she walked in with Ciara. It was something about seeing them together that filled him with a sense of contentment that both surprised and confused him. He had pushed the feeling aside to concentrate on Myra.

She was wearing a long flowing skirt with a pair of leather boots. Her wool sweater made the trendy outfit look sexy as hell. The way her curly hair flowed about her shoulders with this mussed-up look had lust zipping up his spine. He no longer felt guilty about wanting her and accepted that was how it would be. He could no more deny he found her desirable than he could deny his masculinity.

And whenever she smiled, he felt his breath wobble in his throat. He would love to one day take her dancing. He could imagine holding her close in his arms while burying his face in the hollow of her throat and drinking in her scent. One he was getting used to.

And just think, he had come close to not hiring her as Ciara's nanny. She'd been with them for weeks now and he couldn't help but appreciate how well she took care of Ciara and his household in Bonnie's absence. He also appreciated how she'd reminded him he was a man. A man who'd finally realized he hadn't been living but merely breathing, like Bonnie had claimed.

He hadn't counted on such a change in his life. He

had thought he was satisfied with things staying the way they'd been for years. But every time he saw Myra, spent any time around her, he was well aware of what she did to him. A part of him felt he should be fighting it. After all, why get worked up over a woman who would be walking out of his life in a month? She would be leaving Denver and their paths might never cross again. There could never be a future with them and a part of him wasn't sure he wanted one with her or any woman. The only thing he wanted to concentrate on was the here and now. And right now, he was fully aware of Myra Hollister in every pore of his body.

Another thing he was aware of was that seeing them together had drawn a lot of attention. McKays was one of the few eating places in town that was locally owned. The owner, Tony McKay, had been close friends with Pete, Derringer and Riley while growing up and had taken over the running of the restaurant when his old man passed away a few years back.

McKays was a place where locals came to eat and in some cases get wind of the latest gossip. A number of the people in here had known Pete his entire life. They had known his parents and Matt and had encouraged him to run for sheriff. They were also people who'd known Ellen and most, like Bonnie, had told him at one time or another that it was time to find someone and settle down, claiming Ellen would have wanted that for him. In the past, he'd harbored feelings of resentment, thinking they had no idea what Ellen would have wanted. But they'd known Ellen as long as they'd known him. They knew Ellen hadn't had a selfish bone in her body. She'd loved life, embraced it fully.

He could admit now that the Ellen they'd known, and

the one he'd known, would have wanted him to move on and live again.

"Evening, Sheriff."

Pete snapped out of his thoughts to stare at the man and woman standing beside his table. "Good evening, Mr. Karl and Mrs. Inez."

He knew they expected him to introduce them to Myra. In fact, he was fairly certain that was the main reason they'd come over to his table. "Not sure if you've met Myra Hollister. Myra is helping me out with Ciara while Bonnie is away visiting her sister."

They exchanged greetings with Myra. "The Fosters were good friends of my grandparents," he told Myra.

"Yes, Thomas Higgins was captain of our football team back in the day," Karl said about Pete's grandfather. "And I was captain of the basketball team."

"And I bet it was a very good basketball team," Myra said, smiling, causing the old man to blush.

"Yes, we were pretty good. We won the state titles in both football and basketball our senior year."

The older couple moved on, but their approach had somehow broken the ice, and other people trickled over to their table on their way out for an introduction to Myra, as well. Since they were not sitting by the exit door, there was no doubt in Pete's mind that everyone was making a conscious effort to come by.

"This is certainly a friendly town. For such a large city, Denver still somehow presents itself with a small-town atmosphere," Myra said, after what Pete hoped was the last person to interrupt their meal left.

"Only certain parts of the city," he said, taking a sip of his coffee. "Where you really get the big-town feel is downtown and in the newer areas, where a lot of people don't know each other and prefer it that way."

They were about to order dessert when Pete detected someone else had approached their table. He glanced up and saw that Derringer, Zane, Riley and Canyon were out dining with their wives. Greetings were exchanged. No introductions were needed since Myra had met everyone at a Westmoreland chow-down a few weeks back.

Zane told Pete that his sister Gemma had called that day to say she and her husband, Callum, would be coming to town for Christmas after missing Thanksgiving. Riley then chimed in to add that several of their cousins living in Alaska, the Outlaws, would be joining them for Christmas, as well. As much as Pete liked the Westmorelands, he was glad when they'd finally moved on, dismissing the thought that he just wanted Myra's attention for himself.

"You're off work this weekend, right?"

Myra's question reeled in his thoughts. "Yes."

She nodded. "I'll be going back to Breckenridge this weekend."

Her statement gave him pause. "Joining your girlfriend there again?" he asked, in what he hoped was a casual tone. That night when they'd shared peach cobbler, she'd told him where she'd gone over the Thanksgiving holidays. Unknowingly, she had solved a mystery that had plagued him.

She shook her head. "No."

He thought that was all she planned to say, and then she added, "I planned to go there to get away."

Pete wondered if she was making a conscious effort to be gone the weekends he was off. Those first two weekends she'd spent with Ms. Miller, had that been intentional, as well? "Any reason you're going away for the entire weekend I'm off work?" he decided to ask.

She shrugged before saying, "Bonnie said when you

had weekends off, she would use that time to return to her place to check on things. I don't have a place to go, but I want to give you and Ciara some alone time."

That was thoughtful of her but not necessary. "Ciara and I will have that even if you're there. Please don't leave to go somewhere on our account."

"You're sure? I don't want to intrude."

"You won't be." In fact, he wanted her there with him and Ciara. He would question the reason why later. Right now, he just wanted to enjoy her company and he had only another month left to do so.

At that moment the waitress returned with their dessert.

"Thanks again for dinner, Pete," Myra said, when he opened the door to his home. He'd wanted Ciara to ride with him back home and he had an extra baby car seat in the back of his sheriff's cruiser.

"Did Ciara take a nap today?" he asked.

She glanced over her shoulder at him. "Yes, why do you ask?"

He chuckled. "Because she was a lively one tonight. On the way home I made the mistake of telling her to sing that song you taught her and she kept it going until we got here."

Myra couldn't help but chuckle. "You can't say I didn't warn you. But she is getting sleepy. Just look at her."

They both did and although the little girl was fighting it, it was obvious she could barely keep her eyes open. "I'll get her ready for bed," Myra said, reaching to take Ciara out of Pete's arms. Their bodies brushed and Myra felt her heart skip a beat.

Cuddling Ciara close, as if the little girl could serve as a barrier between her and Pete, she took a step back. "I'll let you know when you can come tuck her in." Faking a yawn, she added, "I had a long day and after I get Ciara ready for you, I'm going straight to bed."

"All right."

Why was she feeling a little disappointed that Pete hadn't talked her out of going on to bed? What had she expected him to say? *Meet me in the kitchen later so I can devour your mouth again?* Maybe he regretted the kiss like she wanted to do. Only problem was, she couldn't.

"Is something wrong, Myra?"

Too late, she realized she'd been standing there staring at him. Namely at his mouth. That very sensuous mouth. He had a look in his eyes that almost made her moan. It was a good thing he wasn't privy to her thoughts. "No, nothing is wrong." Holding Ciara tightly in her arms, she hurried on down the hall.

She had given Ciara her bath and had just finished getting her into her jammies when the bedroom door opened. She drew in a sharp breath. This was the first time Pete had ever come into the room while she was here. Usually, he would wait until he knew she'd finished and had gone to her own room. He stood in the doorway looking way too fine.

"You're just in time. She's all ready for you," Myra said, trying to make it seem as if his unexpected appearance hadn't rattled her.

"Good."

He walked over to the dressing table and smiled down at his niece. Myra had wanted to braid Ciara's hair tonight but the little girl had been too fussy to let her do so. Huge locks of curls covered her little head and she could barely keep her eyes open. But when she saw Pete, she smiled up at him and asked, "Want me sing, Da-da?"

He laughed and then quickly said, "No, Ciara, it's my time to sing to you."

Myra watched as he picked up Ciara and carried her over to the rocking chair and sat down. When he was settled in the chair with his niece cuddled in his arms, he glanced over at her. Their gazes collided and too late she noticed her breathing pattern had changed. She wondered if he'd noticed.

She backed up toward the door. "Ahh, I'll leave the two of you alone now. Good night." She quickly reached the door.

"Myra?"

She turned around. "Yes?"

"Please meet me in my man cave in half an hour."

She swallowed while he held her gaze hostage. "Is there something we need to talk about?"

"No."

She nervously licked her lips as she felt the heat from his eyes drift over her. Her body automatically responded to each lingering visual caress. "Then why do you need me to come down to your man cave?"

"I want to kiss you again."

At least he was honest and now she needed to be, as well. "I don't think that's a good idea." No use lying and saying she didn't want him to kiss her again, because she did. However, it still wasn't a good idea.

"I don't think so either but my mind isn't being ruled by what's a good idea or what's not a good idea. It's being ruled by the memory of your delicious taste."

Before she could respond, although she really didn't know what to say to that, Ciara reached up and took a hold of his chin to force him to look down at her. "Sing, Da-da."

He smiled down at his niece and before he could look back at her, Myra had quickly left the room and closed the door behind her.

Seven

She isn't here.

Pete tried downplaying the pang of disappointment he felt in the pit of his stomach. Had he honestly thought she would be? He had hoped. There was no way he'd misread the chemistry between them tonight. Chemistry he was certain Myra had read, as well. But just because she read it didn't mean she intended to act on it.

He rubbed a hand down his face as frustration set in. Not toward her but toward himself. They'd only shared one kiss and one dinner date and he expected her to… what? Hell, he'd been thinking like a typical man when what he was dealing with wasn't a typical woman. He was finding that out while watching her interactions with Ciara. She was definitely a lot different from any other woman he'd dated over the years. Mainly the ones who understood their role in his life was just for pleasure, and he made sure his role in their lives was for the same purpose.

But what if Myra wasn't into taking on a casual lover?

Pete didn't want to think of that as a possibility, especially now that he was on board with the idea. Now that he'd accepted the fact that the attraction between them was way too strong. It had been hard sitting across from her and watching her eat their dessert of chocolate à la mode. Every time she licked her spoon was an erection waiting to happen.

A sound made him turn toward the stairs and his breath caught when he saw Myra standing there staring at him.

She had come after all.

Myra had questioned herself with every step she took down the stairs.

Peterson Higgins was way out of her league. He unsettled her. Made her wonder about things between a male and female that she'd never thought about before. With her lack of experience, a part of her wished she was getting a PhD in sex education instead of child psychology. Then she would know how to deal with this. How to deal with him.

Drawing in a deep breath, she paused on the stair. That was when he turned and looked at her. The minute their gazes connected she knew he did more than unsettle her.

She'd never had a weakness when it came to a man before. She could stand her ground with any of them. Being a sister to Baron made such a thing possible as he befriended some of the worst men alive. Men who had no respect for women and thought their only purpose was pleasuring a man.

Yet here she was. She'd come to Pete even when she knew it was not in her best interest to do so.

Myra had enjoyed their kiss last night even as she

told herself it couldn't happen again. Yet every time she looked at his mouth, she *wanted* it to happen again.

And again and again.

The look in his eyes was telling. So was the erection pressing against his zipper. She should turn and run as fast as her legs could carry her. But she didn't. Something phenomenal was taking place between them and they had yet to exchange a single word. It was so intense it scared her in one sense but fueled the fire within her in another.

She didn't fully understand what was happening but knew it was something she could no longer deny. She didn't want it or need it but wasn't sure how to stop it.

Her father had always told her never to cower. If there was a problem, then you dealt with it. Therefore, somehow and someway, she was here to deal with the likes of Sheriff Peterson Higgins.

"You came."

The sound of his husky voice broke the silence, intruded on the strong sexual chemistry flowing between them. It did nothing to lessen the intensity. If anything, his voice heightened her awareness of him.

"Yes, I came."

She watched the sudden flare of his eyes. It seemed as if her response had ignited something within him. The very thought had her nerves dancing, and her brain racing. Not being able to handle the sexual excitement curling her stomach any longer, she asked, "So what's next?"

He smiled that slow, sensuous, make-your-panties-wet smile. "We talk first."

She blinked. *Talk?* Had he actually said that? Who wanted to talk at a time like this?

Myra's concentration was on him when he took slow, deliberate steps toward her. She hadn't walked all the way down the stairs and now he was coming toward her and bringing all that heat with him. When he reached the stairs, he extended his hand up to her.

She knew she had two options. Refuse the hand he offered and leave, or take it and go where he led.

What did he have to say?

She already had an idea.

Little did he know, although she was innocent about some things, she knew just how a man's mind worked.

Deciding at that moment which option she would choose, she took Pete's hand.

Pete led Myra over to the sofa, fighting hard to stay in control of his senses and his body.

The moment their hands touched, his pulse had done a double kick in response. But he was determined that they have "the talk." It was basically the same conversation he'd had with every woman since Ellen. However, Myra's would be modified somewhat. How? He wasn't sure yet. All he knew was that it would be different because she was different.

He sat down and placed her in his lap. Her sharp intake of breath signaled her surprise. Good, he had a lot more surprises in store for her.

Pete shifted her to face him at the same moment she nervously licked her lips. If she had any idea what that did to him, she would stop.

"What do you want to talk about, Pete? Although I think I know already."

"Do you?"

"Yes. This is where you tell me all you want is sex, sex and more sex and that you're going to make sure I enjoy it every time. However, what you don't want is me getting confused about anything. You don't want me to get sex mixed up with love. You want me to know that you don't do long-term, just short-term, and that your heart is encased in unbreakable glass."

He didn't say anything because what she'd said was true. That was what he'd intended to say, or at least a version of it. Some other man had given her the this-is-how-it-will-be speech before and she fully expected him to give her the same spiel.

Why did he suddenly feel like a total bastard?

"That's right, isn't it, Pete? That's what your talk will be about."

He stared at her, feeling drawn in by the way she was looking at him, by her scent, by the very essence of everything that was her. He drew in a deep breath knowing there was no need to lie, although at that moment he hated admitting the truth. "Yes, my talk would be similar to what you just said."

She nodded and somehow he could detect her disappointment. Had she expected more? Now that she knew she wasn't getting *more*, would she be willing to settle?

"I'm not into casual sex so I'm going to have to think about it, Pete."

A part of him was glad she wasn't going to rush into anything. He wanted her to be certain because once she gave her consent, he planned on taking her on one hell of a sensuous journey.

"I understand and I want you to think about it and not rush into your decision. However, I want to give you something to mull over while deciding."

"What?"

"This."

And then he captured her mouth with his.

Myra groaned. Pete's mouth devoured hers and she tried fighting the desire he was stoking within her. He was laying it on thick, to the fullest. This kiss was even more powerful than the one last night. Again she followed his lead. When he deepened the pressure, she moaned again. *This is what the girls at college would call one of those bone-melting kisses.*

Moments later, when he pulled his mouth away, all she could do was whisper his name. "Pete." She was convinced that she would be consumed with his taste for days.

Nibbling at her, he used his tongue to lick the corners of her mouth over and over again. "Say my name again," he whispered against her moist lips. "I want to hear you say it again."

"Pete." She didn't hesitate and the moment she said it, his tongue slipped back inside her mouth, claiming hers fully. She was tempted to tell him she'd made up her mind already. She wanted to move forward and didn't want any boundaries between them. She would deal with the consequences later.

Shivers rippled through her. If she were to tell him that now, without fully thinking things through, she would be embarking past a point of no return.

She wanted Pete. For her this was a first because she'd never truly wanted any man. She'd been curious about sex but not curious enough to throw caution to the wind. What she was craving wasn't based on curiosity but on something else altogether.

She was being stripped of her senses with this man and so far all they'd done was share kisses. But then he wasn't just kissing her—he was expertly making love to her mouth.

Somehow she mustered up the strength to rebel against her body's desires. No matter how much she was enjoying being in his arms this way, kissing him, she had to hold on to her sanity and not throw away twenty-four years of self-control for one night of passion that would mean nothing to him.

She was the one to pull away and it was only then that she realized he had maneuvered his hands under her skirt and was softly stroking her inner thigh.

Suddenly, memories of a similar scenario with Rick shot through her mind and she scrambled off Pete's lap, nearly falling to the floor in the process.

"Whoa, you okay?" he asked, when he caught her before she hit the floor.

No, she wasn't okay. She needed to breathe in deep, but more than anything she had to get out of there. Now. He must have seen the anxiety in her features. He tightened his hold on her. "Myra? Are you okay?"

She saw the concerned look on his face and instead of answering, she nodded. Drawing in a deep breath she said, "I'm okay and you can release me now, Pete."

The moment he did so, she took a step back. "I should not have come down here tonight. It was a mistake."

Then, without saying anything else, she rushed up the stairs.

Eight

Pete stood at his kitchen window, drinking coffee while looking out at the expanse of his land. This was something he did every morning before leaving the ranch for work. One day Ciara would inherit Matt's share of this place and he was determined to keep things up and running for when that day came.

As he sipped his coffee, he thought about what had happened in his man cave last night. Myra had wanted him as much as he'd wanted her, he'd been sure of it. But when he'd touched her intimately, she'd bolted. Although she had denied anything was wrong, the look on her face had said otherwise. He'd been in law enforcement long enough to know when someone had had a flashback of something they didn't want to remember.

Had she once been the victim of sexual assault? Had some man tried touching her in the same place he had? The thought that what he'd done might have conjured up bad memories had hit him in the gut last night and he could still feel the pain.

That was the reason he was still here, an hour later than he normally would be. He knew Ciara would wake up around eight and that Myra would get up earlier than that to start breakfast. He intended to be here when she did. He wanted to apologize for taking liberties he should not have. Everything they'd done had been consensual. The last thing he wanted was to create a hostile work environment. He had never taken advantage of a woman and wouldn't do so now.

"You haven't left for work yet?"

He turned at the sound of Myra's voice and then wished he hadn't. It took everything within him to ignore the shivers rushing through him. No woman should look this beautiful so early in the morning. She was wearing a pair of jeans and a pullover pink sweater. That color made her look feminine as hell and just as sexy. Then there was the way her curly hair hung loose around her shoulders. He doubted she was wearing any makeup and she looked simply radiant just the same.

Regaining control of the situation, he said, "No, I was waiting for you to wake up."

She wrapped her arms around herself in a somewhat nervous stance. "Why?"

He wanted to cross the room and pull her into his arms. He wasn't sure how he could make up for last night, but he would try. "I didn't want to leave before apologizing, for touching you in a place that made you uncomfortable. That was not my intent, Myra."

She didn't say anything. Instead she studied the floor for a minute. Then she raised her head and looked at him. "You didn't make me feel uncomfortable. Just the opposite, Pete. I liked you touching me there."

Relief rushed through him. And something else. Confusion. He again fought the urge to pull her into his arms. "Then can you tell me what last night was about? Why you ran away?"

She began nibbling her lips and he knew she was pondering what to tell him, if anything. "It's not important. At least not anymore."

He stared at her, wanting to accept what she was saying, but the cop in him knew there was more to it. However, if it was something she wanted to put behind her, she had that right.

"Okay," he said, moving past her to pour his unfinished coffee in the sink and rinse out his cup. When he turned back around, he asked, "Did you decide if you're taking Ciara to that festival?"

"Yes, I'm taking her."

He nodded. "I promised Pam I would help out after I got off."

"Okay, then we will see you there."

He nodded and headed for the door. Before grabbing his Stetson off the rack, he turned and walked back over to her and did what he'd wanted to do since first seeing her that morning. He pulled her into his arms, waited one moment to see if she'd lean in or away and then kissed her. He needed this. He wanted this. Her taste empowered him. When he released her mouth, he stared at her swollen lips.

"Was that your way of telling me your proposition of an affair is still out there?" she asked, staring up at him with a pair of gorgeous hazel eyes. Whenever she looked at him that way, he felt like a man doing a balancing act right above a dangerous cliff. One wrong move and he could fall.

He touched her chin. "It's my way of letting you know I am here if you ever need me."

Pete turned and headed for the door. Pausing, he grabbed his Stetson off the rack and then he looked back at her and said, "Yes, I still want an affair with you, Myra."

He then opened the door and left.

Myra touched her lips that were still tingling from Pete's kiss. When she heard the sound of his truck leaving, she moved to the table and sat down. The man was way too nice for his own good. And way too sexy.

After she'd left him last night she'd had a lot to think about because she'd done the very thing she'd sworn she would not do, and that was to allow the likes of Rick Stovers to dominate her thoughts. He wasn't worth it.

She would never forget how at twenty she'd drawn his attention, that of an older man, one twelve years older. He was a successful attorney and had seemed quite taken with her. She was in her last year of college and was home for the holidays. They'd met at a party and had immediately hit it off. He was a perfect gentleman and had wined and dined her, made her feel special.

And then one night, after plying her with a delicious dinner, he'd given her "the talk." At first she'd thought she was ready. She'd been a twenty-year-old virgin and had wanted to experience for herself what the whispers were about. But "the talk" from him had bothered her. Maybe because he had stated what he intended to do so matter-of-factly; it had given her pause.

They'd kissed and his hand had found its way under her dress. He began getting rough. It was then that she had pushed him away and told him she wanted to leave. He'd got mad and told her she wasn't going anywhere.

She owed him for the four weeks he'd wasted his time with her and he intended to have her with her brother's blessings. That was when Rick had told her everything, including Baron's suggestion that he seduce her. When she'd headed for the door, he had tried stopping her. The moment he put his hands on her, she put her self-defense training to good use. By the time she left his apartment he'd been on the floor, clutching his precious jewels and bawling like a baby.

She had gone straight to her brother's home and confronted him. He hadn't denied Rick's allegations and even said he didn't appreciate her making such a big deal about it. He'd further stated that Rick was a man and had needs and if she couldn't give Rick what he wanted, then she needed to get out of the game.

That was when she'd made the decision to leave older men alone.

Until Pete.

All she'd felt with Pete had been tenderness. His touch had been so different from Rick's. And so was the way he looked at her. After a good night's sleep, even his proposition of an affair didn't bother her. He wasn't looking for forever and neither was she. He was obviously still in love with his fiancée and would remain single for the rest of his days.

And although she wasn't interested in settling down now, a time would come when she would want to do so. She loved kids. At twenty-four she had plenty of time to find a man who wanted the same things she would want. Still, Pete's proposition was something she was thinking about.

Myra smiled when she heard Ciara waking up singing the song she'd taught her. As she left the kitchen to head toward Ciara's room, the kiss she'd shared with

Pete still had her lips tingling and a part of her warned that if she wasn't careful, Pete could start her heart to tingling, as well.

Pete leaned back in his chair and gazed at the two men sitting across from his desk. Navy SEALs, Bane Westmoreland and his teammate David "Flipper" Holloway definitely looked the part even when out of uniform.

"I appreciate you letting me use this camera, Flipper. Now I'll capture some footage of my own to figure out who's trying to scare Katherine Lattimore."

"Any leads?" Bane asked, while sipping coffee.

"None. To be honest, we all thought the ghosts were in her head until she captured the images. It's obvious someone was in her backyard moving around dressed as a ghost. But when I went to check I couldn't find a single footprint."

"You know why," Bane said, grinning.

Pete frowned. "No, why?"

"Because ghosts don't have feet."

Pete shook his head. Having grown up with the Westmorelands, Pete was used to their penchant for humor when there was none. "You're turning into a comedian, aren't you? Maybe it's time for your commander to send you on another mission."

"Ignore Bane," Flipper said, rolling his eyes. "Seriously though, there has to be a reason for that, other than the wisecrack one Bane just gave. Mind if I take a look at the footage that lady captured, Pete?"

"Not at all."

It didn't take a minute for Pete to load the video into his computer and it took Flipper even less time to reach a conclusion. "That's not a real body moving around in her backyard."

Bane joined the two men at the computer. "Flip's right."

Pete frowned and studied the image. It looked pretty damn real to him. "But how?"

"It's fake," Flipper explained. "Made with a high-powered camera similar to what filmmakers use on set. It's so advanced you can basically code in that lady's address, and any sort of image you want will pop up on the property via satellite."

Pete ran a hand down his face. "Then that image could be coming from anywhere."

"Yes," Bane agreed, "but in order for the satellite to pinpoint the target, there has to be a digital receiver somewhere in Ms. Katherine's backyard. It's probably so tiny you either can't see it or it resembles something you wouldn't detect even if you saw it."

"But I bet the two of you probably could."

Flipper chuckled. "Of course. We're SEALs."

Yes, and Pete couldn't help appreciating that such competent men were protecting this country. "Who would go to the trouble of doing this?" he asked, thinking aloud.

Bane nodded. "An even bigger question is why. Ms. Katherine has lived in that house for years."

"It's not the same house that you and Bailey spray painted orange," Pete said.

Flipper glanced over at Bane. "You and Bailey spray painted some old lady's house?"

Bane shrugged. "One of my childhood pranks."

"Why?" Flipper wanted to know.

Bane smiled. "She was my teacher and wanted to promote me to the next grade. I wanted to hang back another year."

Pete contained his laughter when he saw how Flipper

was staring at Bane. "Why would you want to be held back in school?" Flipper asked.

"So I could be in the same grade as Bailey."

Pete chuckled. "Now you see what the city of Denver had to put up with? Bane and Bailey, along with the twins, were holy terrors."

"We learned our lesson, trust me," Bane said. "Dillon made us repaint her entire house and not just the part we'd messed up. Ms. Katherine benefited when she got her entire house repainted." He glanced over at Pete. "So where is she living now?"

"In the house her fourth husband left her."

"The lady's been married four times?" Flipper asked.

"Yes." Pete then glanced over at Bane. "I think she got married again after you left for the military, Bane. She was only married to the guy a few years before he passed away."

"Well, it's my guess that someone is trying to scare her out of that house for a reason, Pete," Flipper said. "And whatever the reason is, they feel it's worth the money. Those kinds of illusions aren't cheap."

Later that day Pete pulled up into the acting school's parking lot an hour later than he'd originally planned. Getting out of his truck, he glanced around. The place was packed, and he knew why. One of Pam's sisters, Paige Novak, had followed Pam's footsteps and pursued an acting career in Hollywood. It seemed she was making a name for herself. No doubt a lot of the people attending tonight were autograph seekers.

He got pulled into several conversations when he was seen by other people. That was fine because the closer he got to the door, the more his stomach became tied in knots knowing he would be seeing Myra.

He finally reached the door and a group of smiling

men stepped out, grinning from ear to ear. He overheard their conversations and they were all muttering about how beautiful Paige Novak was. He thought so, too, but it was his opinion that Myra was even more of a stunner. There was something about the woman that got to him.

"Want a soda pop, Sheriff? It's two dollars."

He glanced down at the young woman. It was Pam's other sister, the youngest, who was working on her PhD at Harvard. "Don't mind if I do, Nadia," he said, fishing a couple of dollars out of the back pocket of his jeans. "I see Pam has you working."

Nadia laughed. "She has everybody working. Even Jillian flew home. She's in a booth dressed as a cowgirl and working the cotton candy machine"

Moments later Pete entered the foyer and could hear sounds coming from other parts of the building. He headed toward the auditorium, passing a number of people who tried getting him to stop and engage in conversation. However, he spoke and kept walking because at the moment he was on a mission to see two certain females. One had already stamped her name all over his heart and the other could…

He paused a moment to draw in a deep breath.

This was the first time since losing Ellen that the thought of another woman getting close to him, especially to his heart, had ever crossed his mind. He couldn't help but wonder what that could possibly mean.

"How do you enjoy living with the sheriff and being nanny to his niece?"

Myra was convinced that if another person asked her that question, she would scream. So far, this was the sixth time. Pete had been right about some people worrying there was more going on under his roof than met the eye.

Regardless of whether or not they were wrong in their assumptions, the bottom line was that she and Pete were adults who could do as they pleased.

"I enjoy taking care of Ciara," was her constant reply. She refused to address whether or not she enjoyed living with the sheriff.

"Evening, Ms. Coffer and Ms. Finley. If you don't mind, I need to borrow Myra for a minute," Lucia Westmoreland said, appearing seemingly out of nowhere, and looping her arm with Myra's.

"Of course we don't mind," the ladies chimed simultaneously and then she was whisked off with Lucia, pushing Ciara in her stroller.

She gave Lucia an appreciative smile. "How did you know I needed rescuing?" Myra asked when they were out of earshot of the two women.

"Trust me, those two are the nosiest on this side of town."

Myra nodded. "Pete tried to warn me that if I took the job of nanny and moved in with him there would be talk, but I didn't believe him."

Lucia lifted a brow. "Why didn't you?"

"Well, mainly because this is Denver and I figured this town was more progressive than that."

"It is, for the most part, but like any place else there are those who thrive on gossip. Besides, for years Elnora Finley thought she had a vested interest in Pete. She was convinced Pete would make her daughter Rose a perfect second husband."

"Oh. Whatever happened to the woman's first husband?"

"He was killed in a motorcycle accident a few years back. Elnora felt since both Rose and Pete had lost the people they loved, they would be the perfect match."

Interesting. "Did Pete and Rose ever date?" She hated asking but a part of her wanted to know. Needed to know.

"Not that I know of. In fact, Pete had to pretty much tell Rose and Elnora to back off because he wasn't interested. For years after losing his fiancée he didn't date at all. And he rarely dates now."

Yet here Myra was, contemplating giving in to his proposition. Drawing in a deep breath, she knew it was time to make some decisions. Pete had brought out desires within her that she'd never dealt with before. To deny him would mean denying herself. She no longer wanted to do that.

"Well, look who just walked in."

Myra followed Lucia's gaze across the crowded room and her eyes connected with Pete's. His mouth edged up in a smile and she knew at that moment Peterson Higgins had gotten to her in a big way.

"Um, my magazine is doing a segment on law and order. I wonder if Pete would agree to be on the cover, posing as a sexy Western lawman. I bet it would definitely increase sales."

Myra knew Lucia was editor-in-chief of a national women's magazine, *Simply Irresistible.* With her gaze still locked with Pete's, Myra said, "Yes, I bet so, too."

Pete felt the force of meeting Myra's gaze like a jolt of sexual energy. Never had any woman consumed so much of his concentration, his thoughts and his desires. That included Ellen. When Ellen had died, she'd been the same age Myra was now. Twenty-four. Now, as a nearly thirty-seven-year-old man, he was facing an entirely different set of emotions. He was dealing with a degree of lust he hadn't had at twenty-four.

She looked gorgeous, standing there beside Lucia

dressed in a long flowing cowgirl skirt, Western blouse
and cowhide boots. Her hair flowed around her shoulders beneath a cowgirl hat. At that moment he wished
he could cross the room and kiss her, regardless of the
crowd of people here.

"I hope you're staring at your nanny and not my wife,
Pete."

He didn't even break eye contact with Myra when
he responded to the person who'd come to stand beside
him. "I have two eyes and can check out both of them."

Derringer Westmoreland laughed. "You're crazy,
man."

"You think so."

"At least you better be because if for one minute I
thought you were honestly checking out Lucia, I would
have to end your life."

It was only when Myra's attention was drawn to a
woman who'd approached her and Lucia that Pete looked
over at Derringer. "Need I remind you of what could happen when you threaten a man of the law," he said, opening
his bottle of pop to take a swig. He felt hot and needed a
drink, even if the contents weren't as strong as he'd like.

Derringer chuckled. "That badge won't matter any
to me. Besides, it won't be the first time you and I have
battled it out."

Pete smiled, remembering that time in fifth grade.
"Oh, yeah, and then when we got home, your momma
gave us another ass-whipping."

"Only because Zane told on us. What we should do
is go find him and beat the crap out of him. I don't care
if it was close to thirty years ago. We can even get Riley
to help us since he was the victim of Zane's snitching a
few times, as well."

Pete glanced back over to where Myra stood, still talk-

ing. "Let's do it another night," Pete said. "I need to go
rescue Myra from Ida."

"Okay, but just so you know, now you have me wondering about something."

Pete lifted a brow. "What?"

"Who's going to rescue Myra from you?"

Instead of addressing Derringer's comment, Pete
moved across the room toward Myra.

Although the woman standing in front of her was
steadily chatting, Myra was aware of Pete crossing the
room toward her. His heat called out to her, encompassed
her. She thought about what Lucia had said about him
being on the cover of a magazine. She could envision him
dressed as he was now, in jeans, a Western shirt, Stetson
and boots. The rugged cowboy type had never appealed
to her before. Now, thanks to Pete, it did.

"Evening, ladies."

Before either Myra or the woman could return the
greeting, Ciara let out a huge "Da-da." Myra watched
the grin spread across Pete's face when he leaned down
to take his niece out of the stroller. Once she was in his
arms, Ciara planted a huge kiss on her uncle's cheek,
nearly knocking his Stetson off in the process.

"My hat, too, Da-da," she then said, pointing to the
miniature cowgirl hat on her head.

"I see. It's pretty."

"Me pretty, too."

Pete laughed. "You certainly are."

"Evening, Sheriff," Ms. Ida said. "I was just telling
your nanny that if she needed more work after Bonnie
comes back that I know a family on the other side of town
who could use her services."

Had the woman said that? Myra wondered. She

couldn't recall anything they'd discussed since becoming aware of Pete's approach. "I appreciate you looking out for me, Ms. Ida, but I'll be returning to Charleston not long after Miss Bonnie returns."

The woman looked disappointed. "Oh, how sad."

Myra wondered what would be sad about her leaving Denver. Before she could ponder that any further, Pete said, "If you don't mind, Ms. Ida, I need to borrow Myra for a moment." He took her arm and steered her off.

"Oh, of course."

Myra didn't say anything as she walked beside Pete, who carried Ciara. There was no need to tell him he could place Ciara back in her stroller since it was apparent he wanted to carry her around.

"I thought I'd better save you from Ida. She's known to be long-winded."

"She seems to be a nice lady."

"Yes, she is. Just talkative."

They didn't say anything for a while, satisfied to let Ciara take center stage as she sat atop Pete's shoulders, pointing out a number of things that caught her attention. "She's alert—that's good."

Myra chuckled. "She won't be for long. She missed her nap today."

"Have you guys eaten yet?" he asked her.

"Yes, we got here early and Pam fed all the helpers before the door opened."

He lifted a brow. "You're a helper?"

"I was. Ciara and I volunteered to take the first hour of face painting."

Pete grinned. "Let's be honest. You did the face painting and Ciara watched."

"She was my little helper. And by the way, I like your look."

He raised a brow. He had nice brows and his lashes were nice, as well. "And what look is that?"

"One of a notorious cowboy." He hadn't left home dressed that way this morning so he must have changed clothes at the office.

He chuckled. "A notorious cowboy? Evidently, you missed seeing this," he said, pointing to his badge. "This makes me a lawman."

As they continued to walk around, stopping at various booths, Myra was not only aware of the man by her side but that several people were staring at them…like they'd done that night at McKays. Pete was a very observant man and she figured he was noticing, as well. "I could kiss you and really give them something to talk about," he whispered close to her ear.

She jerked her gaze up at him and saw the devilish twinkle in his eyes. He was joking, right? "I wouldn't suggest you do that," she said, biting back a smile. "How was your day?" she asked, switching their conversation to a safer topic. The last thing she needed was for the thought of them kissing to dominate her mind. It didn't take much to recall last night when she'd sat in his lap while he'd kissed her into sweet oblivion.

"Busy but hopefully productive. I think we might have a break in the case of Ms. Katherine's ghost."

"Really? How?" she asked him.

They continued walking while he told her. "There's something else I did a lot of today," he said while placing Ciara back into her stroller.

"Oh, what?" Myra asked him. She studied the broadness of his back as he bent down to the stroller. He had nice shoulders bulging beneath his Western shirt. Why were her palms suddenly aching to rub over them?

When he straightened, he glanced over at her. "I

thought about you a lot today, and do you know what I mostly thought about?"

She wished she had the strength not to ask, but she was powerless while staring into the darkness of his eyes. "No, what did you mostly think about?"

"How it would feel making love to you."

She started them walking again, mainly to keep herself from shivering all over. She was glad they were in a somewhat secluded section of the auditorium. No one had heard what he'd said, she was sure of it. But she had heard him, loud and clear, and his words had glided over her body like molten liquid. It was as if she could feel his body's heat and his body's lust. At that moment breathing became difficult.

She knew what all this meant. It was time for her to walk on the sensuous side and be the passionate woman she believed she could be. But only with this man.

Glancing around to make sure they were still pretty much alone, she leaned in close to him and said, "Then maybe it's time for you to find out how it feels, Pete."

Nine

Pete drove home following close behind Myra's vehicle, while images of kissing her again and making love to her all through the night aroused him in ways he'd never been aroused before. It had been hard to remain at the school and work the booth Pam had talked him into doing, handing out fake badges and telling kids about the importance of obeying laws. As soon as his time was up, he'd found Myra and Ciara and escorted them toward the parking lot so they could leave.

He doubted she had a clue what her words had done to him, but she would soon find out. What she'd said had pushed him to the edge. Yet he was determined not to pounce on her the moment they reached his ranch. Besides, she needed to get Ciara ready for bed and he would sing his niece to sleep. After all that, the night would belong to him and Myra.

He released a sigh when they reached the marker to

is land. When had the drive from the acting school to his place become never ending? He slowed his pace, giving Myra time to maneuver her car along the long, winding driveway. His heart began pounding the closer he got to the house and when she parked her car, he pulled in beside her.

He got out of his truck and approached her car to open the back passenger door and take a sleeping Ciara from the car seat. Holding tight to his niece he wordlessly followed Myra up the walkway to the front door. After unlocking the door, she stepped aside when he carried Ciara to her room. Myra followed and after placing his niece on the dressing table, he stepped back.

"I'll be in the kitchen," he whispered, then left them alone. They might have eaten earlier, but he hadn't and he was hungry. Luckily for him, Pam had prepared him a to-go plate of ribs, corn on the cob, baked beans and coleslaw. He just needed to go back out to the truck to get it.

He had just finished the meal when the sound of Myra's voice came over the intercom. "Ciara is ready for bed now."

When he arrived in his niece's room it was to find her standing in the crib, barely able to keep her eyes open. She was getting older and it would soon be time to put her in a kiddy bed. He wasn't ready for the change and part of him wished she could stay a baby forever. A baby who would always wait for her uncle to tuck her in and sing her a lullaby.

Closing the door behind him he noticed Myra had left. Was she somewhere having second thoughts about them sharing a bed tonight? Pete hoped not. He'd barely handled the buildup and couldn't imagine dealing with a letdown.

Taking Ciara into his arms, he moved to the rocker,

and for the next few minutes he sang her to sleep, enjoying this time, their time, together. He had placed her in her bed when he noticed the note that had been slid under the door. A part of him was almost too nervous about what it might say to pick it up, but he picked it up anyway. Was it a note from Myra calling off their plans for tonight?

Drawing in a deep breath, he opened the sheet of paper and read the words.

Mr. Lawman, please meet me in the man cave. Myra

Myra glanced around the room. She'd had to work fast to arrange things in here just right. While going through the pantry the other day she had found a box of candles, probably meant to be used in case of a power outage. However, tonight she intended to put them to a different use.

She'd grabbed a blanket off her bed to place in front of the fireplace, where a bottle of wine sat, along with two wineglasses. She'd even grabbed several pillows off the sofa upstairs.

The lights were dimmed and soft country music played—the theme of Pam's Wild West festival. Myra's goal was for them to continue in that vein and have their own Wild West night. She'd never done anything like this before; never deliberately set out to seduce a man. She should be the last person on earth to entertain thoughts of seducing a man—an older one at that—after what she'd gone through with Rick. But at least she had enough sense to know Pete wasn't anything like Rick. Both were older, good-looking men, but when it came to class, Rick had somehow missed the boat. Whatever foolishness some women had told him over the years had gone to his head and stayed there.

With Rick it had been about conquering. But Myra
believed with Pete it would be about pleasuring. The two
men were as different as night and day. She was experi-
encing emotions and desires with Pete that she honestly
hadn't thought she was capable of feeling. That was one
of the reasons she'd initially gravitated to older men—
because none of the guys her age ever made her desire
or crave anything.

Last night Pete had not only been gentle, but he'd offered her a proposition and hadn't tried forcing it on her.
He'd left the decision up to her and tonight she would let
him know she intended to take him up on it. Literally.
With her lack of experience, that might be an impossible
feat, but she was energized and ready to try.

Pete Higgins had tempted her enough. He aroused
her even when he didn't realize he was doing so, just by
being him.

She glanced down at herself. She had changed out of
her long skirt and blouse and put on another cowgirl outfit. This was one she'd seen while shopping in Breckenridge. Although at the time she hadn't a clue where she
would wear it, it had been way too cute to pass up.

It was a black rhinestone-adorned minidress with an
attached petticoat. What she'd liked most was the metal-
and-rhinestone horseshoe belt buckle that came with it.
The outfit was so short on her that it barely hit midthigh,
and the way the lapels were turned back showed a generous amount of cleavage.

It was simply scandalous. Myra smiled thinking how
much she loved it. She couldn't wait to see Pete's expression when he saw her in it. Feeling a little nervous, she
pushed her hair back from her neck and began pacing to
the rhythm of the country music. A few beats later she

stopped when she heard the door closing on the main floor. She glanced toward the staircase.

Swallowing, she watched as Pete descended the stairs with his eyes glued to her. He had the note she'd written in his hand. He was here and all those things she'd thought she would be brave enough to do and say to him suddenly left her. Drawing in a deep breath, she tried willing them back.

He moved away from the stairs toward her while sliding the note into the back pocket of his jeans. She could tell by the way he was smiling while his gaze roamed over her outfit that he liked what she was wearing. The heated look in his eyes was enough to make her back up a few steps.

"Going somewhere?" he asked, coming to a stop in front of her.

Pete looked like the sexiest man alive and now it was her turn to roam her gaze over him. She'd seen him when he first entered Pam's acting school, but now she was really getting her fill. The only thing missing was the Stetson he'd been wearing. He'd removed it when he'd entered the house, but she was still wearing her cowgirl hat.

She nervously licked her lips. "No, I'm not going anywhere. You came."

His chuckle was throaty and she was convinced the sound made the tips of her nipples harden. "Did you honestly think I wouldn't?"

At the moment, she couldn't think at all. She wanted to run her hands all over him, trace her tongue across his lips and—

"You want to dance, Myra?"

His question caught her off guard, but she quickly recovered, or at least tried to. She had invited him to this party, so she needed to take ownership of it. But still, she appreciated that he was being patient with her.

"Yes, I want to dance."

He opened his arms and she went into them. She wasn't sure what song was playing. At the moment the only thing that mattered was she was here and so was he. Their bodies were pressed close together and his arms were wrapped around her as they swayed to the slow beat. She felt him. All of him. Especially his erection poking her middle. That was a sign that he wanted her and she knew without a doubt that she wanted him, as well.

She looked up at him and the arousal in his gaze nearly made her weak in the knees. He then smiled that same smile that always whacked her senses. Swallowing, she said, "I hope you don't mind me taking over your man cave."

"No, it looks good. You look good. I love your outfit. It's definitely an eye-catcher. I'm glad you didn't wear it to the Wild West show tonight. Otherwise, I would have had to hurt somebody."

His words heightened the beat of her pulse. "You mean you would have arrested them, right?"

"No, I would have hurt them first and arrested them later."

That made her smile because it hinted at a possessive nature she wasn't used to him demonstrating. And when he tightened his arms around her, she felt a throbbing sensation near his middle. Suddenly, he stopped dancing and stared at her. The silence in the room wasn't helping. The air between them seemed to thicken with sexual energy.

And then he leaned in and kissed her. He wrapped his arms around her even more tightly as his mouth took hers with a hunger that she felt in every part of her body. They'd kissed before, a few times, so why did it feel like

every time their mouths joined there was some kind of
awakening in her body? His kisses could arouse her,
make her desire things that simply astounded her. She
was feeling the full impact of Pete's kiss and she couldn't
help but moan her pleasure over and over again.

Pete finally released Myra's mouth on a low, throaty
groan. Then, sweeping her off her feet, he carried her
over to the blanket in front of the fireplace. Never had
he known such a responsive woman and he loved hearing every moan she made.

And he loved touching her, probably way too much.
He couldn't recall ever wanting a woman with this much
intensity…and that included Ellen.

With Ellen he'd had the desires of a young buck feeling his way around. Now he was a man with a different
type of sexual hunger. He wanted to do more than just
seduce Myra, more than merely satisfy primitive urges.
He wanted to embark on emotions he'd long ago laid
to rest. Miraculously, Myra was enticing him to recon-
nect. He'd tried ignoring her and had failed. She was not
a woman a man could ignore, at least not for long or in
some cases, not at all.

Getting on his knees, he joined her on the blanket and
then stretched out beside her. He didn't want to rush her,
was determined to make tonight as pleasurable for her as
he knew it would be for him. After tonight she wouldn't
remember any other before him. Why that was important to him he wasn't sure. All he knew was that it was.

He kissed her again and when he finally released her
mouth, he whispered, "If I ever do anything that makes
you uncomfortable, I want you to let me know. Okay?"

She stared at him through glazed hazel eyes and slowly
nodded. For him it was important that she not only know

that but believe it. The cop in him knew there had been more to her actions last night than she'd shared with him. He hoped in time she would share it all. For now, he'd resolved that whatever bad experiences she might have had, he would replace them with good ones.

"I'm wearing too many clothes," she whispered.

He smiled. Was that her way of letting him know she wanted to get naked? If so, he had no problem obliging her. "Then let me remove them."

Sitting up, he gently pulled her to face him. The flickering blaze from the fireplace was dancing all over her, making him burn even hotter for her. She was so beautiful and he loved looking at her. And this outfit he was about to take off her had been hot. When he'd come down the stairs and seen her, his erection had nearly doubled in size. She didn't look like your ordinary cowgirl—she looked like a cowgirl out of every man's fantasy.

"Let's start here," he said, removing her hat and placing it aside. He loved the way her hair looked all tumbled around her shoulders. Then he reached down for her feet so he could remove her boots and socks. She had pretty feet and her toes were painted a bright red. It occurred to him that he'd never paid much attention to a woman's feet before, just their legs. And tonight, with this outfit, she was showing a lot of hers and they were gorgeous.

"Did I tell you how much I like your outfit?"

Her chuckle was soft and sexy. "Yes, you told me."

"As much as I like it, now it's time to take it off."

She used the tip of her finger to trace along the collar of his shirt. "Do I get to take your outfit off of you?"

"Yes. I wouldn't want it any other way."

His words seemed to please her and he knew what would please him was kissing her while undressing her. So he proceeded to do just that. By the time he had her down to her bra and panties, her lips were swollen. What it was about her mouth that made him want to devour it, he wasn't sure. All he knew was that he did.

"Sexy," he said, running his fingers along the black lace of her matching bra and panties. He was careful not to touch her inner thigh, remembering what happened last night. But then he remembered what she'd told him this morning.

That she liked him touching her there.

"Now for this," he said, releasing the clasp of her bra and easing the straps from her shoulders. His breath caught when the twin mounds were freed from confinement. Her breasts were perfect. His erection doubled in size. Leaning toward her, he lowered his head and eased a nipple between his lips.

Myra was convinced Pete was trying to drive her mad. What man sucked a woman's breasts this way? With enough suction that she could feel the tips hardening in his mouth. With enough pressure that it triggered sensations between her legs. She closed her eyes and cupped the back of his head, to hold him there. She cried out in protest when he pulled his mouth away, but he moved to the other nipple. She sighed out her pleasure over and over again.

When he finally released her breasts, he stared at her as his fingers eased toward her inner thighs. Tentative at first, as if to gauge her reaction. She knew why. To ease his mind, she whispered, "Like I told you, I love the feel of you touching me anywhere."

He smiled. "In that case, now for these," he said, inching his fingers beneath the black lace of her panties. In a movement that was swifter than anything she'd ever witnessed before, he lifted her hips just enough to eased the panties down her legs.

This was the very first time any man had seen her naked and she wasn't sure how she was supposed to handle such a thing. The blatant heat, the fire and desire she saw in his eyes made any awkwardness she might have felt nonexistent. Instead, she felt empowered.

"Now for *your* clothes," she whispered, reaching for his shirt.

She held his gaze while working free the buttons, not thinking about how many there were but about what she would find when she had them all undone. Then he licked his lips. She didn't have a clue as to why.

Myra only licked her lips when she was nervous about something and she couldn't see him being nervous about anything. It must have had another meaning altogether. He did it again and the motion did something to her, made her nipples harden even more.

Evidently he saw the look on her face. "You know what that means, right?"

She wasn't ready to let him know about her lack of experience. He would discover that soon enough. So for now, she lied and said, "Yes."

"Just making sure."

She had reached the last button and removed his shirt from a pair of masculine shoulders. She gazed at his stomach and flat chest and, giving in to temptation, she stroked her hand up and down his chest.

"Sweetheart, if you knew what your touch does to me, you wouldn't do that."

His words nearly undid her already capsized senses. "I'll be able to handle whatever that might be, Pete."

Instead of saying anything, he gave her a long, drugging kiss that had her whimpering. When he released her mouth, he eased her to her feet. "Now for my jeans. Do you want me to take over from here?"

She met his gaze and smiled. "I want to finish, but you can certainly help."

He nodded and ran his fingers across her nipples. "Just let me know when you need me to jump in."

She nodded. There was a first time for everything and it was her first time undressing a man.

Removing the huge belt buckle was easy. Undoing his zipper against a massive erection was another matter.

"Jump in," she finally said.

"No problem."

Not only did he unzip his pants for her, but he inched them past his waist so all she had to do was tug them down his legs so he could step out of them. That left him completely naked except for a sexy pair of black briefs. Hmm, Mr. Lawman had a downright sexy streak.

"One piece of clothing to go," she heard him say.

And she could just imagine what would happen when that last piece was gone. She reached out and gently tugged the briefs down a pair of masculine thighs to uncover what he was packing.

Lordy.

She looked at him and swallowed deeply. Before she could say anything, he said throatily, "I'll take over from here. Time for you to enjoy."

Pete couldn't help it when his gaze shifted down to Myra's womanly core. She was beautiful and he wanted to kiss her there. He *needed* to kiss her there. Brand her. Claim her. Possess her. His erection throbbed at the thought of doing all three.

He fought back a groan at the thought of kissing her all over, especially there. Without saying anything, he gently eased her back down on the blanket and kissed her mouth with a hunger he felt all through his body.

He moved from her mouth and kissed around her face and neck, eagerly making his way down south, kissing every area he traveled.

"Pete…"

He knew why she had moaned his name. It was as if his tongue had a mind all its own and was licking her everywhere, loving the taste and texture of her. When he'd reached the area between her legs, she grabbed his shoulders as if to stop him from going further. He remembered what he'd told her from the beginning. If he ever did anything that made her uncomfortable, to let him know.

Pete lifted his mouth from her stomach to stare up at her. "Has a man ever gone down on you before, Myra?"

She nervously licked her lips. "No."

He nodded and then, wanting to assure her that her lack of experience in that particular area was fine with him, he said, "Then I am happy to introduce you to the wonder of it all. Is that okay?"

"Yes."

He then lowered his mouth back to her stomach to pick up where he'd left off. He licked her, loving the taste of her skin. He kissed below her navel and continued moving lower.

He felt her tense and looked back up at her to make sure she was okay. "We're good?"

She nodded, a tentative smile on her lips. "No, *you're* good. I don't think you know how you're making me feel, Pete."

He wanted to tell her that she hadn't felt anything yet, but decided he could show her better than tell her. He lowered his head and gently nudged her thighs apart. Her

feminine scent was intoxicating. She moaned his name
the moment he slid his tongue inside her.

Not wanting to wake Ciara, Myra fought back a
scream of pleasure. And when his tongue began moving inside her with intense strokes, she fought back another scream while thrashing on the blanket. He finally
used his hands to grip her thighs and hold her still. What
on earth was his mouth doing to her? She wanted him to
stop, but knew if he stopped she would die. Never had
she experienced anything like this. All kinds of sensations were plummeting through her all at once.

And when his tongue went deeper and the strokes became more intense, she did release a scream. Her body
was hit with what she knew had to be an orgasm. Her
very first. Ever. She closed her eyes as she felt like she
was undergoing some sort of out-of-body experience with
Pete's tongue still planted deep inside her.

Then suddenly another orgasm hit, this one stronger
than the last. She felt the intensity of it in every bone.
Her body bucked several times beneath his mouth, but
he held tight to her hips, refusing to remove his tongue.

When the tremors slowly subsided, she felt Pete move
away and she slowly opened her eyes. He was sliding on
a condom. Then he came back and straddled her body.

"You're ready for me now, baby," he said as he eased
into her.

She knew now was the time to tell him that not only
had no man ever gone down on her before him, but none
had gone inside of her before either. Moments later, when
his body suddenly went still and he stared down at her,
she knew it was too late. He'd figured things out for
himself.

Before he could ask her anything, she placed her arms

around his neck to force his mouth down to hers. Before their lips touched, she whispered, "We're good?"

Instead of answering he pushed more into her tight womanly core until it seemed he couldn't go any farther. He went still again, as if giving her time to adjust to the pressure of his engorged erection planted deep inside her.

Then he began moving, slow at first and then with more intensity. More vigor. It wasn't long before his thrusts became long, hard and deep and she unwrapped her arms from his neck to grab hold of his shoulders. It was as if he was riding her the way he would ride Satin and she could feel his every moment.

Suddenly her body was hit with tingling sensations all over again, with more intensity. And this time she wasn't alone. Pete threw his head back and let out a deep, guttural growl as his body bucked several times. They reached orgasmic pleasure together. She held on to him and he held on to her.

When the last of the tremors had passed through their bodies, he eased down beside her. Entwining their legs, he pulled her into his arms. The last thing she remembered before sleep claimed her was the feel of him softly caressing her stomach and whispering, "No, sweetheart. *You're* good."

Pete stopped the alarm before it could go off. The last thing he wanted was to wake the woman sleeping naked beside him. It had been one hell of a night. He'd wanted to be gentle, after he'd learned it was her first time, but she hadn't let him. She'd deliberately brought out the lusty beast in him.

He found it amazing that at twenty-four she hadn't shared a bed with a man until last night. Until him. He'd had the honor of introducing her to pleasure and she'd told him so many times how much she had enjoyed it.

After that first time, he'd carried her upstairs where he joined her in a hot, sudsy tub bath. Then he'd toweled her dry and carried her to his bed. When she complained about them not drinking any of the wine, he'd gone back down to the man cave to snuff out the candles and grab the wine bottles and glasses. They'd sipped wine in bed, then made love all over again before dozing off to sleep.

She was the one who'd awakened him at two in the morning telling him it was her turn to do the licking. He wouldn't let her, simply because having her mouth on him would have killed him and he wasn't ready to die yet. In the end they'd made love again. And from the looks of it, she was sleeping peacefully now, and he figured she was just as satisfied as he was.

He wished he could stay in bed with her all day, but he had a job to go to and she had Ciara to take care of. However, there would be tonight and he was looking forward to coming home to her. Their days of ignoring each other were done.

Pete forced himself to remember that whatever they were sharing was short-term. She would be leaving Denver in a few weeks. He knew it and accepted it. The only thing they had was the present and he intended to take advantage of the time they had left. He refused to dwell on the fact that Myra Hollister was definitely everything a man could want in a woman.

She was everything he not only wanted but also what he needed.

"Good morning, lawman."

He shifted in bed and smiled over at her. "Good morning. I didn't mean to wake you."

"You didn't. I'm too wound up to sleep long after last night."

"Because of last night you should be exhausted."

She chuckled. "I'm not. Are you? Being an old man and all."

He leaned toward her. "But you enjoyed this old man last night, right?"

"Immensely. I can't describe exactly how I feel, Pete."

Myra decided not to even try. All she knew was what they'd shared had been a game changer for her. She knew it and felt assured Pete knew it, as well. Just like they both knew this affair would end when Miss Bonnie returned. She tried not to let the thought bother her. He had his life here and she had hers someplace else.

She had entertained the thought of returning to Denver for the Westmoreland Charity Ball on New Year's Eve, but now she wasn't sure that was a good idea. What she should do was enjoy what they were sharing now, and when it was time for her to move on, to do so without looking back. Without coming back.

In the meantime...

"Pete?"

"Yes, sweetheart?"

She wondered if he knew what the endearment did to her. "Do you know what I'd like?"

From the look in his eyes she knew he had an idea. "No, what would you like?"

"For you to leave me with something to think about all day until you return."

The smile that appeared on his face was priceless. "That can definitely be arranged."

He then pulled her into his arms.

Ten

"So, there you have it, Pete," Detective Lewis Tomlin was saying.

"Carl Knight, who is serving time in prison for armed robbery, claims he buried his loot in Ms. Katherine's backyard underneath that storage shed while he was hiding out from the Feds. It's my guess that he shared that information with a fellow inmate who passed it to someone on the outside who's trying to scare her into selling the house."

Pete nodded. "Did you question Ms. Katherine about anyone trying to buy her house in the last year?"

"Yes," Lewis said, "she did say that someone had shown up twice inquiring if she wanted to sell and both times she told them she didn't. Said he was a nice man and that he gave her his business card in case she changed her mind."

"Knowing Ms. Katherine, I bet she still had that card."

"Yes. We put a trace on it and the name is connected to a trust. But I'm on it. Hopefully in a week I'll have the name of the person that trust belongs to."

Pete leaned forward in his chair. "Okay, and since we're talking about money missing from a bank robbery, at some point we'll need to get the FBI involved."

When Lewis left his office, Pete leaned back in his chair. When would people learn that crime didn't pay? He knew Lewis wouldn't leave any stones unturned. But if whoever owned that trust couldn't scare off Ms. Katherine, then what? He didn't feel good about this entire thing.

He pressed a button on his desk phone. When his administrative assistant came on the line, he said, "Monica, find deputies Anderson and Sims. I want to see them."

"Okay, Sheriff."

He would instruct them to drive by Ms. Katherine's home more frequently, especially at night. They were squad leaders and would make sure it was done. Standing, he walked over to the window and looked out. He would never tire of this view of the mountains.

Glancing at his watch, it seemed the day was dragging by. It wasn't even lunchtime yet. He shook his head. He'd never been a clock-watcher when it came to his job, but now there were two special females waiting for him. Namely, Ciara Higgins and Myra Hollister.

It was hard to believe it had been almost two weeks since the night he and Myra first made love. Things had certainly changed since then. They now shared the same bed every night, and his day would start with them making love every morning. She also joined him for breakfast, usually preparing him pancakes…made of wheat of course…and turkey bacon and sausage. Her kind of food was beginning to grow on him, and he did feel healthier.

What he enjoyed most was at night, after they'd put Ciara to bed, when over dessert he would share with Myra how his day had gone. It felt nice having someone to come home to and share details with. Then they would go down to his man cave and watch a movie or football. When they retired for bed, it was together. He enjoyed sleeping with her at night and waking up with her in his arms every morning.

They spent their time talking about several subjects. However, the one thing they never talked about was the time when she would be leaving. He'd heard from Jason that Myra had approached Bella about staying at the inn after Bonnie came back. He intended to tell Myra she didn't have to do that. He certainly had enough room at his ranch.

Bottom line, he wasn't ready for her to leave and doubted he ever would be. However, he had to face the fact she *was* leaving. Therefore, he would do the only thing he could, which was to make every moment count.

He turned at the sound of his phone and then moved to click it on. "Sheriff Higgins."

"Pete, this is Pam."

He smiled as he settled into the chair behind his desk. "Hey, Pam, what can I do for you?"

"Dillon's birthday is coming up and he doesn't want us to make a fuss since a lot of the family will be here for the Westmoreland Charity Ball. But I wanted to at least prepare a special meal for this Friday's chowdown. I'd love for you to make it, and please bring Myra and Ciara. I appreciated Myra's help at the Wild West show."

"Ciara and I will be there and I will let Myra know the invitation extends to her, as well."

"Okay, thanks."

He hoped Myra would attend with him. It'd be another moment to cherish.

"So, how are things going with that nanny gig?" Wallace asked Myra, after she'd put the casserole in the oven and sat down at the kitchen table to call him.

She'd just put Ciara down for her nap after feeding her lunch. From where Myra sat, she could see the Christmas tree in the living room. She would never forget the day they'd gotten it. And because this would be Ciara's first Christmas with Pete, and he'd never thought of having a tree before, that had meant shopping for ornaments, as well. The two of them, with a little help from Ciara, had decorated it. Myra would never forget the look of happiness on the little girl's face when Pete had switched on the lights for the first time. Even now, whenever they lit the tree, Ciara would sit in front of it and stare at the blinking lights.

"Myra?"

Wallace had asked her a question that she had yet to answer. "It's going great. Ciara is wonderful."

"And Ciara's uncle?"

She wondered why Wallace would ask her about Pete. She wasn't sure who knew that her and Pete's relationship had changed. They seldom went out. They now had a reason to stay in. She certainly hadn't breathed a word about anything to Wallace.

"Why would you ask me about her uncle?"

He paused and then said, "Well, you did say that early on he hadn't wanted to hire you because he thought you were too young."

She couldn't help but smile at the memory. A lot had

certainly changed since then. "Well, once I began working here and he saw how competent I was, his opinion changed."

"I knew it would. I figured you would eventually win him over."

Myra had news for Wallace. Pete had won her over, as well.

She had fallen in love with him.

That fact couldn't be disputed even though she wished otherwise. But she lived with the evidence every day—when she looked forward to him coming home, when he found her in the kitchen, when he would pull her into his arms with a kiss…

"You don't have long now."

Wallace's words pulled her back into the present. "I don't have long for what?"

"To work for the guy. Won't the regular nanny be back in two weeks?"

Yes, Miss Bonnie would be back and Pete wouldn't need Myra anymore. She and Pete never talked about her leaving because it was a foregone conclusion that she would be. She needed to go to Charleston and claim the company back and then turn it over to Wallace. But what then?

Pete was very much aware of when her last day would be. He hadn't shown any inclination that he'd want to see her again after she left. She doubted he knew she planned to remain in Denver until the day after Christmas. If he knew, would he invite her to spend Christmas with him and Ciara?

She'd known she had to leave, but she had fallen in love with him anyway.

On top of that, his heart still belonged to a dead woman.

"Myra?"

Again she'd left one of Wallace's questions hanging. "Yes, Miss Bonnie will be back in two weeks." Then, deciding to change the subject, she said, "How are things going at the office?"

"So far, okay, but I have a feeling Baron and his friends are up to something. I don't know what, but it's not good. They have been whispering a lot amongst themselves."

"They're probably trying to come up with a plan for stopping me from reclaiming the company. I talked to Lloyd the other day and he assures me there is nothing they can do. All I have to do is show up."

Lloyd Kirkland had been the company attorney for years and one of her father's close friends. He'd been appalled at how Baron had managed to manipulate the stockholders into putting him in charge and replacing Wallace.

"According to Irene, they still think you're out of the country. Baron has hired someone to find you."

Irene was one of the department heads and, like Lloyd, had worked for the company for years. She was loyal to Wallace and tried keeping him abreast of what Baron was up to.

"Let them try. I covered my tracks well. They will see me when it's time for them to see me."

When she ended the call with Wallace, Myra decided to grab a nap for herself while Ciara slept. She and Pete made love every night before they went to sleep and in the mornings when they woke up. She wasn't used to such a vigorous routine.

She smiled when she thought about all they'd done together since making love that first time. Once he'd gotten over the fact that she was inexperienced, it was as if he intended to give her all the training she needed. She couldn't keep up with all the positions they'd tried and the rooms where they'd made love. Her favorite spot still remained on a blanket in front of the fireplace.

Myra walked out of the kitchen the same time the front door opened and Pete walked in. "Pete! I didn't know you were coming home for lunch. Had I known, I would have made—"

"I didn't come home for lunch," he said, tossing his Stetson on the rack with perfect aim, all while walking toward her.

"Oh?"

"I came home for you."

The combination of what he'd said and how he'd said it caused the pulse at the base of her throat to throb. And she could only stare as he walked toward her, the epitome of masculinity.

When he came to a stop in front of her, he placed his hands at her waist and a surge of longing ripped through her.

"So what do you have to say to that, Myra Hollister?"

She started to speak and felt her breath wobble. So, instead of saying anything, she leaned up on her tiptoes and pressed her mouth against his. That was another thing she was in training for. Kissing 101. She took her time brushing her lips over his full and sexy ones. And then she used her tongue to lick the curve of his mouth and lower to his jawline.

Myra heard the way he was breathing and decided to exert a little pressure with her mouth and tongue. She was convinced that she hadn't been properly kissed until Pete. She continued to let her lips roam over his while teasingly licking, sucking and nibbling, loving how he let her do her thing while he fought for control. The hands holding her at the waist tightened as she greedily sucked his lower lip.

It didn't take long for Pete to grow impatient with her playing around with his mouth. Suddenly he crushed his mouth to hers. His hands plunged into her hair, as if to pull her head even closer so he could consume her.

Then, with the same intensity, he released her mouth, only to sweep her into his arms and head toward the bedroom.

Eleven

"So are you going to tell her?"

Pete lifted a brow at Derringer. They'd been standing on the other side of the room watching Dillon cut his birthday cake while the women were busy setting out plates. "Tell who what?"

Derringer rolled his eyes. "Myra Hollister. Are you going to tell her how you feel about her?"

Pete crossed his arms over his chest. "And just how do I feel about her?"

Derringer shook his head. "If you have to ask me, then you're in worse shape than I thought. You love her. I can see that."

"Can you?" Pete asked, before taking a sip of his punch.

"Sure can, and I hope you tell her before she leaves town."

Pete didn't say anything as he glanced across the room to where Myra stood holding Ciara while smiling and talking to Bella, Lucia and Bane's wife, Crystal. She fit in well with them, the wives of the men he considered good friends. And Derringer was right.

He had fallen in love with her, even though he knew doing so had been a mistake.

They could have no future. She had a life beyond Denver, although he hadn't a clue what she intended to do with it other than leave here. It was something they never talked about, a subject he avoided because the idea of her leaving was something he tried not to think about. But he didn't have much time left with her so he had to think about it whether he wanted to or not.

What could he offer her? He tried to ignore the voice that said: *You have your love to offer.*

"Well?"

Derringer reclaimed his wayward thoughts. "Well, what?"

"Are you going to stop her from leaving?"

Stop her from leaving?

"Not without a warrant," he said, trying to bring a little lightheartedness into the conversation.

Derringer wasn't having it. "Don't be a smart-ass, Pete. Are you or are you not going to tell her you love her to stop her from leaving?"

"No, I'm not. I might desire Myra but my duty is to my niece."

"Then I think you are making a huge mistake."

Although Myra was contributing to the conversation with the ladies around her, she was conscious of Pete's eyes on her. She was tempted to return his stare but she didn't for fear that he would look into her very soul. And see her love. Feel her love. Discover the thing she didn't want exposed.

"So, Myra, you and Pete share the same birthday?"

Megan Westmoreland's question reclaimed her immediate attention. Did they? She'd had no reason to ever ask when his birthday was. "If we do, I didn't know it."

"Pete is also a Christmas baby," Lucia said, grinning. "That's the one thing I remember about his parents while growing up. They would come into Dad's paint store around the holidays. Mr. Higgins was good with his hands and every holiday he would make something for Pete. Since Pete was a Christmas baby, he wanted to make a special birthday gift for him so he wouldn't feel cheated out of a birthday celebration."

Myra took a sip of her punch, remembering her parents did the same thing for her birthday. They always made it special. This would be her first without them. "If I was going to be around, I would bake him a cake, but I'm leaving the day after Christmas."

"You're still leaving?" Bella asked, surprised.

"Yes, I'm still leaving." Myra could see the confused looks on the women's faces. "Why do you ask?"

"We thought… We were hoping that something was going on between you and Pete," Megan said, hesitating before getting it out there.

Myra knew it would be a waste of time to lie to the three women. Besides, women who were in love would recognize that same emotion in another woman and there was no denying that she had fallen in love with Pete.

"Yes, something is going on, but not what you think," she said softly, feeling the impact of the words she'd spoken. She knew they understood her meaning.

"I think you might be wrong," Megan said gently. "I've known Pete all my life. He's been best friends with Derringer and Riley forever. I remember Dad would often tell him that if he continued to hang around with them as much as he did he would begin to look like a Westmoreland," she said, chuckling. "There were times people thought he *was* a Westmoreland because he would go on a lot of family trips with us."

She took a sip of her punch and added, "I know how hard he took Ellen's death and how he shut himself off because of it. But over the past month I've seen him come to life. He began thawing out when Ciara got here, but now he's back to being the Pete we all know and love. I think you might be underestimating his feelings for you, Myra."

Megan's words remained on Myra's mind all through the ride home from Dillon's party. They were like a seed in her heart that she wanted to bloom. Was she underestimating his feelings for her? Could there really be more between them than sex?

And what if there was? She would still have to leave to return to Charleston and handle that business with the company. It would be a smooth transition if Baron didn't try making things difficult. Yet she couldn't see him agreeing to leave without a fuss. Either way, she would love nothing more than to have it settled and be done with it so she could return to Pete and Ciara—if he truly cared for her like the Westmoreland ladies thought.

On top of that, Myra couldn't ignore the call she'd gotten from Wallace two days ago. Baron had run into one of his old college girlfriends and she'd mentioned seeing Myra in Breckenridge, Colorado, around Thanksgiving. That meant there was a good chance Baron would be moving his search to that area. Wallace felt she should tell Pete what was going on. She disagreed. Baron was her problem and the last thing she intended to do was get Pete involved.

"You're quiet. Is everything all right, Myra?"

She blinked, realizing they had reached Pete's ranch. Forcing a smile, she looked over at him. "I just have a lot on my mind. Miss Bonnie will be returning next week."

"But that doesn't mean you have to move out. Derringer mentioned you intended to stay at Bella's inn for a week before leaving town."

"Yes, those are my plans. I do have to move out, Pete." Surely he didn't think she could stay here and continue their relationship with Miss Bonnie in the house?

As if he read her thoughts he said, "We're adults, Myra. We shouldn't have to sneak around. Besides, I'm too old for that sort of thing."

"This is coming from a man who didn't want to hire me because of possible talk?" she asked, frowning.

"And you're the one who said you didn't care what people might say or think about you living with me."

She rolled her eyes. "We're not talking about people, Pete. We're talking about Miss Bonnie."

"I know. But you don't have to worry about Bonnie. I got a call from her today and she asked if she could remain with her sister an additional week. I think she might feel guilty about leaving her alone for the holidays. I told her I would talk to you to see if you could remain another week. Would you?"

Undisguised happiness swelled inside of Myra. That meant she would have an extra week to spend with Pete and Ciara. That would make leaving even harder, but she would take it and deal with the consequences later.

Drawing in a deep breath, she said, "Yes, I'll remain for an additional week."

Pete woke up the next morning and glanced over at the clock. Although it was Saturday, he usually would get out of bed early anyway since it was his day to take care of

Ciara. Myra was still entitled to two days off even though she never really took them anymore. She seemed content to spend her off days hanging out at the ranch with him and Ciara and he didn't have any problem when she did. Regardless, he didn't want to take advantage of her time in case she had something else to do.

But then he had made sure she would be free this weekend for an entirely different reason.

He glanced at the empty spot in his bed wondering how Myra had gotten up without waking him.

He hadn't told her yet, but he'd asked Charity Maples to babysit Ciara for him tonight because he planned to take Myra out on a date. Two days ago, he'd made reservations at Barnacles for dinner and figured they could take in a movie afterward.

Pete chuckled. He wasn't as slow as Derringer thought. Although the timing wasn't right to tell her how he felt about her. Chances were, she didn't feel the same way, and there was no way he could stop her from leaving. What he *could* do was give her a reason to come back. He no longer felt he had to chose between duty and desire. He could have both.

Getting out of bed he quickly went into the bathroom and washed up, brushed his teeth and shaved. A short while later he was walking out of his bedroom and headed toward the kitchen where the sound of voices could be heard. Namely, Myra and Ciara. They were both singing…or trying to sing.

He couldn't help the smile he felt touch his lips. Myra had made his house a home and he wasn't sure how he and Ciara would handle her absence. Bonnie taking an additional week had postponed the inevitable but for how long?

At least Myra would be here on Christmas Day, since

she was leaving the day after. He had assured her he could handle things for a day until Bonnie got back.

Walking into the kitchen, he said, "Good morning."

Two pairs of feminine eyes glanced over his way. He would give anything for them to keep that look of happiness in their gazes when they saw him.

"Da-da," Ciara said, reaching out her arms to him.

He headed toward her, but not before stopping in front of Myra to place a lingering kiss on her lips. "I didn't hear you leave the bed this morning."

She gave him a mischievous grin. "I guess one of us was exhausted for some reason, Mr. Lawman."

He leaned in close to her ear and said, "I guess I should be thankful you aren't calling me Mr. Old Man."

She threw her head back and laughed. "I must admit I am finding it hard to believe that you're letting this young woman get the best of you."

He smiled. "Only because I'm exhausted from getting the best of you."

Now he was the one to throw his head back to laugh; he had effectively put her at a loss for words. And while he had her in that condition, he figured it would be a good time to tell her about his plans.

"By the way," he said, after taking Ciara out of the high chair. "I hired a babysitter for Ciara tonight."

Myra looked at him dumbfounded. "A babysitter? Why?"

He knew he had to be careful how he answered. "Because I want to show my appreciation for all you've done for me and Ciara while Bonnie has been gone. I want to thank you."

"You don't have to thank me, Pete. Besides, are you okay with a sitter keeping Ciara? She won't stay with just anybody."

He studied Myra's features and wondered if she'd gotten upset with what he'd said. For some reason she sounded annoyed.

"I do need to show you how much I appreciate what you've done and as far as a sitter goes, Charity is seventeen and the daughter of one of my deputies. She's kept Ciara a number of times for me in the past. She's a responsible teen and she and Ciara get along just fine. There's no need for you to worry about anything."

Myra knew she sounded pretty ungrateful and that wasn't how she wanted to come off. Taking her to dinner was truly a nice gesture on his part. Just because she was in love with him didn't mean she should expect him to feel the same way about her.

"Then after dinner we would take in a movie."

She stared at him. Dinner and movie? Did he not know those things constituted a date?

That was probably the last thing he wanted but those were his plans, not hers. He would figure out the mistake he'd made when he ran into people who knew him and recognized her as the nanny, and noted the two of them were out and about without Ciara. She would be leaving after next week. He would be the one left here to deal with talk because he'd sent out the wrong message in trying to show his appreciation.

She wished she could tell him that she didn't want his appreciation but his love, but that was out of the question. She had to take care of her family business, and his heart was still taken.

"Do you not want to go to dinner with me?"

She wanted to go. She valued him showing his appreciation. She'd get over her feelings.

He had explained his intentions from the beginning.

He had not been looking for a lasting relationship. It was only about sex. It wasn't like he hadn't told her because he had, and she'd accepted his terms.

"Yes, I'd love to go out to dinner with you, Pete," she said.

And just like he wanted to show his appreciation to her, she could certainly show hers to him, in her own special way.

It wasn't too late when they returned home. Charity told them what a great little girl Ciara had been, before leaving in her own car.

"I like her," Myra said about Charity, when Pete joined her in Ciara's room. They both stood over the little girl's bed just watching her sleep. Pete knew his niece had captured Myra's heart the same way she'd captured his. Even if Myra didn't care about seeing him again after leaving Denver, she would be tempted to return to see Ciara.

"Want to join me for a cup of coffee, lawman?" Myra said, smiling.

He smiled back. "I don't mind if I do, cowgirl."

Because he had such a wide hallway, they managed to walk down the hall side by side while holding hands, which was something they'd done at the movies. Dinner had been great and the movie had been entertaining, as well. They'd run into a number of people he knew, most of them his age, and they hadn't found it newsworthy that he was out on date with his niece's nanny. In fact, when he had introduced her to them, he'd introduced Myra as a good friend.

He sat down at the table while she got the coffee going. He liked watching her move around his kitchen, loved the movements of her hips and the sway of her hair around her shoulders. When she turned around, catching him staring, she smiled.

"I enjoyed dinner and the movie, Pete. Thanks for taking me."

"I'm glad you did and you're welcome." He wanted to suggest that they do it again, but he didn't want to bring up the fact that she was leaving soon.

She placed his cup of coffee in front of him and then joined him at the table with hers.

Finally, he decided to ask, "Are you looking forward to returning to Charleston?" She didn't answer right away. Could it be that she would miss him and Ciara? He knew they would miss her.

"Yes, I'm looking forward to returning home."

He didn't say anything as he sipped his coffee, wondering how he was going to let her leave when the time came. "You'll be leaving Denver before the coldest part of our winter."

"I won't miss that."

Because he had to know, he asked, "Will you miss me?"

She met his gaze and held it for a long moment. "Most definitely. I'm going to miss you, Pete."

A surge of passionate energy passed between them and they placed their coffee cups down at the same time. Who got up from their seat first, Pete wasn't sure. Nor did it matter. All he knew was that Myra was in his arms and he was kissing her in a way he hoped let her know he would also miss her. Miss kissing her. Miss making love to her. Miss seeing her. Miss talking to her. He would miss her in ways he couldn't even imagine right now.

Their tongues tangled with a desperation and hunger he'd never experienced, never with such urgency as this. The cause might have been knowing they were racing against time. Soon they would have to say their goodbyes. Now, though, they were succumbing to unbridled passion.

Suddenly, he swept her off her feet into his arms. He'd intended to make it to his bedroom, but he only made it to the dining room before he knew he had to have her now. "I need you now, baby. I can't wait."

After placing her back on her feet, Pete yanked his shirt from his pants and proceeded to take it off while watching her remove her own clothes. It didn't matter to him that this was the first time he'd ever stripped naked in his dining room. He knew before it was all said and done, he would be doing a hell of a lot more in this dining room.

She was back in his arms and he was kissing her again with a fervor he felt in every part of his body, especially in his throbbing erection. He broke off the kiss, needing to touch and taste her everywhere. He needed to feel his hands glide over her breasts, enjoying how her nipples hardened beneath his fingers.

He needed to know if she was ready for him, so he lowered his hands to the area between her legs. She moaned when he touched her there, and he eased his finger inside of her. Yes, she was ready for him.

Lifting her up, he placed her on the dining room table and wrapped her legs around his neck. Then, nudging her thighs apart, he thrust into her, going as deep as he could go. And when he was satisfied he couldn't go any further, he held tight to her hips and began moving in and out of her. He was filled with a greed that went beyond anything he'd ever experienced before. It was as if he'd become insatiable, but only for her.

With this position he not only felt her but he could look at her, see the play of emotions on her face caused by his every thrust. He loved watching her expressions and knowing he was the cause. As if she needed to see his emotions as well, she used her inner muscles, as if trying to milk every single thing out of him.

It was then that he grasped he wasn't wearing a condom. That realization must have shown in his expression, because she whispered, "I'm on birth control and I'm safe."

"And I'm safe, too," he said, continuing to pump hard into her.

When he felt her begin to shudder, he leaned in and captured her mouth as the same orgasm that struck her hit him, as well. His body bucked and then bucked again as he poured into her, the first time he'd done such a thing with any woman.

But he was doing it with her. The woman he loved with every part of his being. The woman who didn't have a clue what she meant to him. He wanted her to have it all. He kept thrusting until there was nothing left to give. It was only then that he released her mouth and slumped down on her. Burying his face between the most gorgeous pair of breasts, and the tastiest.

At that moment Pete knew the hardest thing he would ever have to do would come on the day he would have to let her go.

Twelve

Pete tossed the pencil on his desk, leaned back in his chair and placed the palms of his hands at the back of his neck. He'd been doing that all morning, in the middle of reading or writing a report. That was when thoughts of Myra would flash through his mind.

It had been almost a week since their date on Saturday night, when he'd taken her to dinner and a movie and then they'd later made love on his dining room table. He still smiled at the memory and he had new admiration for that table and its sturdiness.

He tried not to think about how time seemed to be quickly going by. Christmas was next week. And he'd fallen deeper and deeper in love with Myra. He tried showing her every time they made love without saying the words. A couple of times during the throes of passion the words nearly slipped out anyway. She still hadn't decided if she would return for the Westmoreland Charity Ball on New Year's Eve.

Although she'd never said she felt anything for him, whenever they made love he swore he could feel her emotion. A part of him wanted to believe a woman like Myra could not share with him what she'd shared, holding back nothing, if she didn't care. Or was it mere wishful thinking on his part?

He would soon find out because he planned on telling her how he felt tonight. He couldn't kiss her again, hold her in his arms and make love to her again, without her knowing that he loved her. She might think it was just sex for him, but it was time she discovered it was a lot more. Then he would convince her that if she gave him a chance, she could love him, too.

At least he was praying that she could.

He looked up at the knock on the door. "Come in."

Lewis came in smiling, looking pleased with himself, and Pete figured he should. A week ago, Lewis had traced that trust to a corporation in New York, and a few days later an arrest had been made. Yesterday, the FBI had brought in equipment to scan the perimeter of Ms. Katherine's backyard and they'd uncovered the loot that had been hidden there. The recovery had made national news. Because of all the long hours Lewis had put in trying to solve the case, Pete had given him extra days off. He would be leaving tomorrow to take his family to visit his wife's parents in Boulder.

"Your first day off and you couldn't resist coming here anyway?"

Lewis dropped down in the chair in front of Pete's desk. "I needed to wrap up a few things before leaving. How are you going to handle things without me?"

Pete chuckled. "I'll manage."

At that moment the intercom on Pete's desk went off. "Yes, Monica?"

"Ms. Katherine is on the line and she says it's important that she talk to you."

Pete glanced over at Lewis and raised a brow as he said, "Okay, put her through."

When the connection was made, Pete placed the call on speaker so Lewis could listen in on the conversation since he was the one who'd worked on her case. "Ms. Katherine, don't tell me you're seeing more ghosts," Pete said jokingly.

"Of course not, Peterson, but there's something strange going on."

"Strange how?" he asked, reclining back in his chair.

"I met with Lucille and Alma today. We're knitting holiday hats for the babies at the hospital. And they told me a well-dressed man was going around their neighborhood asking questions."

Pete lifted a brow. Lucille's and Alma's homes were at least a good four to five miles from where Ms. Katherine lived. "What kind of questions?"

"They were about your nanny."

Pete sat up straight in his chair and frowned. "My nanny?"

"Yes. Ms. Hollister. The man knew her name and even had a picture of her and everything. Said he was looking for her, but didn't tell them why. Of course Lucille and Alma didn't tell him anything. They told me about it and I told them I would pass the information on to you to tell Ms. Hollister. The man didn't look dangerous, but you can't take any chances these days. You don't think he's an ex-husband, do you?"

"No," Pete said, his frown deepening. "Myra has never been married." He was damn well certain of that. "Thanks for telling me. I'll pass the information on to Myra. If the man comes back, tell Ms. Alma and Ms.

Lucille to let me know. Did the man say how he could be reached?"

"No, he didn't tell them anything, which is another reason they found the man odd."

Pete found that odd, as well. "I appreciate the information. Goodbye, Ms. Katherine." He then clicked off the phone.

"Who would be looking for your nanny?" Lewis asked Pete.

Pete stood. "I don't know but I intend to find out. Enjoy your time off."

Lewis nodded, standing, as well. "Is there anything you need me to do? I can delay my trip another day if—"

"No," Pete said, pushing his chair to his desk. "There's no need for you to do that. I was going home for lunch anyway, so that gives me a chance to ask Myra about it."

Twenty minutes later, Pete was pulling into his driveway. On the way home, all kinds of scenarios ran through his mind. It could very well be an insurance agent since her parents had been killed a few months ago. But why would an insurance man be going around showing her picture? Sounded to Pete like a process server or bounty hunter, which didn't make sense. She would have told him if she was in some kind of trouble. Wouldn't she?

Then there was another possibility. She was being stalked…like Ellen had been. She'd told Bonnie she'd come to Denver because of her parents' deaths and that she needed to get away. What if there was more to that story? His hand tightened on the steering wheel, not wanting to go there, but his mind was trying to do that very thing. Now he was getting damn paranoid and there was no reason for that. But the thought of not knowing was driving him crazy.

He started to call out to her the minute he opened the

door, but caught himself. If Ciara was taking a nap he didn't want to wake her. He went into the kitchen and found it empty, but something was baking in the oven. He left the kitchen to head down the hall the exact moment Myra was walking out of Ciara's room.

She saw him and threw her hand to her chest and took a deep breath. "Pete! You scared me. I thought you said you weren't coming home for lunch."

He tried reining in all those rampant emotions hitting him at once. "Do you know why a man is going around town looking for you, Myra?"

Breaking eye contact with Pete, Myra took a slow, deep breath as she stared down at the floor. She should have known Baron wouldn't give up on trying to find her. She should have taken heed of Wallace's warning.

"Myra? I asked you a question."

She snapped her head up and met Pete's gaze. She didn't like his tone. He sounded angry. What did he have to be upset about? It wasn't him with the issue of a ruthless brother. "Yes, I know why he's here. Now, if you will excuse me, I need to check on dinner." She brushed by him to walk to the kitchen.

"Wait just a damn minute!" he said, grabbing hold of her wrist.

She jerked her hand from him. "Pete, what is wrong with you? Please lower your voice or you'll wake Ciara. I just put her down for her nap." She then turned toward the kitchen and he followed.

Myra still didn't understand what he was upset about. She should be the angry one. All her calculated plans to make Baron believe she was out of the country had gotten blown to bits because one of his ex-girlfriends had seen Myra that day in Breckenridge. Well, she had news for her brother and that witch of a mother of his. She would not hide out like a criminal anymore.

Entering the kitchen, she walked over to the oven to check on the baked chicken, very much aware of Pete moving behind her. When she turned around, he was standing in the middle of the kitchen with a fierce frown on his face and his arms crossed over his chest. "You owe me an explanation, Myra."

A part of her knew she did. She was living in his house and taking care of his niece. If someone was going around town looking for her, he should be told why. "Yes, I do owe you an explanation and I will give you one, Pete, but you have no reason to be angry about it. You and Ciara were never in any danger."

He frowned. "Danger? What in the world are you involved in?"

She disliked his accusations even more. "I am not involved in anything and I resent you thinking that. Maybe we shouldn't have this conversation after all—it's not like I have to confide in you. I'm leaving soon, and all we've been sharing is a relationship that's not going anywhere."

She watched him grit his teeth and his neck seemed to expand while he fought for control. He looked like a great specimen of furious masculinity with his tight thighs and heaving chest. She had never seen him this angry before.

He took a couple of steps toward her and pointed at her. "You think that's all it's been, Myra? Nothing but a relationship that's not going anywhere?"

His question surprised her and she lifted her chin and met his intense glare. "What else am I supposed to think, Pete?"

He stiffened. She watched his already tight muscles appear to tighten even more. Then she said, "I clearly recall your proposition. So yes, all we've shared is a relationship to nowhere and I'm fine with that. If I hadn't been, I would not have slept with you." And she didn't regret any of the times she had.

He took a closer step to her. "Don't try changing the subject. I want to know why some man is looking for you."

Myra rolled her eyes. "Change the subject? You're the one who wanted me to explain what I meant by *relationship*, as if you didn't already know."

"Answer my question, Myra," he said in a tone that indicated his patience was running thin.

In a way, she didn't want to tell him. She didn't want to explain how a brother could treat his sibling this way, especially when Pete and his brother had shared such a close and loving relationship. He had suffered a loss when Matt had died and now he was caring for his brother's daughter, giving her everything he knew his brother would want her to have. Especially love. All Myra's brother felt toward her was loathing.

"Myra!"

She jumped. "Will you stop screaming?"

"I am not screaming," he said, lowering his voice somewhat. "Now answer my question."

Moving away from the stove, she walked over to the table to sit down in a chair. She needed to sit. Just the thought that Baron had tracked her here was too much to take in at the moment. She glanced at Pete. He was still standing in the same spot. Still angry. Drawing in a deep breath, she said, "The man was sent by someone to find me. The reason I came to Denver was to hide out and I thought I'd done a good job of leading the person to believe I was out of the country somewhere, so he would have no reason to look for me here."

"He?" Pete all but roared. "You're being stalked? By

whom?" Before she could respond he said, "Some men are crazy. They *want*. Nothing else matters. They will do anything to have you and if you turn them away, they will hurt you because the sick bastards have demented minds."

Stalker? Maybe he assumed that because he was a law enforcement officer. Drawing in a deep breath, she said, "I wasn't being stalked, Pete. I was being tracked. It was imperative to Baron that I not return to Charleston to cause problems, which is why that man is looking for me."

"Baron? Who the hell is Baron? An ex-boyfriend? A guy who doesn't understand the meaning of no?"

None of the above...

She still heard the anger in his voice but now it wasn't directed at her, but rather the man he was inquiring about. She truly didn't want to tell him any more than she had already.

Why did he want the identity of the person involved? She knew the answer. It wasn't because he cared about her, but because he was a cop. A sheriff. It was his job to know details.

Myra met his intense stare. "Baron Hollister is my brother."

Pete was certain he'd heard her wrong. Did she say her brother?

As if she read the confusion in his features, she said, "Yes, my brother. I told you we had the same father but different mothers. His mother, Charlene, was my dad's first wife. They were married only four years and divorced when Baron was only two."

Pete came to the table to sit down opposite her. "Are you saying your brother is stopping you from returning home?"

With a sigh, she nodded. "Yes and no. He's never told me per se but he's sent his warnings through others. I know Baron and how ruthless he can be and decided not to take chances. I needed to leave Charleston anyway and grieve after losing my parents. I chose not to tell him where I was going because I knew he would have someone watch me and let him know when I was on my way back home. Not knowing my location upset him and he's been looking for me."

The thought that she knew someone was out there looking for her and hadn't told him anything about it had Pete boiling in rage. "I think you need to start at the beginning."

He listened as Myra told him everything and the more he heard, the angrier he got. As far as he was concerned, Baron Hollister was a fool. Myra had allowed him to get away with it when she could have reported his threats. She should have told someone. She should have told him. She had been living under his roof and sleeping in his bed, yet she hadn't trusted him enough to confide what her brother was doing to her. Just like Ellen hadn't confided in him about the stalker's threats.

While listening to Myra, that day twelve years ago came back to him. Ellen had told her best friend about the threats but not him. In the end, the man had taken her life. Pete recalled sitting in this very kitchen while listening to Sheriff Harper tell him that Ellen's death hadn't been an accident but an intentional, malicious act. The man had been arrested and, after being told his purchase of the firecrackers had been captured on a video camera inside Paul Markam's feed store, he'd confessed.

Suddenly, those memories became unbearable, almost suffocating to the point where Pete couldn't breathe. He needed to get out of there. Standing quickly and without saying a word, he crossed the room and walked out the back door.

His mind was filled with memories of Ellen's death as well as all the things Myra had just told him. All the things that, like Ellen, Myra *hadn't* told him.

Within minutes he had Satin saddled and was riding off, no particular destination in mind. He had to get away and think. So he kept riding.

In his lifetime he had fallen in love with two women, and neither had trusted him enough to tell him what was happening in their lives, even though he could have helped. He would not have let them face anything alone. He would have taken care of them. He would have been there for them.

It wasn't long before he'd come to the edge of his property, which connected to Gemma Lake. In the distance, across the way, he saw all the wild horses running loose on Westmoreland land. Bringing Satin to a stop, he dismounted and sat on a huge tree stump and gazed at both the lake and the horses. The water indicated calmness while the horses displayed just the opposite. He could feel their untamed energy. Pretty much like the energy flowing through him now. Untamed and unmanageable.

He had to come to terms with the fact that life was sometimes unpredictable. Unruly. Undisciplined. That was one of the reasons why he'd wanted to become a lawman. To battle the bad guys. To bring order. Then after Ellen's death, he'd been even more determined to do so.

Now, twelve years later, he'd fallen in love again. When Myra had walked into his life, he hadn't been ready for her and had tried to fight what he'd felt. But it seemed fate had decreed she was to be a part of his life, for better or for worse.

He had accepted weeks ago that he loved her, but could he accept her not telling him when her life was in possible danger?

Yes, he could accept it because he loved her, mistakes and all. More than anything, he needed to let her know his feelings for her went beyond the bed they shared every night. He needed her to know that he was there to help fight her battles, whatever they were, and that she wasn't alone. She would never be alone because she would always have him and Ciara.

It was time to let her know that.

"Any reason you're sitting here staring into space, Pete?"

He turned at the sound of Riley Westmoreland's voice. "No reason. What are you doing out here and not at the office?" Although Riley might enjoy the outdoors, he worked in an office setting in the Westmoreland family-owned Blue Ridge Management Company. Most of the time he was in a business suit instead of Western wear.

Riley chuckled. "I decided to play hooky today. Everyone needs to do that every once in a while."

Before Pete could respond, his cell phone rang and he saw it was Lewis. "Hold that thought a sec," he said to Riley before clicking on his phone. "Any reason you're calling me? Need I remind you again that you were given time off?"

"Hey, consider it the former FBI agent in me, but I couldn't leave town until I checked out something. Namely, why someone was in town looking for your nanny. I decided to investigate and you won't believe what I found out."

Pete listened to what Lewis was saying and a frown covered his features. "I'm on my way."

He looked over at Riley. "I need to get back to town immediately and I'm closer to your place than I am to mine. Can you give me a ride? I'll get one of my men to bring me back home later."

"Sure."

Pete got on his horse and, like in the old days, he and Riley raced across the meadows to where Riley lived, a few minutes away on one hundred acres of land he called Riley's Station. Minutes later and they were in Riley's car and on their way into town.

"Hey, we traded one type of horsepower for another," Riley said jokingly, as he drove his two-seater sports car down the interstate. When Pete didn't respond to his jest, he said, "I hope what's going on at police headquarters is not too bad."

"Nothing I can't handle."

"Figured as much," Riley said. "So what had you sitting on that stump and looking into space?"

Pete decided to be honest with the man who for years had been one of his best friends. "Women and their secrets."

Riley chuckled. "They all have them. Alpha reminds me of that often."

Alpha was Riley's wife. The one who'd turned the once womanizer into a one-woman man. The one who'd made Riley burn his playa card and decide he wanted marriage instead.

Pete glanced over at Riley. "But when it's a case of their life being threatened…"

"You know what I think, Pete?"

He truly didn't want to know because the last thing he wanted was a Riley Westmoreland lecture, especially after that phone call he'd gotten from Lewis. "What?"

"At some point you need to stop blaming yourself for

Ellen's death. Yes, maybe things might have turned out differently had she told you she was being harassed by that guy, but things could have taken another turn, and I think she knew it and tried to avoid it."

Pete lifted a brow. "What other turn?"

"You had just gotten accepted into the police academy and were still in training. Had she told you, being the hothead that you still were at the time, you would have gone after that guy and whipped his ass. Of course you would have told me and Derringer about it. Then we would have whipped his ass right along with you and all three of us would have gotten into trouble."

"Yes, but at least Ellen would still be alive."

"We won't ever know that for certain, Pete. There's no telling how he would have retaliated. Personally, I think he would have gone after the both of you. If you recall, Sheriff Harper also found that box of explosives in his house. Harper figured the bastard planned on blowing up the church the day of your wedding."

Pete always thought that as well, especially when the address of the church was found on a slip of paper in a drawer in the man's apartment. But although the man admitted to throwing the firecracker, he wouldn't confess to anything he had planned with the explosives.

"I've watched you with Myra, Pete. Don't you think it's time to admit how you feel about her?"

"You're late, Ry. I have admitted it to myself."

"But not to her?"

Pete shook his head. "No."

A frown touched Riley's face. "You haven't told her?"

Pete drew in a deep breath. "No, I haven't told her."

"Damn, man. What are you waiting on?"

Pete didn't say anything. He'd planned to tell her tonight and now he knew those plans hadn't changed.

* * *

Myra stood at the kitchen window and looked out. Pete had been gone for a while now. Where was he? His truck was parked outside, which meant he hadn't gone back to work. Wherever he'd gone it was on horseback and it was now getting dark.

Ciara had awakened from her nap and Myra had played with her while listening for Pete. Maybe he'd found what she'd told him so repulsive that he'd left. What she needed to tell him was what she'd been trying to tell him all along. It wasn't his problem. It was hers and she would deal with Baron when she would have the upper hand. Not a minute before.

She fed Ciara dinner and then played with her some more before giving her a bath. Pete still hadn't returned. She knew he could take care of himself but that didn't stop her from worrying and caring. She loved him and couldn't help being concerned.

"Da-da."

She glanced over at Ciara, who was standing in her crib. The little girl knew this was usually the time of day when her uncle would come in and rock her to sleep while singing her a lullaby. After a while, sleep took over her and Ciara slumped down in the bed and dozed off.

Myra had taken her own bath and was in her bed when she heard the sound of Pete returning. Footsteps passed her bedroom door headed for his bedroom. Then she heard him come out of his room and walk back down the hall. He knocked on her door.

Pulling up in bed, she switched on the lamp on the nightstand and after pushing her hair away from her neck, she said, "Come in."

He opened the door and stood in the doorway looking handsome while staring at her. "Why aren't you in my bed?"

In his bed?

Myra frowned. Did he not see things weren't the same now? Why was he acting like they were? Before she realized what he was about to do, he entered the room and swept her into his arms.

"What do you think you're doing, Pete?"

"Taking you to my bedroom where you belong."

Where she belonged?

"But you don't want me there now."

"Don't know what gave you that idea," he said, leaving her bedroom and heading to his. He closed his door with the heel of his boot before placing her in the center of the bed. "We need to talk."

"You left when we were talking."

Sitting on the edge of the bed he rubbed his hand down his face. "I know and I apologize for that."

"I know what I told you repulsed you. I know it's hard to believe one sibling can harbor that much dislike for another one."

He reached out and took her hand. "You didn't repulse me and it's not hard to believe. As a police officer I've seen and heard things even more far-fetched."

"Then why did you leave like that?"

He drew in a deep breath. "Because listening to what you were saying reminded me of Ellen and how she died. At that moment, I was feeling like I'd let the both of you down."

"Ellen? Your fiancée?"

"Yes."

"I don't understand. Why would you feel that way? Your fiancée died in a horse accident."

He shook his head. "It wasn't an accident but an intentional act by a guy she'd rebuffed for weeks." He shared what had happened with Ellen.

"Oh, no!" Myra tightened her hand on his. "I am so sorry, Pete."

He didn't say anything for a minute and then he continued, "The hardest thing for me to accept was that she hadn't told me anything about him. I had no idea her life had been threatened. That someone had targeted her. I felt as if I'd let her down in that she didn't come to me. I now know why she did it. Mainly because she didn't want me to get into any trouble. But still, as the woman I loved, I felt I should have known to protect her."

Pete paused again. "Do you have any idea how I felt listening to you telling me about your brother? About how you've been hiding here, trying to keep a low profile so he wouldn't find out where you were?"

"It's not the same, Pete."

He'd loved Ellen, but he didn't love her. He might feel responsible for her since she was living in his house, but still, it wasn't the same. Besides, Baron wouldn't hurt her that way. He was ruthless, true, but he mainly wanted to scare her into staying away. He wouldn't physically harm her.

"And why isn't it the same, Myra?"

Why did he need her to spell it out for him? Okay, if she had to, then she would. "First of all, Ellen was your fiancée, the woman you loved. Second, she was murdered. Baron might be ruthless but he isn't violent. The reason I was in hiding was because I didn't want to be bothered with him until I was good and ready, which would have been after my birthday. The only reason Baron is looking for me is because he wants to know where I am at all times."

Pete shook his head. "No, it's a little more serious than that, Myra."

She lifted a brow. "What do you mean?"

"One of my detectives picked up that guy who'd been looking for you. Under interrogation, he revealed the plan your brother had in store for you."

"Plan? What plan?"

"It seems that one of his associates convinced Baron that he could keep the company beyond your twenty-fifth birthday if you signed everything over to him."

She shook her head. "I would not have done that."

"He intended to force you to do it."

"How? By blackmailing me with a video that he was going to get Rick to film? One of me in a compromising position? As if I'd let Rick get within ten feet of me again. Baron's wife, Cleo, overheard him making those plans with his friends and told me about them. That's when I left Charleston."

Pete lifted a brow. "Who's Rick?"

She released a deep breath. "My one mistake in life. He was older, worldly, a guy I thought I could fall in love with. He got rough with me and I didn't like it. When I tried to leave, he told me the only reason he was wasting his time with me was because my brother had encouraged him to seduce me."

Myra saw the way Pete's jaw tightened. "So that's why you had this thing against older men?"

"Yes. All Baron's friends were older and undesirable. And that's why I freaked out the night in your man cave when you inched your hand under my skirt. It reminded me of Rick." She paused and then asked, "So how was Baron supposed to get me to sign everything over to him, Pete?"

Pete didn't say anything for a minute, and then he

said, "By having you kidnapped and taken to some private island in the Caribbean that's owned by someone his mother knows. They would have drugged you up enough to make you do anything. Even say you were happy there and never intended to return to the States."

Myra stared at Pete. "You're kidding, right?"

"No, I wish I was. The guy we picked up, a friend of your brother's, doesn't relish any time in jail and has provided enough proof for us to bring in the FBI on attempted kidnapping charges. So far, the Feds have validated much of his claim, including the exchange of money, text conversations and where the island is located."

She shook her head, not wanting to believe that. "But that is ludicrous."

"Greed will make some people do unbelievable things, Myra."

She fought back tears at the thought that Baron would go that far. "I guess I was wrong about him." A tear she couldn't hold back fell down her cheek.

Pete reached up and gently swiped it off. "You were wrong about something else you said."

Mentally, she wasn't sure she could take much more. "What?"

"That the situation with you and the one with Ellen are different because I loved her. Well, I love you, too, Myra."

She blinked. "What did you say?"

"I said that I love you and as the woman I love, I would have done whatever I could to protect you. Now that I know what's going on, I am doing that. Your brother will not get away with anything."

She swallowed as she stared into his eyes. "You love me?"

"Yes, with all my heart. I honestly think I fell halfway in love with you the first time I saw you. That day you walked into my kitchen. I got pushed the rest of the way when I saw how you interacted with Ciara and what a great job you were doing taking care of her. Taking care of me."

"Oh, Pete, I love you, too. I truly do."

He pulled her into his arms and kissed her thoroughly. When he finally released her mouth, he held her close. So close she could feel his heart beat against hers.

"I can't imagine my life without you and didn't want to tell you how I felt for fear you weren't feeling the same way. But I had made up my mind to tell you tonight regardless and take my chances. Then I got the call about that man in town asking questions about you."

He paused and then said, "I want a life with you. I want me, you, Ciara and any kids we have together to be a family. Will you marry me, Myra?"

Happiness exploded within her and, swiping at her tears, she said, "Yes! I will marry you, Pete."

He pulled her back into his arms and held her, and at that moment she knew how it felt to love someone and feel their love in return. When he pulled back to look at her, she smiled up at him. "I love you so much, Pete."

"And I love you, too." He then pulled her back into his arms for another kiss.

Epilogue

"You look absolutely beautiful, Myra."

Myra smiled at the man who held her in his arms while they danced at the Westmoreland Charity Ball.

Last night, in this same ballroom, she and Pete had exchanged vows to become husband and wife. It had turned out to be the perfect plan since most of his friends had already arrived in town for the ball. Miss Bonnie had returned to town, as well. Wallace was the one who'd given her away. He and Pete had hit it off the moment they'd met. She and Pete would leave tomorrow on their honeymoon, a week in Honolulu. That was the longest they wanted to be away from Ciara.

"Thank you, and I think you look rather handsome yourself."

He grinned at the compliment. "Are you happy?" he asked her.

"Immensely. Especially since that matter with my company has been resolved."

The situation involving Baron had been more serious than Myra had known. It seemed the FBI already had Baron, Charlene and his cohorts under their radar. Baron's friend, the one he'd sent to grab her in Denver, had taken a plea deal. The man's confession and evidence had resulted in the arrests of Baron, Charlene and several of Baron's friends. The FBI had uncovered a number of their extortion schemes. It was also discovered that the island where they'd intended to take Myra was known as a depot for human trafficking.

Pete had accompanied her back to Charleston where she claimed total control of her company and then turned the head job over to Wallace, just like her father had wanted. Christmas morning had been wonderful, waking up to celebrate their birthdays together. Miss Bonnie had baked a huge chocolate cake for them. Later that day they had joined the Westmorelands for dinner at Dillon and Pam's home.

"That woman is absolutely gorgeous," she said, looking over Pete's shoulder.

"Who?"

"Garth Outlaw's date."

He chuckled. "Regan isn't actually his date. They've known each other for years. She took over as his pilot when her father retired. I understand he'd been the Outlaws' personal pilot for over forty years. And by the way, I happen to think you're absolutely gorgeous, as well."

She looked at him and smiled. "Thanks, sweetheart." She then returned her attention back to the couple. Like them, Regan and Garth were on the dance floor. "That might be the case, but I still think they look good together. And I can't get over how much Garth looks like Riley."

Pete chuckled. "I know. Anyone who thinks the Westmorelands and Outlaws aren't related just has to look at those two. Same thing with Dillon and Dare Westmoreland from Atlanta. Those are some strong Westmoreland genes."

Myra had to agree. And regardless of what Pete said about Garth and his pilot, she could detect a romance brewing between those two, even if they couldn't detect it themselves. She gazed back into her husband's eyes and at that moment she knew that he was her joy and her happiness.

She had loved being the sheriff's nanny and now she looked forward to forever being the sheriff's wife.

* * * * *

TEMPTING
THE TEXAN

MAUREEN CHILD

To Mills & Boon Desire readers.
Thanks to you,
I can tell all the stories I love to read.
I appreciate you all so much.

Prologue

Kellan Blackwood was pissed.

His father, Buckley Blackwood, was dead and gone and yet the old man was still pulling strings. Only Buck could manage that from the grave.

Kel glanced at his brother and sister and silently admitted they didn't look any happier than he felt. Vaughn's intense green eyes were narrowed thoughtfully and he was half-sprawled in his chair. Sophie, their baby sister, wore black, and her long auburn hair was pulled back from her pretty face. Her brown eyes were teary, but she still looked as if she were torn between sorrow and anger.

Kel couldn't blame her. This wasn't easy on any of them, but there was no way to avoid what was coming. But at least they had each other to lean on. All three of them had had complicated "relationships" with their father. Buck had never been concerned with his kids or what they were doing. So the three of them, as children, had formed a tight bond that held strong today.

Kace LeBlanc, Buck's lawyer, walked into the office and stopped. "Kel," he said and nodded. "Vaughn. Sophie. Thanks for coming."

"Not like we had much choice, Kace." Vaughn sat up straight and tugged at the edges of his jacket.

"Right." Kace looked uncomfortable and Kel could understand it. As Buck's lawyer, Kace knew as well as they did that Buck hadn't given a good damn about his children—it was his businesses that had demanded his attention.

"Where's Miranda?" Kace glanced around the room as if expecting her to stand up from behind a chair.

"She hasn't managed to come downstairs yet," Kel explained, and his tone said exactly what he thought of the woman who had married and divorced his father.

Miranda Dupree was thirty-six years old. Same age as Kellan. A hell of a thing for your father to marry a woman the same age as his oldest child. But Buck had been a wealthy, lonely old man and she'd swooped in on his checkbook so fast, she'd been nothing but a redheaded blur. Sophie had given Miranda the nickname *Step-witch*, and Kel had to say it suited the grasping, greedy—

"Hello, everyone."

Speak of the devil, Kel thought. He stood because his mother had drilled manners into him from the time he was a child. Then he surreptitiously slapped Vaughn's shoulder to get him on his feet, as well. The one thing Kel couldn't manage was making his voice sound welcoming. "Miranda. Surprised to see you back in Royal."

The woman was beautiful, he'd give her that. Bright red hair, brilliant blue eyes and a figure that would bring some men—including his father—to their knees. But when Kel looked at her all he saw was the woman who'd driven another wedge between Buck and his family.

"Buck sent me a letter asking me to be here—along with a few other things." Miranda gave him a slow smile that he was willing to bet she practiced in front of a mirror. "From what I hear, you're not here all that often, either, Kellan. You live in Nashville now, don't you?"

He gritted his teeth to keep what he wanted to say to the woman locked inside. There were plenty of reasons for his move to Nashville several years ago. And not one of them was any of Miranda's business.

"Why are you even here?" Vaughn demanded. "Not like Buck's alive enough for you to seduce again."

"Like I said, Buck wanted me here," she said simply and took a seat, smoothing her tight black skirt over her thighs. Glancing over to Sophie and ignoring the men, she said, "I'm sorry about your father, Sophie."

"I am, too," she said and turned to look at Kace, in effect dismissing Miranda entirely.

"Can everyone just sit down?" Kace asked, his voice cool but clear.

"Yes," Sophie said, tugging on Vaughn's hand to get him back in his chair. "Come on, you guys, sit down and let's get this over with."

"Right," Kel agreed. No point in dragging this out. He wanted to settle his business and get out of Royal fast enough that he wouldn't run into—he cut that thought off because he couldn't afford to think about *her*. Not now. Not ever.

He scrubbed one hand across his whiskered jaw and told himself that raking up the past wouldn't serve anyone.

"Buck wanted all of you present to hear his will," Kace said from behind Buckley's desk. Instantly, Kel focused on the present.

"But it won't take long." Kace looked at each of them

in turn, then zeroed in on Kellan. "I can give you all the legalese or just say it straight. Which do you want?"

Kel gave his siblings a quick look and nodded. They were clearly of a mind with him. He didn't give a damn what Miranda wanted. So he said, "Just say it, Kace."

Sympathy shone briefly in Kace's eyes and Kel knew he wasn't going to like whatever was coming before the man even said, "Basically, Buck left everything to Miranda."

"What?" Kellan was up and out of his chair in a blink. Vaughn was just a second or two behind him, and Sophie... Well, she sat there looking stunned as if she'd hit her head.

"You can't be serious." Kel glared at Kace.

"Yeah, I am." Kace didn't look happy about this. "He knew what he wanted and he laid it all out pretty clearly. And before you ask, your dad was of sound mind, Kellan," Kace said.

"You call this 'sound mind'?"

"Legally, yeah," Kace said. "I know this is hard—"

It was unthinkable. Buckley Blackwood hadn't been much of a father, but damned if Kellan could understand the old man leaving the family ranch to his ex-wife instead of his children. Slowly, he swiveled his head to stare at her. She didn't look surprised at all. Now, why was that? Had Kace told her what to expect? Had Buck?

"What the hell, Miranda?"

She shrugged and gave him that smile again. "I don't know why he did it, Kellan. All I know is he had a letter delivered to me after his death, telling me to be here for the will reading." She shrugged. "Your father was a generous man."

Not how Kellan remembered him.

"You know what? I didn't want his money or his property anyway," Vaughn said. "I don't need anything from him at this point. But there is no way Dad would do this," Vaughn argued, glaring at their ex-stepmother.

"Yeah, well, he did," Kace said simply.

"He must have hated us," Sophie whispered.

"No," Kellan assured her. "He didn't." Hell, Buck hadn't noticed any of them enough to instill any real emotion—love or hate. Besides, no one could hate Sophie. "I don't know what the hell is going on," he said, giving Kace a hard glare before turning to Miranda. "But I will find out. For now, all I'll say is this isn't over."

One

Kel was still riding a tidal wave of righteous anger when he pulled up in front of the ranch house. Blackwood Hollow was a six-hundred-acre working ranch but the main building looked like a five-star luxury hotel. Sprawling twin wings spread out across the land and climbed to two stories. Lights shone in every window, making the whole place sparkle in the darkness. And with the white Christmas lights strung along the outline of the ranch house, it looked magical.

It was a mammoth place. His little sister, Sophie, sometimes stayed there, but they'd all gotten into the habit of avoiding Blackwood Hollow because they hadn't wanted to see Buck. A part of him wondered if that would change now that Buck was gone.

For Kellan, the memories in Royal were too hard, too painful to welcome him back for anything longer than a short visit to see his siblings even if that meant an extra trip into Dallas to see Vaughn.

Frowning, Kel looked past the main house to the guest quarters. Just as luxurious, the stone-and-glass building held four guest suites, a massive great room and a four-car garage.

"And," he murmured, "not a chance Miranda's staying there."

His father's ex wouldn't settle for anything less than the big house. Especially now, since she apparently *owned* it.

Okay, there was the rage again, in a fresh wave that nearly stole his breath. Shaking his head, he got out of his black Range Rover and headed for the main house. A couple of the ranch hands nodded or lifted a hand in greeting, but didn't try to stop him to chat. Good call.

He was here only because he knew the Step-witch wasn't. His sister, Sophie, had called him to say that Miranda was in town, shopping. Naturally. When you inherit several billion dollars, you want to spend some of it.

Muttering under his breath, Kellan entered the house, crossed the foyer and walked into the great room. He gave a quick look around, to assure himself she wasn't there. He hardly noticed the blazing fire in the hearth or the dark brown leather sofas and chairs clustered in conversational groups.

Deliberately, he kept his gaze off the damn Christmas tree in front of the bank of windows overlooking the front yard. It glittered and shone with multicolored lights and ribbons of silver and gold. The scent of pine hung in the air and stirred more memories, whether he wanted them or not. As a kid, he'd loved this house during the Christmas season because his mother had always gone all out on decorating.

The holidays were always opulent at Blackwood Hollow. It was the one tradition even Buck had kept after

Kel's mother and he had divorced. Donna-Leigh had died a few years ago, but here at Blackwood Hollow Kel could still feel her influence. Tiny lights were strung around every window and there were decorated trees in almost every room of the house. The whole place smelled like evergreen, and as the memories rushed into his mind, Kel fought to keep them out.

He reminded himself that almost before the ink on their divorce decree had dried, Buck had married Miranda DuPree and brought her into the house that had been Donna-Leigh's. So the old man keeping Kel's mother's decorating traditions alive didn't mean squat.

Quickly, he took the stairs to the second story, ignoring the decorated tree on the landing and the twinkling white lights strung along the hallway. He checked the first of the guest rooms. Empty. No sign of anyone staying there. He moved on down the hall, his footsteps muffled on the dark red runner laid out in the center of the gleaming oak floor. Next room. Still nothing. He was down to two now. He didn't know how long Miranda would be in town, though according to Sophie, the woman was being trailed all through Royal by the camera crew that worked on the ridiculous TV show she was on.

Secret Lives of NYC Ex-Wives.

He snorted. So she'd found a way to make even more money out of her divorce from a rich man. And now her costars and the film crew were in Royal, helping to make the Blackwood family even more of a sideshow.

Pushing those thoughts aside, he hurried. He needed time to go through her things and look for this special letter his father had sent her. He wanted to see for himself what Buck had had to say. How he explained cutting his own children out of their inheritance.

Kel had never had much of a relationship with his fa-

ther. Buck had always been too busy swooping down on
failing companies to buy them out and sell them, adding
to his millions. But none of that mattered now. The family
legacy, the ranch, the business, should *stay* in the family.
Blackwood Hollow alone was valued at more than $60
million and that wasn't even counting Blackwood Bank
and Buck's personal fortune.

Why would he leave it all to Miranda? Hell, they'd
been divorced for years. Kel needed to know what was
going on and the only way to get those answers was to pry
them out of Miranda—even if she didn't know about it.

He opened another door and smiled. Another Christmas tree stood resplendent in front of the windows overlooking the back of the house and the swimming pool.
Women's clothes were strewed across the bed, there was
a hairbrush on the dresser and, in spite of the tree, even
the air smelled feminine.

In a rush, Kel pushed that thought aside and headed
for the closet. It was filled with clothes that he absently
noted looked a lot more conservative than what he was
used to seeing Miranda wear. He dismissed it when he
didn't find anything and went to the bedside tables. Nothing. Then he hit the dresser where he found drawers of
sweaters and shirts and yoga pants. Also very un-Mi-
randa-like. No letters, no papers. Nothing.

"Damn it," he muttered, reaching for the next drawer.
"Where the hell did she put it?"

He tugged on the drawer pull and saw a collection of
delicate bras and panties. Black, pink, red, blue—a rain-
bow of lace and silk. Gritting his teeth, he ran his hand
through the silky fabric, tumbling them all, looking for
an envelope that wasn't there. Frustrated, he stopped dead
when sounds erupted from the adjoining bathroom. Was
she here after all? Was Sophie wrong about Miranda trot-

ting around town spending his father's money in front of an audience of cameras?

The door opened, steam poured out—and through that misty fog, a woman appeared as if from a dream. It wasn't Miranda.

It was the one woman Kel hadn't wanted—or dared—to see again.

Her long strawberry blond hair was damp, lying across her shoulders and draping onto the towel wrapped around what he knew from personal experience was a hell of a body. Her dark green eyes were wide and those long legs of hers were displayed like living temptation.

"Irina Romanov."

She actually tightened her grip on the towel she wore. "Kellan? What are you doing in my room?"

God, that voice. Husky. Tempting. With just the slightest tinge of a Russian accent. In an instant, he was thrown back in time seven years. It had been Christmas then, too. For a week, the two of them had spent nearly every waking moment in bed together. Or anywhere else they'd found a flat surface. And then he'd realized what he was doing and he'd left Texas—and Irina—behind him.

If he allowed it, even now, he could hear her whispers in the dark. Feel her hands on him. Taste her hard nipples as he slammed his body into hers until they were both screaming with need. That long, unforgettable week had seared his soul and stirred a heart he'd believed dead.

Still clutching that too-small towel to her like a shield, Irina looked him dead in the eye and said, "Get out, Kellan."

Probably best, he told himself, since at the moment, all he could think about was tearing that towel off her and tossing her onto the bed. Or the floor. Or against the wall. His body didn't care how he had her—just that he *did* have her. His dick felt like stone, his breath was caught in his chest and the slow, hard hammer of his heart thundered in his ears.

Kel took a long, deep breath in an attempt to find steadiness. "Fine. I'll go. But I'm not leaving the house. I'll be downstairs when you're dressed."

The minute he left her room, Irina slammed the door and locked it. Turning around, she leaned back against the solid oak panel and rolled her eyes to the ceiling. Her heartbeat was simply out of control, and what felt like dragons were swarming in the pit of her stomach.

She forced air into her lungs and swallowed hard against the rising tide of tears. Why should she cry? She should be outraged. Furious. It had been seven years since he'd walked away, and her first emotion on seeing him again was teary anticipation?

Just like that, the burning in her eyes disappeared and the burn in her heart began. Seeing him again was a shock, even though she'd known he'd come home to Royal after Buck's death. He had to go to his father's funeral after all.

Irina had thought she was prepared—more or less— to see him again. She simply hadn't been ready to greet him while she was stark naked but for a towel. Being naked around Kel was not a good idea. Not with their past. Not with the temptation he presented simply by settling his gaze on her.

He looked good, too. Even better, somehow, than he had so long ago. He wore that elegantly cut suit the way a medieval knight might wear his armor. He was powerful, strong, gorgeous. All things dangerous. His dark brown hair was still kept short—he thought it efficient— and like always, he had a day or two's growth of beard

on his face. The scruff of whiskers reminded her of how
that stubble alternately tickled and scratched her skin.

The flash in Kel's blue eyes had disarmed her. She had
read heat there and remembered the fire that had consumed them both whenever they touched. She remembered long nights, with the Christmas tree lights the only
illumination in the room. She remembered lazy dawns,
wrapped in each other's arms before she was forced to
get up and go to work as a maid in the big house.

In fact, Irina remembered all of it as if that week with
him were burned into her brain.

Back then, she'd convinced herself she was living a
fairy tale. The oldest son in a dynasty, falling in love
with a maid in his father's house. But the fairy tale ended
with a whimper when Kellan left Texas. There were no
letters, no calls and, apparently, no regrets. Then Irina
was alone again with empty dreams and a broken heart.

She'd long suspected Buck had known about what had
gone on between her and his oldest son. The older man
had been especially kind to her when Kellan left town.
And that kindness—like everything else Buck had done
for her—was something she could never repay. It had
taken her a long time to find her way again and she had
no intention of allowing herself to slide back down into
darkness. Kellan was here, but wouldn't be for long. Her
life was in Royal. Her future was one she would build
for herself.

"I don't need Kellan," she said aloud, more to
strengthen her resolve than anything. "I've built my own
life now. Without him."

Irina wasn't the same woman she had been when she
and Kellan were together so briefly—and memorably.
She'd been to college. She was in law school now and
she was a budding author. She'd grown and taken care

of herself and she wouldn't be drawn back into an affair with a man who didn't value her.

It didn't matter that one look at him had undone seven years of self-discipline. She could be strong. All she had to do was keep her distance. A few miles would probably do the trick.

"All right," she said quietly, lifting her chin and squaring her shoulders. "I can do this. Get dressed. Talk to Kellan. And then this time I will be the one to say goodbye."

Two

Lulu Shepard took a good look at Main Street. She wasn't ready to admit this on camera yet, but she actually liked Royal, Texas. The people were nice; their hotel, the Bellamy, was luxurious and the town made a nice change from Manhattan. People were so friendly, too. Not like Manhattan, where you could probably bleed from an artery and go unnoticed.

She hadn't been sure about coming to Royal with Miranda and the rest of the cast of their reality show. But Lulu was really enjoying herself. And she really loved all of the Christmas decorations. Every light pole on the street was wrapped in garland, banners proclaiming Have a Royal Christmas were strung across the street and every tree and shop front was glittering with tiny white lights.

"Afternoon," a tall cowboy with a wicked smile said as he passed, tipping his hat.

"Well, helloooo." Lulu turned to admire the man from the rear and had to admit that view was pretty good, too.

Oh, there were so many delicious opportunities to get into a little trouble while they were in Royal. If she and Serafina couldn't find a way to shake this town up a little, then Lulu didn't know who could.

She wore a black knit tunic sweater with black tights and black ankle boots with a three-inch heel. Her bright red overcoat swung around her knees with every step and she grinned for no particular reason.

"There's just something about a small town, don't you think, Fee?"

Her best friend, Seraphina Martinez, whirled around, letting her long forest green coat swing in the wind. She, too, was wearing New York black, but for her coat. Her long brown hair was perfectly styled and lifted in the wind. Her brown eyes were shining when she smiled. "You know, I didn't think I'd like it, but I do. It's sort of like a movie set—only real." Then she sent a glance at the camera crew following them. "Come on, guys, we've got some shopping to do. Let's show America how small-town Texas lives."

Lulu laughed and fell into line behind her friend and the other members of the *Secret Lives of NYC Ex-Wives* cast. Zooey Kostas, sweet and vulnerable, was always on the lookout for her next ex. Rafaela Marchesi was never afraid to toss one of her friends under the bus as long as it earned her a few more minutes of screen time. Then there was Seraphina, the take-charge woman in their little group. Fee had a great laugh and a huge heart. And Miranda was the last—sort of a mother-bear kind of woman, which didn't earn her a lot of time on the show, since as their producer was forever saying, "Scandal sells."

But when Miranda DuPree had announced she was coming to Royal for a funeral, the powers that be at the network had decided it would be a great idea for the whole cast to go along.

Though she liked Miranda a lot, Lulu hadn't thought much of the idea at first. Now she couldn't imagine why. An icy wind lifted a lock of her thick black hair and tossed it across her eyes. She plucked it free, grinned and hurried her steps to catch up with Fee. There were so many new and interesting shops waiting.

Kellan had one hand planted on the mantel and was staring at a blazing fire in the stone hearth when he heard her come into the room. Hell, she moved so quietly maybe he had just *sensed* her.

He turned to face her and his breath caught in his chest. Seven years since he'd last seen her and every cell in his body was responding to her presence. Time, it seemed, hadn't cooled off what he felt for her. Damn it.

"What are you doing here, Kellan?"

That voice tugged at his insides and awakened even more memories that had been asleep until that moment. Not good. He'd once walked away from her because he felt he had to. He'd had nothing to offer her then and nothing had changed since. He had to stay cool, keep his distance.

But she was looking at him with a carefully banked fury he'd never seen before. And for some damn reason, that put him on the defensive.

"This is still *Blackwood Hollow*," he said tightly. "I'm a Blackwood. I don't have to explain why I'm in the house I grew up in."

"You don't live here anymore," she reminded him.

Tipping his head to one side, he narrowed his gaze on her. "Yeah. But I didn't know you were still living here."

"Not surprising," she pointed out. "You haven't been back in this house for seven years."

A jab, well aimed. Kellan had avoided this house like it

was haunted. And maybe, he thought now, it *was*. Ghosts of his childhood, memories of his mother. But mostly, it was the memories of his week with Irina that plagued him. Being in this house made those ghostly images in his mind more real. More corporeal. As if he could reach out and touch them, bring back those moments in time to relive at his leisure.

His gaze swept her up and down in a blink of an eye, taking in everything, missing nothing. Her long, wavy hair was still damp, but now she wore a loose-fitting yellow jersey shirt with a neckline wide enough to bare her shoulders. At five feet ten inches tall, Irina had legs that were long and shapely, though at the moment they were covered by a pair of gray yoga pants that clung to every inch. Black ballet flats were on her feet.

Kellan's whole body tensed.

Even dressed casually, Irina was more beautiful than any other woman would have been decked out in diamonds. Heat rushed through him. The sparks in her eyes intrigued him. There was a pride and a self-confidence about her now and he liked it. Irina had once told him that in Russia, she'd been a model, but when he'd known her, she'd been shy, unsure of herself. As if she were lost and hadn't been able to find her way.

This Irina, strong enough to meet his gaze and lift her chin in defiance, was someone new, and damned if she wasn't even more attractive.

She crossed her arms over her chest, unconsciously lifting her breasts, making his mouth go dry. "What were you doing in my room? Going through my things?"

"Didn't know that was your room," he said shortly. "I thought it was Miranda's."

One of her expertly shaped eyebrows lifted and he knew what she was thinking.

"God, no." He shuddered at the idea of sex with his late father's ex. Even if it hadn't been more than a little gross to contemplate sex with his father's former lover, he wouldn't have been interested in Miranda. She was too... practiced at seduction. "Trust me," he said. "It's not that."

"All right." Her arms dropped to her sides. "Then why were you looking for her room?"

He took a deep breath and gritted his teeth. Kellan wasn't used to explaining himself. Mostly, he did what he wanted when he wanted and screw whoever didn't like it. Made life easier. Back in the day, Irina never would have confronted him like this. And maybe that was why he was willing to answer her. Damned if he didn't admire the fire in her eyes. "For something to explain why Buck did what he did. They read his will today and dear old Dad left her *everything*."

"Yes, I know. Kace told me earlier today when he came to tell me about the inheritance Buckley left to me."

Surprise had him speechless for a moment. Kellan never would have imagined Buckley Blackwood even *noticing* a maid in his house, let alone naming her in his will. Buck hadn't been exactly known for being a kind soul. He had marched through his life, single-mindedly focused on his business, his fortune.

Finally, he recovered enough to ask, "My father left you something?"

"Is it really so shocking? Your father was very good to me."

"I know you always thought so." He shook his head as if denying what he was saying. "But Buck was never described as *generous*."

"Fine. Think that if it comforts you."

"Comforts me?" Kellan stared at her for a long minute. "What the hell does that mean?"

"Never mind." Irina swung her long hair back over her shoulder and her shirt dipped just a bit lower over her upper arm. "You've obviously set your mind on who you believe your father was. I can't change your mind."

Maybe Buck was good to Irina, but Kellan couldn't be budged from his own perspective on his father. Hell, he'd lived it, hadn't he?

"But you haven't answered me. Why did you want to look through Miranda's things?"

Hard to keep his mind on business when he was fantasizing about sliding that shirt all the way off, then— "I heard Buck sent her a letter. I want to see it. Need to know what's in it."

"It's none of your business."

"Of course it's my business," he snapped and rubbed one hand across the back of his neck. "I need to know what she knows. I need to understand why Buck left her everything."

For a long moment, Irina just watched him, and the steady stare from her dark green eyes made him uneasy. For good reason, as it turned out.

"No. I can't help you, Kellan. And I won't let you spy on Miranda."

Irritation flared to life inside him. "You can't stop me."

"I can tell her what you did."

"Letting her know after the fact won't change anything," he said quickly.

Even though she was standing between him and what he needed to do, he couldn't help thinking that it was damned good to see her again. *Too* good. He should have been past this, Kellan told himself.

He'd stayed away from her deliberately for years, because being close to her and not having her would have killed him. Hell, she was *part* of the reason he'd moved to Nashville. But even distance from her hadn't been enough to wipe away the memory of her. She'd still been with him. In his dreams. In those quiet, waking moments when he didn't have enough to occupy his thoughts.

And every time she popped into his mind—way too often—he shut it down fast. He spent empty nights with other women telling himself that sex with them was just as good as it had been with Irina. Lies he wanted to believe because they made it all that much easier.

But standing here, with her just out of arm's reach, those lies rushed back to bite him in the ass. So naturally, he buried what he was feeling beneath the anger still riding him since the will reading.

"Since when are you Miranda's friend?" he asked. "You're really ready to stand with her against me?"

"And how do I owe loyalty to you? You disappeared, Kellan."

"I had to."

"Yes, I'm sure." She entered the room but walked a wide path around him to do it. She dropped onto a corner of the couch, curled her legs up beneath her and tipped her head to one side to look up at him. "She's Buck's guest."

"Buck's dead."

Emotion flashed briefly in her eyes. "I know. But this is his home—"

"And mine," he added.

"Not for years," she reminded him. "You walked away, Kellan. From your home. From your family. From Buck. From *me*."

And there it was. The past was in the room with them, with its hungry, snapping jaws, not really caring whom it bit into, just wanting the pain. The blood.

He'd known that the minute they saw each other again,

they'd have to relive this. He'd have to look at old decisions and would be forced to defend them. He didn't know that he could.

"I had to leave." He shoved his hands into his pockets.

Irina looked up at the man around whom she'd once built ridiculous dreams. The oldest son of the man she'd worked for—the man she owed so much. Buck had rescued her. Given her a chance she might never have had otherwise. She'd come to this house broken, to work as a maid, to go to school, to rebuild a life that had been shattered.

Kellan was the man who had touched her in so many ways, he'd left her breathless. She'd trusted him, in spite of everything she'd already been through. She'd believed in him when she shouldn't have. And then, he'd simply *left her*.

Seven years ago, they'd had a week together. He'd been wounded. She'd been hurt. And yet, somehow, for that one week, they'd reached beyond themselves and found something she had believed was magical. Stolen time, stolen passion and her silly dreams of something more. Then it was over and she was broken again.

Irina wouldn't let it happen this time. Wouldn't let her heart overrun her mind. But even as she thought it, she knew that the reason she'd dropped onto the brown leather sofa was because Kellan still made her legs weak. Her heartbeat was racing and there were tingles of expectation, anticipation, at the core of her. It seemed her body didn't care what her mind had to say. It only wanted.

Irina looked up at him and deliberately hid everything she was feeling.

"Yes, you had to leave. You said as much to me. Seven

years ago." The leather felt cold and that chill was seeping inside her. "You said a lot of things. I remember."

Kellan nodded. "Yeah, I do, too. I didn't want to hurt you, Irina."

Her gaze locked on him and she drew a long, shallow breath. Irina didn't want to talk about any of it, either. Didn't want to remember the sound of his voice saying, *I can't be what you want.* Or, *This isn't real, Irina. It can't be. I won't let it be.* So she swallowed hard and hid what she was feeling. "You may not have wanted to, but you did. Still, that's not why you're here now, is it?"

"No," he said, inclining his head slightly. "It's not." He braced his feed wide apart, as if preparing for a battle. "Tell me this. How long is Miranda staying in Royal?"

She shrugged as if indifferent. "I don't really know. She's made no plans to leave as far as I know."

"Of course she hasn't," he muttered, pushing one hand through his short, neat hair. "Why would she? Has the run of this house, all the money Buck left her and plenty of time to cause more trouble."

Miranda had always seemed like a nice woman to Irina. In fact, they'd bonded some over a shared past of heartbreak and mistrust. And seeing how Buck's grown children had treated Miranda had guaranteed that Irina would stand up for her. Since she'd once been an underdog herself, she would always stand up for people she thought were being bullied.

"What exactly, apart from her marrying and divorcing your father," Irina asked, "do you have against her?"

"Isn't that enough?"

"No." Love died. Marriages ended. She'd lived it herself and usually there was more than one person to blame for it.

"It is for me," he countered. "She's got no rights here as far as I'm concerned."

Shaking her head, Irina watched him. "Then it's good it's not up to you."

"What the hell, Irina? I don't understand this," he admitted. "You were always more loyal to Buck than he deserved, so why would you switch that loyalty to Miranda?"

"And you were always harder on Buck than he deserved. Your father was more than you think he was."

"I don't believe it," he snapped. "And that doesn't answer the question. Why are you being so damn protective of Miranda of all people?"

Because, Irina thought, she understood Buck's exwife. She knew what it was to be called a gold digger. Knew what it was to love and lose. Knew how hard it was to start over. To rebuild your life. How could Irina not stand by Miranda, when Buck had stood by her?

"It was your father's fortune to do with as he pleased. Why do you get to say that he can't leave Miranda everything?" Forcing herself to her feet, Irina locked her traitorous knees so they wouldn't wobble on her again and tipped her head back to stare up at him. Looking into those lake-blue eyes of his sent tendrils of heat spiraling through her, but Irina did her best to ignore them. "I *am* being loyal to Buck. To his wishes."

He slowly shook his head and watched her curiously. "What the hell did he ever do for you?"

Everything, she thought but didn't say. Buckley Blackwood had played guardian angel to a lot of people and he'd insisted on remaining anonymous. So no one—not even his children—knew what a good man he really had been. But Irina would never forget.

"That's none of your business, Kellan. You walked

away. You don't get to show up seven years later and demand answers to anything."

He huffed out a breath and took a step closer. Irina steeled herself because she could smell his cologne. That same wild, spicy scent that seemed to chase her through sleepless nights. His jaw was clenched, his eyes snapping with sparks of frustration, and tension practically radiated from him in thick waves.

She felt that same tension pulsing inside her and she hated it. He'd once had so much power over her. One look from him turned her body into a molten puddle of need. One touch and she was burning. Orgasms with Kellan were more than she would have thought possible.

But strangely, what she missed most was lying in the circle of his arms, darkness all around them, while they talked and laughed together. That closeness, that intimacy, had meant everything to her and had hurt her the most when it was gone.

"I used to admire that hard head of yours," he said, his voice lower, more intimate.

Now it was more than her knees that were feeling weak. Everything in her yearned. A slow burn started deep inside and bubbled in her bloodstream. This was dangerous. A temptation to go back rather than forward. She'd fought hard to reclaim her life, her heart, her mind after Kellan left. Irina couldn't let herself be swept into another temporary liaison. And with Kellan, she knew it would be nothing *but* temporary.

"Kellan…" Warning? Invitation? Even Irina didn't know for sure.

"You're still so damn beautiful," he murmured.

And he was still enticing.

"I think I'm going to kiss you," he said, one eyebrow quirking. "Do you have a problem with that?"

Say yes. Say yes. Say yes.

"No," she whispered.

So he did and the first touch of his lips to hers set that slow burn free and turned it into a wildfire deep within her body. She remembered that fire so well. She welcomed the flames, though she knew she shouldn't. Irina was helpless to stop herself. Kellan had always had this effect on her and seven years hadn't changed a thing.

His hands came down onto her shoulders and pulled her toward him. She kept her mouth on his as her arms snaked around his waist. The feel of him pressed against her made her body ache. An aching, molten heat settled in her core and left her hungry for so much more than a kiss.

His tongue swept into her mouth and tangled with hers. She tightened her hold on him, and met him stroke for stroke, need for need. The kiss awakened her from a years-long sleep and the awakening was almost painful. Her body hummed with anticipation. Her mind clouded over with too many sensations rising and falling to make sense of any of them. Her breath caught in her chest as she gave herself up to the wonder of the fire even while a small voice within shouted at her to be careful. To step back. To remember that though his touch was magical, he wasn't staying this time, either.

And that thought was finally enough to penetrate the fog in her brain. To push past what he made her feel long enough that she could remind herself that only pain waited for her if she let this go on.

Irina pulled back, shaking her head as much to convince herself as him. She took a deep breath to steady herself and met his gaze, no matter what it cost her to look into those blue eyes again. "We shouldn't have done that."

He scrubbed one hand across his face, then the back

of his neck. His breath came hard and fast so she knew
he'd been as affected as she had been. Small comfort,
she supposed.

Nodding, he said, "Right. Mistake." His gaze locked
on hers, he added, "A good one."

Her stomach jumped. "No, it wasn't."

"Liar."

Her heart jittered.

"Fine. It felt good. But then, chemistry was never our
problem," she said, remembering. God, how she remembered what happened when they were together.

"No. It wasn't." He stepped back from her as if he
didn't quite trust himself not to reach for her again.

And Irina didn't know if she was sad about that or
grateful.

"I couldn't stay back then, Irina," he was saying. "There
were too many memories in Royal. Too much pain."

She knew that. He'd lost his wife a year before he and
Irina got together. So he'd come to her, a widower with
a broken heart and a shattered soul, and for a very short
while, they'd healed each other.

"So you left and shared the pain."

His head snapped up and his gaze fixed on hers. "That
wasn't my intention."

"And yet it's what you did."

Clearly irritated, he pushed one hand through his hair.
"I didn't come here tonight to argue with you."

"No," she said. "You came here to spy on Miranda."

"I want answers," he countered.

"Get them another way."

A muscle in his jaw ticked. "I hope Miranda appreci-
ates how you're defending her."

"I'm not doing this for her," Irina said. "Or not just for
her. I'm doing this mainly for your father. Buck wrote his

will. It laid out *his* wishes. Kellan, you don't get to disregard them simply because you don't like them."

"Man, I hope Buck appreciated the tiger he had defending him."

A small smile curved her mouth briefly. "He did."

Nodding, Kellan studied her for a long minute. "I'm not going to let this go."

"I didn't think you would," she said. "But you should. And, Kellan, you should know that Buck loved you. Loved all of you."

"Please." He snorted dismissively and waved one hand at her as if erasing her words entirely.

"He did."

"And he proved that by leaving our family legacy to a woman he chose to not stay married to?"

"I don't know why he did that," Irina admitted. "But I always trusted Buck."

"There's the difference between us, then," Kellan said softly, his gaze locked with hers. "I never trusted my father. And I won't start now."

"So you're not going back to Nashville?" She had hoped that after the funeral and the reading of the will that Kellan would once again leave Royal.

"Not a chance," he promised. "I'm not going anywhere until this whole situation is settled." He turned on his heel and headed for the front door. He paused only briefly to look back at her. When their eyes met, he said, "You haven't seen the last of me, Irina."

That sounded like a promise, too, and she hated that she was pleased by it.

"How'd the big spy operation go?"

Kellan glanced over his shoulder at his younger brother as Vaughn walked into the great room and dropped onto the closest sofa. Since Vaughn lived in Dallas now, he was staying at their mother's friend Dixie's ranch, Magnolia Acres. Since Kellan was in Royal for a while, though, Vaughn was dropping in and out. It was good to spend real time with his brother and sister instead of the quick visits he usually made. The only time Kellan stayed at his ranch himself was when he came back to Royal to see his brother and sister. Now he was rethinking the whole drop-in-anytime thing.

Scowling, Kellan said, "As well as you said it would."

Vaughn laughed shortly. "It was a crappy plan, Kel. Face it. Storm Dad's house, snoop through Miranda's stuff?"

Kellan stalked to the wet bar in the corner of the room. Bending down, he opened the fridge and grabbed a beer. "You want one?"

"Hell yes."

Kellan crossed the room again, handed a beer to his brother and then took a seat opposite him. "I never got to go through her things. Irina was there and stopped me."

Vaughn's eyebrows lifted. "Interesting," he mused. "I didn't know anyone *could* stop you once you had your decision made."

Kellan took a swig of beer and avoided looking at Vaughn. His brother was entirely too perceptive. "Doesn't matter."

"Uh-huh. So, how's Irina?"

Now he did fire a hard look at his brother. "She's fine."

"Better than fine, if you ask me," Vaughn said with a small smile. "We both saw her at the service, and gotta say, she's still hot."

"Hot?"

"I'm not blind, Kel. Even if you are."

"I'm not blind, either," he snapped and took another hard pull of his beer.

"Good to know." Vaughn sat up and braced his elbows on his knees. "So you going to do anything about it?"

The taste of Irina rose up in his mind. The feel of her body pressed to his. Her breath on his cheek. The scent of her hair. The silk of her skin. He took another drink of his beer and let the icy brew dampen the fires inside. He really didn't need his brother poking at him over Irina when his own mind and body were doing just fine on that front. "What the hell, Vaughn?"

He held up one hand. "Fine. I'll back off."

"Thank you."

"But," he added, and Kellan frowned at him, "all those years ago, you two had something."

"How do you know?"

"Everybody knew."

So much for a secret affair. "It was a long time ago."

"True. But according to gossip and our baby sister, Irina's still single. So are you."

Kellan's gaze narrowed. "I'm not looking, Vaughn."

"Because of Shea?" Vaughn's voice was a whisper.

Kellan shot off the couch like he was on a spring. It had been eight years since his wife had died in that car accident. Eight years and he still didn't want to think about that day. Remember the staggering loss. Remember that touching Irina only a year after that loss had made him feel like a damn cheat. "Don't talk about her."

"A lot of rules," his brother said softly. "No talk of Irina. Shea, either. What am I allowed to say to you?"

"How about good-night?" Kellan snapped. "Or even better, *I'm headed back to Magnolia Acres.* Or even better, Dallas."

Vaughn laughed. "Yeah, not happening. I'm here for a couple more days. Have some friends I want to see while I'm in Royal. Now that the services and the will reading are done, I'm free."

"Why are you not pissed?" Kellan demanded suddenly. "About Dad leaving everything to Miranda? Why isn't that burning your ass?"

Vaughn's features smoothed out into a blank slate. Only his eyes flashed to let Kellan know he wasn't as disinterested as he was pretending to be. "Because I don't want Buck's money. I made my own way with no help from our father. It's too damn late for him to do anything for me. So let Miranda have it. I hope she chokes on it."

"I call bull." Kellan pointed his beer at Vaughn. "Maybe you don't want the money, but I know losing Blackwood Hollow to that woman has to be eating at you. That's *family land*, Vaughn. It's our land. Our ranch. Our damned legacy."

Studying his own beer, Vaughn was silent for a long minute or two. Finally, though, he said, "Being pissed won't change anything, Kel. So accept the fact that our dad was a dick and move the hell on already."

"No."

Vaughn gave another short laugh and lifted his beer in a toast. "Fine. You go ahead. Charge into the dragon's den and try to come out with the magic sword or whatever. But don't expect me to help you do it."

Kellan said, "Just don't get in my way."

"Deal." Vaughn turned for the door. "Now, I'm going to Dixie's place. I'm too tired to keep jousting with you. Good luck on your next caper, 007."

Life, Kellan thought, might have been a lot easier if he'd been an only child.

* * *

The next morning, Kellan was working at his ranch, wearing some jeans, a dark green flannel shirt and a heavy brown leather jacket. His old boots were scuffed and worn, and stepping into them made him feel complete somehow. You could take a man off the ranch, dress him in a suit and toss him into a city, but it seemed you couldn't take the Texas out of him.

He was tired, though. The argument with Vaughn bothered him, but it was that kiss with Irina that had kept him awake most of the night. He'd played it over and over in his head for hours, like a damn movie on constant rewind and replay. He hadn't been able to turn it off. To ignore what seeing her again, touching her again, had done to his body. So a night of self-imposed torture left him squinting into the early-morning sunlight and wishing for more coffee.

Standing on the wide front porch in the cold, blustery wind, he scanned the property he'd purchased five years ago. He should probably rent it out, but the truth was, it was nice to have his own place to stay in when he was in Royal. He had a great foreman, who took care of the place while Kellan lived in Nashville, and, as an investment, the ranch couldn't be better. The land itself was worth almost twice as much as it had been when he'd bought it and that wasn't even counting the value of the palatial ranch house and outbuildings. Not to mention the stock—thousands of heads of cattle and horses.

But he hadn't bought it for its financial worth. Instead, it was a touchstone of sorts. A reminder that though staying in Royal had been too much for him seven years ago, this corner of Texas was still his home. His roots ran deep here. The Blackwoods had been in this area for more than a hundred years.

Which was just one more reason why he wasn't about to give up his family legacy to a gold digger. Just the thought of Miranda DuPree made his hackles rise and had him grinding his teeth together so hard, he was half-surprised they didn't shatter. He'd thought Miranda was out of their lives when she and Buck divorced—and now she was back, worse than ever. "What the hell was Buck thinking?"

When a bright red Jeep zipped up the drive and came to a screeching halt almost directly in front of him, Kellan smiled in spite of the dark thoughts tumbling through his mind. His baby sister hopped out of the car and shivered in the cold wind.

"Hi, Kel," Sophie said as she tugged her black jacket tighter around her.

People didn't usually think of Texas as cold-weather country. But winters could be harsh and even though snow was rare, the icy wind could cut like a knife.

"What're you doing here so early?"

She waved one hand, smiled, and Kellan realized what a beauty his sister had become. Just an inch or so shorter than Irina, Sophie had long auburn hair, brown eyes and a curvy body that Kellan really didn't want to acknowledge. As far as he was concerned, there was no man good enough for Sophie—so she should just be alone. If they were Catholic, he'd be voting for a convent.

"I've got a ten o'clock appointment at the Courtyard. My client wants to look at the antiques at Priceless."

Sophie, at only twenty-seven, ran a popular YouTube channel on style, was a licensed interior decorator and had her own shop in Royal. And as a designer, of course she would love shopping at the Courtyard. The place had grown from a single rehabbed barn housing antiques into a series of eclectic businesses, including a few artisans and cafés.

"I saw Vaughn at the diner having coffee and he told me you'd be up and moving because when he left here last night, you were too wired to sleep."

"Our brother's got a big mouth," Kellan muttered. "What's up, Sophie?"

She sighed and flipped her hair out of her face when the wind gusted. "I couldn't sleep last night, either. I kept thinking about the will and Miranda and us, and I guess I just wanted to talk to you. See what you think about all of it."

He scowled and tugged his hat down firmer on his head. "I think I'm going to be going into town to talk to Kace later today. See if I can find a way to fight this will."

"Okay, but what if he says there isn't one?"

"Then we fight anyway," Kellan said tightly. "Damned if we just hand over our home to Miranda."

She nodded and smiled. "Okay, good. Because I was thinking maybe I could snoop around a little. Talk to people. See if anyone knows anything about Miranda. Gossip in Royal lives forever. Plus, I know Miranda's come back to town more than a few times since the divorce. I mean, you and Vaughn and I, we haven't really been spending any time at the house in years."

True. They'd all avoided the house because they were busy avoiding Buck. Kellan lived in Nashville now, Sophie had her own house in Pine Valley and Vaughn was in Dallas these days.

"Maybe," she continued, "there's a reason behind Dad doing this to us. And maybe I can help find it."

Three

Kellan looked into her eyes and saw the worry and the hurt there, and if he could, he would have reached beyond the grave to grab his father and curse him for giving Sophie pain. He knew she wanted to help him find answers and, hell, maybe she could. Women talked more easily to other women. If she could pry some secrets loose, it might give them something to use against Miranda.

"Sounds good," he said and saw the flash of pleasure in her eyes. "Where are you going to start?"

"After my appointment, I thought I'd go to the ranch and talk to Irina."

"No." The one word shot from him before he could hold it back.

"Why not?"

Good question. The answer wasn't something he wanted to share. Kellan didn't want to risk his sister and his former lover having a private chat. God knows what

Irina would have to say about him. He certainly hadn't given her any reason to speak well about him.

"I'm going to the house later today." That hadn't been the plan, but plans change. "So I'll take care of talking to Irina. Why don't you speak to some of Miranda's friends in town? Maybe some of the women she dragged here with her from New York."

Sophie frowned thoughtfully. "That's probably a good idea. I mean, she went to New York after the divorce, she probably had plenty to say about Dad when their breakup was fresh."

It actually was a good idea. Then he had another one. If their little sister talked to Vaughn about all of this, maybe he'd change his mind. "Okay, then. And why don't you give Vaughn a call? Tell him what we're up to."

"Oh, he won't be interested." Sophie shrugged. "Soon enough, he'll be back in Dallas running his company. He said he doesn't give a damn what Miranda does with her inheritance. It has nothing to do with him."

So much for that. In a way, Kel understood the attitude. His brother had built his own fortune at Blackwood Energy Corp., so he didn't need Buck's money. But hell, neither did Kel. It was the damn principle of the thing that motivated Kellan. And he wished Vaughn would stick around long enough to stand with his siblings.

"Okay, then, for now, it's you and me, baby sister." He reached out with one arm and pulled her into a hug. She held him tight, then let go.

"I'll let you know if I find out anything and you tell me if Irina has anything to say, okay?"

"Sure." Nodding, he watched her hop back into her car. "And drive slower, will you?"

"Nope!" She grinned, slammed the door and gunned

the engine. Whipping the red car around, she peeled off down the drive, leaving a fan of spun gravel in her wake.

"Damn it." Sophie always drove too fast. As a teenager, she'd had her license pulled first by Buck and then by Sheriff Battle. And that hadn't stopped her. The last time Kellan had been in town, Nathan Battle had told him that Sophie's speeding tickets alone were paying for the remodel of the sheriff's station.

Pushing that thought out of his mind, Kellan headed for the stables. What he needed was some hard work. Work that would keep his hands busy and free his mind to think about what his next step would be.

Though he already knew the answer.

He had to see Irina again.

"I'm meeting my friends in Royal for lunch," Miranda said. "I've told them all about the Royal Diner for years and now they want to try it out in person. Would you like to join us?"

Miranda had been in Royal since a couple of days before the will reading, and in that time she and Irina had become friends. When Miranda was still married to Buck, the two women hadn't really bonded. Irina was more shy back then, too. Less sure of herself. They actually had more in common than she would have thought. They were both divorced—though their situations were wildly different. They were both rebuilding their lives. And they both knew hidden truths about Buckley Blackwood. Each of them, in their own ways, owed Buck a lot.

It was good to be able to talk about the older man with someone who understood. Almost no one in Royal knew the real Buck.

In business, Buck had been ruthless, determined and

unstoppable. But in private, the man had helped more people than anyone would guess. It really irritated Irina that his own children were clueless about that side of Buck. But she'd once promised him that she'd keep his secrets. Just because he was dead didn't give her permission to talk. Did it?

"Thank you, Miranda," she said. "I really appreciate it. But I think I'm going to work on my book this morning. I'd like to finish the chapter at least."

She was so close to finishing the book she'd been driven to write. Her own personal background story was one she thought a lot of women could connect to. Maybe not the particulars of her experience, but the spirit of the story. Picking yourself up and starting over would be a clarion call to those who might be feeling hopeless.

And an agent and a publisher had believed in her, too. She'd sold her book six months ago and it was still a thrill to her. Soon, she'd be a published author and then an immigration lawyer, and her own American dream story would be complete.

Or as complete as it could be without the man she'd once believed to be the love of her life.

Miranda smiled and nodded. "I get it. And I know Buck was proud of you for everything you've accomplished."

"Thank you," she said. "That means a lot."

"And," Miranda added as she picked up her bag, "if you're willing, I'd love to read some of your book."

Irina almost choked. She hadn't expected that rush of wild panic. Someone wanted to read what she'd written? Why was that terrifying? Soon it would be out on shelves and hopefully a lot of people would want to read it. But this was different. This was someone she *knew*. Yes, she'd submitted it to an agent and publisher, but that was business. Letting someone she knew and liked read it was something different.

Miranda laughed. "Okay, never mind. I can see how unnerved you are at the idea."

"No," Irina said, taking a step forward as she got a firm grip on the swirls of what felt like eagles in her stomach. Then she sighed. "All right, yes, I'm a little nervous at the thought. But I really would love for you to read the first chapter and tell me what you think."

It sounded terrifying, of course. But one day soon, everyone in Royal would see it, buy it, read it. It might be a good thing to get an idea of what people would think ahead of time.

"Great!" Miranda gave her a quick hug. "I'm sure it's wonderful, so don't look so worried."

Irina laughed a little. "I think worrying is what I do best."

Smiling, Miranda said, "I'll see you tonight. And remember, you're not a maid here anymore, Irina. You're a guest."

Technically. But Miranda now owned the lovely house and Irina was Buck's guest, not hers. So she would pitch in and help out as much as she could.

"Thank you. I appreciate that." She gave a look around the great room, with its plush but homey atmosphere, and at the Christmas tree, which she personally decorated every year. "But I've worked here for more than seven years now. While I'm here, I'll continue to help the housekeeper."

Miranda studied her for a long moment. "I get that. You don't want to be beholden to anyone. You need to steer your own path. Pay your own way."

"Yes," Irina said.

"You know, I think you and I are very much alike."

Irina smiled. She'd had the same thought. "Have a good time."

"Right." Miranda headed for the front door. "I'll see you later."

Alone, Irina thought about their conversation. About the secrets she held. About promises made and about Kellan, still holding so much anger for his late father. And she made a decision.

Working on the book would have to wait. First, she had to see Kellan. Tell him things he should know.

The diner was kitschy, with the decor set firmly in the fifties—black-and-white tile floor, red faux leather booths and an actual jukebox on one wall. Lulu was charmed. The waitresses seemed to know everyone in there and the camera crew following Lulu and her friends didn't intimidate anyone. Instead, the locals were interested, excited even.

Except for one man.

Of course, he was gorgeous. His brown eyes were flashing with irritation and his rumpled dark brown hair was a little too long. The collar of his dress shirt was unbuttoned and his dark red tie loosened. He had a sheaf of papers spread out over the table in front of him and a cup of coffee at his elbow. The hostile looks he was shooting everyone involved in her reality show left no doubt what he thought of any of them.

Well, if he wanted privacy to work, Lulu told herself, he shouldn't have come to a diner. The scowl on his face seemed to be a permanent fixture and she wondered idly why she found that appealing. A man that inherently cranky shouldn't be so attractive. But he certainly was. He sipped his coffee, made a note on one of the papers and then frowned again at her group and the camera crew.

Fee and the rest of the girls were oblivious, joking together about another day of shopping or perhaps a spa
day at the Bellamy, where they were all staying. But
Lulu couldn't stop watching *him*. So she was aware when
Miranda came into the diner and stopped at his table.
Briefly, the scowl on his face lifted and she wondered
how Miranda had managed that small miracle. While
they talked, Lulu scooted out of the booth and walked
up to join them. She heard her friend saying something
about Buck's will, but she missed the context because
both people got quiet as soon as she arrived.

"Hi, Miranda." She smiled at her friend, then sent a
deliberate wink at the crabby man frowning at her.

"Lulu!" Miranda gave her a hug and grinned. "Did
you guys have another fabulous morning of shopping?"

"We did. It was wonderful. We went back to the Courtyard shops." They'd all enjoyed it so much the day before, they'd returned to hit the stores they'd missed on
their first visit.

"And your camera crew loved it, too?" the man asked
snidely, inserting himself into the conversation. "Get
every little purchase covered, did they? Want to make
sure America sees you spending your exes' money."

"I'm sorry?" she asked, pointedly meeting his less-
than-friendly stare.

"That would be nice, but I doubt you are," he said.

"Um," Miranda interrupted, confusion written plainly
on her features. "Lulu Shepard, this is my ex-husband's
lawyer, Kace LeBlanc. Kace, Lulu."

"A lawyer," Lulu said with feigned, over-the-top sorrow. "That explains it."

His eyes flashed. "What does that mean?"

She shrugged and ignored Miranda's growing confusion to continue the byplay with Kace. "I've rarely met

a lawyer with a measurable sense of humor or any talent for finding joy in life."

"Is that right? Well, my *joy in life* isn't dependent on the presence of a camera."

Their cameramen, Henry and Sam, maneuvered into position so they could capture this whole scene. The guys were experts at this and there was nothing that sold better on film than conflict. They were probably sensing a good one right here and they weren't wrong. But Lulu didn't care. She was starting to enjoy herself.

She tossed her hair back over her shoulder. "What do you like about your job, then? Evicting widows and orphans?"

Henry snorted a muffled laugh.

Miranda said, "Now, Lulu…"

Miranda was always the most altruistic of the Exes. The one who looked out for everyone else. She hated an argument; that was why she was the peacemaker on their show. Lulu sort of liked arguments. Especially when she was trading barbs with a gorgeous man with the most beautiful brown eyes she'd ever seen.

"Seriously?" Kace demanded. "That's the best you've got?" He pushed out of the booth and stood much taller than her, even with her three-inch heels.

"Oh no," Lulu assured him, a small smile curving her mouth. "I can do way better. I promise you. I'm just getting started."

"Ah." He nodded sagely and waved one hand to indicate Henry and Sam. "Had to wait for the cameras to get set. Have they caught your 'good side'?"

"Every side is my good side," she quipped and stared up at him.

He met her gaze and she saw a flash of interest spark in those amazing eyes of his before he said, "Is there some reason you have to have cameras in the diner? Do you guys eat with your feet? Do they need to document you chewing?"

"It's a reality show," Lulu reminded him. "They follow us around. And they probably want to catch some local color in Royal—which you're currently providing. And no one but you seems to have a problem with it."

"Everyone else is too polite to say anything."

"Um…" Miranda's voice slid into the fray but couldn't stop it.

"But polite doesn't occur to you, does it?"

"I'm too busy for social niceties."

"So busy you have to work in a diner?" Lulu countered, really starting to enjoy herself now. He was angry, and that put a fire in his brown eyes that was both magnetic and irritating. "Where's your office? Over a dry cleaner's?"

His mouth worked, then tightened into a grim slash. "My office is being painted. I came here to get some work done, which would be easier if you and your fellow 'actors' weren't making so damn much noise."

"Um, maybe…" Miranda's voice was barely noticed.

"Not actors," Lulu told him. "Just people. Reality show, remember? Do you have memory problems?"

"Oh," he said, glaring down at her, "there's a problem in here, but it's not with my memory."

"Well, you'd think a lawyer would know that a diner wasn't going to give him quiet. Why don't you go to the library?"

"It was fine in here until your crowd showed up."

"Okay, let's just leave it there, all right?" Miranda took Lulu's arm, clearly ready to drag her away. But Lulu wasn't ready just yet. Honestly, she'd wanted to meet the gorgeous, cranky man, but she hadn't expected such explosive chemistry between them. Everyone in the diner was watching them and she had no doubt the cameras had caught the entire exchange between her and Kace LeBlanc. Kace. What a great name.

"We'll let you work, then," Lulu said as he sat down again. "Be sure to tell us if we're too loud, though. Not that we'll get quiet, but I don't want to miss you being annoyed."

His lips quirked briefly. "I don't imagine you're ever quiet."

She gave him a brief, sly smile in return. "Nope. And in certain situations I've been known to scream."

Later that afternoon, Irina pulled up to Kellan's ranch and parked outside the main house.

With the engine off, she simply sat there and studied the place. Two stories, sparkling white with black shutters and black newel posts on the wide wraparound porch. Oaks surrounded the building, offering shade in the summer and stark definition in winter.

It wasn't the first time she'd been there. Since Kellan left Royal for Nashville, she'd been here several times. Well, not *inside*, but she'd driven past it. Parked outside it. Not obsessively or anything. But the ranch had become a touchstone of sorts. The last piece of Kellan to remain in Texas. She could tell herself he hadn't left entirely. And indeed, she knew that he came back from time to time to see his brother and sister. And to check in on his own property.

But he'd *avoided* Irina.

Knowing that had stung her deeply. But she'd gotten past it. She'd focused on work. On school. On building a future for herself. Now she didn't think of him every day anymore. She didn't dream of him every night. But when she did, it was with an ache of remembered loss that was so strong, sometimes she woke up crying. And that infuriated her. Why should she cry for a man who hadn't wanted her? Why should she give her tears to Kellan when he'd made it clear that he was determined to stay out of her life?

She didn't owe Kellan anything. But she did owe Buck. Irina had no idea how long Kellan would be here in Royal, so if she was going to tell him at least some of the truth about his father, she couldn't wait for the perfect time.

"And," she muttered, slanting a look at the fire-engine red front door of the ranch house, "you're stalling."

Who could blame her, though? Being around Kellan was dangerous to the stability she'd been working on for seven years. She had a life now. She was no longer that frightened, shy woman just starting to be on her own. And she felt as if she was risking it all by being here. With him.

But that decision had already been made and putting it off now wasn't going to change anything. She reached for a brown leather briefcase on the passenger seat, took a breath and stepped out. A heartbeat later, though, the ranch house front door opened and a stunning woman with short, spiky black hair walked out. She was wearing a black coat, sky blue dress and mile-high heels, and she was laughing up at Kellan. He pulled his hat on while they talked, then the two of them crossed the wide porch and, at the top of the stairs, they stopped, hugged, then the still-smiling woman walked to her car, climbed in and took off.

Irina's heart felt…sluggish. Stupid. Of course there were other women in Kellan's life. Just because he had walked away from her didn't mean he had signed up to be a monk. It also didn't mean that she would enjoy seeing him with another woman. She hated that it could hurt so much.

Kellan turned his head, spotted her car and started down the steps. Irina couldn't put it off any longer, so she walked toward him. Now, after seeing the beautiful woman with him, she was gladder than ever that she'd taken the trouble to look good. Her long strawberry blond hair was loose, hanging in heavy waves down past her shoulders. She wore black slacks, a deep red long-sleeved shirt and a heavy black jacket. The wind whipped past her as if urging her to get back in the car and leave while she still could. From the corral, she heard a couple of cowboys shouting and the sharp, high whinnies of horses.

But all she could see was Kellan. He looked every inch the successful rancher. His dust-colored hat was pulled down low over his forehead, somehow highlighting the piercing blue of his eyes. The collar of his heavy leather jacket was pulled up against his neck. He wore a dark green plaid flannel shirt and jeans that hugged his muscular thighs and stacked on the toes of his scuffed cowboy boots.

Ironic that he was the epitome of the American cowboy that she had once dreamed about, as a young girl in Russia. But in those childish dreams, there had been love and a happy ending. Not a broken heart and the promise of more pain.

Irina took a breath, but she was afraid it wouldn't be enough to keep her calm. Every nerve ending in her body was awake and on alert. Her stomach did a slow swirl and her heartbeat thundered in her ears.

"Irina. I was coming to see you later today."

Then it was better she'd come to him. She didn't need him so close to her bedroom.

"Did I interrupt something?" she asked, nodding to where the woman's sleek black sports car was disappearing down the drive.

"That's Ellie Rae Simmons." He shook his head. "She's my executive assistant. Flew in from Nashville last night to take care of some business."

"Oh." His assistant. That should make her feel better, but that hug looked far friendlier than boss and employee. "It looked...different."

One eyebrow winged up as he tipped his head to one side to study her. "Jealous?"

She didn't even want to admit to herself that she'd felt a sharp pang of jealousy, seeing him with Ellie Rae. Kellan wasn't hers. Never had been. But seeing him with that woman had twisted her insides into tight knots that were only now beginning to loosen.

"Of course not," she lied smoothly. "I've no reason to be, do I?"

"No, you don't."

Well, that was honest anyway.

He folded his arms across his broad chest. "What are you doing here, Irina?"

"I want to talk to you about Buck."

Instantly, his features went coolly blank. "I don't need you to tell me about my father."

"I think you do." Of course, she couldn't tell him *everything*. She'd made a promise to Buck and she wouldn't break it. But there were things he needed to know.

"Irina," he said tightly, "let it go. Buck's dead and there's nothing you can tell me now that will change that."

"No. But there are things I can tell you that might change what you think of him."

He snorted.

She looked around. The cowboys were watching them

now, curious. She recognized a few of them from see-ing them around Royal, but now wasn't the time to say hello. Fixing her gaze back on him, she said, "Can we do this inside?"

It almost seemed as if he would refuse, but then he said, "Sure. Come on."

He stepped back to allow her to go first, and Irina felt his gaze lock on her. It gave her a chill that swiftly became heat. Apparently she had zero control over her body's reaction to the man. All she could do was hang on and hope her mind would win the battle.

"Let's go in here," he said, crossing the foyer into the great room.

She followed him and couldn't stop her gaze from dropping to his behind, cupped so nicely by that worn denim. He set his hat, crown down, on a table, then shrugged out of his jacket and tossed it onto the near-est chair.

Irina took a moment to look around, since it was the first time she'd been inside. There was no hint of Christ-mas here, unlike at Blackwood Hollow. But the floor-to-ceiling windows on every wall offered amazing views of the ranch land and the yard and outbuildings. Sunlight flooded the space, highlighting the groups of overstuffed furniture covered in shades of blues and greens. The oak floor was gleaming and the wide expanse was broken up with dark red rugs. All in all, it was a comfortable room, with a distinctly male presence.

And, she thought, the words *distinctly male* described Kellan Blackwood perfectly.

Irina took off her coat and tossed it alongside Kel-lan's. She kept a tight grip on the briefcase she'd brought with her as she asked, "Why were you coming to see me today, Kellan?"

He shrugged. "I'm still looking for information, Irina. It's not a secret."

"Well," she said, "maybe I can help with that."

Surprise flashed briefly in his eyes. "I wasn't expecting that. Yesterday you were pretty clear about not helping me with Miranda."

"This isn't about your ex-stepmother," Irina said. "This is about Buck."

"No, thanks."

God, he was as stubborn as ever. His eyes were cool, disinterested, and he might as well have been wearing a sign around his neck that read Not Listening.

"Kellan, he wasn't the man you think he was."

He laughed shortly, but there was no humor in it. "Is that right?" Shaking his head, he added, "Good luck convincing me of that. I knew the man my whole life, Irina. And you think you knew him better than I did?"

"Yes." She lifted her chin and fixed her gaze on his, so even though he was letting her see nothing he was feeling, he could at least see for himself that she was serious. "A father and his children don't always get to know each other as simply *people*. But I did know him like that and I can tell you that Buck helped people. A *lot* of people. Me included."

His gaze narrowed on her. "What're you talking about?"

Well, she'd come here to tell him the truth and she'd known that would mean sharing what he didn't know of her own story. But at least, he was listening. "You know I was married before."

"Yeah…"

She took a breath to steady herself before saying, "What you didn't know was that I was a mail-order bride."

"Are you serious?"

Surprise shone in his eyes again. Understandable. Most people didn't realize that sort of thing was still going on. But it was and she sincerely hoped that in most cases it turned out better for the "bride" than it had for her.

"My younger sister and I were orphaned when we were very young and we used to dream of coming to America." A small smile curved her mouth as she remembered, lying in the dark in the noisy orphanage, she and her sister whispering together. Making up dreams of love and husbands and being able to eat whatever and whenever they wanted.

"When we were older, Olga gave up those dreams and married a government official, but I joined an online dating service that matched up young Russian women with successful US businessmen."

"Why didn't you ever tell me?" His question interrupted her and she paused to answer.

"Because I don't like to think about it," she admitted, though the whole truth was that she hadn't wanted Kellan to know. It was embarrassing. She'd married a stranger in the hopes of a better life. And God, it was lowering for her to admit to having been duped.

Even as a model in Russia, her life hadn't been great. And when Olga's husband was transferred to a post far from Moscow, Irina had been desperately lonely. So when her friend suggested they both register on the mail-order bride website, Irina had taken a chance.

She swallowed her pride and continued, "Anyway, I was matched with Dawson Beckett, came to Texas and married him." She tightened her grip on the briefcase handle as if it were the one stabilizing point in her world. "Dawson was much older than me, and he had certain *expectations* of a wife that I didn't meet." She'd been young and so naive and so far from home or anyone she could go to for help. "He found ways to...convince me to meet them."

"He hurt you?" Fury in his voice warmed her heart even as Irina smiled but didn't answer. She wouldn't tell him what she'd suffered with Dawson. All the petty, demoralizing verbal abuse, along with the slaps, the hair pulling, the bruises in places no one else would see. There were some things she didn't want to relive, even in the telling of it.

"It doesn't matter now."

"Hell yes, it matters," Kellan ground out. "What the hell, Irina? Why did you stay with him?"

"Where was I to go?" she countered, defending herself, remembering her situation. "I didn't speak English well. I had no job skills beyond modeling. I had no friends to run to. I was in a trap that I'd walked into willingly."

He blew out a breath and shook his head. "You should've told me."

"By the time we met, it was over and I didn't want you to know," she said. "But my misery isn't part of the story. This is about Buck."

"How did my dad fit into this?"

She smiled. "I met your father at a dinner party. I was one of a number of foreign brides attending and Buck noticed how badly Dawson was treating me.

"One of my husband's friends was groping me and I slapped him. Dawson took me aside—" she took a breath before adding "—he hit me, in the ribs, where it wouldn't show." And in spite of the pain and humiliation of that moment, she smiled, remembering the rest of it. "Buck saw it all and he saved me."

The memory of Buckley Blackwood getting in Dawson's face and warning him to keep his hands to himself was still one of her favorites.

"Damn, Irina…"

She shook her head. "Anyway, Buck helped me get out of that marriage, gave me a job at the ranch and secured a work visa for me." She lifted her chin, met his gaze and said, "He offered to pay for my college and law school, but I would only allow that if he considered it a loan so I could pay him back."

She laughed a little at that, because in the end, Buck had won that argument, too. "In his will, Buck canceled my debt to him. My life has changed immeasurably, thanks to him. I came to this country looking for a prince to make my dreams come true. Now I am making my own dreams a reality. All because of Buck Blackwood."

"You're amazing."

"No. What Buck did was amazing," she insisted. "He helped me when he didn't even know me."

"I wish I could have seen Buck face down your ex," he admitted, and it sounded almost as if he was sorry it had been his father to ride to her rescue instead of him.

"It's not just me he helped," Irina continued quickly. "Buck paid off mortgages so people could keep their homes. He gave a young couple the money they needed to try IVF when they were desperate for a child. He sponsored children to summer camps. He rebuilt an entire neighborhood after the last hurricane. And he did it all anonymously. I only know because he had me help him with much of it."

While she talked, she watched Kellan's eyes and was pleased to see that he was not only stunned but also a little humbled by his father's deeds.

"The only thing he ever asked," Irina added, "was

that no one know who helped them. Of the few who did know his identity, as far as I know, I'm the first to break that promise to Buck. Because I think you need to know, more than Buck needs secrecy now."

"I don't even know what to say to all of this," he admitted and pushed one hand through his short hair.

Confusion shone in his eyes and Irina took a deep breath. She'd taken a chance in telling Kellan all of this. Especially about her own past. It wasn't something she liked to think about, let alone share.

Her brief abusive marriage was only a small part of her life, but it had been important in making her who she was now. In the years since then, Irina had learned to let the past go. To set that old pain aside and move on.

But she knew that was something Kellan had never been able to do. He'd lost his young wife in a car accident just a year before he and Irina had come together for that oh-so-memorable week. And she knew that pain would always be a part of him.

But he also used it as a club to keep away anything and anyone who might get too close to him, who might invite that kind of pain to revisit him. And as long as his past defined his present, his future would be empty.

Four

"You don't have to say anything, Kellan. But I wanted you to know that there was so much more to Buck than you were aware of."

Kellan felt shell-shocked. In a million years, he never would have pegged his father as some anonymous Santa Claus. Hell, he was surprised Buck had even *noticed* people in need, let alone helped them. Still, the fact that he had been kind to people outside their family didn't absolve him from doing a crappy job as a parent.

"I'm getting that," he said, nodding. "But as a father…"

"I'm not finished." Kellan watched her set the briefcase she'd been holding close on to the coffee table and open it up. There were four file folders inside. She grabbed the first one and held it out to him.

Wary, Kellan looked from the file up to Irina's eyes.

"You need to see these, too," she said and waved the file to encourage him to take it. When he did, he felt her watching him as he opened it, half expecting a snakebite.

"Buck had one of these on each of his children. None of you were talking to him, so he followed you all as best he could."

Kellan flipped through the articles, both newspaper and magazine, the pictures, the letters inside, and he felt the ground beneath his feet shift. There were things in that file he hadn't thought of in years. Big and small, all of his achievements, every piece of his life was all here. From his first newspaper interview to the day his real estate development company became the biggest in Tennessee. Buck had kept *everything*. Even Shea's obituary.

"He saved whatever he could find on you and your brothers and sister," Irina was saying. "He was a part of your lives in the only way he felt he could be."

A part of him softened toward his father. Had Kellan been wrong about Buck all those years? But as soon as he considered it, his mind argued, no. This file didn't excuse Buck's hard-ass attitude. His my-way-or-the-highway rule of life. His habit of cutting his own kids out of his life in favor of devoting every moment to his empire building.

Kellan's gaze snapped to hers. "He should have talked to us."

"Would you have listened?"

There was a ball of ice in the pit of his stomach and he didn't like it. He also didn't care much for that question because he knew the answer. "Maybe not."

She shook her head sadly. "Maybe he felt that it was too late to try to build bridges to all of you. Buck told me that he knew he'd lost all of you long ago. That he hadn't been there for any of his children. It was his one regret."

Again, he felt a twinge of…*something* for the father he'd never really known. Kellan couldn't stop flipping through the damn file. "But he didn't tell us that when he could have."

"No, he didn't. And maybe he should have tried," Irina admitted. "I tried to get him to contact all of you, but Buckley Blackwood was nothing if not stubborn."

"Yeah. I'll give you that much."

"He wanted to be a part of your lives," Irina said quietly. "He just didn't know how to get past the mistakes he'd made."

Kellan thought about that, and then a harsh laugh scraped his throat as he tossed the file back into the still-open briefcase. "Well, leaving our family home to Miranda sure wasn't the way to do it."

"I don't know why he did that," Irina said. "He never mentioned it to me."

"Nobody knows why Buck did anything," Kellan muttered and scraped one hand across the back of his neck. There was too much new information storming in his mind. A new side of his father? What was he supposed to believe?

Irina was standing there, just one long step away, and she was watching him, waiting. It was killing him having Irina here. In his house. He'd steered clear of her for years because being near her was too damn hard. But now that they were here together, he couldn't imagine letting her leave, either. Maybe it was because she'd told him so much. About his father. About herself.

It drove him insane thinking about her all those years ago, alone and abused. If nothing else, he was grateful to Buck for stepping in to help Irina when she needed it most. But he couldn't figure out how he felt about the fact that Buck had been as involved in Kellan's life as he could be.

Thinking of the file his father had kept on him, he

blurted, "He even saved an interview I gave to a tiny Nashville newspaper five years ago. Why the hell would he do that?"

Irina knew he wasn't asking her as much as he was throwing the question out to the universe, but she tried to answer anyway. "I told you. He loved his children. He just didn't know how to get past the mistakes he made."

Kellan lifted his gaze to hers and she saw pain and confusion in those sky blue eyes before he shuttered them to keep her from reading any more of his emotions. He and Buck were more alike, she thought, than either of them would have wanted to admit.

So she tried a different tack. "Buck helped so many people. Two of the stores on Main Street in Royal are only open now because Buck bought their buildings and sent the shopkeepers the deeds."

"What?"

She threw her hands up helplessly. "And a young couple trying to adopt? He paid all their fees and bought them airplane tickets so they could fly to China to get their baby."

He tossed the folder back into the open briefcase with the other three and scrubbed his hands over his face. "I can't decide if all of this information makes things better or worse for me. I didn't know the man you're telling me about, Irina. And bottom line? It doesn't change anything." Voice flat, he added, "Buck's still dead. He still left our family legacy to Miranda and shafted his own children. So all of this other stuff may only mean he was feeling old and trying to buy his way into heaven."

Impatience swamped her. "It can't change the past, true. But it could change how you feel about your father. Instead, you're determined to hate him, aren't you?"

"I don't hate him. Never did," Kellan argued. "But I won't pretend we had a great relationship. Or act as though his kindness to strangers makes up for the way he treated his own kids."

"No," she said, closing the briefcase and snapping the locks. "I don't suppose you will. But I wanted you to know, because Buck deserved that recognition. He wouldn't claim it in life, but now that he's gone, I want you and Sophie and Vaughn to know what kind of man he really was."

He laughed shortly. "And don't you see the irony in that? You have to tell me stories about how he treated strangers to give me an idea about my own father?"

"Yes, I see it. But you don't want to see anything else."

"What else is there?"

She looked around the beautifully appointed but somehow *empty* room. This was Kellan. On paper, his life looked wonderful. Fulfilled. But in reality, he was a man alone and determined to stay that way.

Nothing could have been more irritating. "There's opening your eyes to the present and letting go of the past. I did it. I had to, to be able to have a good life." She wanted to tear at her own hair in frustration. "You are not the only one to have survived pain. But survival isn't enough, Kellan. You're letting bad memories cloud your vision so much that you can't see past them."

"This isn't about Buck, is it?" His voice was low, quiet. "None of this was. Not really."

Irina folded her arms across her chest and held on. She felt a little unsteady. Unsure. But it was too late to back down now. She'd wanted to show him a side of Buck he hadn't known, yes. But in doing so, she'd come up against a door to Kellan's past. One he'd always kept locked and barred from her. And she'd hoped, ridiculously, that he would finally open it—and if not let her in, then at least step out himself.

"No," she admitted. "I suppose it's not."

"I'm not going to talk to you about Shea."

She flinched. Couldn't help it. "I wouldn't think so. You never would before."

One dark eyebrow winged up and his jaw went tight. "And how much did you tell me about your ex-husband? Nothing. That's how much. What did you say his name was?"

"Dawson Beckett," she snapped, and even saying the man's name left a bad taste in her mouth. "What should I have told you, Kellan? That I was foolish enough to marry a man I didn't know? That he was mean? Abusive?

"He used me to make himself look better. And Buck helped me get away. Your father intimidated Dawson into giving me a divorce. And I will always love Buckley Blackwood for that." She hated it, but tears gathered in her eyes. It always happened when she was angry, and right at that moment, she was furious. "I was young and stupid and wanted a new life. I got a nightmare."

Kellan took a step toward her and Irina backed up, holding one hand out to keep him at bay. If he touched her then, she'd crumble, and she didn't want to do that in front of him. Angrily, she swiped the tears off her cheeks and glared at him.

"Damn it," he said, clearly frustrated. "I didn't mean to hammer you with your own past."

She lifted her chin and tossed her hair back behind her shoulder. "Unlike you, I don't hide from my past, Kellan. I face it. I overcome it. I don't lock it away, because it made me who I am now. As much as I hate remembering my marriage, every time I do, it gives me strength to know that it didn't destroy me."

Kellan stared at her for a long moment and the tension building between them arced like a power line.

"And because I don't want to 'share' the most painful time of my life, I'm a coward? Is that it?"

"I didn't say that," she hedged.

He choked out a short laugh. "You didn't have to."

Irina took another deep breath. "Kellan, I know you lost your wife…"

"And my *child*," he ground out.

"What?" She swayed a little, not really sure what she was hearing.

He looked as though he wanted to bite his own tongue off for saying that out loud. But clearly, it was too late to call it back now. He scraped both hands across his face as if he were trying to wake up from a nightmare that had been haunting him for years. "Shea was pregnant. The *coroner* told me. I didn't tell anyone else."

"Oh God." She couldn't imagine what he'd been through, hearing about his lost child from a coroner. Not only had the woman he loved died, but she'd taken a piece of him with her.

Irina's heart ached. Literally ached. She'd had no idea and now she felt terrible for prodding at this wound. For forcing him to face a memory that had to tear at him. No wonder he was locked in the past.

As far as Kellan was concerned, he'd lost his future eight years ago.

"I'm so sorry." For his loss. For assuming she knew what he was dealing with.

He pushed one hand through his short, neat hair. "Don't. That's why no one knows," he said tightly. "I didn't want to hear 'I'm so sorry.' Or see the sympathy, the pity in people's eyes."

"I'm not offering pity," she countered. Though she really wanted to, she had known without being told that it wouldn't be welcome.

"Yeah?" His gaze locked on hers. "Then why do you look like you want to cry?"

"My God, Kellan." Completely exasperated, she continued, "I'm not a robot. I feel badly for you. For what you lost. That doesn't mean I'm offering you pity."

"Exactly what are you offering, then, Irina?"

Well, that was the question, wasn't it?

"I…" She took a breath, tried to settle her wild, racing thoughts and finally had to admit, "I don't know."

Kellan stepped up to her and she felt the heat of his body reaching out for her, wrapping itself around her. She nearly sighed but managed to stifle it. Irina knew she was in dangerous territory here, but she couldn't seem to care. Maybe it was because they'd talked more in the last fifteen minutes about the things that really mattered to them than they ever had before. And maybe, she thought, she was simply responding to the fire in his eyes.

"I think I know," Kellan whispered.

"I didn't come here for this," Irina said softly. She wanted him, of course. She always did. But today, she'd hoped only to reach him somehow.

"Yeah. I know that, too." His hands dropped onto her shoulders and Irina's eyes closed briefly at the rush of heat pouring through her.

This was not wise and she knew it. Worse, though, she didn't care. How could she? It had been seven years since she'd felt his hands, his mouth on her. She'd worked so hard to push thoughts of him out of her mind and yet here she stood, as eager for him as she had been the first time.

What was the definition of insanity? *Doing the same thing over and over and expecting different results.*

By that measure she was completely crazy.

"This is not a good idea," she said.

"Or," he countered, "it's the best idea we've had in seven years."

Amazed at that statement, she stared at him. "Really? You walked away all those years ago. Avoided me every time you've come back to Royal and now you think it's a great plan to slide back into bed as if nothing happened?"

He frowned and let his gaze move over her face like a caress before settling on her eyes again. "I won't apologize for leaving. It was the right thing to do."

"Maybe it was. For you." But she remembered how she had felt when he had left. As if he'd hollowed her out and left her an empty shell. Which she didn't want him to know. And that, she admitted, was pride. For a long time, she'd grieved the loss of him, wallowing in the pain because it was all she'd had left of him.

Eventually, though, she'd reassessed and realized that she didn't want a man who didn't want her. She'd asked herself, if Kellan had thought it was so easy to walk away from her, then why was she wasting tears on him? She'd worked hard to rebuild herself. To discover who she really was and what she wanted. Wouldn't going back now undo all of that work?

Or would it help to solidify her strength?

"Yes. And for you, too, as it turned out." His hands on her shoulders tightened a little. "You went to college. Now you're in law school…"

She frowned. "How did you know that?"

"You told me."

"I don't remember telling you."

"When you were busy defending Buck to me."

She frowned again.

"And now," Kellan said, "I hear you're an author, too."

"I *know* I didn't tell you that."

"Sophie did," he admitted. "What's the book about?"

"It's about starting over," she said. "When your world crashes down on you." That was the easiest explanation, and really, at the heart of it, that was her book.

"Maybe I should read it," he murmured, his gaze moving over her face like the lightest of touches.

"It's not finished."

"Fine. I'll buy a copy when it comes out."

"Why?"

"Does it matter?" He slid his hands to the column of her throat, then up to hold her face in his palms. "I missed you, Irina. Didn't want to. Tried not to. But I did."

"If that's supposed to be a way of flattering me, I don't understand it." His hands on her face, his thumbs stroking her cheeks, his eyes locked with hers.

"Understand this," he said and bent his head to hers. Irina held her breath as he took her mouth softly, almost tentatively at first. Then he deepened the kiss and Irina felt herself drowning. There was no air. There was no help. There was nothing but him. Just like seven years ago.

The moment that thought entered her mind, she pulled her head back and fought for the air he'd stolen from her. "I don't think I can do this again."

"It's just a kiss, Irina," he said tightly.

"It's more than that and you know it," she argued. Her body was humming and her mind was about to take a long vacation. Between them, a kiss was a lit match to dynamite. "And you don't have to look so pleased by that."

"Why wouldn't I?" His lips quirked. "Are you actually going to tell me you don't want to?"

"No," she said, because it would be pointless to lie.

He could see the truth in her—just as easily as she saw the heat still glittering in his eyes. "I do want you. But doing this would solve nothing."

"Why does it have to?" he ground out. "Why can't it just be what it is?"

"Because…" She tried to come up with a reason, but she couldn't find one. Self-respect? Please. She had plenty of that and she wouldn't lose it by giving in to the need to be with him again. Pride? What did pride have to do with anything here? Really, why shouldn't they have sex? They'd always been good at it. Chemistry was never a problem for them. It was what came after that had always been their undoing.

"Not much of a reason," he taunted her.

She gave him a reluctant smile. "I'll find one. I only need a minute."

"Take two. It won't change anything." He moved in, closing the distance between them. "I want you. Always have," he admitted. "That didn't end when I left."

"But you still went."

"And will again," he agreed. His eyes were burning. His jaw was tight and his voice, when he spoke, was low and filled with an urgency that echoed inside her. "No secrets here, Irina. I can't stay."

"Won't."

"Either," Kellan said. "But this is now, Irina. We're here. Together. In this moment. So do we waste that? Or enjoy it?"

Was it that simple? Or was this a road studded with land mines that could blow up in her face and tear her heart to pieces again? Could she just "enjoy" time with Kellan and then let him go?

A tiny voice inside reminded her that she would watch him go anyway. Would it be better to stand strong and

not know what it was to have his hands on her again—o
would losing him be easier if she gave in to the fire siz
zling inside and relished what they had while they had it

Her breathing quickened and her heartbeat jumpe
into a gallop. She couldn't look away from his eyes
Maybe because she didn't want to. That settled it, as fa
as her body was concerned.

Missing Kellan had been like breathing for her. Inev
itable. Unavoidable. Simply a part of her life. Irina ha
tried dating other men, but they had never quite measure
up to the memory of Kellan. So instead, she'd burie
herself in her studies, her job and, eventually, the boo
she was writing.

And somewhere along the way, Irina had convince
herself that she had a full life because to do otherwis
was just too depressing.

But now he was here and she had a chance at—if no
forever—then at least the opportunity to experience th
magic of being with Kellan again. She'd be a fool to tur
away. And she hadn't been a fool in a very long time.

Irina took a step toward him and his eyes flared in re
sponse. But he stayed where he was. He didn't reach fo
her. Didn't make a move. He was leaving this all up t
her. He'd made his case, and now he waited to see wha
the answer would be.

Another man would push. Or try to sweet-talk her int
his bed. But Kellan Blackwood was different. For him, i
was all about people making their own choices. He wa
honest. Didn't make promises he wouldn't keep. Eve
seven years ago, he hadn't guaranteed her anything. S
Irina had had only herself to blame for the misery she'
felt when he left.

Just as she would now.

Looking up into his eyes, she said, "We might regret this."

"We might," he agreed.

"And we're going to do it anyway."

He cocked his head to one side. "Are we?"

Irina gave him a half smile as she surrendered to the inevitable. "Was there any doubt?"

"Only from you," he said and finally, *finally*, reached out for her, his arms going around her with a strength that stole her breath.

She linked her arms around his neck, looked up into his eyes again—those amazingly deep, beautiful eyes—and said, "That's gone now."

"Thank God." He kissed her. Fiercely, desperately. His mouth took hers and his tongue claimed all that she was.

Irina's entire body lit up like the finale in Royal's annual July Fourth fireworks show. Her blood ran hot and fast, and an ache set up shop at the juncture of her thighs. This was what she'd missed. This was what she'd wanted from the moment she saw him again.

He tore his mouth from hers and then ran his lips and tongue along the column of her throat. She tipped her head to one side to give him better access. She shivered, in need, anticipation. How had she lived without this feeling? Without his touch? His kiss?

Her mind blanked out and her body took over. She lifted her right leg, hooked it around his hip and, when his hand cupped her butt to hold her there, she groaned.

"You've got too many clothes on," he managed to say.

"You, too." She ran her hands up and down his broad back, feeling his muscles shift and bunch. Irina wanted the feel of his skin against hers, the heat of the two of them, building, burning together.

"Upstairs." He threaded his fingers through her hair and dragged her head back, to look down at her.

Hunger was etched into his features. A need she shared seemed to be alive and pulsing in the room around them.

She cupped his face in her palms, kissed him, then whispered only "Yes."

Five

Kellan grabbed her hand and headed for the stairs. Thanks to her long legs, Irina matched his stride until they hit the first step, then they were running, taking those steps two at a time.

At the head of the stairs, Irina gave a quick look around. Pale gray walls, white oak floors and a dark green runner carpet going along the length of the hallway. There was a skylight overhead that allowed the watery sunlight to spill down onto them.

Then he was pulling her down that wide hallway to the room at the far end, overlooking the front of the house. He threw the door open and tugged her inside in one smooth move. Before she could catch her breath, Kellan slammed the door, then turned to grab hold of her. Irina went to him eagerly, her body practically vibrating with the tension he'd instilled in her.

All of the years between their last night together and this moment disappeared in a blink. Kellan's hands came down onto her breasts, and even through the fabric of her shirt and the bra beneath, she felt the burn of his touch. He tugged at the buttons, as impatient to touch her as she was to be touched.

A near-electric buzz erupted between them and Irina welcomed that oh-so-familiar feeling. It was as if they'd never been apart.

"Off," he said thickly. "Take that shirt off before I rip it off."

Another shiver because she knew he meant it and it thrilled her that he wanted her so much. She undid the buttons, pulled the red shirt off and tossed it aside. His first glance at her lacy black bra fired his eyes and dragged a guttural moan from his throat. "Man, it'd almost be worth it for you to keep that on—if I didn't want your nipples in my mouth."

"Since I want that, too…" She unhooked the bra and let it drop to the floor. His eyes went hot and fixed. Irina nearly groaned when he tore his own shirt off to expose his muscled, tanned chest. All she wanted now was to slide her palms across all that lovely flesh.

He must have been thinking the same thing, because the next couple of minutes passed in a breath of time and then they were naked, wrapped in each other's arms, tumbling onto his bed and rolling across the navy blue duvet.

The room was still and quiet. Outside, the sky was gray and a winter wind gusted, rattling the windowpanes.

"You're still so damn beautiful," he whispered, lowering his head to take one of her hardened nipples into his mouth.

"And you're still very talented," she whispered, arching her back, pushing herself into his mouth. His lips and tongue and teeth drew on her sensitive skin and sent her into a tightening spiral of escalating need. The duvet

eneath her was cool but did nothing to dim the heat
nveloping her. Irina scraped her nails along his spine
nd Kellan growled low against her chest. "You feel so
amn good," he murmured as he shifted his attention to
er other breast.

"Oh, so do you. And what you're doing… Don't stop."

"Not a chance," he vowed, voice low and guttural.

He swept one hand down her body, following the curve
f her waist, the dip of her belly, to the center of her. Heat
rom his touch soaked through her skin, past her blood,
own to her bones, and Irina felt as if she were burning
p from the inside. *More*, she thought. She wanted *more*.

Then he slid two fingers into her depths, pressing,
troking. Her fingernails dug into his shoulders as she
asped for air. Irina planted her feet on the mattress, lift-
ng her hips into his hand. It had been so long since she'd
elt anything like this, her body was tight and ready to
xplode.

He suckled her and teased her core with steady strokes
nd caresses, and Irina knew she couldn't hold out much
onger. She wanted him inside her when she climaxed,
ut she couldn't wait. Couldn't stop what was happen-
ng and wasn't entirely sure she would have if she could.

When that lovely, elusive feeling began to build at
ightning speed, she braced herself for what was to come.
Then her body came apart in his hands and all she could
o was hold on. Blindly, she stared up at the beamed ceil-
ng and shrieked when he pushed her over the edge into
n orgasm that seemed to roll on and on.

Struggling for breath, body still trembling, Irina barely
elt the surprise when Kellan shifted suddenly. He rolled
ver onto his back and pulled her with him until she was
n top, staring down at him through passion-glazed eyes.

She smiled down at him, licked her lips and stroked

her palms across his chest, her thumbs flicking at his fla
nipples. He was gorgeous. The man's body was a worl
of art, all sculpted muscle and hard strength. Touching
him filled her with the kind of desire she'd felt with no
one else.

"Just a minute." He hissed in a breath and reached fo
the bedside table drawer. He yanked it open and fumble
for a condom, ripped at the packaging, then sheathed
himself in only a few seconds.

"You should have let me put that on," she whispered

He snorted. "If you had, it never would have gotten
on in time. I'm teetering on a narrow ledge here, Irina
Won't take much to push me over."

"You say the nicest things." Irina gave him a small
smile, then lifted both arms high over her head, lifting
her hair and letting it slide down over her like a reddish
golden cape.

"And you're doing that on purpose." He reached ou
and cupped her breasts in his hands.

"You're a very smart man."

"Not at the moment," he said. "Blood supply's no
going anywhere near my brain."

"I noticed." And her insides trembled as she stroked
his chest again. She couldn't get enough of touching him
feeling all that coiled strength and banked heat beneath
her hands.

She wanted him inside her. Deep. Hard. Fast. "How
much more talking are we going to do?"

"I think we're done." He set his hands on her hips
and lifted her up high enough that she felt the tip of him
brushing at her core. Irina took a deep breath. Her gaze
locked with his as she slowly, deliberately slid down hi
length, drawing him deep inside her.

With every inch of him she claimed, she felt that bone

deep stirring of need rise again. Along with a sense of "rightness" she hadn't felt in far too long. Watching his eyes, seeing the flames dancing there, fed the fire burning within her. When Irina rocked on him, he groaned her name and clenched his hands on her thighs. She felt the hard imprint of his fingertips digging into her skin, and she loved it.

Loved that he was so wild for her. Loved that he needed her. Loved that when they came together, nothing else mattered.

Irina threw her head back, braced her hands on his flat belly and rode him frantically. Every stroke pumped up the desire arcing between them. Every movement tantalized. Promised. Her hips set the rhythm that he followed. She listened to his breathing, fast, desperate. And she knew what he was feeling.

Irina took him deeper still, grinding her hips against his, creating a friction that drove them both faster, higher. How could she feel so much, so quickly after a shattering orgasm? How could she be so needy, so filled with the kind of desire that only Kellan could engender?

She looked down at him and etched his image onto her memory, so that she would always be able to draw up this moment in time and relive it. Far into the future, when she was living without him, when he was once again nothing more than a longing in the night, she would wrap herself in this moment and find the beauty and disregard the pain.

His expression was fierce. His eyes flashing. His jaw tight. He was…everything.

Gazes locked, Kellan reached down to where their bodies were joined and stroked that one spot that was filled with every beautiful sensation in the world. The moment he did, Irina's body and soul splintered again. A crashing wave of pleasure a thousand times stronger than the one before washed over her. Rocking her hips wildly, she called his name and rode that crest of satisfaction even as he claimed his own and emptied himself into her.

Then she collapsed onto his chest and felt his arms come around her.

Kellan cradled Irina to his chest and waited for his heartbeat to ease back down. Though the chances of that happening while he was holding a naked Irina seemed pretty damn slim. He'd known going in just how good sex with her was. But even he was amazed at what he'd just experienced. She had completely rattled him. His mind was a muddy blank and his body felt as if it had been wrung out and tossed aside.

If he had half a brain, he'd roll her off him and ease her onto the mattress. Regain a little distance between them. A safety zone. But not yet, he told himself, sliding his palms up and down her body.

She gave a soft, satisfied sigh, then lifted her head to meet his eyes. Her long strawberry blond hair was a tangle around her face and across her shoulders. Her dark green eyes looked like a forest at midnight—cool, impenetrable. And when her mouth curved slightly, his did, too.

"Damn if I haven't missed you," he said, reluctantly admitting the plain truth.

She shook her head and laughed a little and the ripples of the sound slid into his heart. "No, you didn't miss me. You missed the sex."

"Well, yeah. It's pretty damn great." But she was wrong. He'd missed her, too. Missed the way she studied him as if looking for answers. Missed the way her hair smelled, like apples and summer. Missed that slight curve of her mouth and the way her eyes glittered when she climaxed. He missed her famous Russian Chocolate Salami and her ridiculous love of mint chocolate-chip ice cream.

Kellan felt a hard squeeze of his heart. Yes. He'd missed her. And that was a dangerous thing.

"You're right about that. The sex is wonderful." She rolled to one side of him and Kellan instantly wished she hadn't. In spite of knowing he should keep a buffer zone between them—for her sake, of course—he liked the heat of her, the sleek, soft slide of her body against his. Damn it. He might be in some trouble.

Scrambling to get under the duvet, she muttered, "It's cold in here."

"I can fix that." He reached for the bedside table, picked up a remote and clicked it.

Across the room, a gas fireplace leaped into life, with flames dancing across artificial logs. Outside, the wind was still whistling under the eaves and the gray sky looked darker now, more forbidding. And the ambient light in the room dimmed as if in sympathy.

"The fire's nice, thanks." She turned her head to look at him. "I didn't get time for much of a look, but this is a nice house, Kellan."

He glanced around as if noticing for the first time. "Yeah, I suppose it is."

"But you do know it's Christmas, don't you?" she asked.

"What?" That came out of nowhere.

Leaning against a pillow propped against the heavy oak headboard, Irina held the duvet up over her breasts with one hand and waved her free arm to encompass the room. "Well, I really like this room—"

"Thanks," he mused, waiting for the *but*. It was a big

room, with a massive four-poster bed, two leather club chairs in front of the used brick-and-stone hearth and an eighty-inch flat screen hanging above it. Right now, though, he'd have to say the bed was his favorite part of the space. "I'm pretty fond of it myself at the moment."

One corner of her mouth quirked. "I bet—but you need a Christmas tree in here. Right in front of the bay window. And at least one more downstairs in your great room. And lights. A lot of lights."

Kellan frowned as she talked. He knew that Irina was as much a fan of Christmas as his mother had been. As Shea had been. He really didn't celebrate Christmas. Hadn't since Shea died. What was the point? He was alone. He didn't need to be reminded of the holiday so that his solitude could be even more starkly defined.

But he wasn't going to get into that with her. Instead, he snorted and tried to make light of it all. "I don't think so. Just because the Hollow is lit up like a small city every December doesn't mean I carry that tradition on. That was all my mom's idea.

"Actually, it always surprised me that Buck kept that tradition going after he and Mom split up." Now that he thought about it, though, Kellan was pretty sure Buck had done it because it was expected of a wealthy man to put on a big show. And Buck had always done what was expected. Except for paying attention to his damn family, of course.

She turned her head to look at him. "That's a shame."

He shrugged, walked naked to the bathroom to clean up, then went back to the bed and got under the duvet himself. Without her warmth against him, he felt the chill in the room down to his bones. Not something he wanted to think about, or even acknowledge. Even to himself.

"Hardly a shame. I live in Nashville, remember? I'm

almost never here," he said, hooking one arm behind his head.

"So you decorate at your house in Nashville?" Her tone said clearly she already knew the answer.

Kellan frowned. "No. Why would I? Just for myself? Pointless to decorate for Christmas when you live alone."

"That's a terrible attitude," she said, sliding her hands up and down the duvet covering her. "Christmas is a lovely time of year. It reminds us to take pleasure in small moments. To be thankful for what we have. That's never pointless."

Not for someone like her, he supposed. Kellan, though, didn't want to be reminded of heartbreak. Loneliness. Better to just close his eyes and try to get through December unscathed.

"Uh-huh." He glanced at her and attempted to change the subject. "Is this really what you want to talk about? Christmas trees?"

She shrugged. "Probably the safest possible subject."

"Meaning?"

Smoothing her hands over the duvet, she asked, "Would you rather start the sex-doesn't-change-anything-between-us conversation?"

Scowling, he went up on one elbow to look down at her. "Excuse me?"

"You know what I'm talking about," she countered, shaking her head as if shaming a two-year-old. "I can see in your eyes, that a part of you is already writing the speech. You're planning how to tell me that sex means nothing and that I shouldn't start building castles in the sky."

Irritated that he was, apparently, so easy to read, Kellan said, "I don't have to tell you that. You know it already. Right?"

"Oh, absolutely," Irina agreed, shaking her hair back

from her face. Her green eyes fixed on him, she said, "I have no castles about you, Kellan. Not anymore."

No castles. He assumed that meant she wasn't indulging in daydreams about him. About *them*. That was good.

And even more irritating.

Seven years ago, he'd had to tell her that he was leaving Royal—and her—behind. She'd looked up at him like he'd just pulled the proverbial rug from beneath her feet. They'd shared an amazing week of sex and laughter and late-night feasts, naked in bed. But when their time was up, he'd left, determined not to make the mistake of getting too close with her again. He'd watched her eyes cloud with pain as he said goodbye. Heard a quaver in her voice as she realized that their time together was over.

What a difference seven years made. Clearly today Irina was the one in charge. He didn't like it.

"Let me save you the effort this time," she said, "so you can get rid of that worried scowl on your face."

Kellan deliberately eased his expression. "I'm not worried."

"Oh, I'm so glad." Irina's delicate, long-fingered hands still moved over the duvet as if she were stroking a beloved pet. "You don't have to worry about me, or about how I feel, because I won't be hurt again, Kellan."

"Didn't mean to hurt you then."

"And yet you managed." A small smile bloomed on her face, then disappeared again.

He hated hearing that, despite the fact that he'd known it even then. But there'd been no other way. Not for him. Royal had been choking him.

"I had to go. Had to get away from Royal." God, the memories of Shea had been everywhere. Kellan had felt as if he couldn't face the cowboys on the ranch or go into town without meeting a sympathetic face. He'd felt suffocated. Back then, it had been a choice to either leave town or die. And getting away from Irina had been imperative. Being with her had felt like a betrayal of Shea, so every time he looked at Irina, he'd felt that pain, too.

"You don't have to explain," she said, lifting one hand to stop him when he would have continued.

She tipped her head to one side and her hair fell in a strawberry blond curtain. "I survived. And now, I'm not the woman I was seven years ago. I've changed. Grown. And I can accept this for what it is."

Irritation mounted. Irrational? Maybe. But damned if he could stop the feeling. Still, he swallowed it back. "Okay, let's hear it. What do you think this is?"

"Just what you wanted back then," she said simply. "It's easy. No complications. It's two adults enjoying each other with no promises made or broken." Smiling, she sighed, then lifted both arms high and stretched languorously. The duvet dropped, baring her breasts to him, and Kellan wondered if she'd done it on purpose.

Reaching out, she cupped his cheek with one hand and said, "You're still frowning, Kellan, and there's no need. I promise you, I'm fine. We're good together. We're both still single. We're both dealing with the loss of Buck and so it's easy to come together—however briefly."

She looked so patient. So…sympathetic. Kellan wondered if that was how *he* looked when he was delivering this speech. Hell, he was being dismissed. Quite efficiently. Kellan was astonished and just a little dumbstruck. He'd said practically the same damn thing countless times. But this was the first time he'd been on the receiving end, and he had to say, he didn't like it.

Hell, was this what she'd felt all those years ago? Regret stabbed at him. Rubbing the back of his neck, he told himself to get over it. That he should be grateful for everything she'd just said. Instead, he felt like a gigolo being paid his fee and told to leave.

"You're looking worried again, Kellan." She laughed a little as she reached out to smooth his hair back from his forehead.

The touch of her fingers was light as air and yet penetrated right down into his bones.

"There's no need," she repeated. "I told you, I'm fine. My body feels wonderful and my heart is safe."

A fresh frown erupted on his face. He felt it and willed it away.

"So what now? We shake hands and part friends?"

"Oh," she said softly, "I don't think we'll ever be friends. There's too much past between us."

That bothered him, too, damn it.

"Psychoanalyzing us, are you?"

She laughed a little and turned her head until she was watching the flames in the hearth. "Oh, nothing so formal. Just acceptance of the reality of it all."

"I see." He didn't, but he would say it so he didn't look like a complete idiot. Kellan much preferred being the one who laid down the rules in any romantic entanglement—not that this was romantic. Having Irina suddenly become the cool, calm, disinterested voice of reason was annoying.

The fan on the fireplace kicked into life and became a low hum as warm air drifted into the room, chasing the chill into the shadows.

"I know I said sex would be a mistake," Irina continued, and he had to lean in to hear her soft but firm voice. "But I don't think it was."

"Well, how fortunate for us." Sarcasm colored his tone and he wasn't sorry for it.

She ignored his jab and said, "I think it was a good thing for us to do this again."

"Happy to hear it." Sarcasm continued to drip from his words, but apparently, she didn't pick up on it. Or didn't care.

"Because now we know that we share chemistry—but nothing else."

Insult rose up now and tangled with the irritation but he couldn't find anything to say to combat her words. It wasn't just chemistry and they both knew it, in spite of what she said. That was the danger.

He'd always known it. Sensed that Irina was the one woman who could slip past his defenses and put him at risk again. Hell, that was the reason he'd avoided being near her all these years. It wasn't just chemistry. It was *more*.

"So I'm glad we did this." She nodded, as if encouraging herself. "I think it was good for me."

"Happy to help," he muttered. This was not going the way he'd imagined it. Kellan had known going in that sex with Irina was going to be world shifting. It always was. And he'd known that he'd have a hard time leaving her again.

What he hadn't expected was Irina having such an *easy* time of walking away.

"Kellan," she said and the faint music of her Russian accent flavored her speech, teasing him with memories of hushed whispers in the dark. "I almost want to thank you."

"Oh, sure." *Thank him?* He choked out a harsh laugh and nodded even while his insides were churning. "Why not? Be sure to leave a referral on the dresser before you go."

A ripple of laughter erupted from her and she reached

over to give his hand a quick pat. "Why do you sound so insulted?"

"How should I sound?" He sat up, the duvet pooling in his lap, and looked down at her. Hand patting. Laughing. Hell, this whole episode had gone from X-rated to a damn farce. "Did you use me for sex to set yourself free?"

"Why?" she asked, still smiling. "Do you feel used?"

"Starting to," he admitted. Not to mention, more than a little annoyed.

She really laughed then and the sound rolled through the quiet room. He wanted to be angry but she was so beautiful when she laughed, he couldn't quite manage it.

When she caught her breath, she looked up at him and shook her head. "God, Kellan, now you sound outraged."

"Only because I am," he countered. Irritation was back, fiercer than ever, and frustration bubbled in the pit of his stomach. He was off balance. Unsteady, and he didn't like it.

"Damn it, Irina, what the hell's going on here?"

She touched his cheek briefly, then shrugged again, tugging the duvet up to cover her breasts. He couldn't have said why that gesture hit him so hard, but it did.

"The last time we were together, you walked away. And I had to watch you leave." Irina's dark green eyes locked on him. "You said you had to let me go for both our sakes. Well, this time, Kellan... I'm letting *you* go."

Six

Stunned speechless, Kellan stared at her for several long, tense beats. Before he could think of something to say to that, he heard footsteps pounding up the stairs at a dead run. He turned to face the door. Did he lock it?

His brother crashed in and stopped dead at the threshold. *No, he didn't lock it.*

"Damn it, Vaughn! What're you doing?"

"Oops." Vaughn laughed, then nodded a greeting. "Hey, Irina. Good to see you."

She only smiled and said, "Hello, Vaughn."

Kellan glanced at her, astounded by her composure. No frantic tugging at the duvet. No embarrassment. No reaction at all. Seven years ago, she'd been constantly worried they'd be found out. Today, she was stark naked beneath that duvet and she'd clearly just had sex with Kellan and she was as cool and serene as if she were at a tea party with the damn Queen of England. Who the hell *was* this woman?

And why was she even more intriguing now than she had been all those years ago?

Anger pulsing inside him, Kellan demanded of his brother, "Don't you knock?"

Vaughn lifted both hands and grinned. "Hey, middle of the afternoon. Who knew you'd be...busy up here?"

Kellan sighed. His own damn fault. *Should've locked the door.* "Go away."

One eyebrow lifted and Vaughn leaned one shoulder against the doorjamb, clearly going nowhere. "Is that any way to talk to a man who's bringing news?"

"Fine," Kellan ground out tightly. "What do you want? *Then* go away."

Obviously enjoying himself, Vaughn gave a one-shouldered shrug. "I was in town and heard something. Thought you'd want to know. Miranda's got her *Ex-Wives* show filming some scenes at the Hollow."

Kellan's head exploded. "Damn it!"

Lulu loved Blackwood Hollow.

The Bellamy, where the cast and crew were staying, was luxurious, as good as or better than any five-star hotel she'd ever stayed in and she had zero complaints. But this ranch house deserved at least ten stars, she thought.

The rooms were huge but cozy at the same time, and the grounds...from the tennis court to the swimming pools—two of them—to the hot and cold running cowboys all over... Well, she could see why Miranda had always described it so lovingly.

"It's an amazing place, isn't it?"

Lulu looked at Fee. They stood beside an enormous Christmas tree in the front window of what Miranda called the great room. Another point in the ranch house's favor—the Christmas decorations that filled the house. Lulu could only imagine how beautiful it all looked at night, with the lights glittering in the darkness.

"It really is," she said with a little sigh. "I could see myself living in Texas, if it could be like *this*."

Fee laughed. "I'd miss Manhattan, but I'd be willing to make the sacrifice." Staring out the window at the wide sweep of lawn and the seemingly endless Texas sky, now studded with dark clouds, she said, "You forget, don't you?"

"What?" Lulu studied her friend's wistful expression.

"That there's a whole world outside New York." Fee took a deep breath and let it slide from her lungs. "I mean, just look at the *space*. There's so much room here. You can see the entire sky. I'm more used to seeing patches of it with the high-rises crowding the image."

"True," Lulu said, turning her gaze back to the ranch. "And really, the night sky is even prettier. So many stars."

Behind them, the crew was setting up for a shot and the other girls were enjoying the coffee and tea served by the ranch cook. Except for Miranda, who was upstairs looking for Irina Romanov.

"You had a good idea," Lulu said thoughtfully. "Having Irina as a guest star on the show."

Fee shrugged. "When Miranda told us about her, I talked to Nigel and he loved the idea. Said it would really get people talking. I mean who even knew mail-order brides even existed anymore?"

Lulu nodded, because she really didn't have anything to add to that. Nigel Townshend was the head of the studio and the producer of their show. He was smart and intuitive, so if he thought having Irina on the show would be a good idea, everyone else would go along.

Outside, the cowboys were working with horses in a

corral painted a bright, shining white. An old dog pushed itself slowly to its feet and ambled up to one of the men, who absently stroked its head. It was such a different life from the one Lulu was used to; it was as if she were living in a documentary.

"Who," Fee murmured, *"is that?"*

Lulu followed her friend's gaze to the man just arriving in a big black truck. As they watched, he climbed out, slammed the door and tugged his hat on. He had sharp, handsome features, dark blond hair, and Lulu would have been willing to bet his eyes would be either blue or green. He was tall and muscular and walked with a slight limp that somehow only made him sexier.

"I don't know," Lulu said softly, "but he's pretty."

"Oh, he's more than pretty," Fee corrected.

"What are you two looking at?"

Lulu turned to smile at Miranda. "Just enjoying the scenery," she said. "That one in particular. Who is he? Do you know?"

Miranda took a look and nodded. "Sure. That's Clint Rockwell. He's got a neighboring ranch."

"Does he?" Fee murmured, tipping her head to one side to study the cowboy.

"He was a good friend of Buck's," Miranda said. "He used to help Buck out a lot, keeping an eye on things at the ranch. I guess he still is," she added as Clint walked over to the corral. "He's also a volunteer fireman for Royal."

He rested one boot on the bottom rail, then crossed his arms on the top one as he talked to one of the working men. Lulu was willing to bet that Fee was also noticing how Clint's jeans hugged his very nice butt.

"Cowboy *and* fireman?" Fee mused. "Interesting."

Lulu grinned. She hadn't seen Fee this interested in

a man for a very long time. This could be fun. Then she turned to Miranda. "So where's Irina?"

"I don't know. She's not home, but her work is spread out across her bed, so she's probably just out on the property somewhere and will be back soon." Miranda touched Fee's arm. "Thanks for suggesting we have Irina on the show as a guest star. I think it will really help push her book."

Fee tore her gaze from Clint Rockwell long enough to smile at her friend. "It's no problem. I'm looking forward to meeting her."

Lulu hooked her arm through Miranda's and left Fee to enjoy the view. She herself wasn't interested in that cowboy, but she'd like more information about a certain lawyer. "Let's have some tea and cookies and you can tell me all about that lawyer friend of yours, Kace LeBlanc."

Kellan bolted, stark naked, out of bed and grabbed his clothes.

Instantly, Vaughn held both hands up and made a cross out of his fingers as if he were warding off a vampire. Turning his head to one side, he said, "Dude. I don't want to see that."

From Irina's perspective, she thought a naked Kellan was an excellent view. Of course, he wasn't naked for long.

"Kellan, what are you doing?" Irina watched him as he dragged on jeans, a shirt, and then sat down to put on socks and his boots.

"I'm going over to the Hollow to have a 'talk' with Miranda."

"Why bother?" Vaughn asked.

Kellan shot him a furious look. "If you don't care, why'd you rush over here to report it to me?"

Uncomfortable, Vaughn stuffed his hands into his pants pockets. "Thought you'd want to know is all."

Kellan scowled at him. "So you're okay with this ridiculous television show being filmed in *our* house?"

"Not my house," Vaughn argued stiffly. "Not for a long time."

"That's a damn lie. It's *Blackwood* Hollow. You're a Blackwood." Kellan stomped into his boots, then pulled his jeans legs down over the tops.

Irina listened to the brothers argue, but her gaze was locked solely on Kellan. He looked furious and she wanted to kick Vaughn for bringing the news. Not only had he gotten Kellan all worked up over Buck's will again, but he'd interrupted an important conversation. Irina was proud of herself for standing up for herself. For letting Kellan know that she wasn't the shy, timid woman he'd once known. But with the news of the film crew, she had a feeling everything she'd said had flown from his mind.

"It's Miranda's house, Kellan." Irina sat up a little straighter, clutching the duvet to her chest with one hand and pushing her hair back from her face with the other. She could see anger pulsing around him in thick waves, and she tried to calm him down. It didn't work.

"If you think I don't know that, you're wrong," he told her, slanting an angry look in her direction.

"Then what are you planning on doing?" She wished she could get up and go over to him, but she wasn't willing to stand up naked in front of Vaughn. And dragging the duvet with her would only make her trip.

"I'm going to remind her that this isn't over," he ground out. "I'm talking to my own damn lawyers and until this will business is settled, I don't want her putting the family ranch out on television for God and everyone to see." He stood up and glared down at her.

His eyes were frosty and she hated to see it. And still, she tried to talk him down. "It's just a TV show, Kellan. It's not that important."

His expression hardened and she knew that had been the wrong thing to say.

"Blackwood Hollow shouldn't be used as a backdrop to a bunch of silly women whose only claim to fame is being divorced from rich men."

Irina shook her head. "It's a silly show. Why are you so angry about it?"

He took a breath, scrubbed both hands across his face and finally answered, "Because I grew up in that house. Buck might have been a crappy father, but that house means something to me. I'm a Blackwood and so's he—" Kellan jerked a thumb at his brother "—whether he wants to admit it or not. Some things shouldn't be used like a damn sideshow, and my family home is one of those things."

She read that plain truth in his eyes and a part of her could understand it. But at the same time, Irina had to wonder if it wasn't more the pain of Buck overlooking his children in the will that was driving him right now.

"How're you going to stop it?" Vaughn asked and Irina wished he'd go away. Unconsciously or not, he was feeding Kellan's anger.

Kellan swung around to face his brother. "I told you, I'm going to talk to Miranda. Set her straight."

"You're only going to make things worse, Kellan." Irina felt as if she were talking to a brick wall. But if she were, she could at least rap her head against it in frustration. "The fact is Buck left her the ranch. Legally, she can do whatever she wants there."

"You're in law school," he countered. "You know a will can be fought in court. Nothing's settled yet, so why take sides against me?"

She flinched at the jab, but she didn't stop. "I'm not taking her side. There are no sides, Kellan. And even if you are fighting the will, the fact is right now, the will says the ranch belongs to her. You can't change that."

Irina looked from Kellan to Vaughn and back again. Both Blackwood brothers were looking at her with accusatory glares. Apparently, Vaughn was no happier about this situation than Kellan was—he was just better at hiding his real feelings.

"I'm going to challenge that will, Irina, so don't bet on Miranda coming out on top." He walked closer to the bed and stared down at her with a coldness she hadn't seen since he'd walked away from her seven years before. "I'm damned if I'm letting that gold digger slither back here from New York and take what belongs to my family." He pushed one hand through his hair and muttered under his breath, "Buck must have been out of his mind."

"With that, I'll agree," Vaughn said and Irina sent him a look meant to shut him up. Instead, he gave her a smile and shrugged.

"You know the bottom line here, Irina?" Kellan asked. "I don't care about the money. Buck could have left her every single dime and I wouldn't have said a word. But our family home? The ranch? Blackwood bank?" He shook his head firmly. "No. Like hell am I going to sit still and take it." He started out of the room.

"Kellan," she called out, "wait for me. I'll go with you—"

But he was gone. Vaughn was still standing in the doorway, though, so she said tartly, "You set him off. You could at least go with him."

He shrugged. "No, thanks. Kellan wants to fight that woman, it's on him. I'm out."

"You're not fooling me, Vaughn." Irina watched him and saw his gaze shift from hers as if he couldn't bring himself to look her in the eyes "I know you're no happier than Kellan is with the situation."

His features went blank. "You're wrong about that. Anyway. Like I said, good to see you, Irina."

She tugged the duvet higher. "Uh-huh. Close the door on your way out."

Irina was only five minutes behind Kellan.

So when she raced into the house at Blackwood Hollow, the argument was still in full swing.

Miranda and Kellan were squared off in the foyer, in full view of everyone else, who were in the great room. She swallowed a groan when she saw that both cameramen were grinning as they kept their lenses focused on the arguing pair. Kellan had wanted to stop the filming. Instead, he was giving everyone quite a show.

"You've got no right," Kellan was arguing, his voice low and grim.

Irina heard the restrained fury in his voice and had to admire the way Miranda stood her ground against him. Actually, the woman looked completely relaxed, rather than cowed.

"Actually," Miranda said, folding her arms across her breasts, "I have every right. Do I have to remind you that Buck left the Hollow to me?"

He slapped his hat against his upper thigh. "No, you don't. But doesn't mean I'm not going to be right here, Miranda, fighting you every step of the way."

The other people in the room seemed fascinated by the confrontation. Irina saw amusement on the women's faces, and barely suppressed glee in the cameramen's expressions. And, Irina thought, Kellan probably hadn't noticed that the cameras were running. That everything he and Miranda were saying to each other was going to be preserved forever for the sake of the show.

Moving up to him quickly, she laid one hand on his forearm. "Kellan…"

He threw a quick glance at her and shook his head. "Irina. What're you doing here?"

She cast another look at their audience. "Trying to keep you from saying something you'll regret."

"Oh, don't worry," he assured her. "I won't regret any of this."

Miranda laughed a little and Irina sighed. Then she held on to his arm and tugged at him until he moved aside with her. Once she had his complete attention, she said, "The cameras are on, Kellan. They're recording you right now."

"What?" His head whipped around and he glared at the man whose camera was pointed at him. The other guy had shifted his focus to capture the women's reactions.

"Perfect," he muttered. Looking at Irina, he murmured, "Thanks for the heads-up. I didn't even notice. But they'll need a signed release from me to use any of it. And I'm not signing."

Before she could urge him to end this, though, he turned back to Miranda. Voice low, controlled, he said softly, "Miranda, I don't want you filming your silly show in my family home."

The other woman smoothed her hands down the front of her short black skirt. "It's my home now, Kellan. And the show isn't silly. It happens to have very high ratings."

He snorted. "From people with nothing better to do than watch you spend your ex-husbands' money?"

"You know," Fee pointed out from the other room, "there is more to us than that."

Kellan barely spared her a glance. "I don't care. I don't want it here. In my family home."

"I'm not arguing with you over this, Kellan," Miranda said patiently but condescendingly, as if explaining something confusing to a three-year-old.

"Good." He waved one hand. "Then, until this is all settled in the courts, get these damn people out of our house."

"Kellan…" Irina kept her hand on his arm and gave him a little squeeze. "Just stop for now. This isn't the time."

"She's right," Miranda said, pitching her voice lower as her gaze met Kellan's. "You don't like the crew here? Well, you're giving them quite a show at the moment, Kellan. If you'll just leave, we'll be finished with the shot in no time."

"Finish now."

"No," Miranda said and Irina watched sparks fly in Kellan's eyes.

Irina grabbed his attention again. "Kellan, why don't you go talk to Clint? I saw him when I pulled up."

"Taking her side, are you?"

"No," she said. "But I'm not on yours, either. I just think neither of you will look particularly good on television if you don't stop."

His mouth worked as if he wanted to argue. His jaw was so tight it was a wonder the bones didn't snap. And his eyes were molten pools of fury. What did it say about Irina that she found him even more attractive than usual? Kellan was usually so controlled, so in charge, seeing him like this was exciting.

When her ex-husband had been furious, Irina had

made every effort to keep out of his way. But Kellan wasn't a violent man at all, so she'd never been afraid— or wary of him—as she had been of Dawson. Instead, she felt more drawn to him than ever. Did that mean she was stronger now?

Or was it just a measure of Kellan's innate appeal and sexual magnetism?

After what seemed like forever, Kellan said, "Fine." He kept his voice down and his gaze averted from the cameras. Then he shot one look at Miranda. "But this isn't over."

"I never for a moment thought it was," she whispered. Then, ignoring him completely, she turned to Irina and smiled.

Speaking more loudly, for the benefit of the cameras, Miranda said, "Irina, I'm so glad you're here. You're actually the reason we came to the house today."

"Me? Why?" Suddenly, she was the center of attention. Irina hadn't been expecting this. She looked at everyone in turn, then finally, back to Miranda, who was still smiling broadly.

"Because you're an amazing woman and I think the world should know it," she said with enthusiasm.

"Oh, for—" Kellan's muttered words broke off quickly when Miranda kept talking.

"When I was looking for you earlier," she said, "I found your manuscript pages on your bed. And since you did say I could read the first chapter, I did.

"Your book is wonderful, Irina. And I think it's going to have a lot of meaning for thousands of women."

A flush of pleasure rose up in Irina. No one but her agent and editors had seen any of her work, so hearing Miranda rave about it meant more than the woman could have known.

"Come on now, you're a guest on our show and I want to tell the whole country about your book and when to watch for it!"

The whole country. Irina knew that the *Ex-Wives* show was popular, but she'd never really considered just *how* popular until right that moment. Millions of people would see her on this show. And though that thought was intimidating, she also realized that if even a small fraction of that audience bought her book, it would be amazing.

Dropping one arm around her shoulders, Miranda guided Irina into the great room, and introduced her to the women she hadn't met yet. Irina was suddenly relieved that she'd taken the time to dress well before going to see Kellan. And then she wondered if anyone looking at her would be able to see that just a half an hour ago, she'd been in Kellan's bed.

"This is Irina Romanov," Miranda said, showing her off as she would a prize puppy. "She works here at the ranch while she attends law school, and she's written a book that I'm sure will be a huge hit."

"Miranda…" She couldn't look away from the steady red light on the camera aimed at her. She felt like a rabbit being hunted. Or a deer caught in the headlights of an oncoming car.

Irina hadn't expected this opportunity and didn't know what to do with it now that it had happened. While she was both relieved and happy that Miranda had read and liked part of her book, she didn't know how to act in front of a television camera. When she was younger, she'd posed for pictures, but speaking on camera, meeting a roomful of strangers all at once was a little overwhelming.

She looked over her shoulder at Kellan and he was staring at her as if he'd never seen her before. No. It was more than that. The expression on his face spoke of betrayal. As if she'd somehow been in on Miranda's plan from the beginning. Like she'd arranged for this and somehow tricked him into making an ass of himself on television.

And the more she thought about that, the angrier she became. In spite of how close they'd been, it seemed he didn't know her at all.

His eyes bored into hers and Irina straightened her shoulders and lifted her chin in silent defiance. She wouldn't apologize for something she hadn't done. She wouldn't rush off to smooth the feathers of a man who was overreacting in the first place.

Those eyes of his were on fire and she could feel the heat despite the distance separating them. All around her, the women were chattering, throwing questions at her and Miranda gave her a nudge as if to wake her up. But Irina was wide awake already. She could be nothing else while staring into Kellan's eyes. Her body coiled and tightened inside, because it didn't matter what her brain was thinking, her body's reaction to the man was simply instinct.

When he slammed his hat down hard onto his head and stalked to the front door, she watched him go and a piece of her went with him. That, too, was outside her control. Seven years ago, it had nearly killed her to watch him walk away. Not this time. She wouldn't surrender her heart to a man who had made it plain that he wasn't interested in keeping it.

She had built a life without him and now it was time to take the next step.

"Why don't you tell us about the book, Irina?" Miranda was saying, and her tone said it wasn't the first time she'd made the request. Tugging Irina over to sit on the brown leather couch, she continued, explaining to her friends and most of America, "Irina was once a mail-order bride from Russia. She came here with nothing, isn't that right?"

Irina nodded, but didn't have a chance to speak because Miranda rolled right on.

"When her marriage ended, she reinvented herself and built a life." Miranda flashed her a bright, proud smile. "And I know that women everywhere will be inspired by her story."

Irina took a deep breath. Kellan was gone. She was on her own—just her and a few million people. That thought made her smile and Miranda beamed in approval. Lulu handed her a cup of tea and winked at her. Fee leaned in, grinned and asked, "So what was the mail-order husband like? And don't leave out any details."

Irina—overwhelmed, a little unsure of herself in the spotlight—laughed and took the next step.

Seven

It had been a long week.

Kellan hadn't seen Irina since that day at the Hollow when she'd joined Miranda and her traveling circus. The memory of Irina walking into the midst of those women and their cameras was still fresh and it still cut at him. Was she really so eager to sell her book that she was willing to work with the woman who had stolen his family's legacy?

He didn't have any answers and he hadn't had any damn peace since that day, either. When he managed to get a few hours of sleep, Irina was there. In his dreams. Naked. Moving with him—over him, under him—and then he'd wake up, frustrated and furious that she could have that much of an effect on him.

Kellan had met with Kace LeBlanc to talk about the will, and so far it looked like it wouldn't be an easy fight. But then, nothing about Buck Blackwood had ever been easy. The old man was dead and gone and still stomping on his kids.

"Earth to Kellan..."

Still simmering, he came up out of his thoughts and faced his little sister, sitting across the white-cloth-covered table from him. The Blackwood siblings were having dinner at the Texas Cattleman's Club and, since Vaughn was late, Kellan and Sophie were having a drink while they waited. It was early, so the dining room wasn't crowded, though a few of the old guard were comfortably seated at their usual tables.

The TCC had gone through a lot of changes in the last several years.

First and foremost, women were members now, too. A few of the old diehards had had plenty of issue with *that*. But the men who actually lived in the twenty-first century had applauded the change. The women had introduced other changes to the club that had been long overdue.

Now there was a day care center, and the interior of the club was brighter and less like a man cave, thanks to a much-needed paint job and an extensive remodel. The old building now had much bigger windows and higher ceilings, giving the whole place a feeling of openness it had really needed.

"Yeah, sorry, Sophie."

He caught one of the waiters checking his little sister out and Kellan sent him a scowl that had the man scuttling away for the safety of the kitchen. Hard to admit that his little sister was a beauty. Also hard to ignore since everywhere they went, men were constantly admiring her. Tonight, she wore a dark red dress that was a little too short for Kellan's comfort and dipped a little too low over her breasts. Her long auburn hair was pulled back from her face to fall in a thick wave down her back, and her brown eyes were sparkling.

A sign that he hadn't spent enough time in Royal over the years. When he first moved away, Sophie was only twenty years old. In the time he'd lived away from Royal, she'd become a beautiful woman and Kellan felt as if he'd missed more than he'd ever wanted to. Vaughn had changed, too. He'd become more insular, more separate from Royal and the family. Had he taken a cue from Kellan? He didn't like the thought of that.

"I don't even want to know who you're scowling about," she said, then stopped. "No. Wait. I *do* want to know. Irina?"

"No." He fired a hard glare at her. He was specifically avoiding thinking of Irina. When he could. "Where'd that come from?"

She shrugged. "Vaughn told me he caught you two in bed, so I figured you guys were together again."

"Vaughn's got a big mouth," he muttered, then added, "We were never 'together.'"

"Not how I remember it," she said, picking up her dirty martini, "but whatever helps you sleep at night." She took a sip of her drink, then set the glass down again. "Anyway, like I was saying before you zoned out, thinking about Irina—"

"I wasn't—"

She ignored that and rushed on, "For all my big plans of snooping around town to get dirt on Miranda? I haven't been able to find out anything." Disgusted, she toyed with the stem of her drink glass and admitted, "I've asked everyone I can think of. Heck, just hanging out at the diner, I can usually overhear plenty of gossip, but the only thing people are talking about is the televi-

sion show and how exciting it is because someone they
know—Miranda—is on it.

"And the other women on the show? I kind of like
them, especially since they have no problem gossiping
about anything under the sun… But they don't know
anything about Buck's will or why he left everything to
Miranda." She sighed dramatically. "Apparently, if there
is a secret, she hasn't shared it with her friends."

"It's only been a week, Soph," he said, sipping at his
scotch. Though he had to admit that his sister should have
picked up on *something* in that time.

"I know. It's just frustrating." She tapped her dark red
nails against the table. "Gossip is usually much easier to
come by in Royal. And gossip about the television show
does me zero good."

But did it? Irina leaped into his mind again. He
couldn't help remembering how she had sailed into the
ranch house and right onto the TV show like it had all
been scripted. Had it? Was she somehow in cahoots with
Miranda in all of this?

Why the hell else would she have been so cavalier
about sex? That wasn't the Irina he knew. She was definitely the hearth-and-home type—but now she was suddenly live and let live? No. Something else was going on.

Maybe she'd been working with Miranda right from
the beginning. He suddenly remembered those files of
his father's that she'd shown him. Well, she'd shown him
only his own file, but he'd spotted three others in that
briefcase. She'd said that Buck had kept a file on each of
his children… But there had been *four* files, not three.
So what the hell was that about?

"Are you even listening to me?" Sophie demanded.

"What? Sure. Of course."

She rolled her eyes. "Nice recovery. So what's going through your head that isn't me and my complaints?"

He wasn't about to dump all of what he was thinking onto his little sister, so he said only, "Miranda. It always comes down to Miranda. She and that film crew are all over town." And now they had *him* on camera and he knew damn well they would use the footage.

He'd talked to a lawyer about the fact that he hadn't signed a release. Apparently, that would have been enough to force them to cut Kellan from the show if he'd pressed the point. But he'd reconsidered at the last minute. Sure, he wouldn't come off looking great, but neither would Miranda. And it suited him to have the whole damn country knowing exactly what he thought of his gold-digging ex-stepmother.

"Yeah, I know. Vaughn and I talked about it. He pretends he doesn't care about Blackwood Hollow, but he does," Sophie said, taking another sip of her drink.

"Maybe." Kellan shook his head as if to dislodge the dozens of random thoughts scuttling through his mind. It didn't help. His eyes were gritty and there was a constant tightness in his chest. Facing Irina again after all this time had been harder than he'd thought it would be— not to mention dealing with all this other stuff. "Anyway. Like I said, it's only been a week. It'll probably take even *you* longer than that."

"Thanks. I think." Sophie's fingers trailed up and down the stem of her glass. "But I was thinking…"

"Never a good thing."

"Funny." She nodded to him. "What do poor, lonely women do when they don't have brothers to irritate them? Anyway, if I can't discover anything here, I think I'll go to New York. Talk to Miranda's friends. Maybe go to the studio, see what I can find out."

Frowning thoughtfully, he said, "They're not going to let you into the studio. Or tell you anything once you're there."

"Please." She waved that off. "People always talk to me. Especially men."

He held up one hand. "I don't want to hear that."

She grinned. "Anyway, I think New York is where we might get some answers."

"Fine. But give it another week or so. Poke around some more in Royal, see what you get."

She sighed. Sophie had always been the impatient one. She wanted things done and done *now*. But in this, she'd have to slow down, Kellan thought. All of them had to agree to a plan before they made a decision.

"All right. A week."

"Maybe wait until after Christmas," he said suddenly.

"I'm sorry. Did you just say you're going to be here through Christmas?" she asked.

He hadn't planned on it, but now... He couldn't see going back to Nashville before he got this mess settled. And he was already here, so why not? "Yeah. Probably."

"A Christmas miracle!" She clapped her hands and gave him a grin. "The Blackwood siblings together at Christmas? Who would have thought that could happen again?"

A twinge of guilt pinged inside him as he realized that in cutting the holiday and Royal out of his life, he'd done the same to his siblings. Why had he never considered that before? He was fighting so hard for the ranch, the family legacy, but he wasn't paying close enough attention to his *actual* family? Made no sense.

Still, seeing the gleam of excitement in Sophie's eyes had him backtracking a little.

"Don't make more of it than it is," he warned.

He wasn't even sure why he was doing this—staying in Royal through Christmas. Since Shea died, he hadn't celebrated the holiday—had, in fact, avoided even thinking about it. But now things felt…different, somehow. Was it Irina? Was it fighting for his family's legacy? Hell, was it as simple as actually spending time with Vaughn and Sophie again? He didn't know. All he was sure of was that he wasn't ready to leave. To go back to his empty house in Nashville.

"Oh God, no," Sophie said, laughing. "This is enough for now."

"Agreed."

"What're we agreeing on?" Vaughn pulled out a chair and sat down. Then he lifted one hand in a signal to the waitress. "Let me guess. Is it that we hate Miranda? Or is this about Kellan and Irina hooking up?"

"What are you talking about?" Kellan demanded.

"You know exactly what he's talking about," Sophie said with a sad shake of her head. "So spill. You and Irina. Together again?"

"No." His gaze narrowed on her.

"They looked pretty together to me," Vaughn mused, then said thanks to the waiter who delivered his usual, a longneck beer.

Sophie smiled and picked up her drink, lifting it in a toast. "Vaughn says Irina looked very cozy in your bed."

He swiveled his head to glare at his brother. "You had to shoot your mouth off?"

"Didn't have to," Vaughn corrected. "Wanted to." He grinned and took a swig of his beer.

"You're not a monk, Kellan," Sophie reminded him. "You and Irina are both adults. Irina's great, so why are you so touchy about it? Tell me everything."

"Nothing to tell."

"Oh, that's sad." She shook her head slowly in mock sympathy. "A naked woman in your bed and nothing to tell? Well, you are getting older…"

Vaughn snorted.

"Not what I meant." Kellan downed the rest of his scotch and signaled the waiter for another. He was already rethinking the plan to spend more time with his siblings. "I meant, it's none of your business. Either of you."

"If it was," Vaughn pointed out, "it wouldn't be as much fun."

"True," Sophie added.

"Enough."

His sister held one hand up for peace and shot a warning look at Vaughn. "Okay, we'll stop."

"Good."

"I'll just say—"

He sighed.

Sophie rolled right on. "—that I like Irina. And it would be good to see you happy again, Kellan."

"I am happy."

"Yeah," Vaughn mused sarcastically. "You're a blazing ball of sunshine. Nearly blinding just to be around you."

"Why're you here?"

"You invited me." He shrugged.

"You're not happy," his sister argued. "At best, you've been content, Kellan. That's different from happy. You haven't really been happy since Shea."

Where was that waiter? "Not going there."

Even Vaughn looked surprised that Sophie had brought up Kellan's late wife. But she wouldn't be stopped.

"It's been eight years, Kellan," she said softly. "You lost Shea and we lost *you*."

He winced at the well-aimed jab.

"I know how much you loved her," Sophie added. "We all did. But maybe it's time to let her go."

His sister's words echoed in his mind, his heart. Memories of Shea weren't as clear as they had once been. Even the pain had been muted over time, though he knew that a part of him would always grieve her and the loss of what they had had. But, Kellan admitted silently, even if it was time to let Shea go, he wasn't sure he knew how.

Two days later, the whole town was buzzing.

The "teaser" trailer for Irina's upcoming episode on *Secret Lives of NYC Ex-Wives* had gone viral and now it was all anyone in town was talking about. Irina simply had *not* been prepared for the reaction to the video.

"Irina! Hi!"

She turned to wave at a blonde high-school girl working for Jillian at Miss Mac's Pie Shack. "Hi, Trina."

"Really looking forward to your show." The girl grinned. "You must be totally excited!"

"Thanks, I am," she said and silently added, *I think*. She kept walking down the crowded sidewalk, smiling and nodding at those she passed. How did celebrities handle this all the time? People watching you. Wanting to talk to you. She gave another wave to the town barber and then the florist, and still, Irina walked, headed to the diner.

It was Christmas-shopping time in Royal. The streetlamps were twined with garlands and winking white lights. Banners hung across the street wishing people Have a Royal Christmas in swirling golden letters. And the sidewalks teemed with busy shoppers. Parking was impossible on Main Street since it was packed with cars, so she'd been forced to park at the other end of town. And this long walk was proving, beyond a doubt, the power of the internet.

She'd lived in Royal for more than seven years, and yet this was the most notice anyone had ever taken of her. She'd never had the time to make real friends. When her marriage ended, Irina had withdrawn into herself, needing time to rediscover herself. Remember who she had been before Dawson Beckett entered her life.

Then between working at the Hollow, going to night school and finally law school and writing her book, Irina's life had been fairly insular.

Until today.

Irina felt exposed in a way she never had before. People she'd never spoken to had seen that viral video. Had seen Miranda and the others talking to her about her marriage. Her book. They knew about her divorce. That she'd been abused. It was mortifying and she had no idea why she hadn't considered the consequences before she'd agreed to appear on that show. Still, the whole story would be out when her book was released, so maybe it was good to get used to this now. Maybe.

But it wasn't only *her* people were speculating about. Everyone was talking about Kellan's confrontation with Miranda, too. She'd long heard that there was nothing the town of Royal liked better than juicy gossip. And thanks to that video, she was seeing the proof.

She wondered what Kellan thought of all this. But she was wondering about him a lot lately. Like, what he was doing? Was he thinking of her at all? Did he miss her even a tenth as much as she missed him? She'd tried to deny it to herself, but the plain truth was she ached to be with him.

"Irina," someone else called out, splintering her thoughts, "that show sure looks like it's going to be fun!"

She smiled at the hairdresser and kept going. What was she supposed to say to people she barely knew?

"Can't wait to read your book," someone else said in passing.

Her smile never wavered as she walked. Her book. That was what she should concentrate on. Surely this publicity had to be good for potential book sales. So she would suffer through being stopped every few feet and keep in mind that she was helping herself in the long run. Irina plastered a smile on her face and determined to find the silver lining.

Until someone came up behind her, slid one arm around her waist and said, "Hello, darlin', it's been a while."

Irina stiffened instantly. She would never forget that voice. How could she? She still heard it in her nightmares. Instinctively, she tried to shift out of his grasp, but Dawson Beckett only tightened his hold and gave her a hard, bruising pinch at her waist. "Don't. Just keep walking. Everyone will think we're old friends. We'll talk a minute and then I'm gone."

"Go now," she said, nodding at a woman who passed her on the sidewalk.

"I don't take orders from you, bitch." He kept a tight grip on her, holding her pressed against him. "I saw your video."

She closed her eyes briefly. In all the rush of the book and the TV show, Irina had completely forgotten that with the teaser going viral, Dawson would be sure to see it. It was clear that he was furious, too. And in spite of how far she'd come, she felt a ribbon of fear slide through her.

"Let me go, Dawson," she muttered, drawing on courage she had lacked completely when she was under this man's thumb. Yes, there was fear, but she wouldn't surrender to it. "Or I will scream so loudly, Sheriff Battle will hear me."

"Oh, you shouldn't do that." Dawson smiled down at her and it was feral. He hadn't changed, except to get more gray at his temples. He was about five foot ten and was still barrel-chested, with small dark eyes and a grand handlebar mustache he waxed and turned up at the ends.

Another hard pinch. "And you best watch how you talk to me."

Wincing from the pain blossoming in her side, she ground out, "What do you want, Dawson?"

Another hard pinch. Tears burned her eyes but she blinked them back. She wouldn't cry in front of him. Never again. He liked it too much.

"Well, that's the question, isn't it?" He stared off down the sidewalk. "What do I want?" He paused as if thinking about it. "I don't like being talked about, Irina. People who know you were my wife are doing some whispering and that's not good for my business."

Irina took a deep breath to steady herself.

"And that book of yours," he added, "is already causing me some grief and it's not even out yet. I've got people looking at me different…"

"No more than you deserve."

"You should know better than to make me mad, Irina." Another vicious pinch and he gave her a tight smile. "I figure you owe me, girl. Without me, you'd have had nothing to write about after all."

Stunned, she stared at him. "Really, you would take credit for what you did to me?"

His voice dropped to a dangerous note she had hoped to never hear again. "There you go, making me angry again. Don't you remember what happened when you didn't do what you were told? You know it doesn't work out well for you."

A chill swept along her spine because she did remember. All too well. She'd lived with Dawson for two years of hell, and had thought that she was doomed to be there forever. But he was out of her life now. She was free of him. She'd fought hard, with Buck's support, and she'd carved out a new reality for herself. Damned if she'd be dragged back into Dawson's web. She didn't answer to him anymore.

He grimly steered her through the crowd and Irina caught more than a few people looking at her in curiosity. Could they see pain on her face?

"The book isn't about you, Dawson. It's about overcoming misery and building a new life for myself."

"You calling me a misery?"

"Among other things," she said tartly and refused to be afraid of him. All he could do was briefly cause her pain. He couldn't rule her life any longer.

They were almost at the diner, and the crowd of people outside seemed to give him pause. He drew her to a stop, turned her to look into his eyes and said, "I had a deal go bad on me today thanks to that video. Cost me ten thousand. You owe me that money."

"I owe you nothing," she said and began to get angry at herself for allowing him to hurt her. She didn't have to do what he said. Didn't have to fear him, either. That Irina was gone.

"Not a good idea to treat me this way, darlin'," he murmured.

"I'm not afraid of you anymore, Dawson."

"Well, you better rethink that, because if you don't get me that money, I can find ways to make you miserable, little girl."

He probably could. Though he wasn't as rich as Buck Blackwood, he had money. And worse, he knew influential people with as few morals as he had.

"You're blackmailing me?"

"Well, you don't have big-shot Buckley Blackwood standing guard over you now, do you?"

No, she didn't. It shamed her to admit that she missed having Buck to rely on. Briefly, she thought about reaching out to Kellan, but it had been a week since she'd seen him and the way they'd left it, she couldn't imagine him standing up for her. So she'd have to do it for herself. "I don't have ten thousand to give you."

"You will once that book of yours comes out."

"That's not how publishing works." She'd gotten a small advance and wouldn't get the other half until she turned the completed book in. As for royalties, she hoped she would get some eventually, but there was no guarantee. So if Dawson wanted money from her right away, he would be disappointed. And a disappointed Dawson, as she knew, could be dangerous.

"I don't give a good damn how it works. You find that money or—"

"Or what, Dawson?" Disgusted with this ghost from her past and her own response to him, Irina finally pulled away from his grasp. She just managed to not rub the spot on her side that he'd pinched so hard.

"Or I'll remind you with more than a pinch."

She hated that even though she was different now, he could still make her afraid. Hated that her old response was still the first thing that occurred to her. "I'll go to the police."

His eyes went hard and cold. "Wouldn't advise that, darlin'. I've got a lot of important friends in Dallas.

They'll sit your small-town sheriff down and tell him how things'll be."

She met his gaze. "You don't have friends, Dawson. You have people you use."

His eyes narrowed. "Gotten mouthy, haven't you? Just remember. Accidents happen all the damn time. Pays to be careful."

"Irina!" Lulu called her name from outside the diner and waved one hand to get her to hurry up.

Thank God. Irina took a deep breath and looked at Dawson. "I have to go."

"That's fine." He took a step back. "I'll be around."

He would, too. She knew this wasn't over. Walking away from him now was just a small reprieve. Dawson wouldn't go away until he had what he wanted. And even then, there was no guarantee he wouldn't come back. Irina walked on and didn't look back. She didn't have to. She could feel Dawson's dark eyes boring into her back.

But she smiled for Lulu and happily listened to the woman laughing and chatting as they went into the diner. Ordinarily, Irina would have enjoyed spending time with her and Miranda and Fee. She didn't know the other girls as well, but these three women had become important to her over the last week or so.

They were her first real friends since leaving Russia. When she was married to Dawson, he'd kept her on a tight leash. She hadn't had a lot of opportunity since to establish friendships. And over the last week, she'd realized how much she had missed having another woman to talk to. Insularity was good, but apparently, she still needed people, too.

"Who was that old guy you were with?" Lulu tugged her over to a booth where the others were gathered.

"He's just…an acquaintance of Buck's." She didn't

want to talk about Dawson. Didn't want anyone to see the remnants of fear still clinging to her.

They accepted that, these new friends, and she was grateful. She was also grateful for the noise, the laughter and the tableful of food and drinks. The film crew had decided to have a "wrap" party of sorts at the diner. Of course, they'd still be filming for a while, but they'd finished what they'd wanted to accomplish at Blackwood Hollow, and as Fee had said, "Any excuse for a party!"

Irina picked up a glass of iced tea and sipped at it while she listened to everyone. Glancing around the crowded diner, she smiled to herself. The locals were loving it, really enjoying watching these reality television stars in their own hometown. Everyone seemed relaxed, happy... except Kellan.

How had she missed him when she'd walked in?

She caught his eye from across the room. He was seated at one of the red vinyl booths and across the table from him sat his "assistant," Ellie Rae Simmons. Naturally, the woman looked beautiful, dressed in a navy blue long-sleeved dress and black heels. She was smiling at Kellan, apparently not noticing that *he* was looking at Irina.

The power of his gaze locking onto hers was nearly a physical jolt. A week since she'd seen him and he hadn't been out of her thoughts longer than a few minutes at a stretch. She'd missed him. Missed his touch. Missed his scowl. Missed the way his mouth moved when he was trying not to smile.

Kellan's gaze fired and Irina's body responded with a flush of heat that swamped her. Didn't matter that she was in a room full of people. It was as if she and Kellan were completely alone. All that mattered was the arc of electricity buzzing between them. Every cell in her body was shouting at her to do something about this now that he was there. *Right* there.

But she didn't want to see him now. Couldn't deal with him and what she was feeling. That buzz of attraction to Kellan was tangling up with the irritation and fear she'd felt at seeing Dawson again. Her body was still jumpy and she felt in desperate need of a shower to wash away her ex-husband's touch. Nope. She couldn't do it. Couldn't stay at the party—not with Kellan there.

She told herself that no one would miss her. The crowd had gotten thicker in just the last few minutes, with the locals and the Exes, as Fee called them, laughing together like old friends. So Irina set her glass down on the lunch counter and left, forcing herself to avoid Kellan's gaze.

The wind was cold and snatched at the hem of her coat, blowing her hair into a tangle. She put her head down, determined to avoid speaking to anyone. She wasn't worried about Dawson approaching her again. He'd said what he had to say and he wasn't a man to repeat himself—as she had reason to know.

Besides, after the viral video, Dawson wouldn't hang around town because he wouldn't want to run into people he knew. Dawson's tentacles reached all over Texas. She could almost understand that—now that she'd talked about her failed marriage, it wasn't only excitement she'd seen around Royal that morning. Irina had also seen the same kind of interested, curious, sympathetic glances Kellan had complained about. Now she knew what it felt like, having people discuss her life. To have them watching her with kind, but curious, eyes. And she felt a whole new sympathy for him.

"Which," she told herself, "he wouldn't want at all."

"Talking to yourself?"

Eight

Irina jolted. For the second time that day, a man had come up behind her. She really needed to pay more attention to her surroundings.

"Sorry," Kellan said. "Didn't mean to scare you."

She took a breath and blew it out. "Well, you did." She kept walking, ignoring the ache in her side that Dawson had left with her as a reminder, until Kellan took her arm and drew her to a stop.

"What's going on with you? Why'd you leave the diner?"

"It's nothing, Kellan. I'm just not in the mood for a party."

"Yeah," he studied her. "Looks like more."

"Well, it's not." Now he had to get insightful? She pulled her arm free, nodded at the woman hurrying past them with several shopping bags. "Shouldn't you be with your 'assistant'?"

"Meeting's over."

"Looked like a friendly one," she said and immediately wished she hadn't. She sounded jealous. Maybe she was. How pitiful was that? He'd already made it clear, both in the past and only last week, that there would be nothing more than sex between them. And hadn't she taken a stand, as well? Told him she was letting him go? That she wasn't going to have her dreams crushed again?

But she *hadn't* let him go. That had been pure bravado and she hadn't been able to back it up, damn it.

"I didn't come after you to talk about Ellie Rae."

Irina stopped on the sidewalk, dragged windblown hair out of her eyes and stared up at him. "Then why did you?"

An older man stepped out of the hardware store and grinned. "Kellan. Boy, my granddaughter showed me that clip of you going after Miranda. Want you to know I'm going to be watching the whole show."

Kellan grimaced. "Great. Thanks, Bill." When the man walked on, Kellan muttered, "My own fault for signing the release just so the country could see what a fortune hunter Miranda really was. Now I can't go anywhere without someone talking about that stupid show."

"Then maybe you should stay home." Maybe she should have, too.

"Why the hell would I hide?"

"I don't know." She shook her head. Tired. She was suddenly so tired. "And I don't care, either. Goodbye, Kellan." *Just walk, Irina. Just walk and get somewhere quiet. Somewhere safe. Where you can think.*

He tugged her to a stop again.

Once more, she pulled free. The difference between him and Dawson was that Kellan didn't hold her against her will. At the moment, though, Irina felt pushed beyond what she could deal with and she just needed to be alone. "I'm not in the mood for this, Kellan."

"That's why I followed you." He looked into her eyes and she wondered how much he was seeing. How much he could sense. She tried to take the fear, the worry, out of her gaze, but that was impossible. All she could hope was that he either wouldn't notice or wouldn't say anything.

"You're shaken."

"It's cold," she said defensively.

"I didn't say *shaking*," he countered and gave a quick glance at the heavy Christmas-shopping traffic on Main Street. "Come on," he said, taking her hand and pulling her along beside him.

"Stop it, Kellan. I'm going home."

"Right again," he said. "*My* home."

"No." She stopped dead. If he wanted her to go with him, he would have to literally drag her behind him. Her emotions were too wild, too uncontrolled right now. Too close to the surface. She couldn't trust herself with him. Couldn't be sure she wouldn't blurt out something stupid. Something she wouldn't be able to take back.

"Damn it, Irina," he said and idly lifted one hand to greet someone behind her. "Something's wrong. I can see it."

His blue eyes shone with concern, and at any other time, she'd have been happy to see it. But she was too needy now and if she gave in to the urge to lean, even just a little, on him, she would end up dumping everything on him. She didn't want to do that. "If there is, it's none of your business."

"Maybe not," he admitted. "And I can see why you would believe that. But…if you think I'm going to back off when you're clearly in trouble, you're crazy."

A huge part of her wanted to accept what he was offering. Yet at the same time, she didn't want to draw him into the mess that was Dawson Beckett. "You can't do anything."

"Try me."

His eyes met hers. She stared up into those deep blue eyes and saw determination, tangled with worry, and Irina sighed. Kellan wasn't going to give up on this. Though he had walls built around his heart, he was also the kind of man who would badger her until she told him what was wrong. Even if that meant they stood on that crowded sidewalk all day.

"Fine," she said, surrendering to the inevitable. "I'll go to your house. But I'm taking my own car because I'm not staying for long." When he nodded, she turned to walk away and stopped when he spoke again.

"I'll wait for you. You can follow me home."

She tipped her head to one side to look at him. "Worried I won't show up?"

"No," he said coolly. "Worried you're too upset to be driving. So I'm going to make sure you get there in one piece."

Instantly, Irina knew he was remembering that his late wife had died in a traffic accident and she regretted being so snotty. God, talking to Kellan sometimes felt as if she were tiptoeing through a minefield.

Nodding, she said, "Fine. I'll follow you."

In fact, seven years ago, she would have followed him anywhere. Then he broke her heart. How humiliating was it to admit, even to herself, that nothing much had changed?

"Is Vaughn here?"

Kellan watched her wander the great room, unable to sit. Unwilling to let her guard down. She kept moving as if she could avoid talking if only she was busy enough. Her arms were folded across her chest and her teeth continually chewed at her bottom lip.

He'd known the minute he spotted her in the diner that something was very wrong. Irina's features were so expressive and her eyes so open to the world that she was easy to read if you knew what to look for. Kellan didn't like seeing her this way. It bothered the hell out of him that she was this agitated and still keeping the reason for it from him.

And it was shocking as hell to him to silently admit that seeing her upset tore at him until he felt as if he couldn't breathe.

"No," he said, finally answering her question. "Vaughn went back to Dallas for a couple of days to take care of some business."

Kellan hadn't expected to miss his brother's presence. Hell, this was the longest they'd been together in years, and yet having him around had been…good. He'd enjoyed being able to spend time with his baby sister, too. In fact, he'd actually enjoyed simply being back in Royal, and he hadn't expected that, either.

Kellan had spent years avoiding his hometown, his family, *anything* that would remind him of his loss. Of Shea. Now being here, that old pain was somehow lessened. For some reason, he'd thought that Royal would remain unchanged, as if it was in a bubble, and coming back here he would be assailed with memories so thick he wouldn't be able to see clearly.

Instead, the town had moved on, his family had, too, and it was only Kellan clinging to the past. Coming back, he'd rediscovered a sense of belonging, while at the same time he'd learned that his memories of Shea were softening, until they looked in his mind like a Monet paint-

ing—misty, shrouded in wisps of remembrance that hid
the pain and left the happiness. He didn't know what to
think about that, so he put it away and focused on the
woman who haunted his every thought.

Even knowing something was bothering her didn't
take away from the bone-deep attraction he felt for her.
In her dark blue jeans, forest green tunic-style sweater
and black boots, she looked…amazing. Her strawberry
blond hair tumbled down her back in a tangle of curls
and waves, tempting him to thread his fingers through
that silky mass. But drawing on his willpower, he buried
his need and focused on her.

"Tell me what's going on."

She whipped her head around to look at him. "Is that
an order?"

"Where's that coming from? When have I ever *ordered* you to do anything?"

She waved one hand and admitted, "You never have.
I know that."

"It's a request. Talk to me, Irina."

"Why?" She stared at him. "Why is this important
to you, Kellan?"

He couldn't explain that. Not to her. Not to himself.
He only knew that having her trust him enough to talk
to him was more vital than anything ever had been before. Maybe he didn't have the right to her trust. Maybe
he'd given that right up seven years ago. But he was here
now. And that had to count for something, didn't it? "Because maybe I can help."

She shook her head. "Why would you want to? There's
nothing between us, Kellan. You've made sure of that."

Yes he had. Seven years ago. But only a week ago,
it had been Irina calling a halt to whatever it was that

burned between them. "You're the one who pulled away this time, Irina."

"Before you could do it—which I'm sure you were about to do."

"We'll never know now, will we?" Though inside, he had to acknowledge that she was probably right. "It doesn't matter, anyway. Tell me what's wrong."

She pushed both hands through her hair, turned around to face him from across the room until she was backlit in front of the window. Outside, the wind was blowing and the pines growing in the yard bent and dipped in the strength of it.

"Fine," she said, releasing a pent-up breath. "My ex-husband found me on Main Street. He's—" she laughed harshly "—unhappy about the show. About my book. He wants money and I don't have it to give him."

"He's blackmailing you?" A surge of anger charged through Kellan with a strength he wouldn't have believed possible.

"*Extortion* would be the technical term." She folded her arms across her chest again and whipped around to stare out the front window, avoiding his eyes. "Are you happy now?"

"Happy?" He stalked across the room in a few long strides. Grabbing her shoulders, he turned her to face him. "Hell no, I'm not happy. I'm pissed. That he came at you. That you were alone. That I had to browbeat you to get you to tell me."

She pulled away from him. "Don't. Don't grab me, Kellan."

He let her go instantly. He didn't like the slight tinge of panic he'd heard in her voice. "I'm sorry."

Sighing, she said, "No. I'm the one who's sorry. It isn't

about you, Kellan. It's Dawson. He always grabs hold of me—like I'm a rag doll or something."

"I'm not him." And it pissed him off that she would compare him to her dick of an ex even for an instant. He could understand it, but that didn't make it any less annoying. He'd never hurt a woman in his life and loathed the men who did.

"I know that." She laughed again and it still sounded pained. "God, I know that, Kellan." Taking a deep breath, she looked up at him and whispered, "This was a mistake. I shouldn't have come here."

"Why not?"

"Because I need some time to think."

"Bullshit."

"What?" She blinked at him.

"You heard me." Kellan laid both hands on her shoulders—gently, carefully—to make sure she knew that his touch was nothing like her ex's. Thankfully, she didn't flinch or try to get away. "You don't need to think about this, Irina. You already know what you have to do. You need to talk to Sheriff Battle. Nathan will know how to handle this guy."

She laughed harshly and the sound was like breaking glass. "I told Dawson I would and he said he would have important people step in and make sure the sheriff couldn't help me."

"And you believe him?" Kellan shook his head and kept his gaze locked on hers. "Come on, Irina. The man's a bastard. He specializes in hurting you. Making you afraid. Why would you take his word for anything?"

She stared into his eyes for what felt like forever, before she slowly nodded. "You're right." Pushing her hair back from her face, she took a deep breath. "I should have realized that on my own—" She held up one hand.

"And I probably would have once I'd had some time to myself to think it through."

"Yeah, you would have," he said with assurance. "I just helped you see it sooner is all."

Frowning a little, she asked, "Do you really believe that?"

"Of course I do," he said and wanted her to believe it, too. She'd picked herself up after a disastrous marriage and built a wonderful, successful future for herself. Kellan admired the hell out of that. "You're a smart woman, Irina. You'd have figured out that the bastard was just trying to keep you from going to the police for help."

She huffed out a breath. "God, he was, wasn't he?"

"Yeah." Kellan nodded and gave her a half smile. "But you're stronger than he thinks you are. You survived him. You built a life. His coming after you like that tells me that *he's* the one who's afraid."

One corner of her mouth turned up at the thought. "You think so?"

"Count on it. Now. You're going to see Sheriff Battle, right?"

Her head cocked, she looked up at him. "I am. That's what I have to do."

"I'll go with you." And he wouldn't take no for an answer on that point. He was going to stand beside her until Dawson Beckett was sent back to whatever rat hole he'd climbed out of.

She nodded again. "Yes. Thank you. I'd appreciate that."

"Okay, then." Glad that was settled and that he didn't have to push her to accept his help, Kellan pulled her in for a hug, wrapping his arms around her and holding her tight.

"Ow!" She pulled away and he had to admit he really hated when she did that.

But not nearly as much as he hated the flash of pain in her eyes. "What's wrong?"

She rubbed her side and shook her head. "It's nothing."

"Irina…" While she avoided his gaze and brushed off his concern, Kellan focused on where she was rubbing. Fury rose up within him like waves crashing against the base of a cliff. "He hurt you." It wasn't a question.

"It's nothing."

He kept his voice even, though his blood was pumping thick and hot. "Show me."

Her mouth worked as if she would argue, and then finally, she walked away from the wide front window. She kept walking until she was in the empty foyer, standing beneath a skylight through which watery sunlight drifted into the room.

"Vaughn's not here, you said. Is anyone else?"

"No," he ground out, looking down at her. "It's just us."

Nodding, she slowly pulled up the hem of her sweater. Kellan spotted the angry reddened skin at her ribs and knew that by tomorrow, she'd be black-and-blue. He fought for control. Fought to contain the rage that raced through him. His hands fisted at his sides and everything in him wished he had that bastard in front of him. He'd make the man pay for putting a mark on her skin and fear in her eyes.

"Dawson prefers pinching to punching," she said, already dropping her sweater.

"Don't," Kellan urged and caught the hem of the heavy knit fabric. Lifting it again, he smoothed his fingertips gently over her burgeoning bruise and saw her eyes mist over. From pain? Humiliation? Anger? He couldn't be sure, though she had the right to feel all three and more.

Slowly, he went down on one knee in front of her.

"Kellan…"

"Shh." He leaned in and kissed her bruise. Gently, carefully, his mouth, his lips covered every inch of the mark Dawson Beckett had left on her as if he were trying to wipe the man out of her memory.

She sighed and swayed toward him, and that soft sound fed a different kind of fire inside Kellan. His hands slid up her legs and cupped her behind while he continued to kiss her bruised skin.

"That feels good," she murmured.

"So will this." He tipped his head back, smiled at her and then let his hands find the waistband of her jeans. With her gaze locked on him, he quickly undid the snap and zipper and then dragged the denim down. Kellan saw the flash of passion dazzling her eyes and was grateful that every trace of fear was gone now.

"You have great legs," he whispered. "Always did like them."

He glanced at the lacy pale pink panties she wore, then hooked a finger in the waistband and pulled them down, as well.

"Um, Kellan. What're you doing?"

"I think that's pretty clear," he said with a wink.

"I thought you wanted me to go to the sheriff…"

He smiled. "Later. Unless, you want me to stop."

She pushed her fingers through his hair and pulled his head closer to her. "No. Absolutely not."

Desire flashed hot and fast inside him, and Kellan immediately fed that need. "Lean against the wall."

"Now, that's an order," she said, "but I'll take it."

He grinned and eased her legs apart, before covering her with his mouth. She gasped and then tugged his hair, pulling him tighter to her body. His tongue swept out, tasting, teasing. She shuddered in his grasp, but she held on, demanding more.

He gave it to her. He slid one hand from her butt to the inner depths of her heat while his mouth worked that tiny bud of sensation. Again and again, he licked her, suckled her, while his fingers claimed her from the inside. He couldn't get enough of her. The tiny sighs and sounds slipping from her throat electrified him. His skin was buzzing. His blood, pumping. His heartbeat thundered in his ears.

Kellan couldn't feed the need inside him fast enough. Touching her. Tasting her. He wanted her more than he ever had. Needed her more than he would have thought possible. She was strength and vulnerability and confidence and anxiety all at once, and that incredible mix drove him crazy with desire. With a want that never left him.

And now he knew she'd been hurt.

Someone had threatened her and he hadn't been there to help. Someone had abused her and Kellan hadn't been there to stop it. Regret, fury, pain whipped through him, twisted with the desire still churning inside him and fueled the need to touch, to claim.

"Kellan—I can't—" Her breath was wild now, her speech broken in short bursts. Her body trembled but she opened her legs even wider, instinctively wanting more of what he was giving her.

He delivered. His tongue flicked madly against that sensitive bud until he felt her shudder, heard her muffled shriek as her body splintered under his attentions.

While her breath was shattered, her pulse racing, he stood, drawing her jeans and panties up as he did. Then he swept her into his arms, lifting her off her feet.

"Or," she said breathlessly, "we could wait until my knees stop shaking and I could walk on my own."

He didn't want to wait. Didn't think he *could*. Kellan dropped a fast kiss on her upturned mouth and said, "Let me feel manly."

Her laughter spilled out around him and Kellan was glad to hear the real pleasure in it. At the top of the stairs, he paused, looked down into her eyes, held her close and felt something shift inside him. Something fundamental. Something…elemental. And while the world around him swung out of its usual orbit, Irina lifted one hand and cupped his cheek.

He turned his face into her touch and kissed her palm. "You dazzle me."

A half smile curved her mouth and completely did him in.

Then she stilled, her forest green eyes shining with secrets she wasn't saying. And maybe that was all right for now. Because in this moment, they didn't need words.

Irina cupped his cheek in the palm of her hand and Kellan turned his face into her touch. Silken heat filled him along with another, more nebulous feeling he didn't want to identify. Didn't want to think about. Yet he remained *dazzled*.

"Show me," she whispered.

There was nothing he wanted to do more. Kellan carried her to his bedroom and inside. He closed and locked the door—just in case—then set her on her feet. Like a dance, she moved into his arms, lifted her face for his kiss, and when their lips met, Kellan felt the spark of it right down to his bones.

The kiss was gentle, passion muted, but there, simmering between them as they gave and took and shared breath by breath, Kellan fell into the spell of her.

Slowly, they undressed each other, hands skimming over flesh, exploring, caressing. She tipped her head to one side and he kissed the curve of her neck, inhaling her scent. He could have spent hours like this, simply reveling in the feel of her soft skin beneath his hands. Still, cupping her breasts, feeling the soft sigh of her breath, made him want more. Feeling her hands moving over his back, his chest, and then down to his already aching erection, made him need.

He saw her eyes blaze with heat and knew that her desire, like his, had climbed to a fever pitch. When he walked her back toward his bed, she smiled up at him as he eased her down onto the bed. She smiled again and undid him. His gaze locked onto hers. "Feels like it's been forever since I was with you."

"It always feels that way for me," she admitted.

"I missed you, Irina." A part of him couldn't believe he was admitting the truth to her after all this time, but he didn't stop. "And it wasn't just the sex. For seven years, I missed *you*."

"I missed you, too, Kellan. So much."

His right hand skimmed over the marks that Dawson had left on her and he felt another jolt of helpless fury. "I hate that he put his hands on you."

"I don't want to think about him now. I never want to think about him again, but especially not now. Besides," she added as she stroked one hand across his chest, "you already kissed it and made it better. Remember?"

His mouth tipped up in a small, knowing smile. "Well, then, I'll focus on the rest of you now. How's that?"

"A wonderful idea." She reached for him, but he shook his head and stepped back. If he didn't get suited up right away, he'd lose all control and forget to stop. He dipped into the drawer of the bedside table for a condom and quickly put it on. Then he stretched out on the bed alongside her and focused entirely on Irina.

It was as if he were seeing her—really seeing her—for the first time. The gray half-light in the room seemed only to illuminate her. She shone. Everything about her was breathtaking.

Her hair spilled out on either side of her head, her deep green eyes were fixed on him. Her mouth, that amazing, wonderful mouth, was curved in a knowing smile, as if she could sense what he was thinking, feeling. And if she could, she knew what would happen next.

Kellan dipped his head to claim one of her nipples and he felt the sharp jolt of desire as it whipped through her body. He was attuned to her, too. He knew what she liked, and he did everything he could to push her beyond her limits. To take her to the very edge of sanity and then to join her there.

He ran his hands up and down her body, while her hands curled into his shoulders, her short, neat nails digging into his skin. Abandoning her breast, his mouth took hers in a deep kiss that demanded as much as it gave. Their tongues tangled together and their strained, desperate breathing was the only sound in the room.

He slid one hand down to the nest of strawberry blond curls at the juncture of her thighs and then beyond, into the heat. Into the tight, wet core of her. She came off the mattress, rocking her hips into his touch. He lifted his head, stared down into her passion-glazed eyes and watched her frantically try to find the release his fingers were promising her.

"Kellan," she managed to say around a gasp for air, "be inside me. Let me feel you fill me."

Now it was his turn to feel that desperation, Kellan

admitted silently. With those words, she'd pushed him beyond the limits of his patience.

"Yes. I need that, too." And he did. More than his next breath.

Kellan shifted position and in one long, slow thrust, claimed her body and gave his to her. She took his face in her hands, pulled him down for a kiss. Her long, beautiful legs came up and hooked around his hips, pulling him deeper and higher inside her. He rode her hard, then gently, changing the rhythm up to keep them both off their guard. To chase the climax and then let it go before it could end everything.

Kellan never wanted it to end. If he could stop time, he'd do it now, he thought, with his body buried inside hers. Kellan's heart raced. His eyes locked with hers and he saw the first glimmer of satisfaction hit her and watched it build as she brokenly cried out his name. She held on to him, as if he were the only safe place in the world, and he felt the same. This moment. This incredible, moving moment was all that mattered.

His hips pistoned, because the climax was more important than the journey now. She held him, shuddering, shaking, and finally, he took that wild jump, following her into that bright oblivion.

Minutes later, Kellan's heart was still pounding and he was still reeling from the power of that orgasm. He felt her hands smoothing up and down his back and knew that no matter what, he would always be able to draw up the memory of those butterfly caresses against his skin.

He looked into her eyes, their bodies still joined, locked together, and he felt his world take another hard jolt. Kellan didn't want to think about what it might mean, but he couldn't deny it was happening. Slowly, silently, he rolled onto his back and drew her with him, until Irina was lying on him, her head on his chest, her legs tangled with his.

And if he could have found a way to manage it, he'd have stayed like that forever.

Nine

"Do you want to press charges?"

Two hours after leaving Kellan's bed, the two of them were in the sheriff's office in Royal. She'd told Nathan Battle everything and he hadn't said a word through the whole thing. He'd simply listened intently, letting her know he was taking in every word. Now he looked her square in the eye and waited for her answer.

Irina took a deep breath, glanced at Kellan, then back to Sheriff Battle. "No."

"Are you sure about that?" Kellan asked, his voice quiet.

Half turning in her chair, she looked at the man she'd been so intimate with just a couple of hours ago. His eyes were fixed on her with heat and understanding and…an emotion she couldn't read. But she knew that something had changed between them. Something monumental. Irina had stopped hiding from the truth.

She was in love with him. Still. Always. She could tell

herself she was going to walk away. Heck, she'd told *him* that she was letting him go. But the truth was she would love him until the day she died. It was as simple—and as sad—as that.

Because she had to accept that Kellan wasn't looking for love. Would never be able to move past the memories of his late wife to build a different future than the one he'd once seen. Whatever love he had to give, he'd already given to Shea. There was no room for anyone else in his heart. Irina couldn't pretend otherwise.

But she also couldn't deny her own feelings. Couldn't deny herself the opportunity to be with the one man who touched her heart and soul and body.

"Yes," she finally said, wanting Kellan to understand. "I'm sure. I don't want anything else to do with him, Kellan. I don't want court dates where I'll have to see him. I don't want him to be a part of my life at all anymore. If he leaves me alone, I'll do the same for him."

He looked as if he wanted to argue the point, but she was relieved when he didn't. Irina was sure that if he had his way, Dawson would be charged, arrested and slapped into jail. But for her, it was enough to beat him. To let him know she wouldn't be cowed or threatened or afraid. To show him that she would stand up for herself. Once he understood that, Dawson would move on to an easier victim. She knew that much about him.

Still holding her gaze, he nodded slowly.

"All right, then." Kellan looked at the sheriff. "What do you think, Nathan?"

Nathan Battle shrugged and leaned back in his chair. He ran one hand through his short, brown hair and turned his gaze on Irina. "I think the decision is yours, Irina. Whether or not I agree with it isn't important. Either way, I'll be having a talk with Beckett. I'll make sure he knows we frown on hurting women. And that blackmail's not going to fly around here, either."

Irina closed her eyes briefly. She'd already shown Nathan the bruise Dawson had given her and she'd seen the same fury in his dark brown eyes that she'd seen in Kellan's gaze. Strong men, she thought, were especially furious at a man who abused others.

"Thank you," she said.

"No need to thank me," he said. "It's my job. And my pleasure to take care of this for you. Don't you worry about Dawson Beckett. He might think he has friends who can shut me down, but he's wrong.

"The man's well-known to law enforcement in this part of Texas," Nathan added, tapping a pencil against his desktop. "He straddles the fence between crook and entrepreneur and usually manages to keep his balance. But he's been known to slip from time to time."

"I feel like even more of a fool now," Irina said. She'd believed Dawson when he said that the sheriff could do nothing against him. But he wasn't a businessman; he was a criminal and the law knew it.

"Well, you shouldn't. Beckett's the one who was a fool." Nathan smiled at her. "He should have recognized a strong woman when he saw her."

She took a breath and smiled. "Thank you."

"Yeah, thanks, Nate," Kellan put in, and then, as if to lighten the mood in the small, ruthlessly organized office, he asked, "How's that new baby of yours?"

Nathan's face lit up. "She's great, but not so new anymore. Coming up on a year old already."

"How many kids does that make for you now?" Kellan's grin widened.

"Four. Two boys, two girls," Nathan said with satisfaction. "And Amanda's already talking about having a tie-breaker in a year or so."

Irina felt a sharp tug of envy for the home and family the sheriff had. She'd seen him and Amanda together at the diner she owned and they always looked...connected. Happy. She'd once dreamed of having that with Kellan, and knowing it wouldn't happen created an ache around her heart that throbbed with every beat.

"You know, Kel," Nathan said, getting serious again, "it's been good having you back in Royal. Usually you blow in and blow out again so fast, nobody gets a chance to say hello."

"Yeah." Kellan looked a little uncomfortable. "It was hard to be here before..."

"I get that," Nathan said, his features somber as both men remembered Shea and the legacy of pain she'd left behind. "But I'm glad to see you. Hope it's not the last time."

Kellan glanced at Irina, then back again. "I don't think it will be."

"Good to know."

Irina felt as if an entire conversation was going on between the lines of what she could see and hear. She didn't know what it meant, but she was willing to cling to hope just a little while longer.

"Anyway," Nathan said, getting back to business, "I'll make a few calls. Got a friend on Dallas PD. He'll go have a talk with Beckett and see if he can get through to him. If I have to, I'll go in and have a sit-down with him myself." He looked at Irina. "Don't you worry, though. He's done."

It was as if every tangled knot settled in her chest suddenly slipped free. Tension drained away and Irina finally released a breath she hadn't realized she'd been holding. When Kellan reached for her hand, she twined her fingers with his and squeezed briefly.

"Thanks, Nate." Kellan stood up and held out one hand to him.

Nathan shook it, then turned to Irina and shook her hand, as well. "I'll get on this today, so don't give your ex another thought."

"I won't," she said, though saying it and doing it were two very different things. Until she heard that the police had taken care of him, Irina would probably still worry about Dawson and his threats.

"I'm sorry this happened to you, Irina." Nathan spoke solemnly. "It shouldn't have. Not in my town."

She shook her head. "It wasn't your fault, Sheriff."

"I've got a wife. I've got daughters," he said, his eyes holding hers. "Nothing pisses me off more, excuse my language, than some guy preying on women."

"Right there with you," Kellan muttered.

Irina smiled. Normally, she liked to handle her own problems. She hadn't been raised to wait for rescue, but rather to forge her own path—which, ironically, was what had gotten her involved with Dawson in the first place.

But she had to admit that it was reassuring to have the local sheriff ready to take care of her problems with Dawson. And if she were to be honest with herself, that was what it would take to get through to her ex. The man would never go away if it was only Irina demanding it. She never should have doubted that going to the sheriff was the right thing to do. "Thank you."

"You bet," Nathan said. "I'll call the Hollow to let you know when it's taken care of."

"Call her cell," Kellan said and gave Nathan the number. Then, catching her eye, he said, "Irina's going to

Nashville with me for the weekend. I've got some business I have to take care of in person."

Well, this was a surprise. He wanted her to go away with him? Hope leaped up in her chest and Irina frantically fought to tamp it down. A weekend with him wasn't a future. It wasn't a declaration of love. And yet, she thought, it was more than Kellan had ever given before. "I am?"

"Aren't you?"

He looked at her and she saw that he wasn't issuing a command. He was asking. In the way that Kellan always would. She thought about it for a moment. Going away with him was only prolonging the inevitable. She'd give herself more to think about, more to miss. She'd add to the pain that would eventually find her when he left. She shouldn't dig an even deeper hole for herself, but how could she say no to a weekend away with the man she loved?

More important, why should she?

"Yes. I am."

"Perfect," Nathan said, completely oblivious to the undercurrents between Irina and Kellan. "This'll be straightened out before you two get home. And, Irina?"

She looked at him.

"I guarantee Beckett won't be bothering you again."

Lulu stepped into the foyer of Blackwood Hollow and shouted, "Miranda? Irina?"

"In here, Lulu."

Smiling, she walked into the great room and found Miranda curled up alone on one of the overstuffed couches. The twinkling white lights were blazing and the Christmas tree was lit against the gloom of the December day. It should have looked cozy. Welcoming.

Instead, Lulu took one look at Miranda and said, "Oh, honey, what's wrong?"

"Nothing, nothing." She shook her head and plastered a very unconvincing smile on her face. "I'm fine. What are you doing here?"

"Okay," Lulu said, dropping her black leather bag on the nearest chair before walking to join Miranda on the sofa. "Now I know there's something wrong. I'm here to pick up you and Irina for a fun-filled Christmas-shopping day at the Courtyard. The other girls and the camera crew are already there waiting for us."

"Oh God, I completely forgot." Miranda smoothed the wrinkled-up tissue in her hand and used a corner to dab at her eyes.

"It's no reason to cry," Lulu said, trying for a little humor. It failed miserably. "Sweetie, come on. Things can't be that bad. Just tell me what's wrong. Do you need me to go bitch slap someone?"

Miranda gave a short, choked laugh. "No, but thanks for the offer."

"Not a problem." Lulu paused and looked around the empty room. "Where's Irina?"

Waving that aside, Miranda said, "She's not here. She went with Kellan to Nashville for the weekend."

"Well, that's interesting." She tapped her finger against her chin, then stopped and demanded, "Wait a minute. Did Kellan make you cry?"

"No," Miranda muttered in disgust. "Kellan made me furious and *that* made me cry."

"Man, I hate when I do that. It always makes me even more mad, which makes me cry harder. Vicious circle. So what happened?"

"What always happens when one of Buck's kids comes anywhere near me. Arguing. Name-calling. Tempers."

Grimly, she shook her head and said, "I should just leave Texas altogether. That would show them all."

"Uh-huh." Lulu wanted to be supportive, but she needed more information. "Why?"

"I can't tell you, damn it."

"Why not?"

Miranda huffed out a breath and ground her teeth. "It's a secret. It's Buck's secret."

"Well, now I'm intrigued." Settling in, Lulu swung her hair back from her face, propped her elbow on the back of the sofa and stared at her friend. Miranda was always the composed one. The one of them who knew who she was and where she was going. She never failed to be coolheaded and rational. Seeing her like this was a little unsettling.

"How does a dead man have secrets?"

"If anyone could, it'd be Buck."

"Just tell me, Miranda. It's clearly upsetting you. So share."

Miranda watched her for a long minute, considering. Her eyes were still teary, but the expression on her face was pure frustration. "Can you keep a secret, Lulu? From everyone?"

Lulu didn't even try to laugh that question off. Miranda's gaze was straight and more serious than she'd ever seen it before. So she looked into her friend's eyes and said solemnly, "I'm a good friend, Miranda. I'm *your* friend. You can trust me."

She continued to study Lulu for another few seconds, as if deciding whether to continue or not. Then, decision made, she sighed. "I believe you. And maybe you're the one person I can confide in. Especially since you have no attachment to any of the people involved in this whole mess."

"You can tell me, Miranda."

Nodding she said, "Thanks for that. Okay, you already know that I got a letter from Buck, after he died, telling me to come here and about the will—"

"You mean about leaving you everything and ensuring his children will hate you? Yeah. I know."

"In the letter, he also said I could share this with someone as long as that person wasn't from Royal—which is why even Irina doesn't know what I'm about to tell you." Miranda gave her a weak smile, but at least the tears had dried up. "The thing is, I'm putting up with all of this crap and I'm not actually Buck's heiress."

Okay, whatever she might have expected, it wasn't this. "What do you mean?"

"I mean," Miranda snapped, "this is pure Buck. Even dead, he's pulling strings." She took a breath. "He said I'd be receiving three letters. So far I've only got the first one."

"And what did it say?" Lulu was caught up in the secrecy of the whole thing. She'd had no idea people actually *did* things like this.

"He wants me to be the steward of his estate. Temporarily." She tore at the tissue, deliberately creating flimsy pieces of confetti that pooled in the lap of her black skirt. "I'm supposed to work with Kace—"

Kace, the yummy lawyer, Lulu thought and wondered when she'd see him again.

"It's going to take several months to straighten all of this out. Months where I get to be insulted, gossiped about and driven to total craziness." She shook her head fiercely, as if denying the whole mess. "But here's the really hush-hush part, Lulu. In the end—" she threw her hands up "—his kids are going to inherit after all."

"What?" This just kept getting stranger.

"Oh yes. Torture Miranda for months and then they all get their reward. Damn Buck anyway." Her eyes fired. "For example, Kellan's going to get this ranch, though he doesn't know it yet. And I can't tell him—so I have to put up with all of his bull, knowing that he's got no real reason to dish it out. Sophie and Vaughn will be inheriting a huge chunk of the estate, too, in spite of the way they're treating me, like I poisoned Buck to get all his money."

"This is so weird."

"Tell me about it. And before you ask," Miranda added, "I'm doing this because Buck left fifty million to my charity, to compensate me for seeing this through. The damn man knew I'd put up with anything to see Girl to the Nth Power fully funded."

"Wow." Lulu laughed shortly. "I don't even know what to say to all this."

Miranda laughed, too. "That's a typical reaction to one of Buck's plans. You know, his kids hated me before and this isn't helping anything. This whole thing is driving me nuts. I loathe secrets and Buck knew that, damn it."

"Your ex really wins the prize, doesn't he?" Instinctively, Lulu took Miranda's hand and gave it a squeeze. "You're not alone in this anymore, Miranda. You've got me. And when things get tense, you can dump all over me, I promise."

Her friend laughed a little and gathered up the confetti from her skirt. She blew out a breath. "Thank you. Seriously, thanks. It really helps having you to talk to."

Lulu gave her a quick hug and said, "You know what else helps? Shopping. Why don't you go freshen up your makeup and we'll go meet the girls?"

"Right. Okay, I won't be long."

When she left the room, Lulu sat alone, her mind buzzing. She'd keep her friend's secrets, but she had to wonder if all superrich people were crazy, or if it had just been Buckley Blackwood.

Kellan wasn't sure why he'd wanted Irina with him on this short business trip. Hell, he didn't even know why he was planning on going back to Royal. Ordinarily, he'd have stayed in Nashville, gone back to his normal life. But now nothing seemed "normal" anymore.

It was a short flight to Nashville from the Dallas airport, just under two hours. But rather than fly commercial, Kellan preferred his private plane. Usually, he got work done during the flight, burying himself in reports, prospectuses and plans. But today was different.

Today, he had sipped champagne with the most beautiful woman he'd ever seen. If he felt a stab of guilt over that, because it seemed disloyal to Shea, he suppressed it. The two women couldn't have been more different, and it was as if he was only now realizing that.

Irina had a strength that Shea, in her more sheltered life, had never been forced to develop. Irina went her own way while Shea had done what was expected of her. At that notion he *did* feel disloyal, so Kellan shut those wayward thoughts down and focused on Irina.

"This place," she said, doing a slow turn on the teakwood porch floor, "is amazing. The house itself is beautiful and the grounds…" She shook her head a little and glanced over her shoulder at the yard, with its manicured lawn and surrounding trees. "It's like a painting. But… don't you get lonely here?"

"I'm not here often enough to get lonely," he admitted.

She choked out a laugh. "So you own a three-story house on five acres of land and you're not here often?"

He knew how that sounded, but he shrugged it off.

"Most often, I simply stay in town at the Heritage Hotel. It's more convenient for work."

"Then why—" She waved both arms, encompassing the house.

"I guess you can take the boy off the ranch but you can't take the ranch out of the boy." It was a glib excuse, but one he'd used before. Kellan looked at the house, with its wraparound porches, elegant lines, and knew that buying it had been more of an investment than it was a true expression of him looking for a home.

He liked Nashville—hell, he owned half the buildings in the city—but it wasn't home and never would be.

Maybe he hadn't consciously admitted it before today, but the truth was, Texas was home. Royal, Texas. And more than that, his home was Blackwood Hollow. Funny that it had taken him this long to acknowledge that simple fact. Shea's death had chased him from Texas.

But now it was time to go back and fight for what was his. The question was, did that include Irina?

"Well, it's beautiful," she said and turned around to lean on the iron scrollwork railing. She lifted her face to the sunlight and sighed a little, simply enjoying the moment.

And Kellan enjoyed the view. She took his breath away. Punched at his heart and shook him right down to his bones. Irina wore a pale yellow dress with a full skirt that kicked around her knees paired with mile-high heels that did incredible things for her already gorgeous legs.

All he wanted to do was take her inside to the master bedroom and lose himself in the wonder of her for a few hours. But when she turned her head to him and grinned, he felt another hard jolt and knew that if he gave in to temptation, they'd never leave the bedroom all weekend. He had other plans.

When her cell phone rang, Kellan's thoughts shut off as Irina's features went tight and worried. Without glancing at the screen, she said, "That's probably Sheriff Battle."

Kellan hoped so, if only because hearing that Dawson Beckett had been dealt with would ease her anxiousness. He got up and went to her as she pulled the phone from her purse.

"It is him."

"Well, let's hear him out. Put him on speaker, Irina."

Nodding, she answered and said, "Sheriff, you're on speaker so Kellan can hear you, too."

"That's fine. Irina, I wanted to tell you that Beckett's been warned off."

She looked up at Kellan and he could already see worry draining from her eyes. "What happened?"

"That detective friend of mine in Dallas had a talk with Beckett. Told him in no uncertain terms to stay away from you."

"Will that work?"

Kellan dropped one arm around her shoulders and hugged her to him. If it didn't take care of the problem, Kellan would have a "talk" with the man and end this once and for all.

"It will," the sheriff said, "because Beckett's got a couple of legal problems at the moment already. He has a court date coming up in a week or two. So, if he bothers you again, he was told we'll add the attempted blackmail to his list of charges and that won't go over well with the judge."

She smiled and seemed to sag against Kellan. "That's wonderful. Thank you so much."

They could hear the smile in the sheriff's voice. "Like I said, it's my job and I'm happy to help."

"Thanks, Nate. We both appreciate it," Kellan said.

"Not a problem. Now, enjoy Nashville and I'll see you when you get home."

Home. There it was again, Kellan thought as Irina disconnected the call. Royal was home and it was resonating with him in a way it hadn't in years. Why now?

Even while he thought the question, he knew the answer was Irina. She had drawn him back into his family, into his hometown. What that meant, he wasn't sure—and didn't want to think about it now.

"I'm so relieved," she whispered, tucking her phone back into the tiny brown leather bag she wore draped on one shoulder. "I can't believe it. He's really not going to bother me again. Dawson, I mean."

"No," Kellan said, holding her shoulders and turning her to face him. "He won't."

"Thank you. For helping me with this."

He slid his hands up until he was cupping her face with his palms. He looked into her deep green eyes and something stirred inside him. "Dawson Beckett's out of your life, Irina. This time for good."

She took a deep breath and smiled. "I can't even grasp that. Not really. He's always been on the edges of my mind. Always a regret. A worry that somehow he'd find a way to reenter my life."

"Let it go now. Because you can," he whispered, and bent his head to kiss her. A slow, soft brush of the lips that had her sighing and swaying into him.

That unidentifiable *something* stirred within again and Kellan broke the kiss in response. He steadied himself and even then, the stars in her eyes when she looked up at him were nearly blinding.

They'd crossed a line in their relationship by coming to Nashville. Things were different here. *They* were different. Right here, right now, they were just two people with no past, no future. They had this weekend and it lay before them like a gift. Kellan was determined to appreciate every damn minute.

"I feel so good," Irina was saying and pulled away from him long enough to do a quick spin that lifted the hem of her skirt halfway up her thighs.

"Look good, too." He winked at her and she grinned, stealing his breath again.

"Thank you for bringing me here, Kellan." She looked out over the grounds, then back to him. "You know, since I came to this country, I've never been outside Texas. This has made a lovely first trip."

"We're just getting started," he said and took her hand. "We've got a lot more to see."

"We do?"

Looking into those beautiful green eyes of hers, he could happily lose himself and everything else in the world that wasn't her. And Kellan wanted more than anything to keep that smile of anticipation on her face. There was so much he wanted to show her. Share with her. And no better time to start than now.

"One tour of Nashville," he said, tugging her along behind him, "coming up."

A few hours later, they were in a crowded bar, with flashing neon on the walls and country music streaming from speakers. Waiters and waitresses moved through the crowd like dancers, delivering drinks and laughing with their customers. And Irina took it all in with a big smile.

"You like country music?" Kellan asked. "I thought I knew everything about you and now you're throwing me a curveball."

There was still so much he didn't know, Irina thought. Like just how much she loved him. How much she wished they were any other ordinary couple out for the evening. But they weren't. There were secrets between them. And a ghost. And seven years of mistrust.

She'd been going along for the last couple of weeks, taking the days and nights for what they were. But she'd always known that things would change. This time with Kellan would end again, as it had so many years before. And when it was done, she wanted these memories. Wanted to be able to soothe her broken heart by drawing up images of him.

Deliberately then, Irina pushed all of those thoughts aside, because for tonight, she wanted the fantasy. She wanted to *believe*.

"I've lived in Texas since I came to this country from Russia," she reminded him with a smile. "So yes, I do like country music. In a lot of ways, the music itself reminds me of folk songs I grew up with, and that's comforting. I am a little surprised that you like it, though."

Both eyebrows winged up and mock insult was stamped on his features. "I'm born and raised in Texas, honey. Country music is sort of rooted into my blood."

Her smile softened until it became almost wistful. "That must be nice."

"What?"

"Growing up in one place. Feeling that connection." She sipped at her vodka again, then set the glass down. "My father died when Olga and I were very young and our mother moved us all over Russia while she looked for work. Being in Royal was my first try at developing…roots."

"Funny. I always thought that roots just tied you down."

"No, they anchor you," she said, wishing he could see his home as she did. "You can go wherever you want, but there will always be a place where you belong. Where people know you and are happy to see you." She looked at him. "People in Royal have enjoyed having you back home. Your brother and sister especially."

He snorted. "Not Miranda."

She had to laugh at that, too. He and Miranda were truly oil and water, and it was a shame, because she thought if there weren't so many obstacles forcing them to see each other in the worst lights, the two of them might be able to be friends. "True. But Miranda is only there because your father wanted her to be."

"And we've circled around back to Buck," he said, sipping at his scotch as he leaned back against his chair.

She hated that every time his father came up in conversation, Kellan shut down. Yes, she knew that Buck hadn't been a perfect father. She knew that now, more than she ever had before. But at least he had cared. And Irina wondered if Kellan would ever accept that. Especially once he knew everything.

"He loved you," Irina said, feeling as though she still had to defend Kellan's father to him.

He smirked at that and had another taste of his scotch. "Had a strange way of showing it."

"His only regret was how he'd treated his children."

"Even if I accept that," Kellan said quietly, "it doesn't excuse him. Doesn't make me sad he's gone or wish for more time with him. Because frankly, every minute I ever spent with Buck turned into a contest of wills. The old man had a head like rock."

Her eyebrows lifted and Kellan grinned unexpectedly. What that smile did to her was lethal. How would she ever live without him in her life?

"Okay, so I inherited some of Buck's stubbornness."

"Some," she agreed, then tried to make him understand again. "Kellan, you have regrets. We all do. Can't you believe that Buck did, too?"

Before he could answer, the stereo shut off and live music erupted. They both turned to look down at the stage from their balcony table. A country band of five men in jeans, boots and hats were playing and singing and the crowd was already moving onto the dance floor.

Kellan stood up and held out one hand to her. "Dance with me."

He was full of surprises today and Irina was charmed. Everything about this trip had disarmed her. The private jet, his beautiful home, his easy smiles and the fun they'd both had touring this amazing city. But Kellan himself had touched her more than she ever would have believed possible.

He was attentive and sexy and funny and sexy and chivalric and sexy, and every second she spent with him made her love him more.

She slipped her hand into his, and when his fingers folded around hers, Irina felt the sharp blast of heat slam into her heart. As he led her down the stairs to the dance floor, all she could think was that when she lost him this time, the pain might actually kill her.

Ten

For the following week, Kellan fell into a pattern of filling his days with work and his nights with Irina. His assistant, Ellie Rae, kept him up-to-date with what was happening in Nashville via email, but for now, he was content to remain in Royal and oversee his businesses long-distance.

And the longer he stayed in his hometown, the less he wanted to leave it again. Even the ghost of Shea seemed less haunting. Maybe because things had changed enough that he was able to be in Royal now without expecting to see her around every corner. Or maybe, he told himself, it was simply time.

But everything in Royal wasn't rainbows and sunshine. There was still the will, Miranda and even the mystery of those four file folders he'd once seen in Buck's briefcase. He needed answers and Kellan wasn't going anywhere until he got them.

Sitting on a sofa in the great room, he briefly thought

that by rights, he should have been behind the massive desk in Buck's study at the Hollow. Yet another reason to stay in Royal—fighting Miranda for his legacy. Grumbling under his breath, Kellan opened his email. He fired off some instructions to Ellie Rae, checked out a new property he was thinking of buying and then deleted a few emails from people wanting him to donate to whatever cause was the favorite that week.

He almost deleted the last email when he saw that it was from Dawson Beckett. He hadn't given the man another thought since Nathan Battle had called Irina in Nashville. So why was he contacting Kellan?

Against his better judgment, he clicked Open.

Blackwood, thanks to you and your bitch Irina, my businesses are folding.

Kellan smiled to himself. Good news after all.

Your daddy was a bastard and you're no better.

Chuckling now, he kept reading. If Beckett was miserable, Kellan was happy to hear all about it.

And speaking of bastards, Beckett continued, got some news for you, boy. Your daddy left you another brother.

What the hell?

Found out Buck's secret twenty years ago and held on to it for the right time. Well, this is it, you son of a bitch. Hope to hell it tears what's left of your family apart.

Kellan slammed the lid of his laptop shut. Scraping one hand across his face, he stared at nothing while his mind raced. Another brother? Was it true? Buck had been a lousy husband and it was common knowledge that he'd cheated on Kellan's mother regularly. But had there been a child?

And if so, why hadn't Buck done anything about it? Was his soul really so small as to ignore his own child?

Even as he considered it, Kellan knew it was very likely to be true. Though Dawson wasn't exactly a beacon of truth. Buck had ignored his legitimate children. Why not one whom he could keep hidden?

But who, besides Dawson Beckett, knew about this?

He stood up, stalked across the great room to the wet bar in the corner and poured himself a scotch, neat. He downed it in one gulp and relished the river of fire filling him. His breath came fast and his brain raced with information he had and speculation on what he didn't.

Did Miranda know about this other sibling? Did Kace? Did Irina?

In the week they'd been back from Nashville, they'd been together every night. Mostly she stayed at his ranch since there was no way in hell Kellan would stay at the Hollow as long as Miranda was holding court there. Irina had become an integral part of his life. Seven years ago, he'd run from the woman who he feared could make him forget Shea and the pain of loss. Today, he had been grateful for her.

Now all he could think was maybe it had all been a lie.

"Hell," he muttered, glancing at the bay window, "I even put up a damn tree because of her." The gigantic pine, regally decorated, shone with lights that he and Irina had strung themselves.

Briefly, he remembered that night and how they'd celebrated that tree, naked in his bed, with the door firmly locked.

And in all the time they'd spent together, Irina hadn't said a word to him about this. She'd never again spoken about those files that she'd brought him a couple of weeks ago. Never even hinted about the possibility of another Blackwood sibling.

But there had been *four* files in that case. Files she claimed that Buck had kept on each of his children. And that told Kellan she had to have known.

She'd simply chosen not to tell him.

He glanced at the time. Irina's night school class had ended by now, so she'd be home soon. As anger rippled inside him, Kellan made a decision. Until he had more information, he'd be the one keeping secrets.

A few days later, the Texas Cattleman's Club was decorated for the season—and the annual holiday party.

Twinkling lights lined the branches of the trees in the parking lot and surrounding the club. Inside, the lights continued along the ceilings, and twined through pine boughs that lined the mantel and wound around the stair rails. There were several Christmas trees set up in different areas of the club with wrapped gifts destined for local charities gathered beneath them. Balls of mistletoe dangled from the ceiling on red ribbons and every white-cloth-covered table boasted red candles and a tiny vase filled with roses and pine sprigs.

Christmas music pumped through the speakers and everything seemed perfect—but wasn't. Irina was on edge. She felt as if her nerves had nerves. For the last couple of days, Kellan had been different. Quiet. Introspective. Cold. She'd caught him looking at her with speculation in his eyes, but when she asked him about it, he brushed her concerns aside. When they made love, he didn't hold her afterward, but rolled to his side and stared at the ceiling.

There was definitely something wrong, and the fact that she didn't know what it was was making her crazy.

She had thought that the two of them were becoming closer. The trip to Nashville had done that, she thought. Because they'd had a chance to get away from everything that was hanging over their heads here, in Royal. Miranda, the will, Dawson. Secrets. Shea.

There was so much going on that at times it felt as if she were running in place. But since Nashville, she'd sensed a change in Kellan. He'd been happier, more open, more…involved than ever before. Until three days ago.

She missed that new Kellan. Missed that sense of rightness between them. She wanted him back. But she didn't know what to do to get him.

He was across the room from her at the bar getting them drinks. She picked him out of the crowd easily, though it had to be said that Royal, Texas, had more than its fair share of tall, well-built, gorgeous men.

Kellan wore a tuxedo as if born in it. His dark hair and beautiful blue eyes gave him a dangerous look that set off licks of heat inside her whenever she looked at him. Would it always be like that for her? She sincerely hoped so.

"Who are you checking out?"

Irina smiled when Lulu walked up. Though the party was a private one every year, meant for TCC members and their families, for some reason, the ladies of the reality TV show had been invited this year. Irina, for one, was glad of it. She enjoyed Lulu, Fee and Miranda.

Lulu's strapless, floor-length ice-blue dress skimmed her figure and outlined every curve. Her hair was done up in a twist at the top of her head while allowing soft tendrils to lie against her cheeks and neck.

"You look beautiful."

Lulu grinned. "Thank you. So do you. I love that dress."

So did Irina. It was dark red, with spaghetti straps and a deeply cut V bodice and a thigh slit. When Kellan first saw her in it, his eyes had flashed with the kind of heat that made her want to forget all about the TCC's annual formal party.

"So who are we watching?"

Irina smiled again. "Kellan."

"Ah... And, ooh, he's talking to Kace." She made almost a purring sound. "Isn't that interesting? Well, well, the lawyer looks very studly in a tux, doesn't he?"

"I suppose," Irina said and noted that Kellan was frowning as he talked to Buck's lawyer. What did that mean?

"Come on, Irina. I want you to see Miranda's dress. She went into Dallas to find it."

"All right, but—"

"Come on." Lulu threaded her arm through Irina's and pulled her along. "Kellan's not going anywhere. It's a party, remember?"

"You've got nothing to say about this?" Kellan demanded.

Instead of answering, Kace LeBlanc ran one finger around the inside of his shirt collar. "Why do they make us wear these damn things? Feels like I'm being hanged. Slowly."

"You're avoiding the question." Kellan had been gnawing on this other-sibling thing since that email from Beckett. He was unsettled. Uneasy. There was a cloud over him when he was with Irina now, because he couldn't be sure she wasn't working with Miranda against him.

He glanced over his shoulder to where he'd left Irina and saw her walking away with Lulu. Just that one look at her and his body tightened. His heart ached and he didn't like it. She was beautiful, though, no doubt.

When he first saw her in that red dress it had nearly knocked him out. Her long, silky hair was pulled back from her gorgeous face to fall in a curtain of curls down her back, and the thigh-high slit in her dress, not to mention the deeply cut bodice, was designed to drive him a little wild with desire.

Yeah. She was beautiful. And desirable. And so many other things that were now impossibly important to him. But was she treacherous, too? That was something he had to know.

Keeping his voice low, he demanded, "Damn it, Kace. Talk to me. Did my father have another kid?"

Kace looked around, to make sure no one was listening. He didn't have to, though. The banquet hall at the TCC was packed with what felt like the whole damn town. The noise level was just shy of deafening, so no one would be overhearing them.

"I can't talk to you about this, Kel," the other man said tightly. "I'm your father's lawyer..."

"Buck's dead."

Kace winced, then shrugged. "Yeah, I know. Doesn't end my responsibilities toward him and his estate."

"This is bull, Kace," Kellan insisted. "What about your responsibility to me? To Vaughn? And Sophie? We've got a right to know what the hell's going on."

Kace shook his head. "Not yet."

Frustration roared through him and Kellan had to fight to keep his temper in check. Last thing he needed was that damn camera crew swinging around to catch him in the middle of another argument. Besides, standing here giving Kace a hard time wouldn't do him any good anyway. He knew Kace. The man was loyal to a fault and as stubborn as Kellan himself. If he felt honor bound to stay silent, then there was no way Kace going to break a confidence—or the law.

"Fine." Admitting defeat, he nodded abruptly. "I'll find out on my own."

"Damn it, Kel," Kace said quickly. "Just leave it alone. Always so damn impatient."

"I think I've been plenty patient."

"God," Kace muttered, "it's like dealing with Buck again." Louder, he said, "You'll know everything eventually. Wait for it. You don't have a choice in this, Kel."

"Wait? You want me to wait?" he repeated. "How much longer? I've got Buck's ex living in the family home, inheriting *everything*, and now I'm supposed to quietly sit back and wait to find out if I've got another sibling out there? Really?"

Kace shook his head. "Yeah, I didn't really think you would."

"If you're not going to help," Kellan said, "then just stay out of my way."

"Well, don't do anything stupid."

Kellan just looked at him for a long minute. "*Stupid* would be to stand by and *trust* that everything will be fine. I don't do waiting."

He threw one last look toward Irina, surrounded by Miranda and the women of the *Ex-Wives* TV show, not to mention the camera crew. Miranda was here, so that meant he could get into the Hollow and look through Buck's office without being stopped or hassled. And if he was fast enough, Irina wouldn't even notice he was gone.

Standing in his father's office, Kellan half expected to hear Buck's voice telling him to get out. This study had been the old man's inner sanctum and no one was allowed inside when Buck wasn't there. Or when he *was* there. Or ever, really. Naturally, it had been the one room in the house that Kellan was always fascinated with.

"You can't stop me now," Kellan muttered as he walked to the closet. That was where Buck had kept his briefcase and so it would be the first place Kellan looked.

He found it, carried it to the desk and laid it down. For a second he paused, because once he opened this case, there would be no going back. But to go forward, he had to know the truth.

The four manila folders were inside. Kellan set aside the ones labeled with his, Sophie's and Vaughn's names. Then he picked up the last one and opened it.

Darius Taylor-Pratt.

Kellan stared at the photo of a smiling man younger than himself, but with the clear stamp of their shared father on his features. Brown hair, brown eyes and clearly a Blackwood. He quickly scanned everything Buck had kept on the man and finally came back to the picture. There was no denying it. Darius Taylor-Pratt looked too much like Buck to even think about pretending otherwise.

Kellan had another brother. Another should-be heir to the fortune that Miranda had already stolen.

He thought about the lost years, time that he and his *three* siblings had lost. Time together they'd never have now. "Dad, you bastard. You should have told us. We should *know* our brother."

But then, there was a lot Buck should have done differently in his life. Gritting his teeth, Kellan used his phone to take a picture of Darius's file, then packed everything away again, set the case back in the closet and left the Hollow. Sitting in his car, Kellan tapped his fingers against the steering wheel as his brain ran with all of the new information. But there was one thing he kept coming back to.

Irina.

Did she know about Darius?

Was she in on all of this with Miranda?

Was her part in Miranda's plan to keep him so busy in bed he didn't ask questions?

Kellan needed to know.

Forty-five minutes after he left the party, he was back and scanning the room for Irina. When he spotted her, a flash of need jolted him. In spite of his questions. In spite of the sense of betrayal echoing inside him, everything in Kellan screamed at him to hold her. Kiss her. Touch her. Claim her.

Irina was on the dance floor with Kace, smiling and laughing up at his father's lawyer. Under the twinkling white lights, she looked ethereal. Like something that had stepped out of a dream. And yet all he could think was that she'd tricked him. Lied to him. Kept the truth from him.

And still he wanted her.

Pulse pounding, he stalked across the room, tapped Kace on the shoulder and said, "Cutting in."

His friend grinned. "I don't know, she's awful pretty."

Irina smiled up at Kellan and even as his heart turned over in his chest, he wondered how she could do that. How could she look so pleased to see him, if she'd been betraying him all along? Was she that good an actress?

"Yeah," Kellan ground out. "Find your own girl." He swept Irina into his arms, dismissing Kace without another thought. He steered her through the crowd, swaying to the music—some old song from the fifties, romantic, haunting.

The other dancers swirled past them in jewel tones, but he didn't see them. He could see only *her*. Irina's right hand in his, her left on his shoulder, she leaned into him and tipped her face up to his. She was so beautiful that, for a moment, he almost forgot the fury driving him.

All he could think was that he'd come so close to letting go of Shea. Letting himself love Irina. Had it had all been a game?

"Where have you been?" she asked.

"I went to the Hollow." He waited to watch her reaction, but all he read in her eyes was confusion.

"Why?"

"I had to get some answers," he said. "Now I have them—along with more questions."

"What are you talking about, Kellan?"

He dipped his head close to hers and whispered, "I'm talking about Darius Taylor-Pratt."

She stiffened in his arms and that told Kellan all he needed to know. He lifted his head and saw the truth written plainly in her eyes. She was aware of his half brother. Had known all along and hadn't told *him*.

"We need to talk," he muttered. Keeping a tight grip on her hand, he led her off the dance floor and through the crowded party room. He nodded to those they passed but didn't slow down.

If she said anything, it was lost in the rise and fall of the noise level in the building. Laughter, snatches of conversation came to him, but he ignored it all. He passed a couple under the mistletoe and wondered if there were secrets between them, too.

It was too cold outside for the conversation he wanted, so Kellan led her to the back, where the currently deserted childcare center was located. Drawing her into the room, he closed the door behind him and looked at her, trying to see her with new, more jaded eyes.

The room was filled with tiny chairs, short tables and colorful rugs. Shelves held what looked like hundreds of storybooks, and there were at least a dozen easels arrayed along the back wall, standing like soldiers waiting to be called into battle.

Irina rubbed her hands up and down her own arms as if she were chilled and he almost offered her his jacket, when he realized it wasn't cold she was feeling, but nerves.

"What's happening, Kellan?"

"Don't," he ordered, shaking his head and steeling himself against the shine in her forest green eyes. "Don't pretend you don't know. Not anymore."

For a moment, it looked as though she might try to put on an act after all, but then she sighed and admitted, "Yes, I knew about Darius."

"And didn't tell me," he ground out, feeling that hard slam of truth steal his breath.

"I couldn't," she argued. "It wasn't my secret to tell."

"That's crap, Irina," he said tightly, keeping a close rein on the temper pumping inside him. "You brought that briefcase—those files—to my house. You showed me my file."

"Yes," she said. "I wanted you to see it. To know that Buck cared. That he knew about you and your life. That you *mattered*."

Amazed that she was still defending what she'd done, he asked, "But you didn't think that my half brother mattered? Is that it?"

"Of course he does," she snapped. "You're putting words in my mouth."

"Because you're not telling me why you did this." He

took a step closer to her and a part of him noticed that she didn't back up. Didn't retreat. And he admired her for it even while furious. "You should have told me, Irina. I had a right to know. So did Sophie and Vaughn."

"I know you do and you would have found out. When Buck wanted you to."

He threw both hands up. "Why do we care what the hell Buck wants? He's *dead*. What he wants doesn't matter anymore. The rest of us are still here. Still living. Still wanting answers."

Her chin tipped up and her eyes narrowed on him. "And you'd do anything to get those answers?"

"Damn straight." He pushed his jacket back and stuffed his hands into his pockets, more to keep from instinctively reaching for Irina than anything else.

Nodding, she locked her gaze on his and he read sorrow and anger there. "That's why you've been so good to me," she said quietly and Kellan was stunned.

"What?"

"This," she said, waving her hands to indicate her dress, his tux. "You asking me to this dance. You taking me to Nashville. Spending every night with me in your bed." She huffed out a breath. "God, I'm a fool again. It's all been a ploy, hasn't it? To get information about the will. To expose Buck's secrets."

"Are you kidding?" he demanded. "You're actually trying to say I'm the one who was sneaking around? Holding back information? *You're* the one who's been using *me*."

She laughed shortly and it sounded painful. "How? How, Kellan? Did I seduce you? Were you swept off your feet and made to feel important? Were you caught off guard by romance? Did you fall in love?" Her eyes filled, but she blinked the tears back, thank God.

Panic jolted him. "Who said anything about love?"

"I did. Weren't you listening?"

"Damn it, don't turn this around," he said. Kellan didn't want to think about *love*. Love wasn't the point. Trust was. "And don't change the subject. This is about you betraying me."

"No, it's not, Kellan," she said, slowly shaking her head. "This is about you finding a reason to leave. To walk away from me and whatever future we might have had in favor of clinging to memories of Shea."

"This isn't about her," he said, feeling a brand-new jolt of anger.

"It's always about Shea," Irina told him, walking closer so that she had to tip her head back to meet his gaze. She didn't back down from him or what she was saying. Instead, she stared him square in the eye and said, "You're constantly telling everyone 'Buck's dead,' expecting people to brush the man off and move on. According to you, he doesn't matter. His wishes don't matter.

"Well, Kellan, Shea's dead, too."

He flinched.

"You're not married to her any longer, Kellan. She doesn't decide your present or your future. She's your past. A big part of it and one that should never be forgotten. But you cling to her ghost. You use her as a weapon, to keep everyone else away from you." She drew a deep breath and said, "Congratulations. It worked. You're alone. You'll always be alone.

"And I feel sorry for you."

"I don't need your sympathy." How had this turned on him?

"You have it anyway. Because I love you, Kellan."

Pain shot through his chest, because it wasn't love he

read on her features, but goodbye. And still she wasn't finished.

Her green eyes were shining with temper, sorrow, regret, and all three of those emotions reached for his heart and squeezed.

"You'll never know what it would be like to have my love in your life every day. Neither of us will ever know what we might have had together. Because time after time, you choose the past over the future." She stepped around him and walked to the door. Opening it, she paused, looked back over her shoulder and said, "I wish you and Shea good luck."

Then she was gone.

Eleven

"He makes me so angry." Two days later, Irina was still fuming as she paced the length of Blackwood Hollow's great room.

"Yes, that's what men do," Miranda supplied, her gaze following Irina's every step.

"Well, Kellan is very good at it." She turned around to face the other woman, curled up on a couch in front of the roaring fire. "He thinks I lied to him."

"Well…"

"It wasn't a lie," Irina argued when she thought Miranda might see Kellan's side of things. Because she really hadn't lied to him at all. "I simply couldn't tell him the whole truth about Darius because it wasn't my secret to tell."

And yes, she'd felt guilty about that. Every time she was with Kellan and had to remain silent about his brother and other things she knew he would want to know, she'd felt pangs of regret. But she had owed Buck so much she couldn't break the promise she'd made him.

"I know that." Miranda held up both hands, one of which was holding a glass of straw-colored wine.

"Buck told me about his other son, before he died, Miranda. I think he needed to talk to someone. I blame Kellan for not understanding." And she did. It had been two days since the Christmas party and she hadn't heard from him. It was as if he had packed up his ghost of Shea and left town. But she knew he hadn't. Gossip was still the oil that kept Royal moving, so she'd heard that he was still on his ranch.

"Of course he's staying," she said to herself more than Miranda. "He won't leave until he gets to the bottom of everything."

The twinkling lights in the room seemed to mock her with their electric joy. Thanks to Kellan, she couldn't even appreciate the trees or the lights. Instead, they were all a reminder that she would be alone this Christmas, too.

"Just like his father," Miranda said wryly. "Ironic, don't you think, that Kellan considered his father a giant pain in the ass and he's turned out just like Buck?"

Irina dropped onto the sofa, picked up her own glass of wine and did what she could to wind down. It wasn't working, of course, because she could still hear Kellan's voice. Could still see the look in his eyes when he accused her of betraying him. He thought she'd been working against him. How could he believe that? How could he be with her and not know her—the core heart of her?

"I'm so angry and so—"

"Hurt?" Miranda offered.

"Yes," Irina admitted. "That, too. And disappointed.

How could he believe I would do anything to deliberately damage him?"

"And we come back to… He's a man. They don't really think, you know." Miranda took a long sip. "For men, it's all about the penis."

Irina snorted her wine. "Excuse me?"

"Sorry, did I embarrass you?" Miranda didn't look sorry. "What thinking they actually do is done with their penises." She tipped her head to one side to consider. "Or is the plural *peni*? Doesn't matter. Anyway, it's all about whatever could be considered the 'manly' thing. What makes them bolder, stronger, richer. That's what drives them. It always comes down to size with a man."

"Miranda…"

"Sorry," she said again and this time it looked like she meant it. "I think I'm a little drunk. My point is, I am sorry you, too, are getting screwed by trying to help Buck."

"It's all right. I'll live."

Miranda groaned. "God, this is all such a mess."

"It really is." Irina agreed. "As far as my life goes, this is all on Kellan. If he'd trusted me. If he'd waited. Given Buck the benefit of the doubt…"

"I get why he couldn't, you know." Miranda laid her head back on the sofa. "Buck could be a son of a bitch at times." She sighed. "When I first met him, I sort of liked that about him. He was the take-charge type. And I did love him, you know. Once." A sad smile crossed her face briefly. "But he didn't make it easy. And being one of his kids had to be more difficult than being his wife. At least, when I'd had enough, I could leave."

Irina knew that Kellan's father had been a hard man. But it wasn't all Buck was. And Kellan didn't have to carry on that tradition, did he? Miranda was right. Kel-

Ian was so much like the father he still resented and he just didn't see it. He could have come to her. Asked for answers instead of demanding them. Could have believed in her enough to listen. Instead, he chose to think the worst, and for that...

Her heart hurt. She felt as if she could hardly breathe. She hadn't slept since the party. All she'd been able to do was go over and over that last conversation with him. She wished it had gone differently. Wished especially that she hadn't told him she loved him, because now she didn't even have her pride to keep her warm.

Sighing, she took another sip of wine, looked at Miranda and said, "We're so wrapped up in the drama it's hard to see past it all. But, when this is all over, what will you do?"

"That's a very good question." Miranda studied her own wine and said thoughtfully, "I guess that depends on how it ends."

"He looks a lot like Dad, doesn't he?" Sophie studied Kellan's phone and the picture he'd taken of Darius Taylor-Pratt.

"'Course he does," Vaughn said, taking the phone from his sister. He glanced at Kellan. "We all do. Why should our brother be any different?"

"We have another brother," Sophie said with a laugh. "For me, another *older* brother. Yippee."

Kellan smiled briefly. Sophie had always complained about how he and Vaughn had hovered over her. Keeping the boys at bay, checking up on her all the time. He wasn't surprised at her attitude. "Yeah, you're still the baby."

"Great," she said. "Hey, maybe Dad has another one who's younger than me out there somewhere. I could finally get the chance to push someone around."

"Like you don't do that to us?" Kellan shook his head. Sophie just smiled.

"Wouldn't surprise me to hear there are more siblings out there." Vaughn said. "The old man wasn't exactly a saint."

"True." Kellan took his phone back to study his half brother's face. It said something, didn't it, that none of them were really shocked at the news. Buck had left behind a legacy of secrets. What was one more?

"So, does he know?" Sophie asked and Kellan smiled again.

She'd always had a soft heart. Of course Sophie was worried about how Darius was taking this.

"I don't think so. Not yet, anyway. Hell, *we* weren't supposed to know yet." And it still bothered him. How much more was there that he and his brother and sister weren't being told? Correction: *brothers*.

"Where does he live?" Vaughn asked. "Darius, I mean."

"California. Pasadena, I think the file said."

"Well, of course he doesn't live around here," Sophie put in. "If he lived anywhere near Royal, we'd already have known about him. No one keeps a secret in this town."

Except Irina. Kellan frowned to himself, remembering their last conversation. She'd looked hurt. Insulted. He pushed one hand through his hair, trying to somehow wipe her image from his mind. It didn't work, though. She was with him. All the time. Her smile. Her frown. Her voice. Her laugh.

Irina had become a part of him and without her...

"I like your Christmas tree," Sophie told him. "I'm surprised to see one in your house, but I like it."

He should have taken it down after that confrontation

with Irina. She was the reason that tree was in the room and now every time he looked at it, he was reminded that she wasn't at the house anymore. Kellan shot Sophie a quelling look, but as usual, it had no power over his sister.

"You did it for Irina, didn't you?" She gave a dramatic sigh. "So romantic."

Vaughn snorted. "A Christmas tree is romantic?"

"No," Kellan interrupted before the two of them got going. "It's not." Not anymore, anyway.

"So where is Irina these days?" Vaughn looked at him. "Haven't seen her lately."

"She's busy," Kellan said shortly. He didn't want to discuss any of this with these two. Hell, Kellan didn't want to even think about it.

But that wasn't happening. He hadn't been able to think of anything *but* Irina since that night at the TCC. He could still see her eyes, swimming in tears she refused to shed. The defiant tilt to her chin when she faced him down. And he heard her, too, in his mind, his heart. Heard her tell him she loved him when she'd called him out about dismissing his father after death and enshrouding his wife after she died.

He hadn't argued. Hadn't been able to. Because it was all true. He had done exactly that and it pissed him off now to realize that for seven years, he'd been stalwartly holding on to Shea's memory like a damn flaming torch. He always said he didn't want people's sympathy, but wasn't that exactly what he was silently demanding when he couldn't let her go?

God, his head ached.

"Hey, you don't look so good," Vaughn commented. "You're not mad about a new brother, are you?"

"What? No. Hell, he might be an improvement on you."

"Thanks very much." Vaughn slumped in his chair and took a sip of his beer.

"What about you two?" Kellan asked. "How do you feel about Darius?"

"I'm kind of excited by it," Sophie admitted. "I mean, when you're an adult, you don't often get a new brother or sister. So I'm looking forward to meeting him."

"What about you?" Kellan asked.

Vaughn shrugged and gave him a sly smile. "Hey, I'm all for having a younger brother for a change. Maybe I can order him around like you do me."

"Takes practice," Kellan warned.

"Well, hell, no wonder you're so good at it."

"So did you and Irina have a fight?" Sophie asked out of the blue.

Kellan looked at her. Were all women psychic?

"Just apologize for being a boob and everything will be fine."

Insulted, he asked her, "How do you know it was my fault?"

Sophie laughed. "Please. Of course it was your fault, Kellan. You're *you*." Shaking her head, she said, "You're as bossy as Dad was and just as inflexible sometimes. So apologize. Fix it. I like her."

"I like her, too," Vaughn said. "And yeah, it was your fault."

"Thanks for the support." Disgusted with his family, Kellan hoped to hell that when they finally met, Darius Taylor-Pratt would take *his* side for a change.

Apologize. He could. He'd been considering it for days. But what if he hadn't been wrong?

Kace LeBlanc faced Kellan the next morning over a cup of coffee in the diner. Kellan wasn't really in any frame of mind for talking to his old friend, but when Kace called, asking for a meeting, he felt like he couldn't say no. Now he was second-guessing that decision.

"Why are you still working in the diner? How long does painting an office take anyway?" Kellan finished his coffee and set the mug down.

Kace shook his head. "Billy Talbot and his son are doing the painting—"

"Well, that explains it." Billy was good at his job but he was a notorious perfectionist. Painting the office could take a month or more.

"Yeah. But he swears he's almost finished."

Kellan really didn't care. "What's this meeting about, Kace?"

"About you and your inability to wait for a damn thing," Kace muttered. "I was asked to explain a few things to you."

"Asked by whom?"

"Not saying."

Kellan lifted his coffee and held it between his hands. "So, when *some* people ask you to do something, you do it?"

Kace sneered at him. "You know, I'm glad I went to school with Vaughn, not you. You're too damn annoying."

Kellan laughed shortly. He'd scored a point and they both knew it. "What are you supposed to explain?"

"It's about Irina."

"Nope." Kellan started to slide out of the red vinyl booth, but Kace stopped him. Kellan contemplated climbing over the leg blocking his way. It wouldn't exactly look dignified, but he wasn't about to sit there and listen to someone else tell him about Irina.

"Damn it, Kellan, listen to me."

"Why the hell would I?"

"Because if you don't, you're a damn fool. I'm willing to admit that you are many things, but I never figured that foolish was one of them."

"Fine." Kellan eased back and signaled Amanda Battle for a coffee refill. If he was going to do this meeting, then he needed the caffeine.

"Hi, boys," she said as she poured fresh coffee into their cups. "Anything else I can get you?"

"Not for me," Kellan said. He didn't plan on being there long enough.

"Once I'm done with Mr. Personality," Kace said, "I'll have bacon and eggs."

Amanda laughed, patted Kace's shoulder. "You bet."

When she was gone, Kellan said, "All right, talk."

"Irritating. Just irritating." He took a breath and said, "I was asked to explain that Irina knows nothing about your father's will."

A knot in Kellan's chest tightened. "I didn't think she helped write it. But she did know about—" he glanced around the diner, making sure no one was listening "—about my *brother* and said nothing."

"She couldn't." Kace muttered something under his breath, clearly fought for patience, then said, "Buck told her about Darius before he died and asked her to say nothing. She promised Buck she'd do as he asked. I happen to know that when you give your word on something, you don't break it, no matter what."

"And that's important why?"

Kace looked exasperated. "Because for some reason, you expected Irina to break *her* word. You seem to believe that keeping it is a betrayal of you."

He hadn't thought of it like that, and he didn't much care for it now. She'd tried to tell him the same thing that night, but he hadn't wanted to listen. He'd been too wrapped up in his own anger—at his father, at the will, at the damn universe for keeping his *brother* away from them.

"Look." Kace kept talking and Kellan listened. "I don't know how much you know about Buck and Irina…"

He frowned. "I know some. She told me."

"Good. Did you know that Buck offered to pay for her schooling, but she turned him down? And after he died, she found out he had paid it all off, so she has no debt."

"Yes. She told me that."

"And Buck's the one who arranged a work visa for her. Gave her a job. A home. Somewhere to feel safe from that bastard she'd married."

Kellan idly turned his heavy coffee cup in circles on the tabletop. His heart felt like a lead weight in his chest. All of the things Irina had been through and survived humbled him. Hell, it made him proud of the way she had thrived. And as much as he hated to admit it, her loyalty to Buck was understandable, given his father's role in her life. "Yeah. I know most of that."

"And still you can get pissed at her for not breaking her word to Buck?" Kace looked amazed. "He was the one man in her life who helped her and expected nothing in return. The one man who offered her safety. The man who gave her a shot at a future."

"Damn it, Kace." Kellan was feeling lower than dirt.

"And on his damn deathbed, this man told her a secret and asked her to not say anything about it. She gave that man her word." Kace gave him a hard look. "And you give her a hard time for that? Call her out? What the hell, Kellan? You used to be better than that."

Kellan gritted his teeth and swallowed hard. He didn't argue, because how the hell could he? He'd come to most of this on his own already. Hearing Kace say it all out loud only underscored it. And made him feel worse than ever.

"Irina's sense of loyalty is every bit as strong as yours," Kace said. "You shouldn't be punishing her for it."

And that pretty much said it all, Kellan told himself. He'd given her grief for doing exactly what he would have done in her place. For three days, he'd been kicking himself for turning on her. For three nights, he hadn't been able to sleep because he needed her and he'd pushed her away.

He should have known. Should have realized that betrayal wasn't in Irina's nature. She was too loving. Too open, kind, in spite of what she'd been through in her life. And instead of seeing that, appreciating that, Kellan had attacked her for being who she was.

"I made an ass of myself," he grumbled and, man, did that cost him.

"Damn." Kace shook his head. "Never thought I'd hear you admit something like that."

"Yeah," Kellan grumbled, scraping one hand across his face. "Me, either. Didn't enjoy it."

"Not surprising." Kace shrugged. "But I'm not the one you should be saying it to."

He looked at his old friend. "You're right. I need to find Irina. But just know this, Kace. Our fight against Buck's will isn't over. Whatever happens between me and Irina… You and I aren't done."

Sighing, Kace only said, "Of course we're not. Now go away so I can have some breakfast."

Kellan slid out of the booth and marched out of the diner, headed for his truck. He needed to talk to Irina. Needed to tell her that he had been wrong. That he missed her. Needed her. And damn it, he wasn't going to lose her.

* * *

Irina needed to get out of the house. She'd moped enough. Missed Kellan enough. Now she needed to be with people, try to recapture her joy in the Christmas season and avoid all thoughts of Kellan.

"Good luck with that," she murmured, digging into her purse for the keys to the ranch truck.

The icy wind slapped at her and Irina tugged her coat closer around her. It wouldn't help, though, because since that last night with Kellan, she'd been unable to get warm. It was as if the chill in his eyes had seeped right into her bones. He was the one man she wanted and the one man who didn't trust her.

Shaking her head, she pushed him out of her mind. She climbed into the truck, adjusted the mirror, then stopped dead and stared as Kellan's luxury truck came roaring up the main drive like a dragon swooping in on a castle.

Her heart gave a solid jolt, but her mind sent a firm warning to keep calm. Inviting hope now would only make her feel worse when it didn't work out. He was probably coming to yell at Miranda again.

But he jumped out of his truck and ran to hers. He yanked open the driver's-side door, looked into her eyes and Irina's foolish heart began to hope.

"Thank God I caught you," he said. "We have to talk, Irina. Or I have to talk, anyway, and I want you to listen— no." He stopped, scrubbed one hand across the back of his neck and said, "I'm *asking* you to hear me out."

His eyes fixed on her and she realized that he'd never *asked* her for anything before. His hair was ruffled by the wind. He wore a dark brown leather jacket, a red sweater, black jeans and boots, and he looked so amazing, he took her breath away.

While he waited for her decision, she knew there was nothing to decide. Of course she'd listen to him. And she'd hope this conversation went better than their last one.

"All right, but let's go inside. It's cold out here." She grabbed her purse from the bench seat.

Kellan took her hand to help her down, then released her immediately. Irina curled her fingers into her hand because she missed his touch.

"Is Miranda home—never mind," he said, holding up one hand. "I don't care if she's there or not."

She smiled and shook her head. "She's not here. She went shopping. I was about to join her and the others. I want to buy some Christmas presents for my sister and her family."

"I'm glad I caught you, then." He took her hand again and led the way into the main house, through the foyer and into the great room.

"What is it, Kellan?" she asked, slipping out of her coat and tossing it onto the nearest chair. "What's so important?"

"You," he said quickly. "Us. We're important, Irina."

There went that thread of hope again. She clung to it and waited. Her heartbeat jumped into a wild gallop and she took a deep breath, trying to steady herself. It wasn't easy. Because she'd missed him so much, that just being near Kellan now was electrifying.

He came to her, and looked down into her eyes. "The other night, I was angry."

She laughed a little and folded her arms across her chest in an unconscious defensive move. "I know. So was I."

"You had a right to be," he said solemnly.

"Really." It wasn't a question, though she was curious about what had changed his mind. Why he was here. What had made him see the truth.

"Yeah." He scrubbed his face with one hand. "I'm sorry for all of it. If I'd taken the time to think it all through I would have known that you'd never trick me. Betray me. Lie to me.

"It's not who you are, Irina. And I should have remembered that."

Hope continued to grow in spite of the fact that she tried to rein it in. "I didn't want to keep that secret from you, Kellan."

"I know that. I do." Kellan laid both hands on her shoulders. "And I know that your relationship with my father was different from mine. I'm glad he was so good to you, Irina. I'm glad you had someone you could count on."

A sheen of tears filled her eyes and she blinked them back frantically. Releasing a breath, she nodded and said, "Thank you. That means a lot to me."

His hands on her shoulders sent spears of heat shooting through her body and she welcomed it after the soul-deep cold she'd lived with for days.

"The truth is," he continued, "I don't think I ever knew the real Buck and that is a shame. But through you, I'm getting a different picture of my own father."

"I'm glad." She met his eyes and saw so many emotions shining there, she couldn't identify them all. And Irina wondered if her eyes were reflecting the same thing.

"Yeah, me, too," he said. "But I didn't come here to talk about Buck. What you said the other night, about Shea?"

"Oh, Kellan…" She still felt bad that she'd thrown those words at him—though she still believed he'd needed to hear them.

"No. Don't apologize. You were right." He took her hands in his. "I've been holding on to the memory of Shea for all the wrong reasons. I thought I was protecting myself, but I wasn't. I was hiding. And, Irina, I'm done hiding."

"What are you saying, Kellan?"

Behind him, winter sunlight pierced the front windows and lay across the floor in a soft golden pattern. The lights on the Christmas tree flickered, and in the hearth, a gas fire burned against the winter cold.

But all Irina could see was Kellan's eyes.

"I'm saying I love you, Irina."

She swayed under the impact of those words.

"I'm not afraid to say it anymore," he went on in a rush. "In fact, I want to say it every day. To you. I never thought I'd be in love again, but I am. And it's real and rich and everything to me. You are everything to me."

"Oh, Kellan, I love you so much."

"Thank God," he said with a choked laugh. "I was worried that I'd blown it completely. I'm so sorry I didn't listen to you. So sorry I didn't trust you."

The pain she'd carried for days began to drain away and Irina smiled up at him as he went on.

"You gave your word to my father and I respect that you kept it in spite of me being an ass."

She laughed again and covered her mouth with one hand to muffle it.

"You changed everything for me, Irina. Hell, I've got a Christmas tree in my house. But it's not Christmas without you. Come home with me. Be with me. Marry me."

"Marry you?" She blinked. He loved her and that would have been enough for her. But marriage? Family? This was the greatest Christmas gift she'd ever known.

"Yes. Marry me. Make a family with me." He cupped

her face in his palms. "Irina, losing Shea broke my heart. You healed it. You brought me back from a dark, lonely place that I never want to visit again. Don't leave me out here all alone. Without you, I've got nothing."

Tears spilled from her eyes, but she was smiling at him.

"I know this inheritance fight isn't over—" He kissed her. "But it can wait. What can't wait is living a life with you. Marry me, Irina. Love me."

It was all she'd ever dreamed of. Kellan was here, loving her, holding her, promising her a shared future that looked so bright, it almost hurt to imagine it. Hope soared and love sailed with it.

"I do love you, Kellan. I always have," she said softly.

"So that's a yes? You'll marry me?"

"Of course I will," she said, joy bubbling up inside her.

He pulled her in tightly to him, wrapped his arms around her and buried his face in the curve of her neck. "You're everything to me, Irina."

Her heart was so full now, her chest felt tight. "Oh, Kellan, I've loved you since the moment we met. Nothing will ever change that."

"Then you'll come home and spend Christmas with me?" He straightened up and looked down into her eyes. "This one and every other one for the rest of our lives?"

"Yes."

He grinned. "I'll even ban Vaughn from the house so he can't storm in on us if you want."

Irina laughed again and it felt wonderful, to be so light, so full of wonder and hope and anticipation. "No, you won't. I love your family. All we have to do is remember to lock the door."

"Trust me on that." He nodded and asked, "So, fiancée, do you want to go buy those presents for your sister? Because we could do some ring shopping while we're at it."

"A ring?" She swallowed hard, but it didn't stop the tears from flowing again.

"Of course a ring," he said, pulling her up against him again. "Any one you want." He kissed the top of her head. "And you know, if you'd like to deliver those presents in person, we could fly to Russia. Surprise your sister."

She stared up at him, jolted. Visiting her sister had been a secret dream, but one so out of reach she rarely even let herself think about it. "Are you serious?"

"I am," he assured her. "Or we can bring her and her family here for a visit, if you'd rather."

"Kellan, you keep touching my heart so deeply."

"Irina," he said softly. "You are my present, my future, my *heart*. Whatever you want, it's yours."

She smiled and looked into those beautiful blue eyes, seeing love shining back at her, and Irina knew that she'd already received the gift of a lifetime. Love.

"You, Kellan," she whispered. "I want you."

"I'm all yours, honey. Now and always."

As his arms came around her, she felt everything in her world slide into place. When he kissed her, she felt their souls link, felt their lives entwine and knew that this once-in-a-lifetime love was everything she'd ever dreamed of.

* * * * *

COMING SOON!

We really hope you enjoyed reading this book. If you're looking for more romance, be sure to head to the shops when new books are available on

Thursday 12th December

To see which titles are coming soon, please visit

millsandboon.co.uk/nextmonth

JOIN THE
MILLS & BOON
BOOKCLUB

* **FREE** delivery direct to your door

* **EXCLUSIVE** offers every month

* **EXCITING** rewards programme

50% OFF YOUR FIRST PARCEL

Join today at
Millsandboon.co.uk/Bookclub

MILLS & BOON
MEDICAL
Pulse-Racing Passion

Set your pulse racing with dedicated, delectable doctors in the high-pressure world of medicine, where emotions run high and passion, comfort and love are the best medicine.

Eight Medical stories published every month, find them all a

millsandboon.co.uk

MILLS & BOON

THE HEART OF ROMANCE

A ROMANCE FOR EVERY KIND OF READER

MODERN

Prepare to be swept off your feet by sophisticated, sexy and seductive heroes, in some of the world's most glamourous and romantic locations, where power and passion collide.
8 stories per month.

HISTORICAL

Escape with historical heroes from time gone by. Whether your passion is for wicked Regency Rakes, muscled Vikings or rugged Highlanders, awaken the romance of the past.
6 stories per month.

MEDICAL

Set your pulse racing with dedicated, delectable doctors in the high-pressure world of medicine, where emotions run high and passion, comfort and love are the best medicine.
6 stories per month.

True Love

Celebrate true love with tender stories of heartfelt romance, from the rush of falling in love to the joy a new baby can bring, and a focus on the emotional heart of a relationship.
8 stories per month.

Desire

Indulge in secrets and scandal, intense drama and plenty of sizzling hot action with powerful and passionate heroes who have it all: wealth, status, good looks…everything but the right woman.
6 stories per month.

HEROES

Experience all the excitement of a gripping thriller, with an intense romance at its heart. Resourceful, true-to-life women and strong, fearless men face danger and desire - a killer combination!
8 stories per month.

DARE

Sensual love stories featuring smart, sassy heroines you'd want as a best friend, and compelling intense heroes who are worthy of them.
4 stories per month.

To see which titles are coming soon, please visit

millsandboon.co.uk/nextmonth

LET'S TALK

Romance

For exclusive extracts, competitions
and special offers, find us online:

f facebook.com/millsandboon

🐦 @MillsandBoon

📷 @MillsandBoonUK

Get in touch on 01413 063232

For all the latest titles coming soon, visit
millsandboon.co.uk/nextmonth

MILLS & BOON

HEROES

At Your Service

Experience all the excitement of a gripping thriller, with an intense romance at its heart. Resourceful, true-to-life women and strong, fearless men face danger and desire - a killer combination!